DON'T
ASK,
DON'T
FOLLOW

DON'T ASK, DON'T FOLLOW

a novel of psychological suspense

MARY KELIIKOA

OCEANVIEW PUBLISHING
SARASOTA, FLORIDA

ISBN 978-1-60809-609-1

Published in the United States of America by Oceanview Publishing

Sarasota, Florida

www.oceanviewpub.com

10 9 8 7 6 5 4 3 2 1

Of two sisters one is always the watcher,
the other the dancer.

louise gluck, poet

To Marilyn, my Big Sister

Lindsay's long red hair glimmered in the moonlight. My big sister. By only three years, I'd reminded her a million times when she acted like fourteen was so much more mature. Her silhouette filled the window as she strung her purple purse across her body.

I sat up in bed with a yawn. "Where you going this time?"

"Just go to sleep, Beth. But cover for me, okay?"

In other words, don't ask. Always the same. I huffed out a breath that sagged my shoulders and made the back of my throat tingle. "You always tell me that. But it's so late."

"Not that late."

"Can I go with you?"

"Like you would. Besides, you wouldn't have any fun."

"You don't know that."

"Yes, I do."

"You're going to meet a boy, aren't you?" It wouldn't be the first time. The last escape had her talking nonstop about some freshman quarterback and how they'd made out. Boys were cute, but way too distracting. Not that I knew a lot about that. My time hadn't come yet, according to Nova, our nanny.

"It's not a boy."

I scanned her face. She didn't blink. "Then where?"

She sighed as she pulled her hair back and wrapped it with one of the bands on my dresser. "No following either."

Great. Don't ask. Don't follow. Wait—somewhere close? The center of my stomach took flight.

Lindsay stared out the window and then back at me, everything perfect from her nose to that straight flowing hair. For some reason, I'd been given the *gift* of dark curls. Nova said that too, anytime my hair stuck out in ten different directions.

My sister leapt onto the side of the bed. "Look. I'm just meeting a few friends. I won't be gone long." The flat silver flask tucked into her purse said otherwise. And I'd be the one trying to make up stories if Dad came in. Which he might. He could. Not that he had . . . I didn't worry about Mom waking up after her pills kicked in.

I flopped back onto the pillow. "Fine."

She smiled, her teeth sparkling. "You've always been the good daughter."

I huffed. "One of us has to be."

Lindsay jumped off the bed, startling me. "You're the best."

She hopped into the window frame.

"Lin?"

"Yeah?"

I sat up again and hesitated, wishing she'd crawl under the covers and talk like we used to. To tell me her plans. She always had big ideas about life and how it would unfold for her. But she'd changed. This past year especially. She'd be in high school starting next month and we'd be in different schools. I was no match for girls her age. I missed her already. "Love you. But if you're not home before morning..."

"You always worry, Curls. Don't. I'll be okay."

"I hate when you call me that," I said.

"Love ya."

She disappeared.

I slid out of bed, padding across the fuzzy rug before my feet hit the cold wood floor. I shivered, watching her shuffle down the roof to the edge. Like a ninja cat, she dangled over on her stomach, her feet brushing the fence. *Be careful.* She dropped, hit the ground, and took off running.

At some point, she'd climb back in the same way since my room had access to the lower roof. Otherwise, I'd be as much in the dark about what Lindsay was up to as our parents. I'd never thought about what I'd say if Dad came through that door asking where she'd gone, but he was the other reason I hadn't followed. His disappointment in me would outweigh any fun with Lindsay and her friends.

But tonight, her lack of an answer about where she was going bothered me.

I watched her shadow across the property expecting her to be catching a ride. The light of the single streetlamp would track her on the road.

Instead, she veered to the right of our family's property... which led to a trail at the edge. The trail led to an open field, and on the other side, a river where an old wood trestle crossed over. No tracks on either side, removed long before we moved here. You could get to it from the main road, but only if you knew it was there. It was isolated. Quiet. Perfect. *Our place.*

My heart sank, joining the thump in my stomach. Lindsay might have decided it was better not to tell me, knowing I'd be upset that she'd told her friends about our spot. My eyes stung with tears.

Knock it off! I shouldn't have been surprised.

Except it was the first time I'd caught Lindsay withholding the truth.

CHAPTER 1

present day

preferred things black or white. Fact or fiction. Fact: I hate office parties. Also, fact: had I kept my butt in my chair, head down working, the night would have ended differently.

Gray—or the unknown—happens when you let others influence you. That's what happened when instead of sticking to what I knew, I got sucked into the holiday spirit.

My closest office friend, Mandy Perkins, had everything to do with that. She was another paralegal at Ralston, Higgins & Schroeder, my father's Portland-based law firm.

She bumped my shoulder. It was after office hours and we stood at the edge of the lobby that resembled the Four Seasons with its marble floors, maple and glass fixtures, and waitstaff drifting about, their trays filled with mini quiches and bacon-wrapped scallops. The pre-holiday *holiday* party had begun.

"This must be killing you, but you can't hide in your office forever."

The open bar flowing with hot-buttered rum and mixed drinks would help with my social anxiety, but Mandy was only half right on the other. Working endless hours without a break was one of my superpowers. "I have a ton to do. Don't you have a stack yourself?" I fought the urge to run and dig back in.

She wrinkled her mouth in a *quit making up excuses* sort of way. "It'll be there Monday, Beth. One drink won't hurt. It might even make you more fun."

"Fun doesn't pay the bills." Or get you ahead in life. Or a better interior office with a view of the Willamette River. An office I'd coveted since Day One at the firm, even if snagging the *view* required the attorney's door be open.

That part wasn't up to me though. The associate I worked for, Craig Bartell, had to make senior partner first. My hard work could help him get there. "Besides," I said, "my plus one was a no-show."

Another *something* I had little control over. My older sister, Lindsay, had blown me off without a reason. She'd never exhibited the same obligatory pull that I was cursed with, but it still stung that she hadn't bothered to text.

"I'm your plus one." Mandy smiled, cheesy as hell and showing teeth. "I just wish you'd dressed for the occasion. After all, Ms. Ralston, I do have a reputation to maintain."

My gray chinos and a black cardigan made the appropriate statement: up and coming, serious about being a lawyer, someday. But I'd ditched the ballet flats for strappy sandals and taken an extra twenty minutes to straighten my shoulder-length brown hair.

"What's wrong with this?"

Mandy's twinkling red sweater screamed *Ho Ho Ho* at me.

She shook her head. "You need a drink worse than I thought."

With no escaping my fate, I scanned the guests. Two of the attendees were my parents: Frederick Ralston III, drink in hand and with his usual ramrod posture, semi-retired as of last year, and my mother, Shelby. My father hadn't seen me yet, and I avoided eye contact to delay the inevitable.

Judge Evelyn Johnson, who'd come up through the ranks of the law firm before her election to the bench, stood next to my father and laughed at everything he said. She glanced up, flashing me a quick smile before stepping away and becoming engrossed in another conversation with a few lawyers—about Oregon Revised Statutes and compelling arguments, no doubt.

I should have chosen to hide instead of focusing on her because the inevitable became reality. My father motioned me over to his group that included several unfamiliar faces. I turned to Mandy and dropped my voice to a whisper. "This is why I should've kept working."

"Just do your daughterly duty and get back here. I'll nab you a martini."

"Make it a double." I stuck my tongue out at her. "See, I can be fun."

She laughed as I swooped a bite-sized quiche from a passing tray, shoved it into my mouth, and started across the room.

My boss, Craig, intercepted me before I got two steps. "Beth. We need to talk." His green eyes bore into mine with a huge dose of seriousness.

Most of the secretaries thought my very single associate was quite handsome. The fact he was great to work for, most of the time, meant more to me. "Can it wait? My presence has been requested." I tilted my head in my dad's direction.

Craig raked a hand through his dark wavy hair. "I didn't realize he'd be here." His eye twitched and his ever-present smile was MIA. Droplets of sweat covered his top lip. The same thing happened to me when I was nervous.

It wasn't an odd reaction to the *great Mr. Ralston* being in the house—he made most associates quiver. "Even when he's fully retired, he won't miss a party." *Have to make sure the firm's profits aren't wasted on frivolities,* he liked to say.

Craig frowned harder as he gripped my arm tight. "About that, you could use more billables this month. Being out here won't accomplish that."

Whoa. Did he expect me to blow off my father? Not that the thought hadn't crossed my mind.

Matching Craig's serious look with one of my own, I stepped away enough to make his hand drop from my arm. "That deposition summary you wanted will be finished over the weekend. And I've already crushed this month's required billables."

He nodded and forced a smile that didn't look right on him. "Sorry. Of course, you have it handled." More surprising, that perspiration had progressed to his forehead.

"You feeling okay?" I asked.

"Yeah. Go ahead. We'll talk later."

I squeezed his upper arm. "Wish me luck."

Still thinking about Craig's off behavior, I approached my father and his fan club. "Dad."

My father wrapped his arm around my shoulders and introduced me to his inner circle, lingering on the people I hadn't recognized. Turned out they were city councilmen. Word on the street was Dad was vying for political office and had formed an exploratory committee to begin early stages for a mayoral campaign.

Mom hadn't said much at the "mandatory" family brunch last Sunday—not so mandatory, it appeared, since my sister hadn't attended the last three and was a sporadic guest before that. But the way Mom had taken to chatting with Dad's longtime paralegal at the far corner of the room instead of being at his side spoke volumes about what she thought of the idea.

"I'd like to introduce you to my new campaign manager, Ericka Hough," Dad said, puffing his chest.

"Guess it's official then?" I asked.

Ericka reached out a cold thin hand. "Pleasure." She held my gaze with her cool blue eyes. "I've heard about you."

"All good, I hope?"

Her lips-only smile response had me shifting my feet.

My father took a drink from his ice-clinking glass filled with scotch—that's how he rolled—and cleared his throat. "How's my little girl?" He gave me no time to respond. "She's a paralegal here, working for an associate by her own choice. She could have been through law school and practicing as a full-fledged attorney by now if she'd accepted my money. Determined to make it on her own or forget about it."

They all nodded. They either admired me or thought I'd lost my mind. But Dad's money never came without strings, and while I worked at the firm to maintain peace, I was determined to control some portions of my life. A part of me resisted blazing the same path he did—and the mountain of debt that loans brought held no appeal. Even more true, with no idea what I wanted yet, staying buried in work made it easy not to decide.

"Stubborn, this one," he added as an underscore.

"Chip off the old block?" one of the councilmen said.

My father chuckled.

He introduced me the same way every time, so what came next was no surprise.

"Now her sister, Lindsay. She's an investigative reporter bent on changing the world." It was subtle, but he rolled his eyes.

The group burst out laughing—my cue to bow out. Even though my father and Lindsay butted heads on environmental issues, he had an image to uphold as the ever-supportive father. My sister's resume would now take the stage and, love or hate her causes, she had the ability to dazzle.

Except when it came to communicating.

I yanked my phone from my cardigan pocket and shot her off a text: *You're missing a great party. You really should be here. Dad's speaking your "praises"!*

My phone remained silent.

I was being petty. She was always busy out "saving the world," as Dad said. Anyway, unlike her, I never stayed upset with her for long.

Tucking my cell back into my sweater, I found Mandy holding my double martini. "Thanks." I took it and searched the room for Craig. "You see my boss anywhere?"

"He disappeared after you left for your chat. You guys are clearly Virgos—never stop working. You're perfect for each other."

Our birthdays were a day apart, and the rest might be true, but I shrugged and took a long sip of my martini with a wince. "Did you triple this?"

She giggled. "Nice dodge."

Over the next hour, I finished my drink, mingled with a few of the staff, gave my mom a hug goodbye as she ducked out because *one of those horrific migraines is coming on*, and avoided getting caught by Dad or his campaign manager. In an effort to be *more fun*, I even let Mandy talk me into another dirty martini instead of generating billable hours.

When Mandy headed to the bar for her third—or fourth—drink, I snuck out to the bathroom. On my return, I used the rear entry that led to the hall near my office and keyed in my security code. The introvert in me had hit a socializing wall, and I hadn't gotten back to Craig, whose door had been closed when I passed by. I'd circle back in a few. He'd appeared a little *maxed* himself and I'd touch base with him on my way out.

In my office, I gathered a couple of depos in the wrongful death case going to trial next month that needed to be summarized and shoved them into my bag. The CEO's deposition had been on my desk when I left for the party. *Shoot.* Craig must have grabbed it. Guess we'd chat sooner rather than later.

As I stepped out of my office, a woman with a jean jacket, electric blue tennis shoes, and straight red hair darted out of Craig's office and sprinted to the back door at the end of the hallway. The woman looked like my sister, especially with those signature bright-colored shoes.

She turned her head as her hands smacked through the exit bar. It *was* my sister.

"Lindsay," I hollered, wondering why she'd been in Craig's office. More to the point, why hadn't she texted if she'd planned to make an appearance?

Maybe she'd tried to find me instead. Between Mandy dragging me around and that second martini, we might've missed each other.

"Lindsay?" I called again as the door latched shut.

The least she could do was offer an explanation. I ran to the end of the hall and shoved open the exit door. An elevator dinged in the lobby. By the time I rounded the corner, the doors had closed.

I caught the next car down and sent another text. *Saw you. Wait up.*

Lindsay would park in the underground lot where the firm-paid stalls were located, but she hadn't responded by the time I stepped out of the elevator. The dim lights on the low ceilings did a poor job of illuminating the concrete cavern. It reminded me of the building's dungeon—at least that's what I called the firm's basement, where archived files and wills were kept. No one went to that floor voluntarily, often leaving the task to the administrator. This area gave off the same tomb-like sensation. Unlike the "basement," exhaust hung in the cool air. A shiver ran through me.

During the day, every stall would be filled. Now, half the cars remained, which accounted for the partygoers upstairs, and none included Lindsay's white Prius. I scanned the lot one last time to see if she'd caught a ride with someone else.

And that's when I saw him. A man slunk low behind the steering wheel of a black sedan, dark hair his only distinguishing feature. The lighting made it hard to tell anything else about him except that he seemed to be watching me. The hairs on my arms raised.

I listened again for footfalls or the sound of an engine turning over. Nothing. Either Lindsay hadn't parked here, or she'd left before I'd made it down.

When I turned back to the elevator, it had closed. Looking paranoid might offend the guy in the car if he was a chauffeur waiting for one of the bigwigs upstairs. Offensive or not, I refused to be too comfortable in this setting. I glanced at the black sedan once more.

The man was gone.

My heart kicked into a hard knock while I searched the area and punched the UP arrow like I was sending Morse code. When it arrived, I hustled in and slapped the *CLOSE DOOR* button.

Once inside the safety of the elevator's walls, I balked at my paranoia, until the sound of heavy footsteps gaining speed grew louder. I squashed the impulse to hold the ride and willed the closing doors to hurry. My jaw remained clenched until the metal pressed together.

It took ten floors before my breath released. One martini would be my limit in the future. The guy in the car could have dropped something and bent over to pick it up, and anyone could have been running to catch the elevator.

Even so, my skin had not stopped tingling, and I was relieved to be back upstairs.

The party had started to clear when I came through the front doors this time, and that included Mandy, and my father and his entourage. Only a handful of hangers-on remained at the bar. Guests had been going downstairs while I was coming up. The footsteps I'd heard must have been one of those partygoers rushing to their car.

I started in the direction of my office and kept walking toward Craig's. He might know why Lindsay had stopped by, and I'd yet to retrieve the CEO's file.

Craig's brown leather chair was turned away when I tapped on the door. "Sorry to interrupt. Coming for the Graham depo. I promise to have it done first thing Monday."

He didn't respond.

The files were stacked on the credenza against the wall in front of his desk. "About earlier." I headed that way. "I apologize for not making time right then to talk. My dad has a way of throwing me off when he's here." I swooped the files into my arms. "But hey, I saw my sister. Was she looking for me?"

Craig still didn't respond. If he had his headset on, he wouldn't hear me. Mandy was right about one thing—we were both workaholics.

To avoid startling him, I stepped to the side of his desk. Craig's head was at an odd angle. God, he'd passed out, and I'd been rambling on.

"Wake up, sunshine. Party's over." I touched his chair. His head fell forward, his chin bouncing on his red shirt.

I clutched the files to my chest.

That shirt was pale blue an hour ago.

Now it was soaked in blood.

CHAPTER 2

Alone in my office, head between my knees, I sucked in air. My rib cage constricted with every breath to the point I worried my bones might crack. My throat was raw, my jaw hurt, my heart ached.

Time blurred as I'd stood in Craig's office screaming. The firm administrator, Phil Garrett, dashed past me at some point, shock creasing his face at the sight of my boss drenched in blood.

Dead.

Mr. Garrett's steadying hand on my back had guided me into my office. He'd been with my father since the firm's inception, but I doubted he'd ever come across anything like this. Still, he remained calm as he led me to my chair.

"Stay put until the police arrive," he'd said.

I must have nodded because he disappeared down the hall again to join the few lawyers who'd run past my office in the meantime. Thank goodness no party guests remained on the floor at that point.

Craig.

My right leg bounced at the memory of him in that chair. His throat had to have been slashed to explain that amount of blood. Had he been surprised from behind? Or . . . My stomach acid stirred, threatening a comeback. I couldn't think about the blood or how he'd died. The question was why? Were any of us safe with a killer on the loose? The police were on the way . . .

Someone needed to notify his parents. Although he'd never spoken of them. Once he'd mentioned not having siblings. His immediate family consisted of Murphy, a gray tabby he'd adopted as a kitten.

I sat upright. My parents. Mr. Garrett hadn't called them, or my phone would be exploding. That's if my mom hadn't taken her pills and already gone to bed. Or if my father hadn't continued the party elsewhere.

And what about Lindsay?

If she went into Craig's office and found him dead, why run? Why not come find me, call the police, tell *someone*? Unless . . . Dizzy, I dropped my bag on the floor to put my head between my knees again and dug out my phone.

I shot off another text to Lindsay. *Call me. Now!!!*

While I pulled up my *FAVORITES* list in contacts for Dad's number, the ding of a cell phone echoed from deep inside my purse.

My gaze stuck to my bag like it contained a poisonous spider.

I owned one phone—the one in my hand.

The commotion continued down the hall. I reached into my purse and pulled out the source of the ding—a white iPhone wrapped in a zebra striped case. My grip tightened around it. Lindsay's phone.

She'd long used her birthday for her passcode, and it opened on the first attempt, landing on the text screen. The text was written to me but not sent: *Don't ask! Don't follow!*

Don't ask. I'd heard that a million times since we were kids. But *don't follow?*

That was reserved for when she was up to something questionable.

My stomach turned again. Had she been in Craig's office when I'd passed by a few minutes before? Why had she shut the door? And her phone—she had to have dropped it in my purse after seeing Craig . . . which meant she'd gone back in? How could she know I'd see her in the first place?

So many questions, and none of the answers hopping into my head were good. Including the worst of them—that she'd left her phone behind so the police couldn't track her. It could be why she hadn't sent the text. An unsent message couldn't be tied to her contacting me at about the same time Craig was murdered.

That felt like premeditation . . . but I didn't, couldn't, believe that. Not about Lindsay.

Forcing my leg to stop bouncing, I clicked back to the main conversation screen and scrolled through the texts, desperate to find why she'd been here in the first place. Proof that she'd been looking for me when she'd gone inside Craig's office. In shock at the sight of him, she'd run . . . that had to be the case, right?

That's not what I found.

Earlier in the day, Lindsay had received a text from a 503 number. I'd texted that number many times myself—it belonged to Craig.

One message remained in the history: *I have the information you wanted.*

What information?

"Excuse me." A voice came from my doorway.

I dropped Lindsay's phone into my bag and bolted to my feet. "Yes."

The man shadowing my office had *detective* written all over his somber face. His wire-rimmed glasses framed weary green eyes. The gray weaving around his short dark hair suggested he had ten years on me. Under different circumstances, like sitting next to him at the paralegal ethics class I'd enrolled in for next spring, I might find him attractive.

"Are you Beth Ralston, the individual who discovered Mr. Bartell?"

"I am. I'm Craig's . . . was Craig's . . . paralegal."

His eyes softened. "How long had you worked for him?"

"Five years." My voice shook remembering my first days at the firm. My father had insisted I be assigned to a partner and allow him to put me in a better office. I declined, insisting I start from the bottom and earn any promotions the way everyone else did— with hard work.

He relented and when an opening with Craig, a newer associate, became available, I applied. We hit it off right away. Our drive to succeed, coupled with neither of us having a social life, helped. But it was more than that. Unlike so many other lawyers, Craig had a heart. I'd seen it in the way he took interest in pro bono work. How he'd picked up elderly clients nervous about testifying so he could make them feel comfortable before court.

How he cared for Murphy.

"You're understandably in shock," the detective said, returning my attention to the room. "But if you're up to it, I have some questions. May I come in?"

"Okay." I eased into my chair and rested my elbows on the desktop. Using my foot, I guided my bag underneath the desk.

My mouth became the Sahara Desert debating how much I could tell him. Not about the message from Lindsay. Not about seeing her run out the door. Now I suppressed a cringe at the thought of meeting this man in an ethics class.

He pulled a card from his waist-length jacket and handed it to me. *Detective Troy Matson. Portland Police Bureau, Homicide.*

I forced down a swallow. "Have they removed Craig yet?" The question sent a ripple of anxiety through me. But his being left in the state I'd found him bothered me.

"No. The DA's working to get a special master assigned before the medical examiner will release him."

"I see." A special master would ensure that attorney/client privileged items were protected while the scene was processed. They'd taught that in one of my first criminal procedure classes.

"Can you tell me your version of events starting with the last time you spoke with Mr. Bartell?" he said.

"We were in the lobby," I began, and recounted speaking with my father and not seeing Craig again until I'd gone to retrieve a file.

"How did he appear during that initial interaction?"

"Stressed, but there's a trial coming up and there's always the pressure to bill around here. Time is money."

He nodded. "Anything about that case that could have led to this?"

We both knew I couldn't talk about client business. "Not that I know of."

"He have problems with anyone? Outside of the case files. A co-worker perhaps?"

"Craig got along with everyone. I mean, I guess not everyone, but . . ." *Oh geez.*

He tilted his head to the side. "How so?"

"Nothing specific, but he's a lawyer. I'm sure he's upset the other side, a witness, a defendant."

Had he upset my sister?

"True enough," he said, "Where were you this evening at seven thirty?"

"I'd gone to the ladies' room and came back to my office about that time."

"How long were you in your own office?"

I closed my eyes. The thought of Craig dead or dying at that point pushed me to the edge of tears. "I didn't check the clock."

"When did you decide to go into Mr. Bartell's office?"

The blood rushed out of my face. From the time I'd seen Lindsay, chased her down, and returned upstairs couldn't have been more than ten minutes. A couple more to get through the lobby.

"Ms. Ralston?" Detective Matson said.

"Yes?"

"Approximates are fine."

I sighed. "I'm sorry. It was probably twenty minutes before I decided to retrieve a file I planned to work on over the weekend."

"And during that time, did you see or hear anyone in the hallway or around Mr. Bartell's office?"

I couldn't implicate Lindsay. I wouldn't. Because *don't ask, don't follow* implied another equally crucial directive—*don't tell.* Anyone. As kids, that meant our parents. Until I knew more, it would now include the detective.

"Everyone was out enjoying the festivities. Craig had disappeared, and I figured he'd gone to put in more work. I'd done all the partying I could handle—that's why I came back here. If I'd known someone was attacking him . . ." Tears stung my eyes now. "If I could have done something to help him . . ."

The detective's eyes wrinkled. Warm. Understanding. "It's okay, Ms. Ralston. It's going to be a long night here and you've answered my initial questions. You're free to go."

"Thank you." I lifted my purse and grabbed the workbag with the files, slinging it over my shoulder.

"You'll need to leave the files, Ms. Ralston."

Right. They could be relevant. Setting the bag on the chair, I followed him out of my office and headed for the lobby, desperate to leave.

"Ms. Ralston," he called after me.

I held myself steady and turned back to him. "Yes, Detective?"

"You planning any weekend escapes I should know about?"

I shook my head, too hard.

"Good. Might be best if you don't."

Unsettled, I flashed an inappropriate smile and raced down the hall.

When I was twelve and Lindsay was fifteen, she'd snuck a boy into her bedroom on the second floor for a sleepover. The boy had broken my mother's favorite crystal vase on his way to the bathroom during the night. The next morning, Lindsay begged me to take the blame. Otherwise, our father, a stickler for everything to be in pristine condition, would have grounded her from the next night's Homecoming dance.

As I'd done countless times before, I covered for her and spent the weekend relegated to my room. Surrounded by my favorite books, I didn't mind.

But we were no longer kids, and this wasn't a boy in the bedroom. This was my boss dead in his office.

Covering for my sister this time could cost me everything—and I couldn't let that happen.

Whether she liked it or not, I needed to get to the bottom of this.

CHAPTER 3

Craig's cat, Murphy, met me at his door.

I smoothed the strip of fur on his head that stood up like a mohawk and Murphy's chest rattled with a purr. I often watched Murphy when Craig traveled. The last time, Craig had been attending a friend's funeral back east and I put gel in that mohawk and shot off a pic to him. By the amount of LMAO emojis that came back, it had done the trick to raise his spirits.

Halfway home, that image and the one of Murphy waiting for his friend who'd never come had drifted into my mind, forcing me to make an illegal U-turn. Also concerning, once Craig's family arrived, they could place Murphy in a shelter. Since Craig hadn't spoken about them, they might not be close—and not everyone loved cats. Even before that, if the detective sent a team to search the house, Murphy could sneak out. I'd never encountered Craig's neighbors, but a Welsh corgi sprinted the fence line across the street, and that alone would put Murphy into hiding.

Neither scenario was acceptable.

Detective Matson wouldn't approve of my unannounced drop-in, but keeping Murphy safe and well cared for was the least I could do for Craig.

"You're coming home with me," I told Murphy, who let out a yowl putting an end to the loving. It was after nine. The boy was hungry.

Craig's modern kitchen reflected the life of a busy bachelor. A mixture of breakfast dishes in the sink, and a pile of clean plates and cups on the drying pad. A container of protein powder and vitamins on the counter, along with his sports watch. He'd likely logged a few miles before work.

How quickly things could change flitted through my mind. He'd likely expected to put those dishes away tonight when he got home. Maybe even prepare a midnight snack. I lifted his watch off the counter and rubbed my thumb across the clock face. He might have set his alarm for another run in the morning. He often spoke about how he enjoyed starting the day that way.

Now the space felt empty and cold . . . sad. Like it too knew Craig was gone forever.

I wrapped my arms around myself to stave off the impending grief. How did a man so young and fit get taken down? I'd seen no signs of struggle in his office. Had he been surprised, or was it someone he knew—someone he trusted? How did Lindsay play into that—or did she?

I both wished for and dreaded the answer to that question. Returning the watch to the counter, I refocused on why I'd come here—to get Murphy, and his bowl sat empty.

A pantry shelf contained a stack of pâté dinners. I opened a can of chicken and shook the meaty gel into his bowl. Before dislodging Murphy from his home, I'd let him eat. It would give me time to find his crate. Since he visited my house on occasion, I already had some of his essentials, but I had to get him there first.

The hall closet, the usual place for Murphy's crate, came up short. Same with the garage. I ended up in Craig's office, where the crate sat on top of the credenza with a comfy striped bed inside. Knowing Murphy, he'd traipsed across the desk, messing with the paperwork one time too many, so Craig had given him his own space. The idea of how much Craig loved that cat squeezed my heart.

Slumped in Craig's chair, I scanned his messy desk, quite unlike the organized workspace he maintained at the firm. Not that I was privy to his habits at home, but he was clearly two different people.

Earlier in the day, he'd texted Lindsay to say he had the information she wanted. But what information? I'd been in and out of Craig's office all afternoon, long before the party, rummaging through his desk, grabbing files. Not once did anything strike me as odd or unrelated to our cases. I'd even gone through his briefcase that morning to find a file he'd taken home.

The message hadn't indicated when they were meeting or where.

I reached to open his drawer, and then pulled back. Nothing felt right about snooping in Craig's desk. But I couldn't fathom what information he had for my sister.

Lindsay championed environmental causes, putting her investigative nose to rooting out toxic waste being dumped into the Willamette River, or the decimation of forestland where the spotted owl lived. And a million things in between. To that end, she took risks when protests she attended got violent. She'd also infiltrated extremist groups a time or two.

When she was back safe though, Lindsay got an earful. Which hadn't helped our relationship in the past several years.

But that was beside the point. While she'd met Craig a couple of times over the years, Craig didn't handle environmental law. Even if he did, how could I see the man for ten hours a day and the topic of him assisting my sister never come up?

It could be a side project, I supposed. There was only one way to find out.

Craig kept several "working files" in his home office filled with thoughts, strategies, and directives that would find their way into my inbox for my never-ending list of To Dos on a matter. In case the police expanded their search to Craig's home office, and I had to admit to being here, I wouldn't mess things up. Otherwise, the detective could accuse me of having an ulterior motive.

I started with the top drawer. The organizer was turned upside down. Odd, but I left it. The second was filled with blank legal pads and extra pens. The third drawer down contained hanging files, which I fingered through. Last year's taxes. A file labeled ST. LUKE'S with the edge of a medical report sticking out. There was a health clinic by that name in the southwest part of town. Craig's medical history was none of my business.

Nothing looked out of the ordinary . . . until a manila folder laid flat on the drawer bottom peeked through. I shifted the hanging files and retrieved it. The words "LR-Query" and "Confidential" were scrawled across the top in Craig's handwriting.

LR could be short for dozens of things: lost receipts, local restaurants, lobster risotto. The file could have fallen out of one of the hangings and slipped down by accident, and here I was rifling through his personal stuff. It could also have been put there to conceal it, and *LR* was short for Lindsay Ralston. The word *confidential* left me no choice but to check.

I'd just cracked open the file when the distinct sound of rubber-soled tennis shoes against tile came from the entry. Someone hollered, "Anyone home?"

Slapping the file closed, I hopped out of the chair, almost toppling it. "Just a second." I shoved the file under the bed in Murphy's crate before grasping the handle and rushing in the direction of the voice.

Coming out of the office, I stopped short of slamming into a stump of a man, a few inches below my five-eight frame. His eyes were dark brown, almost black, and his hair was the color of a Shetland pony I'd ridden when I was six. Not unattractive; not natural either. He seemed familiar, but I couldn't place him.

"You're not Craig," he said.

"I'm his assistant. And you are?"

He scrutinized my face like he was deciding whether I was telling the truth. "His neighbor, Henry."

That explained it. I must've seen him in passing before when I'd stopped by. "Where do you live?"

"Across the way."

"With the corgi?"

"Right." He paused. "You stealing his cat?"

"Why would you think that?"

He nodded toward the crate in my hand.

Geez. "I'm sorry, yes. I mean, no." He hadn't heard about Craig, and I'd leave it to someone else to tell him. "Craig's out of town."

"I see." He didn't move. "You taking the little guy to your place then?" He peered inside the empty enclosure.

Empty except for the bed—and the file. I dropped my arm, letting the crate dangle at my side. "I am. Or will be when I put him in here."

He didn't make way for me to get by him.

Had my boss not been murdered—followed by my sister's message and the guy who'd creeped me out in the parking lot—this conversation wouldn't have fazed me. I'd interviewed hostile witnesses and dealt with pompous judge's clerks enough to navigate most any conversation.

But what kind of neighbor spent their time late at night spying on their other neighbors? Okay . . . well, mine. But who came over to investigate? "I should go . . . do that. Take Murphy home."

His gaze drifted past me into Craig's office. I shut the door and smiled. Well-meaning neighbor or not, there were legal files inside that room.

"Guess I'll let you get to it," he said. "To be honest, I thought maybe you were that other chick that stopped by earlier."

The hairs on the back of my arm pricked. "What other woman?"

"Small thing. Red hair. Flighty. I'd planned to talk with her, but she was in and out so fast . . . What do you suppose she was doing here?"

"No idea. She doesn't sound familiar." I turned so he didn't see my eye twitch. "About what time was that?"

"Two, maybe three hours ago."

Not long before I'd seen Lindsay at the firm. After Craig was dead. I'd have to think about what that meant later. "Yeah, no idea." I lifted the crate. "It's getting late. Better go."

I walked Henry to the door and found Murphy in the kitchen. He'd finished dinner and had moved onto licking his paws. I swooped him inside the transporter and latched it.

"Sorry, bud." I put the extra cans into a bag, thinking about how having a cat full-time in my life would work. I'd never made room for a pet, let alone a man, and my apartment didn't allow animals. Murphy had always been snuck in because it was for no more than a week at a time. Now Craig was gone. My chest tightened. I'd worry about long-term and Murphy later.

In my car, I set my new roommate on the passenger seat. It was almost ten o'clock. The neighbor who'd thought to check on me had gone to bed because his house was dark.

Before I'd left the driveway, my phone rang. Lindsay? I dumped the contents of my purse on the floorboard to find it lit with a private number. Maybe . . .

"Hello," I said.

"Beth Ralston?" a man said. Not Lindsay.

I drooped into the seat. "Yes."

"Detective Matson here. We'll need to have another conversation sooner than I thought."

Trepidation marched across my skin. "Back at the office?"

"No. Meet me downtown at the precinct."

That didn't feel any better. "Now?"

"That would be best."

CHAPTER 4

Murphy and I entered the downtown police precinct on the first floor. I would have taken him home first, but the quicker I got this over with the better.

While I'd stomped all over Portland for work, I'd never set foot inside the sea green and glass building that housed the inner workings of the police force, and the holding cells upstairs. Craig's murder being the reason now—and the fact I withheld my sister's presence at the firm—had every part of me in knots as I approached the desk sergeant.

The file I'd absconded with from Craig's place was secured under the driver's seat of my car parked a block away. I'd look at it later. Explaining Murphy would be plenty.

The sergeant led me to a conference room where I could have been cast as the suspect in a crime show the way Detective Matson sauntered in a few minutes after that, his face pinched in concentration. He'd lost his jacket and rolled his sleeves up to his elbows. He held two cups of coffee and set one in front of me.

"Hope you like it black," he said.

"Thank you." My hands shook as I reached for it. I set them into my lap instead, hoping he hadn't noticed.

"You brought a friend?" He sat across from me, lifting his chin toward Murphy.

Might as well just yank the Band-Aid off. "He's Craig's. I'd just left his house when you called. It's too cold to leave Murphy in the car."

The detective's chin pressed into his chest. "You went to Mr. Bartell's home?"

"Yes. I realized after I'd left that Murphy had been alone all day. He needed to eat, and I've been Murph's designated pet sitter since he was a kitten."

"You've been around law your whole life, correct, Ms. Ralston?"

"Yes," I said, my leg bouncing. I pressed down on it. I swear it had a mind of its own.

"Then you know better."

Having him annoyed was no way to begin—but had he given me an escort, I wouldn't have gotten a mile near Craig's desk. "I was only thinking of Murphy."

His eyebrows raised. "Did you touch anything?"

"Just the cat and what he needs." I shifted, trying to get comfortable. "Why did you want to see me again?" I scooted to the chair's edge. "Have you found Craig's killer?" If he had, at least that part of the nightmare would be over.

Unless Lindsay was involved somehow. My leg started up and I stopped it again.

Detective Matson took a long sip of his coffee. "After you left, a few of your co-workers at a bar nearby saw the commotion and returned to the office."

"What co-workers?"

"Mandy Perkins, for one."

When she'd disappeared without saying goodbye, I figured she'd gone home after one too many. "Sure, Mandy. We're friends."

"Good friends?"

"Yes."

"So, she'd have no reason to embellish or lie about anything as it pertains to you?"

Huh. That sounded like a trap. "Not that I'm aware of, but I wouldn't attest to that."

He flashed a smile that didn't reach his eyes. "Have you had any recent interactions that would lead her to lie about you?"

"No," I said, a little terser than I'd intended. "Why all these questions?"

"What were you and Craig Bartell speaking about during the party?"

"Nothing. He said we needed to talk but didn't say what about. And my dad had motioned me over, so that's where I was headed. I told you that earlier."

"Is that all?"

"He also wanted me to put in more hours for the month."

"Did that make you angry?"

"Craig's tone surprised me, but I wasn't angry."

"How about when he grabbed your arm?"

Damn it, Mandy. "He did that for emphasis." Though it had been out of character. "Did my *friend* also tell you that I squeezed his arm too? It's not unusual. We'd worked together for years. We're friends as well as co-workers." I nodded at the crate. "Clearly."

The detective folded his arms across his chest. "What time did you say you returned to the offices through the back?"

Had I said? "I can't be exact. Seven-thirty. Forty . . ."

"You used a passcode?"

"That's the only way to access that door."

"Anyone else know it?"

My lower jaw quivered. I bit down hard before saying, "I don't think so. Why?"

But someone did—Lindsay.

"We pulled the computer records on the lock. Your passcode was used two other times that night. Once at seven. Another at seven twenty. Care to explain?"

A bead of sweat formed above my lip. I rubbed it away before he noticed. "The code is the six-digit version of our birth dates and the numerical equivalent of our first and last initials. It's the same for all employees."

His eyes narrowed. "You're saying it wasn't you then?"

I squared my shoulders. "I told you the one time I came through there. Are you sure the computer records are accurate?"

He smirked and leaned his forearms on the desk, peering in at Murphy. "Cute cat."

Murphy stared back, unflinching. I'd have given anything to channel his cool demeanor because my body wanted to betray me in a full out tremble. Lindsay's actions could get me arrested or at least detained. Did that thought cross her mind when she used my info?

"Let's say you're right," he said. "Someone else came through that door. Who knew your code? More to the point, who'd want to set you up?" He wiggled a finger at Murphy.

This merry-go-round had me dizzy and I needed off. "Can't think of anyone. But if you were a killer, you wouldn't be using your own code."

His eyes locked on mine.

Murphy reached his paw out to scratch the detective, who pulled back. It was enough to break the tension in the room.

"If there's nothing else, Detective, I'd like to get him home and settled."

"I have a feeling we're just getting started."

My mouth opened to protest.

He cut me off. "However, it's late. In the meantime, don't go anywhere near Mr. Bartell's house again. Are we clear?"

I held back a relieved sigh but didn't avert my eyes. "Yes, sir."

A loud voice came from outside the room and the door swung open. "That will be all."

My father was here?

Detective Matson rose. "Mr. Ralston. To what do we owe the pleasure?"

My father bristled. "You. I thought I recognized the name when we spoke earlier on the phone."

Okay, then. They had history, and it didn't sound good.

"Right," the detective said. "Again. What can I do for you?"

My father cleared his throat. "You can cease questioning my client and refrain from doing so in the future without my presence. You do know how rights work, don't you, Detective?"

"Dad," I said. "Please."

His hand shot up to silence me. "Is that understood?"

Detective Matson sat down and took a long sip of his coffee. "Your daughter and I were having a friendly chat. She's not under arrest."

Friendly was a stretch. "I have it handled, Dad."

"Good, then she'll be leaving," he said, as if he hadn't heard me.

The staring contest between the detective and my dad filled the room with an unbearable level of testosterone.

"Thank you, Detective Matson." I shot out of my seat. "Let me know if you need anything else." Crate in hand, I hurried out. My dad caught up with me as I cleared the second glass entry door.

"You should have called," he said.

"How did you even know I was here?"

"Phil overheard the detective and then notified me."

Ears were everywhere in that firm. And eyes. Mandy's quick assumption had thrown me right under the suspicion bus without a warning. More than a little upsetting. Maybe we weren't as close as I thought.

Just like Lindsay and me.

No, that was different. We didn't always talk with our crazy schedules, but we were sisters. Yes, we had history. History that included difficulties in seeing each other's perspectives. But hadn't I proven over the years, regardless of her questionable ways, that I had her back? Maybe I believed that meant she'd have mine. Using my code to gain access to the office though . . . *Thanks, big sis. I don't mind looking guilty at all on your behalf.* This wasn't a broken vase. This was murder.

"While I appreciate you running down here, Dad, I don't need rescuing. And what was that back there with the detective?"

His eyes narrowed. "I don't trust him, and neither should you. He was set to testify for the defendant in a matter I handled years back. His testimony would've ensured my client walked. Instead, he got on the stand and flipped, burning my case to the ground. Bottom line, I don't want you talking to him."

I was good with that. "Hopefully there won't be any more rea-son to."

"I'd like to think that's true."

"By the way, did you see Lindsay at the party tonight?" I asked.
He stiffened. "No. Did you?"

His reaction suggested he'd invited her, but she'd shunned him
as well. Classic Lindsay—except Fred Ralston the Third wasn't
used to being ignored. "I didn't, but she's not answering her
phone," I said.

His shoulders rounded in a way that made him look older and
exhausted. "You know Lindsay. A wild child, that one. Unlike
you, stubborn like your mother, by the way." He pulled me in for
a sideways hug at our inside joke—I'd never been anything like
my mother. "But Lindsay . . . I wouldn't worry about her even if
sometimes I wonder if she'll burn out too soon."

I pecked him on the cheek. "Who're you kidding? Her drive is
all yours. You and she will burn bright forever."

He gave me a sad smile, as if that could be a problem. "If
Detective Matson reaches out again, call me."

I watched my father disappear into a waiting town car.
Lindsay's need to save the world, and his to rule it, didn't mesh.
Though tonight, he'd spoken about her in a way he hadn't before.

Maybe he was just tired—and I'd been a little hard on him
since he'd come all this way to assist. Even if he'd never felt com-pelled to help me in the past, at least not when I was in trouble.

In ninth grade, I'd been accused of shoplifting a tube of mas-cara. My so-called friend at the time had dropped it into my back-pack and dashed out the door. A security guard reeking of sweat
and onions nabbed me, and my father let me sit in the old guy's

dim, closet-sized office for five hours before he'd allowed a driver to pick me up.

Of course, a Ralston involved in a murder investigation and a shoplifting offense were worlds apart. But he couldn't possibly think I was involved . . . so why the rush to help me now?

CHAPTER 5

I t was after two when I got home, got Murphy settled, and collapsed into my lumpy queen-sized bed. At some point I'd replace it, but every extra penny went toward savings. If I decided to take the leap into law school, it would be on my terms, and without being indebted to my parents—despite their willingness to help. Lindsay and I were more alike on that than she could see sometimes.

"Why would you want to be anything like Dad?" she'd said more than once. "Join me on the front lines. We could change the world."

A noble idea for sure, but I had not seen her change the world. I'd seen chaos and her cohorts dragged off to jail. Good intentions turned ugly when people with extreme ideas joined the movement. When Lindsay was in college, I thought she'd always be a die-hard tree hugger and nothing more. Then she channeled her energy into investigative reporting, which she did with a vengeance.

While I agreed with her causes, I chose a different path. "You keep approaching the problem from the outside. You have to hit them where it makes a difference. In the courts. In the regulations. On the political side."

"That's a sellout."

"It's not."

Round and round we'd go. Maybe sisters just butted heads, but I still couldn't reconcile why she'd been at the firm tonight, or why she'd leave me such a cryptic message.

Sometime after three I fell asleep. Murphy had to reacquaint himself with the surroundings, which meant jumping on counters, walking on the bookshelf, toppling a good portion of my favorite romance novels, and deciding there might be a mouse in the kitchen.

After that, it was hit or miss. Dreams of slamming cell doors and finding myself in an orange jumpsuit had me waking drenched in sweat—and then reality set in. Craig Bartlett, my boss, and a man I'd truly liked, was dead.

The tears came then, and Murphy snuggled next to my shoulder, sensing my grief—perhaps even his own. But I couldn't spend time stuck in that emotion. My sister had fled the scene and the police were questioning my involvement. My dreams might be foretelling my future if I didn't find Lindsay and answers soon.

When I crawled out of bed around seven, I plodded barefoot into the living room and turned on a small table lamp before hitting the kitchen to toss a pod into the Keurig machine.

While the coffee brewed, I gazed at the living room from the pass-through window. Murphy, tired of my thrashing last night, had found his way to the sofa where he was curled in a tight ball of fluff.

In a daze from the night's events, I hadn't taken notice of my apartment when I got home. Now as I inspected the surroundings, the smell of coffee in the air, something felt off.

The books on the shelf nearest the TV had toppled from the second shelf down, and the cabinet door was ajar. My laptop sat askew on the desk that looked out over the park.

"Did you do that, Murph?" I asked, shutting the cabinet.

He fell to his side and stretched in response.

From the window over my desk, I glanced outside. The oak trees dripped moisture onto the concrete path that wound through the park. It had rained some last night.

On a summer day, people and their dogs, joggers, roller skaters, old couples holding hands, and street musicians called the park home. More than a few billable hours had been accumulated while hanging out on the fire escape and listening to my favorite reggae band when it showed.

Now, one old man scurried through wearing a long raincoat and cradling a small dog. Another man dressed head-to-toe in rain gear huddled on the last bench at the end not illuminated by the streetlamp. He seemed focused in my direction. As the old man passed him, the benchwarmer glanced down.

Probably nothing. Just the same, I pushed down on the window, confirming it was locked tight.

My apartment might not be in the best part of Portland—the homeless found their way up this far on occasion—but a guard made sporadic rounds at night, and I'd never had a problem with break-ins. There'd be no reason to bother. Jewelry I'd received as gifts over the years was kept in a safe at my parents' house. My four-year-old laptop had no street value. The senior citizens in the building with their assortment of medications would be a more desirable target than my place.

The Keurig gurgled and I retrieved my cup from the kitchen. The events of last night had me uneasy and paranoid. Yesterday, like most mornings, I'd rushed out. I'd gotten into the cabinet without remembering, and Murph shifted the laptop sideways with his wanderings. Really, the one thing of value I had in this apartment was . . .

I set my cup on the dinette on the way to the bedroom. Under that lumpy mattress, strapped inside the box spring, was a blue neoprene bag my dad had given me from one of his continuing education conferences. Lying on my back, I twisted it out of its secure location. It wasn't much of a twist—it floated into my hands.

My face warmed as I got upright and unzipped the bag. Empty.

For the past ten years, I'd stored emergency funds in that zippered case. Only one other person knew I'd squirreled away three thousand dollars.

Lindsay had been here.

My face went from warm to hot with anger. If she needed money, all she'd had to do was ask—I'd give her anything. My anger slid into fear. Why would she need the money at all?

Lindsay, what have you gotten into?

The file. I'd set it on the dinette along with the cat crate when I'd walked in last night. That's where I found it.

Searching for answers, I settled in and sifted through the numerous pages. Each sheet detailed some kind of test result; I couldn't tell what kind in the dimness of the room. I got up long enough to flick on the overhead light. On closer inspection, it became obvious these were DNA test results on someone with some Spanish descent.

I sipped my coffee.

The reports didn't specify who they belonged to. *LR Query— Confidential.* It could be anything, right? A reach to think it had anything to do with Lindsay . . . unless Lindsay had asked Craig to obtain the information? As an investigative reporter, she had sources I'd have no clue about. Craig could've been one of them. Whatever their connection, she would've had to provide the DNA to be tested. Was that even possible without the person's permission?

An idea niggled in the back of my brain like an unreachable and painful itch. No. I wouldn't go to where it wanted. Not without more data.

I dug out Lindsay's phone from my purse. At my office, I hadn't thought to check the call log after finding the text from Craig. When I did now, my chest tightened. There'd been several calls between Craig and Lindsay over the past month. Too many to be casual.

That's about how long it had been since Lindsay and I had met for lunch. She'd seemed fine then. A little flighty, but that was Lindsay. And the couple of times we'd caught up in between were via text—although she'd mentioned not feeling well. Nauseous, she said. I'd texted the invite to the party that she agreed to, and then ignored.

She and Craig had made up for our lack of communication. Were they working on something together? Or . . . ? DNA tests . . . nausea . . . avoiding me . . . avoiding the family.

The coffee turned acidic in my mouth. Had she been trying to tell me something that day in the park? God, was she pregnant? It's not like she hadn't been before . . .

But why call Craig? Why go to his office?

My mind leapt to a dozen theories, one particularly unsettling. Craig had dark hair and eyes. His light skin tanned a shade of roasted almonds during the summer. We'd never spoken of ethnicity, but if he had Spanish in his background, it would come as no surprise.

Lindsay and Craig? No way. I nearly laughed at the ridiculousness of that idea. Craig worked more than I did.

Still, he had a DNA test in his desk drawer in a file with Lindsay's initials, and he'd texted her that he had information.

Information that would cause Lindsay to get angry enough to kill him, causing her to steal money and run in the middle of the night?

Nope. I couldn't buy that either, even if Lindsay had a history of violence.

One night years ago, she'd assaulted a bouncer. The guy had come on to one of her friends and turned mean when rejected. Lindsay, defending her friend, hauled off and punched—more like unleashed—on the Neanderthal. Luckily, the man was too embarrassed to press charges.

Even if I believed she couldn't kill someone, though, that didn't mean the police wouldn't dig into her background and believe otherwise.

My head pounded with swirling ideas that offered no proof of anything. I had to get to her place. It might provide a clue about what was happening, or where the hell she'd gone.

Just as I finished my coffee, my phone rang. I jumped and found it near the bottom of my purse. Mandy. Not ready to talk after what she'd pulled, I rejected the call.

A minute later, my phone dinged with a text.

Sorry about last night. Drunk off my ass. Hope you're not in trouble. Can we get coffee? I'm here for you . . . M. Followed by a heart emoji.

I blew out a breath. *Can't. Heading out. Later.*

Maybe.

Don't tell me you're going into work?

If I didn't give her something, she'd keep asking. *Family.*

Another heart emoji followed.

Whatever. I was over it.

Dressed and Murphy's bowl filled with food, I headed out. I'd no sooner locked my apartment than my landlord, Harold Logan, hobbled down the hall, leaning with each step on his cane.

He sneezed when he got to my door.

I double-checked the lock and faced him with a smile. "Good morning."

He frowned. "You got a cat in there?"

"Excuse me?" I struggled to keep my voice even, and willed Murphy to not rub up against the door and start purring.

"My allergies kick up when those critters are a mile away. Someone's brought an animal into the complex." He tapped the side of his nose. "I'm sure of it."

They'd never kicked up when I'd brought Murphy before. "You sure it's not mold? It's been raining buckets this year."

"Mold's never been a bother."

Cat hair hadn't either. I changed the subject. "Did you happen to see my sister come by last night?"

"You think I have time to watch everything that happens around here?"

We both knew he did. "Just asking, in case."

He let out a hmph.

"If you do happen to see anyone around my apartment, will you let me know?"

DON'T ASK, DON'T FOLLOW

His eyes narrowed. "You got some problem I should be aware of?" He lifted his cane and pointed it at me. "We don't need any trouble."

Most of the building's tenants were seventy and older. I'd chosen to live here for that reason alone. It was easier to work when the parties were kept to a minimum—unless I counted bridge and bunko. I also didn't mind that there were busybodies, even if no one wanted to admit that. It felt safer.

"No, sir. Just trying to catch up with my sister."

He "hmphed" again and I headed for the stairwell to avoid waiting at the elevator. My landlord's allergies, if true, were a new wrinkle.

I'd figure something out or my place would only be a temporary solution for Murphy. After finding out who belonged to those DNA tests, where Lindsay had gone with my money, and why she'd been blowing up Craig's phone.

CHAPTER 6

ONE MONTH EARLIER

W hat do you want for Christmas?" Lindsay asked.

"World peace." I'd met her for lunch at the gyro food truck on Fifth. We didn't often have time—make time—these days, but I cherished the moments we did.

"Don't steal my line," she said, and then turned to the cashier. "Lamb, please."

"I feel baaad, for the lamb," I said, laughing.

She rolled her eyes. "Like chicken's any better, Curls."

"I hate . . ." I sighed and then smiled at the dreadlocked kid taking orders. "I'll take a falafel sandwich, please."

We shifted from foot to foot to stay warm and made small talk until we got our orders. Then we headed for the South Park blocks while we ate. It had drizzled earlier in the day, but as we crossed Sixth, the sun had started to peek through the clouds. Not everyone was as brave—the park was empty.

"You planning to be at Thanksgiving?" I said in between bites, hoping she wouldn't leave me to contend with the family alone this year.

She kicked through the amber leaves that had blown onto the walkway and I knew the answer before she'd said it. "Working."

"You know you're allowed to take a break, right? Even the whales won't mind."

"Ha ha, you're one to talk," she said. "But I'm on a story."

As usual. "About?"

She smiled.

"Right." Don't ask. "Anyway. I don't want anything for Christmas except for you to be at Christmas."

"And watch the spectacle of Dad giving Mom another fur this year?"

I winced. "It's hard to stomach. I get that, but . . ."

"Fred, darling. It's glorious." Lindsay fanned herself with her free hand. "Seriously, Sis, how do you stand it?"

I wondered that too sometimes. But they were our parents. Even if Nova had done more to raise us than either of them. "Sad thing is she never even wears it."

"Oh, there's plenty of sad things about this family," she said.

"Don't be so hard on them. They do their best."

She cocked her eyebrow. "Always one to defend."

I cringed at that. "That's what Dad says when he hounds me about being a lawyer."

"Screw that. You should be on the lines with me."

I chomped a bite and smiled. Despite my ability to *defend*, I never won arguments with Lindsay. "Anyway—what do you want for Christmas?"

"To know who I am."

I almost choked on my food. "You're Lindsay Ralston. A little crazy, but good-hearted." I bumped her shoulder. "You know exactly who you are." I envied that about her. She'd never had a problem saying no to my parents or traveling her own path.

She stopped mid-stride. "I mean it. Don't you ever wonder who you are, really?"

I'd gone ahead but turned back. "I know who I am."

"I mean besides a spitting image of the old man."

Working at the firm did not make that true. "Am not."

"You're following in his footsteps."

"That's not fair." Sometimes she just liked to argue—and I didn't. "We've talked about this. We want the same things."

She shrugged and started walking again. "Right. Doing it differently. Maybe I'm jealous they like you best."

Her smirk suggested she could care less about that. "They love us both equally, and you know it."

"Seriously, Beth. You're toeing the line. I often don't even feel like I fit in."

I bumped her shoulder again. "Don't steal my line." I scanned her somber face. "What's with you, Lin? You're being weird."

She shrugged again.

Truth was, I'd felt that way too and her question bothered me more than it should. "I do want world peace," I said.

Her face lightened. "You just want peace in the family."

"That's true too."

CHAPTER 7

The rush of running water hit my ears the moment I entered Lindsay's one-bedroom apartment. The shower. There'd been no sign of her Prius in the parking lot or her assigned parking space, which I'd pulled into. She might've had car trouble or parked it elsewhere. It didn't matter. She was here now.

I dropped my purse near the sofa and burst into her bedroom. "Lindsay, what the hell's going on? Are you okay? Where've you been?"

A wide-open gym bag sat on top of the made bed. She hadn't slept here last night. Nothing happened in Lindsay's world until after a couple of shots of espresso and a shower. I didn't recognize the bag, or the T-shirt strewn across it, but much about my sister had become unrecognizable in the last twenty-four hours.

The bathroom door was ajar, and a whistle drifted out. Seriously? Glad to see she was feeling so happy-go-lucky.

I stuck my head into the steamy room. "Lindsay, get rinsed and get out here. We need to talk."

The shower turned off and the curtain rolled back. A naked man reached for the white towel hanging on the bar. My irritation turned to shock as my eyes locked onto the rest of him.

Six-pack perfect abs. Taut arm muscles. Tattoos covered him, including one that snaked from his back and reached over his shoulder onto his chest. And I mean snaked, as in a python with an open mouth and flicking tongue.

What had he done with my sister? "You're not Lindsay."

"Nope." He wrapped the towel around his waist, his mouth turned up in amusement. My eyes had remained above his waistline. Okay, I peeked. And damn—had Lindsay snagged a boy toy she hadn't mentioned?

"Why are you here?" I said. "And who are you?"

"Lindsay's neighbor. Um . . . you mind giving me a minute? I mean, you can watch if you're into that . . ."

My face burned as I backed out of the room and worked to regain my composure. "Of course. Yeah. No. Sorry."

When had my sister started letting men shower in her apartment? Hopefully, I'd have that answer in a few minutes. In the meantime, I'd come here to look for clues about the DNA test and Lindsay's whereabouts, so I got started.

I'd made it halfway through her kitchen drawers when the tattooed man appeared. He'd traded the towel for a pair of blue board shorts and nothing else. His thick combed-back hair gave him an alternative rocker vibe.

"You must be Beth?" He flopped down onto the couch, tossing his gym bag next to him. He withdrew a pair of socks that he pushed his feet into.

"She's talked about me?"

"Just said you two didn't look anything alike, but you liked to mother her, so I'd know if I ever met you."

My jaw twitched. We didn't look alike, true. I'd come by my nickname, Curls, honestly, and it was a stark contrast to her long red hair. There was also my height, and her lack of it. But if she didn't do dumb things like run from a crime scene, or steal money, I wouldn't have to be so responsible.

"You still haven't told me your name, or why you're in my sister's apartment."

"Easy enough. I'm Kai and my shower's on the fritz. Manager takes a day to respond. She said I could use hers anytime I needed."

"Whether she's home or not?"

"Yeah, she gave me a key a while back. Your sister's cool like that."

To some degree, but I didn't buy it. "What's the real story?"

He reached in his bag and withdrew a joint. "Want to share?"

I leaned back. "No, and don't even think about lighting up."

"It's legal here, you know?"

I glared at him.

"She's right. You are intense."

Yeah—when I wasn't getting the full story, or on deadline, or—whatever. "Spill it. Please."

"Fine. She was working a story a while back on what restaurants did with their grease and food waste." That sounded like Lindsay. "I tend bar at the Meta and I had information she found useful. Turned out we were neighbors. She's been nice to me ever since."

"You guys dating?"

He stared at his joint. "Sure you won't let me light up?"

"Positive."

He sniffed the length of it before placing it back in the baggie. "I wouldn't mind, but no."

"Have you seen her since last night?"

He shook his head. "Not since yesterday morning. We didn't talk. She was running out. She does that, you know, and disappears for days at a time."

That was also true. If she was investigating, it could be up to a week or more before anyone heard from her. This was different. Her investigations had never resulted in my boss being murdered while she ran from the scene.

Kai retrieved a sweatshirt and popped it over his head, taking his time drawing it over his bare torso.

I looked away, glad the python had stopped its death stare. "She seem okay to you this last month?"

"No more crazed than usual." He chuckled. "I mean, she's chill, but intense herself when it comes to her work. Probably not telling you anything you don't know."

"Right." The desire to succeed was one of the few traits we did share.

He zipped up his bag and headed for the door. "Well, see you around."

"What apartment did you say you live in?"

He pointed to the ceiling. "405."

He hadn't offered any information on Lindsay's whereabouts, so I followed, and locked the door behind him. In the kitchen, I resumed digging through the drawers that contained everything from the usual utensils, Life Savers to batteries, pens, and matches. Nothing of interest there.

Returning to her bedroom, I stared at her nightstand. She'd kill me if she found me snooping through her personal stuff, but she'd left me no choice. I opened the drawer, relieved the contents were rated PG: nail file, a memoir she'd dog-eared, a bottle of melatonin. Guess we both suffered from hyper minds that kept us up at night.

The bathroom cupboards and medicine cabinet were equally mundane. A pregnancy test would support my pregnancy theory . . . not much else. And if it had been taken a month ago, it would've gone out with the garbage by now.

Any confirmation for or against would be enough though.

I found nothing.

Back in the living room, and at a loss of what to do next, I dropped into the same spot Kai had vacated, my shins brushing up against the square coffee table. Two wicker baskets were nestled on the bottom shelf of the unit. The first one contained the TV remote and a few worn paperback horror novels. The next basket had a collection of brochures, and a notepad that had never been used.

I spread the pamphlets on the table. There were a dozen of them, from various local adoption agencies, including Catholic Charities and the Boys and Girls Coalition.

I sunk into the couch, gripping one of the brochures.

Eight years ago, Lindsay had gotten pregnant. She'd *had a moment*, as she'd described it, with some guy at a climate change rally. She never got his name.

"Whatever you need," I'd said. "No judgment. And there's always adoption."

She'd shaken her head. "I don't have time to be pregnant or for kids. How can I be on assignment and . . ." She'd curved her hand over her stomach. "I mean, if this was years down the road and I had my career handled, you know, I'd consider it. But now . . ."

After the abortion, which I drove her to, we never spoke about it again. Our secret.

Our parents didn't even notice.

If Lindsay was pregnant again, she might be researching agencies to place her child with this time. Her career might be in a better place, but she was no less busy. Or driven.

My hand hurt from holding the paper too tightly. I couldn't understand why she wouldn't have shared that with me. The brochure floated to my lap. As kids, we used to hash out life and our thoughts at the train trestle near the river and my parents' country estate. If we had a fight, that's where we'd go. If a boy broke our hearts, or we just wanted to get away from the parents, we ran there and talked for hours, a pop in hand, feet hung over the tracks. There was nothing that time spent there together couldn't fix.

But I had to admit, treks there diminished as we got older . . . and busier . . . until they stopped. Phone calls became texts, and texts often took a while to get answered. Sometimes we stole a few minutes to walk through a park while eating.

I should have done better. Had it come to my sister bypassing me and reaching out to Craig for help instead?

We didn't handle family law at the firm, but she could have gone to him for legal advice anyway. The DNA test could be for the father. She might have needed confirmation, afraid he'd cause problems if she placed the child for adoption.

Craig's murder might be unrelated. If only I believed in coincidences.

One thing was certain: these brochures had nothing to do with a current story she was working on. Toxins seeping into the soil from corrupt corporations and baby adoptions had less than nothing in common.

Lindsay's email could offer something. I scanned the room for her computer, not finding it on her desk, or any of the flat surfaces where I thought it would be. She must have it with her . . .

Which meant she might check messages. I tapped out one from my email account on my phone:

RE: Where the Hell Are You
Call me. Please. I'm worried.

As for checking her email for any clues, it would have to wait until I got home. Last year she'd dropped by my house to use my computer while hers was in the shop and it had saved the credentials. She might have changed her password by now, but either way, I'd check into it later if she didn't respond.

I gathered up the agency brochures and stuffed them into my purse, just as Lindsay's phone chimed in a way I hadn't heard before.

When I retrieved it, the screen showed only five percent battery life left. I'd come across a charger in the junk drawer earlier. Once I plugged in the phone, an unheard voicemail reminder flashed on the screen.

I tapped PLAY and then SPEAKER.

Craig's voice came through in a shaky whisper. "Don't come. Your father's here."

He must have been calling from the party. I swallowed hard at hearing his husky voice, his behavior last night making more sense. He and Lindsay *were* meeting at the office, and Craig hadn't expected my father to attend the function. That's why he'd been stressed.

Lindsay hadn't gotten the message . . . but what would cause Craig so much concern if my father was there? I rubbed my eyes, unsure of where to begin to find the one person who might have the answer to that question.

Sitting here would get me no closer.

I secured Lindsay's apartment. As I approached the stairs, my Honda came into view—along with Kai standing at the driver's-side window, his hand cupped over his eyes as he peered inside.

Before I could ask what he was doing, he tried the door and then pounded it with his fist like he was frustrated to find it locked.

What the hell. "Looking for something?" I called from the top.

He startled but didn't respond.

I raced down the stairs. "Did you hear me?"

"Your lights were on."

I stared at the front of my car. "No, they weren't."

"Huh. Seemed like it with the glare . . . you know, from above."

There'd been no glare. My skin tingled. "Why did you come out here in the first place?"

"Had to get something off my bike."

Kai didn't meet my eye.

I stepped toward my car; he didn't move. Uncertain whether I was with a friend of Lindsay's, or a foe, I felt exposed with no one else around. "Maybe you should go do that now then."

He nodded. "Yeah."

"Okay." I drew my keys out, my thumb resting on the alarm.

"Have a good one." He brushed past me. Too close. The tingle turned into a shudder.

He kept his eyes on me as I slid into my car. I backed out and raced out of the parking lot, leaving Kai standing near his bike.

CHAPTER 8

By midafternoon, I'd found a quiet corner table inside the coffee shop at Glisan and Forty-Second. The chill of the early December rain had dampened my clothes. I soaked in the warmth of the place, amused at the string of customers ordering their blended iced mochas, no whip, and caramel lattes, extra drizzle, while waiting for Mandy to show.

After leaving Lindsay's, I drove around for a while, shaken by Kai's lame excuse for skulking around my car. Even more so because I'd only found adoption brochures in my sister's apartment and nothing else to suggest where she'd gone, or why she'd wanted Craig in the mix.

I was no closer to finding out what had changed in Lindsay's world, or why she'd left me her phone with that cryptic unsent text. I couldn't jump to conclusions when all I had was supposition.

Finally, tired of being in my head, and desperate to not feel so alone, I'd called Mandy. Now was as good a time as any for her to make amends for her *drunk off her ass* comments that landed me at the police station.

The barista called our order just as Mandy came through the double door.

Dressed in a black velour warm-up suit with a cloud of perfume hanging around her, she swooped in for a hug.

"It was supposed to be my treat," she said as I led her back to our table. She plopped herself in the chair across from me.

"I was early, and I know what you like." I took a sip of my café au lait, which warmed my insides.

She slurped out the foam of her triple shot vanilla latte. "Yes, you do. And I want to apologize again. The minute I'd said something to that cute detective, I knew I'd screwed up." Her eyes crinkled, reminding me of a shar-pei puppy.

Both Mandy and Lindsay had a way of dissipating my frustration with a look. But not so fast this time. "Yeah, that wasn't cool," I said. "I had to drive to the precinct to answer more questions because of that."

"Shit. I didn't realize. It won't happen again."

I drew in a breath.

"Promise." She put her hand over her heart.

I didn't have the energy to stay mad and it appeared she got the point. "You're forgiven."

She flashed a smile. "Good. Now tell me what's been happening. Have you heard any more about Craig's murder? Are they saying who slit his throat?" The milk soured in my mouth. "I mean, was it horrible when you saw it?"

Horrible didn't describe finding someone you worked side by side with every day bleeding out in front of you. There were no adequate words, and the combination of dizziness and being gut-punched hit me at the same moment. I set my cup down and clutched the table to steady myself.

"Oh man, I'm sorry, Beth. I didn't mean to upset you."

"It's not your fault. I can't outrun it forever." Although I'd been trying. "I've stayed busy to keep my mind out of that room." Tears stung my eyes. "But I have to accept that Craig's really gone."

"Crazy," she said, hushed. "Are you managing okay though? Staying occupied is important, but I hope you don't mean work."

I nodded. "I've been getting Craig's cat settled." I scoffed. "Although my landlord has suddenly developed cat allergies."

She tilted her head. "Is that it?"

"Pretty much." Forgiven or not, I didn't feel comfortable telling her about Lindsay after her overshare with Detective Matson.

"What's your dad say about it?"

Other than don't trust the detective in charge? "We haven't talked much since then."

"I'll bet he's shocked. Wonder who they'll assign you to work for now?"

Who cared? Even though at some point I'd have to go back to my life at the firm, the idea made me uneasy. "I'll probably hear about that tomorrow at brunch." I lifted the cup of coffee and started to sip.

"So why were you at Lindsay's?"

I swallowed before I could spit it out, the hot liquid scorching my throat. "How'd you know I went there?"

Her face scrunched. "You said you were seeing family, and that you hadn't talked to your dad. Lucky guess?"

Right. *Quit being so jumpy.* "Yeah, not much. I went to water her plants because she's been swamped with work." Note to self. Never invite Mandy to Lindsay's place. The one plant I'd seen had shriveled and died years ago.

"Cool. Hey, you spilled coffee on your shirt."

A quick glance confirmed I had a wet spot on my chest. Guess I hadn't swallowed quick enough. "Damn it. I'll be right back."

"I'll grab us a croissant. My treat this time, okay?"

"Sounds good."

After a few minutes of running cool water on a towel and blotting the stain, I slipped the sweater I'd had tied around my waist over my head, which made my hair stick out. I reached for my purse to find a brush, only to find my purse not there. I was more rattled than I'd thought. Smoothing my curls with water would have to do.

"Better?" I said, approaching our table.

"Much," Mandy said.

"Let's try this again." I sat down and took a drink, but Mandy's eyes tracked my every move. "What? Another stain?" I inspected my shirt once more.

"Aren't we friends?"

Weird question. "Yeah. Why?"

She frowned. "And you can tell me anything."

"I do." Generally. "What makes you think I don't?"

She sighed, sounding like a deflating balloon, and held up one of the adoption brochures, the one entitled *What to Know When Putting Up Your Child for Adoption*. "When were you going to tell me you're pregnant?"

I shook my head to untangle the logjam of thoughts piling up. "You went into my purse?"

"No. You left it by your chair, and I took it with me when I went to the counter. The brochures are right there on top."

While I appreciated her not leaving my purse behind, it had been zipped. Hadn't it? My phone had the coffee shop app, and I'd used it to pay for the drinks. Maybe I'd forgotten to close my purse again. "Huh. Okay. Well, it's not what you think. I'm not pregnant."

"Then why do you have them?"

"They're for a friend."

"Why so many places?"

"She wants choices." Her expression pinched like she wasn't convinced. "I mean, who wouldn't? It's a big decision," I said.

Mandy's face lit up. "It's your sister, isn't it? You're going to be an auntie?" Then she frowned. "Oh no, she doesn't want to keep it? From everything you've said, she'd be a great mom. In fact, I had a cousin who'd planned to do the same thing and changed her mind. We could arrange for them to meet. Give your sister another perspective."

Whoa. "Thanks for the offer, except it's not Lindsay."

"Who then? Someone at work?"

I reached for my cup. "I can't break her confidence."

She slumped in the chair, holding her coffee close to her chest. "You're a good friend."

"I try." Though I didn't feel like one and regretted having called Mandy. The desire to get home and go through the various brochures and figure out my next steps had me glancing at my watch. "Well, I should go."

"Already?" she said. "Look, I apologize for being all twenty-questions and yammering on about Craig."

"It's fine."

"It's not. Let's change the subject. What do you want to talk about?"

The way she said it had me on edge with a realization. This was the only subject important to me—and who could I trust with what I was discovering? Not Kai, who'd creeped me out. Mandy was up for debate—she'd always been inquisitive, but her questions felt more like a drilling. My parents and Nova . . . but I wouldn't worry them too soon. Especially after Dad had already shut down my concerns.

In answer to Mandy's question—there was nothing I could share. "I'm all good. Thanks for the coffee." I gave her a quick hug before she could argue.

"They haven't even called us for our croissant yet."

"I'm sorry," I said, with a promise to see her Monday—unsure it was a promise I could keep.

CHAPTER 9

That night, dressed in comfy sweats, I pored over the adoption brochures while nursing a beer and devouring a turkey burger. A couple of the agencies had their phone numbers and addresses circled. Could be they'd piqued Lindsay's interest. Some offered open adoptions, others closed. I spent part of the time repositioning Murphy, who was determined to sprawl out and roll on the leaflets like they were catnip, and refreshing my inbox.

By the time I'd crawled into bed, there'd been no word from Lindsay. I stared at the ceiling, a pit in my stomach. If she was pregnant, she had to be freaking out. But that was a big *if*, and I was no closer to understanding what the adoption pamphlets meant.

Even if Lindsay opted to carry a pregnancy through, her staying involved with the child or the new family didn't jibe with what she'd told me in the past. But people could change . . . Had Lindsay? There'd been no evidence of that.

I never doubted she loved me, but I felt it more when we were kids. She'd tell me a spooky story under the covers, then reassure me it was all make-believe when I cried. She'd let me hang out, on occasion, with her cool friends. When I was in a funk, she'd unleash a few quirky jokes to pull me out.

After we got older, Lindsay's world of sneaking out for parties turned to saving the world. I didn't even know who her friends were anymore—we'd long lived in different circles.

All that aside, Mandy's notion that Lindsay had a maternal side was curious. Lindsay had never been a topic of conversation with Mandy, except to say when she'd flake on me.

Another restless night followed. What few hours I slept were spent chasing Lindsay through a black forest and ending up at the edge of a cliff, where she'd disappeared. The other hours were filled with listening to Murphy use my couch as his scratching post. When morning did arrive, I'd slept through my alarm.

Not good. I rolled out of bed and skipped the shower. I couldn't be late for Sunday brunch with my parents on the off-chance Lindsay would join us and, in her nonchalant way, offer a full explanation. When she got to the office, she found Craig dead. Not wanting to be caught up in a police investigation when she had no information to offer, she panicked and ran. *Curls, don't be such a worrier*, she'd told me more than once, and would say again.

At that point, I'd go off on her about running in the first place. I mean, who did that? Not me. Even when I wanted to. I yanked my clothes on and shoved my feet into a pair of loafers.

Who was I kidding? Under the cursing, I'd pull my sister in for a long hug.

That familiar funk threatened to take hold—I didn't believe she'd be there at all. But maybe my parents had heard something by now.

Murphy taken care of, I arrived at my parents' estate with three minutes to spare. Parking under the thick-columned portico, I dashed up the stairs to the massive mahogany doors.

Inside, I sloughed off my coat. Nova, who'd moved to the live-in housekeeper position after Lindsay and I moved out, met me at the door in a gray dress that fell above her saggy knees. Despite the required formality of her hired-help attire and my parents' old-school approach to what being wealthy looked like, I wrapped my arms around her and squeezed.

"How are you?" I said.

"Good," she said, but her hands shook, and her eyes were red.

"Are they working you too hard?" My parents should know better. None of them were getting any younger.

"No. Your family is fine. Slowing down." She gave me a wan smile. "Aren't we all?"

"You'll never grow old," I whispered in her ear. "Not to me."

She laughed, but it lacked any joy. "You good girl. How are you after what you saw?" Her face narrowed in pain.

Her concern nudged me to the edge of the grief and anxiety that'd I'd worked to hold back—and explained her demeanor. Not wanting her to worry, I stood a little taller. "I'm fine. But Lindsay, have you seen her since Friday?"

She arched an eyebrow. "The last time she was here—"

"There you are," my father boomed from the top of the stairway. "A few more minutes and the food would be cold."

Nova straightened without finishing her sentence. Eyes averted, she took my coat and disappeared down the hall toward the kitchen. I'd catch her later.

"Sorry, Dad." Even three minutes early was late in this house. "I slept through my alarm."

"M-hmm. And I see you're still driving that Honda." He descended the stairs, clutching his phone, dressed in a wool suit and an oxford shirt. Missing was the tie, which came off right after the church service they rarely missed, and before breakfast.

"Yep. She's my girl." I smiled.

"Hmm. Well, might be time to let the old girl rest and let me buy you a vehicle befitting a Ralston."

Lindsay's Prius didn't befit a Ralston either, but he knew better than to take issue with that. "Never. I love my car."

He waved his hand. "Because it was purchased with your own money, you've been clear about that. Still, you should be driving a Porsche."

Did he know me at all? "I like reliable and affordable." And to say it was mine, without one single string attached.

"You're far too young to be so . . ."

"Predictable?" I smiled again, and he shook his head, not appreciating that trait in me like I did in him. Except this morning he carried his phone, and that was unusual. "Not to change the subject, but . . ." I pointed to his cell. "Mother will have your head if you bring that to the table."

He hooked my arm and led the way to the massive dining room. "Things are heating up in the mayoral race. You met my campaign manager, Ericka, on Friday evening. She's a stickler for being able to get hold of me at a moment's notice."

Before I could respond, my mother rang her water glass. "Enough talk already. Let's eat. The chef has prepared a wonderful brunch for us this morning."

We knew not to argue. "Should we wait for Lindsay?"

Dad released my arm and moved to the front of the table. "Haven't heard from her, and she hasn't graced us with her presence of late." His tone contradicted his attempt at indifference.

I took the chair across from my mother. "I'm trying to get hold of her but haven't had any luck. I hope she's okay."

"She's no doubt working some new cause," my mother said. Mom had never been impressed with Lindsay's career either.

Normally I let it slide, but with Craig dying and Lindsay in the wind, her tone grated on my nerves. "She's had several good ones, you know."

"Of course she has, dear. That time she followed those horrid brothers who were dumping hazardous materials after an accident was . . . admirable."

Yes, it was. "Can you imagine how much damage they would've done to the bird sanctuary in that area if it had continued?" That had been a few years ago, but it woke the city to the hard-core investigator they had living among them.

"Now if she'd channel her energies in more productive ways," my father said.

I sipped some water. *Not touching that one.*

Mom blew out a quick burst of air. "Ignore him. He's in a tizzy because, in politics, nothing stays in the past. Someone always tries to drum up something. And his corporate donors aren't a fan of, what do they call them, dear, environmental zealots?"

Nova appeared with a tray of eggs Benedict and a bowl of hollandaise sauce just in time. The other items on the table included a bowl of fruit with plump strawberries and blueberries, warm biscuits, and jams.

While Nova served us, my father's phone dinged. Once. Twice. Three more times in quick succession.

"Silence that thing," my mother said.

He scowled and tapped the side button. She continued to be unenthused by Dad's campaign, which seemed odd given her love of status. My mother was hard to understand sometimes.

I picked at the Canadian bacon on my plate. "What kind of things are they drumming up?"

He waved me off as he drank his juice and Nova disappeared into the kitchen. "It's not just Lindsay's passions. You represent someone that has a past, and they hold that against you too. As a lawyer, you'll find out that you don't always have the luxury of agreeing with your clients. We're all entitled to fair representation."

In my ideal world, I'd have that choice. Maybe I was naïve, and Dad was right, but I had to go to law school first—and I didn't want to start that conversation . . . again.

As if he could read my mind he said, "When are you planning to enroll? I'd like to make you a partner at the firm. Soon. Someone needs to carry on my name."

His phone dinged. Saved by the bell.

"Damn it, Frederick," Mom said.

"Shelby, I can't help that I must stay in the loop. However, I'm happy to finish my breakfast later so as not to bother you."

He scooched his chair back, stood, and strode out of the room toward his den. A moment later a door slammed.

Stunned, I didn't move. Tension between my parents had not been common throughout my life. At least none they exhibited in front of me or Lindsay. Something had happened, and I wasn't convinced it centered around the campaign.

My mother nibbled on her eggs Benedict, frowning. "The man is nothing but a bundle of nerves these days. That phone never stops making godawful noises, more so since Friday night when that poor man died."

"Craig Bartell."

"Right, did you know him?"

Had she not been listening to our conversations over the years? "I worked for him, Mom."

Her brow creased. "Oh dear, I didn't realize."

I let that slide. "Didn't Dad tell you that I'm also the one who found him?"

She looked away and checked her hair. "He didn't. How troubling." One way to put it. "Have they arrested anyone yet?"

"Not that I know of. I thought you and Dad might have heard more on that."

"Like he tells me anything." She dabbed a napkin to her lips. "Well, you'll be fine, I'm sure, darling. You're a Ralston." Right. We never let anything bother us. Even when someone we knew was murdered in cold blood. The food in my stomach turned to rock. "As for me, between the Royal Garden Society and the Zoo Foundation Board, I've been keeping busy. Spring is around the corner, after this Christmas chaos subsides, of course . . ."

She didn't come up for breath for the next half hour—going on about gardenias and roses. This interaction represented the extent of our emotional relationship. Some moms might yank out the tea and biscuits—or a bottle of scotch—and worry about the mental scars their kids might develop after witnessing a tragedy. Mine changed the subject to mundane things. Or herself. As if doing so would make it disappear. Feeling invisible was nothing new, but today it felt like a weight on top of me.

I ate the remaining fruit on my plate as she finished the last sentence about the bouquets she had planned for the firm's reception area for next year. But I'd hit a wall.

"Thanks for brunch, Mom." I set my napkin on the plate. "I have to go."

"Work? On a Sunday? You're just a paralegal with none of the same obligations as lawyers . . . yet anyway." *Yeah, that stung a little.* "We could talk to your father about minimizing those even more."

"It's all good," I said, with no intention of billable hours today. I'd decided during my restless night that I would step into Lindsay's investigative shoes. Maybe figuring out where she'd gone would lead me to her. "Have you heard from Lindsay at all, though? Like I mentioned, she's not responding."

She shook her head. "I haven't seen her in a while, dear. Though she doesn't often come here for me." That was true. Shelby Ralston was emotionally unavailable to both of us.

I hugged my mother goodbye and waited in the entry for Nova to bring my coat.

My father, as if on cue, emerged from his den. "I'm sorry for my hasty exit," he said. I hadn't noticed before that his eyes looked as tired as Nova's. They were all getting old on me, and my heart hurt at that notion.

"I understand. But you might want to apologize to Mom."

"I will." His phone began to explode with notifications.

"You might also want to start by silencing that thing, at least on Sundays."

"If only it were that simple." As he said it, an odd look crossed his face. Overwhelmed? Regret that he'd chosen to get into public life?

"Are you okay, Dad? I'm sure what happened to Craig has put a strain on the firm in more ways than one."

That odd look turned to bewilderment and then recognition. "Yes. Mr. Bartell. His loss is tragic. Is that detective still bothering you?"

"No." Thankfully.

"Good . . . I don't want you talking with him. Let the firm handle any questions that arise. And, Beth, please don't concern yourself with your sister. You know how she can be. You have no time for distractions."

"I'm not. I'm sure she's gotten busy, and she'll show up." Whether I believed that or not, I wouldn't stop protecting her, even now. "I'd like that to be sooner than later. That's all."

He grimaced. "You worry about her too much—and I do too. But her investigations have taken her into places before where she was unreachable. Might be best if you don't look right now."

If Lindsay was investigating, she'd be all in. I'd have given him that, except the way his face had tightened didn't feel right. "Do you know what she's investigating?"

Nova interrupted with my coat but didn't linger.

My father hugged me, holding on longer than normal, before turning away and leaving me at the doorway without an answer.

I'd give anything to go back to my life and Craig would be at work Monday morning and Lindsay was . . . well, being Lindsay. Things were simpler then, or at least predictable. But I had no choice with Craig's murder and Lindsay out there.

And simple had never defined our family. Everything about the past forty-eight hours said things weren't normal.

After that interaction with my dad, I also wondered how much he knew and wasn't sharing.

CHAPTER 10

I dropped into my Honda Accord, which was quite adequate, thankyouverymuch, Father, and made my first stop: the Catholic Charity for Youth. Being Sunday, it had a chance of being open.

Or not.

I cruised past the lifeless beige building on SE Powell a half hour later. That might be the case with the other agencies whose brochures sat on my passenger seat. On the off chance that someone was a kindred workaholic, I had to check. The person might not blurt out private information about a woman considering adoption—if they even remembered her—but if I added the element that she was missing . . .

Missing was inaccurate. Maybe running. My shoulders hunched. I'd take the risk of every agency being closed because I couldn't sit around waiting for her to show up. And doing nothing gave me too much time to think about what little I knew about my sister. *Don't ask. Don't follow.* She knew how much I hated being told that. Sometimes the ask was too much.

The only thing I could do was not tell at this point and hope that decision didn't come back to hurt her.

As I headed to the farthest side of town to work my way back, my mind wandered to another person who seemed to have changed. My father. His dinging phone played in my head. If Ericka had been sending all those messages, why had he been so sketchy? *Messages* . . . Shoot.

Making sure no one would rear-end me if I made a sudden move—only a dark-colored vehicle was on the road a couple of blocks behind—I pulled to the curb and retrieved Lindsay's phone from the bottom of my purse. More concerned about whether she'd responded to me last night, it had slipped my mind to get into her personal email from my computer. I hadn't considered that her phone might give me that access without the need for a password. If I could get into her messages now, I'd know if she'd been checking them.

It took a few seconds to find the mail icon and for it to load. Her email might even provide a clear direction in finding her. But as the screen populated, it was clear that this was Lindsay's work email from the newspaper she'd been at a couple of years. I slunk into my seat at the dead end.

Or maybe not. I scrolled through the read messages. Lindsay didn't delete much. The most current emails related to staff meetings, new benefit offerings, and one from an editor that she'd flagged a month ago. "Where's that story on construction traffic?" *Huh*. As a reporter on the environmental beat, Lindsay hadn't reported on anything like that in the past.

Nothing indicated what she was currently working on. I kept scrolling through the administrative type emails and hovered over one from human resources. The regarding section read "COBRA."

COBRA. That was what a company offered an individual who wanted to continue medical coverage after they left their job—or had been fired.

I opened the email and deflated further into my seat. "Ms. Ralston. Your request for leave of absence has been accepted. You are not eligible for COBRA benefits during this time." The email was filled with legalese and equaled one thing—Lindsay had left her employment.

Another item she'd failed to mention. And there'd been time— the email was dated three weeks ago. If Lindsay was pregnant, she'd need medical coverage. Did adoption agencies handle those types of expenses? She must have wanted to keep her condition private. That's the only way leaving her job made sense.

Or was she on an investigation? I scrolled back to the top of the screen to see if I'd missed anything—and found nothing.

There might be another way. Finding her editor's email address, I switched to my phone and typed him a message with my contact information. *I need to speak with you about Lindsay Ralston as soon as possible.*

Now to wait for his call. I eased back onto the empty road. The one glimmer was that she'd requested a leave, which meant she intended to go back to work. It also suggested that if she was on a story, the assignment hadn't come from the paper. The editor being able to help might be a long shot.

What the hell was happening with you, Lindsay?

My thoughts lost in that question, I turned onto Seventh and noticed a black sedan a block and a half back—very much like the one I'd glanced before pulling over. Come to think of it, that car hadn't passed by.

Eyes glued to the rearview, I swung right on Greeley and found myself alone on the road again. Convinced I was wrong, I settled back into my seat. A minute later, I spotted the same sedan making a right turn, but the vehicle hung back on the long stretch of road and braked a few times. I tried not to read too much into it even as my heart thumped. He could be lost or out for a Sunday drive.

The world is full of dark cars, Beth. Chill.

The light had just turned yellow by the time I reached the intersection. I slowed, but the sedan accelerated, closing the distance. Fast. As it drew closer, the driver and his dark hair came into view. The image of the creepy man in the parking lot Friday night flashed into my memory. I stomped the gas pedal, jolting forward as the engine kicked in, and fishtailed as I cranked the wheel left.

The sedan kept coming, increasing speed, intending to follow. My jaw tensed. At the last minute, he slammed on his brakes. A truck and trailer ran their red light and sailed through the intersection, crowding my bumper. If the sedan had proceeded, he would've been crushed.

My hands gripped the steering wheel, my heart now ricocheting inside my chest. The image of Craig's body flooded back, and I sucked in multiple breaths to calm down at the idea of another person dead—or dying—in front of me. Except no one had died. I was okay. And my fast reaction had lost him.

Still, it took me until arriving at the farthest adoption agency, located in a strip mall, before my pulse returned to normal. I parked in front, not expecting such a "retail" setting, and got out to look inside. Dark. And empty. A FOR LEASE sign was taped to the bottom corner of the window. The agency's address had been circled on the brochure, but the reason why was unclear. The nail salon on one side and the small electronic repair shop on the other were both closed. Coming here was a bust.

Finding the next five agencies proved no better. I wound through the city's outskirts, hitting them one by one, only to find each one closed for the weekend. My eyes darted back and forth from the road to the rearview the entire time. No black sedans tailed me again, however; my efficient plan was turning out to be anything but.

By the eighth location, it was late afternoon. My low back ached and my right leg was numb from driving around. The earlier scare and the lack of progress had left me tired and hungry. Both Murphy and I could use dinner soon.

The next agency was near my favorite Peruvian restaurant, and it was the other agency whose address had been circled.

One stone, two birds. Couldn't get any better than that.

But when I followed the Google Map directions, it turned out Alliance Adoption was located in the warehouse district off North Russell. Not as close as I'd thought to my restaurant, and in a rough part of town. Garbage lined both sides of the street and a few abandoned grocery carts littered the sidewalks. The doorways with black trash bags and blankets might be someone's bed for the night.

I got out, traversing around a light pole, and approached the run-down building. Shades covered the larger windows—the glass door gave a clear view of a whole lot of nothing. The lights were off, and a paneled reception desk blocked the space beyond it.

The building appeared to have no other businesses. Although near the end, a door was propped open by a couple of books.

The first signs of life I'd seen at any of the locations, and worth checking.

Light shone through the cracked door and several voices drifted out, growing louder as I approached. Before I could reach for the handle, the door opened, and a stream of people poured through it.

Standing off to the side, I smiled at the clusters of men, then women, and more men. They nodded and smiled in return as they headed toward the main road. Could be that a church service just ended.

A woman with jet black hair stepped out alone. "Excuse me," I said. "What kind of group is this?"

"NA. You want salvation from drug addiction, this is your place." She looked me up and down. "The only thing you look hooked on is designer clothes."

At first, I hadn't noticed her threadbare jeans and stained sweatshirt under her vinyl jacket. Now I pulled my raincoat closer, self-conscious. "You're right, I'm not here for the meeting." I pointed to the agency. "I was checking to see whether they were open and saw your door ajar."

She reached into her backpack, pulled out a pack of cigarettes, and lit up. "You don't look pregnant."

Not much got past this girl. "I'm not. I have some general questions for them."

She took a long drag and glanced up the street as the group she'd come out with disappeared around the corner. "Got to go. I'd be careful about that one though."

"About what? The agency? Asking questions?"

Her eyes widened and she started to walk away.

There had to be a reason for that comment. "Why?"

She turned and walked backwards. "Last chick I saw around here asking questions wasn't so well received."

"Who was that?"

She shrugged. "You've been warned."

Warned? "What's your name? Can I buy you a coffee? The woman asking questions, did she have red hair?"

Her eyes flashed wide again in response. A man came around the corner at the same time. "Rhonda, you coming or what?"

She ran toward him, offering nothing else.

The door they'd exited from had closed. If Lindsay had gone to the agency to inquire about adoption, that shouldn't pose a problem. Or had others come here asking questions? How did Rhonda know about them? I'd been *warned* . . . something had happened.

Consumed in thought on the way to my car, I almost ran into the light pole. Like most in Portland, it served as a billboard of *What's Happening* in the city. Flea markets, concerts, even missing children. None were current, but sad nonetheless. There was also a large percentage of *LOST* dog and cat posters. Those made me think of Murphy. He'd lost his friend, which no poster would ever bring back. The idea of both of us losing Craig settled over me like a storm cloud, and I got back in my car feeling no closer to finding out why my sister had gone to see him.

Or why an adoption agency had issues about being questioned.

I couldn't imagine Lindsay choosing this agency to manage the adoption of her child just from the overall vibe of the area. But like the other agency across town, the address had been circled. Maybe she chose it because it *was* out of the way and thus more private. Otherwise, it didn't make sense. Then again, nothing I'd uncovered so far did.

On my way home, I stopped for Peruvian takeout and rushed inside my apartment before my landlord noticed. Murphy met me at the door, pressed against my shins, and darted between my feet on my way to the kitchen. He didn't stop until he was fed. It was after five, and dark before I settled on the couch and opened my laptop to check Lindsay's personal email.

I took a bite of chicken in spicy green sauce just as my phone rang with a number I didn't recognize. "Hello."

"Beth, this is Steve. Lindsay's editor." Finally, someone who might have answers. "I got your message. She okay?"

I gulped my food. "I was hoping you could tell me. I saw she'd taken a leave of absence a few weeks ago, and . . ." I hesitated, unsure of how to put it, ". . . well, we've had a hard time catching up with each other since."

"Your guess is as good as mine on what she's up to," he said, crushing my hope. "She'd finished her last assignment on the plight of the houseless, and I was ready to assign her another piece when I got the request for leave."

Houselessness. Maybe not the natural environment, but a cause Lindsay could get behind. "Did anything odd happen during that investigation?"

"Nothing she shared. Seemed routine. But you know Lindsay."

It didn't feel that way. We talked for a few more minutes, but he had no other information: Lindsay had seemed physically and mentally fine before her request. "Will you let me know if you hear from her?"

"Absolutely."

I continued my log-in attempt into Lindsay's email and took a bite of rice as the signal icon swirled several times. Lindsay could have changed her password—what then? If her editor didn't know why she wanted a leave, what were my chances of figuring out where she'd gone or what she was doing? The man who she might have confided in was dead.

Frustrated, I reached out to cancel the request and start again when the account opened. *Thank God.*

Unlike the work account that indicated she'd seen the messages, the screen illuminated bright blue with unread emails that had come in over the past few days. Including mine. There were several older ones, too, all marked unread, but she could have marked them that way.

Although she wouldn't do that to junk, of which there were at least a hundred of. I didn't want to think about what that meant yet.

It took me several minutes to scan and delete the *Amazon suggested buys* to *Netflix What's Coming* and big box stores trying to entice her to spend. The other emails seemed routine—until they weren't.

Lindsay Ralston, your personal DNA results are in.

She'd had a DNA test done on herself?

I opened the file that had been read and flagged. It was dated six weeks ago and the lab seemed different from the one in Craig's file.

To confirm, I retrieved the report on the dinette and compared. They were different labs, but the basic results of ethnicity were nearly identical—off by only a few percentage points. More Spanish than anything else, but a combination of French and German, and a bit of Irish, made up the rest.

Trying to grasp what the results meant, I leaned forward on the desk, my heart pounding. Her comments at our lunch a month ago made sense now.

The DNA test in Craig's file was for Lindsay and had nothing to do with her being pregnant. She might have ordered the second test because she couldn't believe the original results. But the proof glared at me from the screen.

The problem was—both our parents were Scandinavian.

CHAPTER 11

M y head buzzed with this information. My father had referred to Lindsay as his wild child over the years and had remarked she wasn't *like us* far too many times. I'd thought he was being flippant because she had no interest in law. Clearly, that's not what he meant.

That didn't explain why he'd hide the fact she was adopted. Adoption was a wonderful option for many, including the children, and would never change how I felt about Lindsay. One of my third-grade friends celebrated two birthday parties each year—her actual birth date, and the *gotcha day* she came into her family. So much love and joy exuded from their little group that I'd often wished we were more like them.

I reached for my cell to get answers—then opted to wait. At this time of night, my mother would be out of it and Dad might dodge the question. After all, they'd hid the fact for this long; they wouldn't likely admit to anything over the phone. No, this was a question asked face-to-face.

My focus returned to the DNA test, and what it also meant— Lindsay wasn't pregnant. Okay. But she'd reached out to Craig, and he'd gotten her information of some kind. It could be about her birth parents. The investigator part of her would want to know their identity.

Craig had clerked at the courthouse for a family law judge while in law school. If nothing else, he could direct her in navigating the system. Bottom line, he would have helped her, giving her no reason to be involved in his murder. While I had no clue who had been or why, the police had that matter in their hands. If they left me alone, I'd let them do their job and I'd stick to mine—tracking down my *sister*. Regardless of what some DNA test said.

Still—too many secrets. My favorite dinner lost its appeal. I headed for the kitchen to put it in the fridge for later and grabbed out a bottle of Chardonnay. Murphy had followed and meowed for more food, which I obliged before opening the wine, comforted by its nutty vanilla smell. I generally reserved wine for celebrations—like a favorable verdict for the firm. Tonight, I had nothing to celebrate and didn't care that it was a work night, reaching for the largest glass in the cupboard and filling it to the top.

I drained half the glass, then refilled it to the brim. In the living room, I turned off the lights and returned to my computer.

Trying and failing to understand what I'd read, my eyes drifted out toward the park, glued to the evergreen holiday wreaths that hung on the lampposts since yesterday. At least the world around me continued as normal. Those decorations went up at the same time each year. The wreaths blurred. I blinked a few times. The wine worked fast, and my arms felt weak.

I took another drink, my gaze now fixated on a man in rain gear sitting on the bench, at the far end of the park, out of the light, looking in my direction . . . with binoculars? I set my glass down on the ledge. It looked like the same man I'd seen yesterday morning. What the hell was he doing, casing the place? Or spying on me?

I glared, making sure he knew he'd been seen. He averted his eyes, tucked the binoculars away, and got up.

He *was* watching me.

It could have been the wine or the shock of what I'd found, but I was tired of not having answers. Phone and keys in hand, I ran out the door. With no time to wait for the elevator, I scrambled down the stairs two at a time, cleared the building, and sprinted toward the park.

If people wanted to watch me, then I wanted to know who they were and why they found me so interesting. But when I reached the park, the man had disappeared. My run turned to a walk the farther I went into the park. The wind blew through my light sweater, and I shuddered. What was I doing chasing down a stranger in the middle of the night? This was crazy. A bird or bat swooped down from the trees. I stumbled back, then caught sight of the man from the bench at the main thoroughfare.

The need to know outweighed my common sense, and I started in his direction.

"Hey, you," I hollered, my fear dissipating with each stride.

He picked up speed, which I struggled to match with my shorter legs. He probably hadn't just chugged two glasses of wine either. He was across the street, a block up before I'd reached the edge of the park.

"Stop already."

At the block's midway point, I crossed and rushed to the corner. By the time I'd rounded it, he was gone.

Damn it. Two young women exited a bar a few doors down. "Hey," I said as they approached. "Did anyone go in there a minute ago?"

"Nope. Place's nearly empty." The blonde giggled. "That's why we're leaving. Looking for some action."

"Thanks," I mumbled and searched farther down the street in case the man decided to show himself.

All was quiet except for the hum of cars passing on the road behind me. He was gone.

A gust of wind blew through the alleyway. I wrapped my arms around me and glanced up at the sign on the bar where the girls had come from. *Meta.*

That sounded familiar . . .

Kai. Lindsay's neighbor.

Hadn't he said he bartended there?

Inside, the dim space smelled of stale smoke and beer. A couple made eyes at each other in the corner, and at the bar, two old men watched a pre-recorded football game on the set above the bartender's head. Their team was losing based on their scowls.

I climbed onto a barstool.

"What'll you have?" the forty-something man said. The stud piercing his bottom lip looked painful.

"Is Kai working tonight?" I rubbed my arms, glad to be away from the wind, which at least had sobered me some. That and chasing a stalker through the park.

"Not Sundays." He winked. "Can I help?"

I nodded. "If you'd just tell him that Lindsay's sister came by, that would be great."

"Lindsay, the cute redhead?"

She'd been there? "She's my sister."

"Really?"

"What's that mean?"

He polished the counter. "Nothing. Just wouldn't know it."

His comment stung. And after what I'd learned, it didn't feel as innocuous as he'd likely intended.

"Do you remember when you saw her last?" I asked.

"Friday night. Maybe. It all blends after a while. She came by to see Kai."

"Late?"

"Around close."

That would be two o'clock in the morning—hours after leaving the law firm. "Any chance you know what they talked about?"

His eyes drifted to the men at the far end of the bar, and he lifted his chin. "Hold on," he said to me. He grabbed a fresh glass from the rack and filled it with whatever was on tap before walking it down. When he returned, he said, "Sure I can't get you something?"

"I'm good. But Lindsay—do you know why she came by?"

"You'd have to ask Kai." He snagged a rag and wiped down his workstation.

You bet I would. "When does he work next?"

"Thursday night."

"Shoot." Too long to wait, which meant returning to Lindsay's apartment building. Although right now wasn't an option.

"It's a bummer," he said, "because you just missed him. He was here an hour ago picking up his paycheck."

Figures. It seemed I was always a step behind.

Back at my apartment, I refilled my glass of wine, made sure the window overlooking the park was secure, and stroked Murphy's fur until the muscles in my shoulders unwound.

Whoever had been watching at least knew I'd seen him. If the guy was a pervert, he might think twice about pulling that stunt again. What were the odds he was some random creep though? Those shoulder muscles bunched again. This was the second time he'd been hanging out in the park—the first being right after Craig's murder. He might know I'd worked for Craig . . . did he or someone think I'd seen something?

The thought that I'd chased anyone involved in Craig's death had me finishing that glass in a few swallows. I'd seen nothing except for Lindsay, who'd run off, taking three thousand dollars from my apartment. The wine soured. What if the person watching me thought I could lead them to her?

What would they do to her if they found her? Tears pushed into my eyes, which I swiped away. *Not happening*. It would be easier if I understood why they wanted her in the first place, but it didn't matter.

I filled my glass again, this time taking a sip. My thoughts turned to my parents . . . my father . . . and the fact they'd kept Lindsay's adoption a secret all these years. Did it not fit into his image of the perfect power family? Though that made no sense. We'd stopped resembling that long ago when Lindsay and I took our own paths. Lindsay even more so than me.

What I did know from our brunch and having met Dad's campaign manager: now would be a bad time for a family secret like that to become public knowledge. And Lindsay was never big on doing things for appearance's sake. To find out she was adopted was not the issue. Like me, she'd known lots of loved people who were adopted. But the fact it had been kept from her would have raised too many questions. If left unanswered, that would upset her. The question was—would she threaten to use that information against my father?

I curled into a ball with Murphy next to me and imagined my father's campaign manager would have plenty to say about that.

CHAPTER 12

Banging on my front door jolted me from my sleep the next morning. *Go away.* I shifted to my side, only to have Murphy's claws dig into my curls. The rascal had nested on my head during the night. I had him detangled when another pounding rattled the door.

Someone's persistent. Who would even be knocking so early?

The possible answer to that question forced me into a sitting position and staring at the door with a fair amount of dread.

Murphy meowed around midnight. I think. More than once. Maybe. The near empty bottle of wine on my coffee table contributed to that uncertainty.

"If it's my landlord, we're both screwed," I whispered to Murph before I grabbed him and rolled off the couch. I shut him in the bedroom with a *shhhhh* signal, hoping he understood.

At the door, I leaned close. "Who is it?"

"Detective Matson."

Huh. The landlord might have been preferable because the detective's tone sounded less than pleasant. I wasn't up for more accusations, the idea causing a flicker of nervousness; I couldn't ignore him either. Smoothing my hair, I ran my tongue over my teeth, tasting the staleness of my breath. I had the same clothes on from yesterday—my sweater wrinkled from sleeping in it.

"Just a minute." I ran into the kitchen, peeling out of my sweater to the blouse underneath, and rinsed my mouth with water before greeting him. "Good morning, Detective. You're up early."

He glanced at his watch. "It's eight thirty."

Perfect, Beth. Yesterday I'd slept through the alarm. Last night, I forgot to set it. "And as you can see, I'm getting ready for work."

"You might want to rethink the shirt."

The creases in my silk blouse were even worse. "Planned on it."

"Was hoping we could talk. Unless we need to set up a time with your father?"

Dad. Yeah, he wouldn't be happy the detective was here. "Depends. Am I still a suspect?"

"You're not."

About time. Though did he have to tell me the truth . . . ? Dad had his reasons for not trusting him. But I didn't want to appear uncooperative. "Guess it'd be fine." I didn't move.

"Would you like to invite me in?" He glanced down the hall toward my landlord's apartment and I did the same.

Mr. Logan's eyeball showed through the crack in his door. "By all means," I said as he shut the door behind him. "I'd offer you coffee, but I'm running behind."

As if on cue, Murphy scratched on the bedroom door, and I let him out.

"No worries. Nice place." The detective wandered over to my dinette and scanned the computer area.

"Thanks."

Murphy followed the detective, hopped up onto the desk and settled on my laptop keyboard, cleaning his paws, unfazed by our morning guest.

Before either he or the detective wandered further, I hurried over, dropped Murphy to the ground, and closed the computer. I might share the DNA info with Detective Matson at some point, but Lindsay's birth status didn't seem relevant to Craig's murder. "Work," I said.

He did another visual scan of my apartment before settling in the armchair next to the sofa.

Make yourself comfortable. "What did you need to chat about?" I stood, hoping he'd take the hint to go sooner than later.

"You should sit," he said.

So much for that strategy. His tone had my anxiety rising. I eased into a chair at the dinette.

"I wanted to go over your version of events that took place Friday night," he said.

My version again. "Okay."

"Is there anything you'd like to add?"

I shifted. "Not a thing."

"How about that you encountered someone you failed to mention?"

There had to be a reason he'd frame the question that way. Cameras. *Of course.* They were located throughout the building. I laced my fingers in my lap, wishing I'd listened to my father. "I told you what I remembered."

"What you remembered?"

"Yes, sir."

"Sir?" His eyes locked onto the wine bottle on my table. He could be deciding whether I had a drinking problem he could leverage. "You've worked at your father's firm for several years."

"Correct."

"Any other family members on the payroll?"

My shoulders inched up. "Not that I'm aware of."

"Your sister perhaps?"

The tension spread into the rest of my back. "That's a question for the administrative department, don't you think?"

He scooted to the chair's edge and rested his forearms on his thighs. "I'll get right to it, Ms. Ralston. Why were you chasing your sister down the elevator on Friday night?"

"Chasing?" I resisted the urge to grab the wine bottle and finish it off.

"We saw who we believe to be Lindsay Ralston enter the elevator on the firm's floor near the time you indicate finding Mr. Bartell's body."

We believe . . . ? "You don't know if it was Lindsay?"

"You didn't answer the question." His lips pressed into a hard line.

"Neither did you," I said.

His eye twitched. "The woman kept her head bent toward the ground. That doesn't alleviate our suspicion that it was her or that you went down the elevator within minutes of her departing."

"I did, but not because of my sister. I didn't see her at the party that night. If I used the elevator after she did, it was purely coincidence." My face remained stoic, but I was terrified that any minute my body would betray me with perspiration springing across my lip and my leg pumping like a piston. *Relax.* He didn't know it was Lindsay—for sure. And despite speculating as to why she'd been at the firm, she didn't kill Craig.

"Quite a fluke," he said. "In my business, I don't rely on those much. Did you catch up with her?"

"I went to the parking lot, and I rode back up. That's all."

He smirked. "Why would you do that?"

"To have a break from the party." Yeah, that sounds believable.

His jaw muscle twitched this time. "Is that your story?"

A thump came from the bookshelf, and I jerked. *Murphy*. He'd toppled a hardcover novel.

Sucking in a breath, I got up and grabbed the troublemaker from the shelf. "It's not a story. It's the truth. It slipped my mind, or I would've told you before. But if you watched the footage, as you say, you'd have seen I wasn't gone long."

He rose from the chair and strode to my desk. "I have a different theory in mind." He glanced out my window into the park. "One that says your sister was the last person to see Mr. Bartell alive."

It's only a theory. "Why would you say that?"

He smiled his reply.

It was more than a theory. Had someone else seen Lindsay there? Or was there evidence tying her to the scene?

My stomach hurt, and not from last night's wine. They didn't think I killed Craig—they believed Lindsay had—ensuring that I had to keep our silent vow a while longer. Maybe I hadn't kept to the other orders of don't ask and don't follow, but with the police viewing her as a suspect, and knowing how Dad felt about the detective, I'd be sticking to *my version*. "Well, I don't know anything about that."

He nodded and got up, focusing on a picture I had of Lindsay and me on my bookshelf. It was from some lame Halloween party she'd dragged me to after college. She went as a Green Peace activist, no surprise, and I went as an orca whale. The shit I did for her.

He looked at it for a long while. There was some warmth and amusement in those green eyes. "Are you and your sister close?"

"Sure," I said.

"How close?"

Closer than some. Not as close as I'd believed a few days ago though. My heart squeezed. "Very."

"When was the last time you two spoke?"

Other than text, we hadn't. Not unusual with our busy lives, but his question underscored again that I should have done better. "Weeks ago."

"That doesn't sound close to me."

"She's an investigative reporter—always on a story—and I work a lot." Or I had, until this. "But I adore my sister, and she feels the same." The need to declare that came out of nowhere. Maybe with her leaving me in the dark, I needed to convince myself.

I glanced at my watch, hoping he'd catch the hint. If he wanted to learn anything more, he could do his own digging.

"Good to know. Well, if you do hear from her . . ."

"I'll let you know."

"Appreciate that, because she's not answering her phone, nor has she been home for a few days, according to the neighbors." He peered out at the park again, and my eyes darted to my purse. Had he traced Lindsay's phone here? That didn't make sense. He would've asked about it by now. He didn't strike me as the holding back type.

But if he found it in my possession, the conversation of why I had it would blow my version apart.

He saw himself to the door. His hand on the handle, he turned back. "Ms. Ralston, if I find out you're lying to protect your sister, or are involved in any way, no amount of legal talk will help you."

He didn't wait for my response as he stepped out and shut the door.

I ran for Lindsay's phone and powered it down, right before I called the HR department and told them I wouldn't be in.

CHAPTER 13

B efore showering and changing into fresh clothes, I made a call to Alliance Adoption. Rhonda from the NA meeting could be confused in her perception of how Alliance didn't appreciate questions, but her eyes had flashed when I described Lindsay and asked if she was the one doing the questioning.

Even if I had read her body language wrong, with no other clear direction, I had to check. The detective's insinuation that Lindsay was a suspect added to my desperation to find her. But I was riding a fine line to keep peace with my father who didn't want me talking to the detective in the first place, and my unspoken promise to Lindsay to not tell. Except I was a grown woman . . . and it was my ass on the line if things went wrong. Just how far would I go to protect my big sister?

That question remained as Alliance's voicemail answered and I hung up. It might work better if I went there instead. They might not be any more receptive to me poking around, but experience had taught me that witnesses had a harder time telling you to *bugger off* in person than they did on a phone where they could disconnect with the push of a button.

An hour later, I pulled up in front of the agency. Dressed in business casual, I hung my bag over my shoulder and carried a six-by-nine notepad and pen. If Lindsay or anyone else had been there and riled people enough for Rhonda to be aware of the agency's stance on being questioned, I'd employ a different strategy.

This time I found Alliance's door unlocked. A receptionist about my age with long sandy hair peeked out from behind her computer when I entered.

Her smile was warm and genuine. "Can I help you?"

"I hope so." I tried not to sound as nervous as I felt. "I'm with a local magazine and we're doing an article on the good people of this city who're finding homes for children."

"That's awesome. We do amazing work here, and I've been telling my boss forever someone should do a story on her."

I rested my elbows on the paneled counter. "Then I'm in the right place. Who is your boss?"

"Margaret Ottoman. She's thought of everything for our clients and she's wonderful."

"What do you mean she's thought of everything?"

"Well, we deal with low-income women, many without insurance, and desperate for resources."

My thoughts turned to the last article Lindsay had done for the paper. "Houseless?"

"Some, but not all. Those down on their luck. People who've fallen through the cracks for one reason or another."

Lindsay might have believed her birth mother had come through here. That didn't answer how she'd gotten this far though. My parents, perhaps . . . or Craig? "How far back do you go with records of the adopted children?" The question was out before I realized how it sounded.

The young woman frowned. "What's that have to do with the good work we do?"

Insert foot. "Sorry, I meant how long has the agency been around?"

Her frown softened. "Not sure. I've been here just a few years. But Ms. Ottoman has been doing this a long time." Her smile brightened again. "She would be such a great candidate for your article."

"Absolutely. Could you give me an example of what kinds of resources she connects the women with?"

"Like I was saying, many don't have insurance. We work with a midwife so that the women don't have to deal with hospitals and those exorbitant fees. Isn't that incredible?"

Before I could answer, a well-dressed woman pushed the door open. Her gray hair had been rinsed with an auburn brown, but it was her lips drenched in bright red lipstick that I noticed first.

She gave me the once-over and hesitated before those lips pressed into a hard line. "Are you here for adoption services?"

I had no time to respond.

"No, Ms. Ottoman." The receptionist hopped out of her seat. "She wants to do a story on you—on the agency. I was just telling her how well-deserving you were of that."

Ms. Ottoman's eyes narrowed. "Not interested."

"Just a few questions—it would be quite simple," I said.

She smacked those red lips together. "You reporters are something else."

My ears perked. "Have you recently had a bad experience with one?" *Lindsay?*

She waved me off. "Bailey. Coffee." She breezed past me without a response and rounded the paneled counter.

"I understand your reluctance," I said. "But this piece would focus on your accomplishments." I'm sure they had many in their quest to find loving homes for children who needed placement for what I imagined were a million different reasons.

Ms. Ottoman didn't break stride as she passed a few more desks and proceeded down the hall, turning into an office.

Bailey held up her index finger and ran in the same direction, disappearing into another side room and reappearing a minute later with a cup of coffee. A few offices down, she vanished again. When she reemerged, Ms. Ottoman had followed her out but went the opposite way. The creak of a door closing sounded before Bailey trotted back to her desk.

"My apologies. She's not always like that. I'm sure she'll warm to the idea." She grimaced. "Today's not that day though. If you leave a card, she'll call you—later."

After that dismissal, I'd be waiting forever for that call. *Shoot.* Not at all how I planned things to go. Given Rhonda's description, I'd expected resistance to come from the gatekeeper, not the person in charge.

But my gut, along with Ms. Ottoman's comment, said Lindsay had been here asking questions. Perhaps not only those pertaining to her birth mother. If I understood more about how this place worked, that might explain Ms. Ottoman's aversion to reporters. And Bailey was beaming a pleasant smile my way.

"Okay, here's the thing," I said. "Some people are so selfless they don't want their good deeds recognized."

Bailey's head bobbed in agreement.

"Your boss is clearly that person. Sounds like someone else was here making inquiries and put Ms. Ottoman on guard, but not all reporters are the same."

"Like any profession, I suppose."

"Indeed. It would help to know who that person was, so I don't make the same mistakes. Do you know?"

"Well," Bailey said, just above a whisper. "I never saw the woman. I only overheard Ms. Ottoman tell someone on the phone that she didn't like what was being asked."

Not fool-proof confirmation, but enough to suggest it was possible that Lindsay had been here. Maybe she didn't like the answers she got about her own parents, or the adoption had been closed and they were tight-lipped about the whole thing. Lindsay didn't like being told no.

"Look, I know you're busy, so how about we meet after you get off work and chat more?" I said. "I can get some background for my story, and you can expand on how Ms. Ottoman helps women. I'll show her in a positive light and keep references anonymous. How about it?"

She bit into her lower lip. "My boss is pretty secretive and doesn't like attention." Bailey glanced down the hall. "She's been quite adamant that I don't talk about things that cross my desk."

"I won't ask for names."

"I'm mostly a friendly face for the company, so I don't know a whole lot . . ." She drummed her fingers on her desktop. "I do think she'd enjoy the limelight just this once though." Bailey looked back over her shoulder one more time. "Okay. Yes. Let's do it."

We arranged to meet at a place I knew well—Highland Café— at five o'clock for coffee, and I got out of there before Ms. Ottoman returned or Bailey changed her mind.

I slid into my car as a text came through from Mandy:

Thought you were coming in today?

My debate on what to tell her took too long because my phone rang seconds later.

"Hey, I was just texting you," I said.

"Too late. Why aren't you here?"

"Woke up not feeling great."

"Girl, it's been a shock. I get it. We're all feeling it." She lowered her voice. "But you need to get your butt back behind your desk. You know how they are about hours, and I heard you're getting reassigned to a partner."

"Great," I said, with zero enthusiasm.

"I thought you'd be excited. Isn't that what you always wanted?"

I frowned at the phone. "Not like this. Not even close."

"I just meant . . ."

Dial it back, Beth. "I know you didn't. I'm sorry. It's just been a lot."

"It's okay. I understand."

I cleared my throat—she meant well. "How's it going there?"

"The police were here looking for you earlier, which is why I got concerned when you didn't show."

"Maybe they've got information on Craig," I said. Telling her they'd already found me at home would invite more questions.

"Not sure, but they seemed interested in your office. They were in there with Mr. Garrett, rummaging through your drawers and stuff."

Did they think Lindsay had hidden the murder weapon in there? I sank further into my seat at their persistence. "I've got nothing to hide. I didn't kill Craig." Neither had Lindsay.

She laughed. "Good to know my friend's not a killer. At least the cops are gone, although there's still yellow tape across Craig's door."

My head ached. "I should go."

She paused. "Beth, are you in trouble? Is there something I can do?"

"No. I'm fine."

"I can tell you're not. How about we get together later? I'll buy you a drink?"

I thought of last night's wine and winced. "I've had one too many of those lately."

"Coffee then."

I hesitated.

"Please, I want to be there for you."

Her sincerity stopped me. Maybe it was time to trust someone with what I'd found out about Lindsay being adopted. Maybe she could help me figure out what it all meant. "Okay."

"Good. Our usual spot, five thirty?"

"Perfect. I'll already be there for another meeting."

With a few hours until then, I knew where I had to go next.

CHAPTER 14

Mom trotted down the stairs in a stunning green wool dress suit to a waiting limo as I pulled my Honda under the portico and off to the side. Her diamond flower brooch sparkled in the slice of sun that had managed to peek out of the overcast sky, as did the matching earrings dangling below her stylish hair. She was headed somewhere fancy.

"Mom." I hurried out of my car. "Where are you off to looking so nice?"

She smiled at the compliment. "Board meeting, darling. Catch you another time?"

"It can't wait. We need to talk."

Perhaps it was my tone, or the intensity of my stare, but my mother slowed her stride. "I don't have time, Beth. I can't be late."

"I'll drive you."

She looked at the limo and then my Honda. To her credit, she pretended to debate. We both knew she wouldn't be caught dead in anything so ordinary. "Another time would be best. The board is waiting, and Devon here is on the clock."

She blew me a kiss and slipped into the limo. Devon shut the door without glancing my way and circled to the front driver's side.

Oh no you don't. My mother had never been into deep or uncomfortable conversations. Questions on what to wear to prom or other social decisions were met with enthusiasm. Other concerns were diverted to my father, or more often, Nova. However, there'd be no avoiding this one.

I ran to the driver's-side passenger door and opened it before Devon could object.

"How about I join you then?" I said, sliding in.

She eased back into the seat. "Sure, darling, I should have thought of that. Devon can return you and then circle back for me later. I have a full day ahead and a dinner tonight at the MAC."

My parents had been members of Multnomah Athletic Club since before I was born. Membership was exclusive, acquired through lottery, and never given up once obtained. Portland's elite held their upscale events in the venue, which explained her dress on this dreary Monday afternoon. Lindsay and I'd been there once—even though membership extended to the entire family.

She withdrew a compact mirror from the silk-embroidered clutch she'd tucked under her arm and popped it open, a rim light illuminating her face. Teeth-smiling, she ran her tongue over her gleaming whites. "Any smudges?"

"Looks good," I said, knowing better than to interrupt her routine.

She snapped the mirror closed, dropping it in her bag, and gripped her cell. "So, what's so urgent . . . and why aren't you at work? Even your father made an appearance today."

That explained the quick assignment to a senior partner. I pressed the button to close the privacy screen between us and the chauffeur, ignoring the perplexed look on my mother's face.

"This must be serious."

I had expected to come in with guns blazing about what I'd found. But my mother appeared so small and frail in the seat next to me, I hesitated. Mom's answer to confrontation was to feign a migraine and go to bed. She and my father had kept the fact of Lindsay's adoption hidden all these years—I'm sure she wouldn't want to discuss it now. But whether it was connected or not, my boss was dead, and weird things had happened since. Staying silent and playing the good girl wouldn't help me to find Lindsay or the truth.

"Why didn't you tell me Lindsay was adopted?" I said.

My mother's eyebrows drew together—right before she burst out laughing. "What are you talking about, dear?"

Surprised at the response, I cleared my throat. "Lindsay. Adopted."

Her laugh disappeared and her face pinched. "Where did you get such a crazy notion?"

Heat crept up my neck like it did every time she'd scolded me as a kid, and another unsettling theory set in. Had my mother had an affair? She'd always been beautiful, and Dad worked a lot. No. There'd been no trace of my parents in those tests.

I wavered, but Lindsay was out there with this information. Alone.

"Lindsay had a DNA test done on herself. And, Mom, there's no Scandinavian in her."

"That's what you're basing your claim on?" She shook her head. "Beth, tests *can* be wrong." She turned in her seat and held my face between the palms of her hands. "You are both my girls. No more nonsense. All right?"

Tests couldn't be *that* wrong. "But, Mom . . ."

"Ah," she said, as her phone rang. She glanced at the screen. "It's one of the ladies about tonight's event. I told you about the gala, didn't I? Beautiful flowers from the Garden Society will be everywhere."

"Can't you talk to her—"

She held up her finger to shush me and took the call.

I bounced back into the seat, clutching my hands in my lap so as not to swat the phone out of her hand. *Incredible.* My gaze drifted to the passing high-rises as she went on about displays and arrangements and rack of lamb with fingerling potatoes to whoever was on the other end of the line. After ten minutes, I had the impression she'd started to make things up to avoid our conversation.

When we reached the MAC, Devon parked and ran around to her side. She muted her phone and said, "You have a good rest of your day, my darling." Before I could protest, she got out and began to walk away, then rushed back. Devon reopened the door. "And, sweetie, perhaps this is something you shouldn't mention to your father. He has enough on his mind these days. Agreed?"

Roadblocks now. Seriously? I nodded, but had the same thought about my father as Mom disappeared into the MAC building. Her desire that I not broach this subject with him, however, said there was more to the story. While she talked around my question, she'd never come right out and said Lindsay wasn't adopted. I doubted Dad would be any more truthful.

One person might be, though.

It was cleaning day in the Ralston household, and as expected, after Devon dropped me at the front door a half hour later, I found Nova in the basement laundry room. She startled when she saw me and almost dropped the basket she had cradled in her arms.

"Child, you shouldn't sneak up on an old lady." She set the basket on the long folding table.

"Sorry," I said, still feeling off-balance from my conversation with Mom. I used to surprise Nova all the time as a kid and got the same response. There were few places I'd rather be than hanging out with Nova while she did her chores.

"Your parents aren't here. Your father left quite early for work. Your mother's out socializing the rest of the day."

"I know. I rode with her to the MAC." I wrapped my arms around Nova's shoulders and hugged her as she folded a towel. With Mom always at some gala or board meeting, Dad at work, and Lindsay off with friends her own age, Nova had taken the loneliness out of my childhood. I gave her an extra squeeze.

She patted my hand. "What's on your mind?"

Untangling myself, I leaned against the dryer. "That obvious?"

She cocked an eyebrow.

Silly question. "Yesterday, I asked when you'd last seen Lindsay."

She tri-folded a bath towel and snapped up another one. "You did."

"But my dad interrupted your answer." My turn to arch a brow. "So?"

Another trifold completed and another towel grabbed before she answered. "Friday morning."

"Just stopping by, or . . . ?"

"I did not get that impression. She was upset. I can tell when Lindsay is upset."

We all could—she turned the color of a beet. "Do you know why?"

"No, but your father's office door slammed shut and their voices raised several times. I thought it wise to be someplace else when they came out."

My father hadn't given any indication that he'd been angry with Lindsay before the party, or since. In fact, he'd said he hadn't seen her for weeks when I asked. "Nova," I said. "You've been here forever."

"It feels that way." She chuckled.

"Were you here when Lindsay was born?"

"I was not."

"When did my parents hire you?"

She shifted from one foot to another. "After you were born. Your mother was overwhelmed at corralling a three-year-old and a baby, as well as keeping up a house."

"Did you ever get the sense that Lindsay was adopted?"

She stopped mid-fold. "No. What makes you ask that?"

I longed to tell Nova about Lindsay's DNA test and the adoption agency, but I didn't know what I had yet. "Just curious. I figured you might've overheard my parents talking about it over the years or seen something that made you believe she was."

She turned to take the last towel from the dryer. "Hmmm. Are you and Lindsay fighting?"

I wish. I'd take every stupid argument we'd ever had and let her win if she were here right now. "Not at all. I haven't been able to get hold of her."

She frowned. "She's a stubborn girl. And she was furious with your father. When she left, she said she'd never be back."

"That's not a first." Or second. Or third . . . Unlike me, Lindsay showed every one of her emotions in the moment.

"No, but the way your father looked after her, I believed it might be true this time."

Dad knew Lindsay always came back after blowing off steam. What happened that felt different to him? "Did he say why?"

"No. But I'd just come out from the kitchen. That's why I'd witnessed the exchange at all. But I was quite certain he said, 'Lindsay, what have you done?'"

CHAPTER 15

Nova's words hung in the air. My father had lied to me. Sure, parents lied—white lies. Like when answering *is Santa real?* This didn't compare. He'd seen Lindsay the morning before Craig's murder, and they'd fought. Did he know what Lindsay had been doing and why she'd disappeared too?

While I wished my mother had been less sketchy on the subject, or Nova had been around during the time of Lindsay's birth to confirm, the idea that Lindsay had confronted my dad about her adoption had some teeth to it. As did the thought that he wouldn't want her anger at him to go public in the form of a scathing article during his campaign. Appearances were everything to my parents.

"Are you sure that's what he said?" I asked Nova.

"Positive." She dropped the folded towels from the table into the basket and transferred another load from the washing machine into the dryer. "Honey, I must get moving. I have shopping to do, and your father will want a snack when he returns. You know how your parents are if I fall behind."

After today, I felt no certainty that I knew them at all. That could be true about most kids and their parents. I just thought I'd figured them out to some degree. My father was driven by success, and by how others saw him as a leader. My mother shined with the status that afforded. We weren't a perfect family—was there such a thing?—but we'd functioned. To learn they'd kept Lindsay's birthright a secret was confusing. What else had they'd kept from us?

Nova headed for the stairs, and I grabbed the basket of towels from her and followed. She left me in the entry with a hug to finish her duties.

My father's den was just down the hall. The afternoon had sped by, and I had that five o'clock with Bailey across town. After learning Dad had lied though, I wondered if there might be something in his office that would help me figure out what happened between him and Lindsay or where she'd gone. I had to check before leaving.

As usual, he kept the massive mahogany door to his office closed. Not as usual, it was locked. I jiggled the handle a couple of times for good measure. *So much for that idea.*

In the past, only the desk drawers with client files were secured when my father was gone. The sudden need for an extra layer of security could be new. Or perhaps it had been that way for a while.

Regardless, it added to my uneasiness.

On my way out, I stopped at the edge of the living room where several boxes of holiday items waited to be unpacked. Soon, there'd be a tree in front of the picture window and festive decorations adorning every flat surface. Every family gathering happened in this room. Lindsay being adopted didn't change that we were family, but our parents hiding it felt wrong. Mostly for Lindsay. As a kid, it could have been a celebration. As an adult, it felt deceptive.

My mind drifted back to our lunch in the park over a month ago now when Lindsay wanted to know who she was. She must have known then and struggled with what she'd discovered. And I'd missed it. Too busy with my own work. With my drive to be something.

What kind of sister had I become? Not a very good one.

My heart squeezed as a row of photo albums on the bookshelf caught my eye. Had there been signs of Lindsay being adopted all along and I'd missed those too? Probably not. At least those signs wouldn't be in some album since we'd never been great picture takers.

In my car, I headed to meet with Bailey and took the on-ramp leading to the interstate, hitting commuter traffic. Since working late most nights, I avoided such things and hadn't accounted for the slowdown. If Bailey showed without me waiting, she might take off, sending me back to square one. I pounded the steering wheel. *Not happening.*

I took the next exit that would put me onto Broadway. From there I'd shoot across to Hawthorne, near the café. However, the moment I crested the overpass, more traffic came into view. Of course, the vehicles on the highway began to pick up pace. *Damn it.*

At the light, I willed the mob of people to cross the street faster. Though they could care less. They were heading toward the Moda Center where the digital sign announced: "Blazers against the Suns." I hadn't thought of it being basketball season. Why would I? That would mean having a social life.

I'd always prided myself on racking up billable hours, working late nights, giving up weekends. I'd sacrificed sleep, relationships, decisions about my future—and worn that grueling work ethic like a badge of honor. During this search for my sister, I realized how small my life had become. How few people I had to rely on. Without Lindsay . . .

A horn blasted. The light had turned. I waved a *sorry* and whipped back across Broadway, hitting the highway once again. One minute to five, I arrived at the café, parked, and grabbed my purse to wait at the curb. Bailey, in a bright red puffy jacket and a beanie cap, was running up the sidewalk on the other side of the street.

She approached the intersection and spotted me. One of her hands was stuffed in her pocket. The other, she lifted in the air as a hello. I did the same and took the moment to formulate my questions, starting with how the adoption process worked. If a person had been adopted and wanted to seek out their birth parents, what were the steps? Bailey might know the common obstacles. Then I'd end with what I really came for—was there some way to find out if Lindsay had been by to talk with Ms. Ottoman as she'd implied when she said *you reporters*?

I thought back to Rhonda from NA. Perhaps she'd run into my sister on her way out of the agency, and that's when she'd gotten the impression that they didn't like questions. Or had there been others nosing around?

These ideas ticked off in my head as Bailey stepped into the marked crossing on a blinking *WALK*. An engine roared, a car coming out of nowhere.

Bailey's name formed in my mouth to scream a warning, but Bailey saw the vehicle just in time. She stumbled back onto the sidewalk as a dark-haired man in a black sedan sped through the intersection, passing her so close her beanie cap flew off her head and something white went up in the air.

My stomach nose-dived as it clicked back to the car in the garage. To the sedan that had followed me that day as I wandered the city looking for adoption agencies. To the man in the park that I'd chased last night.

Get the license plate. I grabbed my phone and punched in 911. I repeated the plate number in my head several times until the operator answered.

"What's your emergency?" the woman asked with all the calm she'd been trained to project.

"A pedestrian was nearly run down. The driver . . ." What could I tell them? "Look, he's driving reckless. He's going to kill someone if they aren't paying attention." I kept describing the situation over and over until the operator pulled me back for a description of the car. Which I gave, along with the plate number, my voice shaking with fear at Bailey's near miss. That this black sedan kept showing up in my world.

"What's your name?"

"Beth. Beth Ralston. It doesn't matter. The guy's driving like a maniac. You need to get him off the road."

I hit END, my eyes searching the sidewalk for Bailey and not finding her. Had she ducked into a building, scared to death? My whole body trembled, and I'd been nowhere near the car.

Making sure the sedan hadn't circled back, I ran across the street where she'd stood minutes before. In the distance, a figure with a red puffy jacket rounded a corner moving at breakneck speed. My heart sunk. She was getting far away from me.

I'd never learn more about the agency now. That's when I caught sight of a piece of paper fluttering near the edge of the walk, the wind about to catch it.

I plucked the paper off the street and glanced at what was written on it. *Sherry Smith, Midwife*. Bailey had spoken about the agency's midwife and must have been bringing the note to me. Before I could think any more about it, my phone rang.

"Hello," I said, stuffing the paper in my coat pocket.

"This is the 911 operator. Detective Matson has been notified and has asked you to stay on premises. He's on his way."

They'd told him I'd called?

"I'll wait in the café."

I tucked my phone into my purse, afraid of another meeting with the detective. But maybe I shouldn't be. Despite my dad's views to the contrary, it could be time to share some of what I'd learned because one person had already died, and someone from an agency Lindsay likely visited had almost been run down.

I crossed back to the café with thoughts returning to the man behind that wheel. He had to be the same man downstairs in that black car the night of the party.

Had he been the one to murder Craig?

My skin prickled. If so, his showing up here today couldn't be a coincidence.

Was I being watched?

CHAPTER 16

Detective Matson sat across the table from me, his arms folded over his chest. "So, you called," he said.

"Not you exactly. I did call 911 to report a reckless driver though. How did you know?" I took my time sipping my coffee. I'd contemplated sharing all an hour ago, but the warmth of the café and time had me rethinking just how much was safe to disclose to the detective who'd implicated Lindsay in Craig's murder.

"Your name came across as a witness in an active investigation. Tell me more about the car."

"Black sedan. Four-door. Man had dark hair . . ." I closed my eyes and envisioned it careening through the intersection. Bailey's beanie in the air. God, so close.

"You also reported something else."

"The license, of course."

"And?"

I thought back to what I'd told the operator; nothing came to mind. "I don't remember. The whole thing had me rattled."

"You said you thought the driver aimed for the woman, and it was because of you."

Great. So afraid for her, I had rambled about something. It was possible that's what I'd said. "It did seem that way at the time. The aiming part."

His gaze bore into me for more. "Who was the woman?"

"Bailey. She works for an adoption agency I'd visited."

The detective leaned back, his eyes widening. "You didn't mention you were pregnant."

"I'm not."

"Then why go to an adoption agency?"

Did I tell him that I thought Lindsay could be looking for her birth parents? My parents denied she'd even been adopted. "I've been trying to get in touch with my sister and she could have been on a story." Not implausible. "I'm just checking a few places she might have gone, and Bailey had agreed to answer a few questions over coffee. That's all."

"And almost lost her life because of that?"

I gripped my hands to stop them from fidgeting. "No. I mean, it just seemed odd."

"Huh," he said. "Anything else?"

I wasn't sure what more to tell him. The DNA angle would betray my family, and Dad would be unhappy to hear I'd been talking with the detective in the first place. I also had no proof that the man behind the wheel was involved in Craig's murder. Or that Lindsay visiting Alliance had anything to do with that either.

Still, the car and the man resembled who I'd seen downstairs that night. "Back to the car . . ." I said. "It felt familiar. When I went downstairs the night of the party, I saw one similar to it. A guy was behind the wheel." I'd have mentioned the guy following me, but I didn't know for certain he had been, and I already sounded para-noid. "Anyway, that was the other reason I was concerned."

His face grew serious, reminding me of that night at the pre-cinct. "Do you think Bailey was targeted, or is it you?"

I'd tried to avoid that thought and shifted in the chair. "I'm not sure."

His eyes narrowed. "It's something to consider because first your boss was murdered. Now you claim this young woman was almost run down. You've been in proximity to both."

I reached for my coffee again and lifted the cup to my mouth shakily. "That's insane." But was it? I set the cup back down with-out drinking. "I'm sure the special master has gone through Craig's files and found that we were working on run-of-the-mill defense stuff." Although that would be irrelevant if someone was following me, expecting I'd lead them to Lindsay. The coffee burned in my stomach at that thought.

He shrugged. "I'm paid to look at all angles."

Wait— "I thought you believed my sister was involved?"

"She's still one of those angles."

I figured as much. "She's innocent, Detective."

He stood. "Well, if you do hear from her . . ."

"Right."

"In the meantime, if it'll make you feel better, I'll look into the vehicle."

"Thank you." He started to walk away, but a question had nig-gled at me since our last meeting. "Detective, you'd suggested Lindsay was in Craig's office. Why do you think that?"

He turned back. "Fingerprints."

"I see." My sister felt like a stranger at this point. "Why are her prints on file?"

"She applied for a concealed weapons permit."

Concealed weapon? Lindsay hated guns. "Did she get the permit?"

"No. The application was filed a few weeks ago. It hadn't been approved yet."

I pulled the coffee cup close to my chest. Lindsay's entire world appeared to have changed—our family never owned guns. Something had frightened her. In her search for her birth parents, and crossing paths with Alliance, had there been an incident? After Bailey's near miss, anything was possible. What I couldn't understand was why Lindsay hadn't come to me with her concerns.

I drove home in a daze. Once in my apartment, I fed Murphy, and crashed into bed. No wine. No dinner. Nothing. It was midnight when I woke to pee that I realized Mandy had never shown for our coffee date.

*　　*　　*

When morning came, the sun rose, along with my determination to find my sister.

On my way to the bathroom last night, the note with *Sherry Smith, Midwife* on it had fallen out of my pocket. Bailey had said she was only the *friendly face* of Alliance. She must have been bringing me the midwife's name as someone who had more information about the agency.

I tried calling Alliance at eight thirty, then at eight fifty in hopes of speaking with Bailey about the note and see if I could get her to meet me for coffee again. Both calls went to voicemail. It had been a long shot. After her near miss, she'd probably opted to take the day off.

At least I had a lead to follow and settled in front of my computer.

But in no time, I hit a wall. The state of Oregon kept a database of licensed midwives, but among the few dozen Smiths, no Sherry was listed. Google didn't help either, other than to mention that "Smith" took the number one spot for a last name in Portland, and then proceeded to show over a thousand names. It would take me a month to narrow it down, maybe. Sherry could be a middle name or nickname.

The fastest way to find out was to return to the agency—this time as Lindsay's sister. I left a message with HR that I'd be out for the rest of the week and was on the road before nine thirty. Ms. Ottoman would either be receptive, or she'd tell me to leave. I'd soon find out.

My thoughts on how to get Ms. Ottoman's cooperation, I turned onto the street where Alliance was located, only to be stopped by two fire trucks parked in the middle of the road. The activity explained why no one had answered at the agency. I squeezed my Honda into a spot and walked down the opposite side. Firefighters dressed in full protective gear stood on the sidewalk.

"Lady, you shouldn't be here," one of them said as I drew closer.

"I know this place." I wrapped my arms around myself and nodded toward the agency. "What happened?"

"Fire gutted part of it. We saved the building, but—" His walkie-talkie crackled. He was summoned inside. "Don't go anywhere near it." He pointed at me for emphasis as he walked away.

"If you knew anyone who worked here, stick around. Detectives are on their way."

Knew . . . and *worked* . . . as in past tense. Detectives, not police . . . My stomach tightened at the thought of a body inside that building.

It could be anyone . . . Ms. Ottoman. The midwife. Bailey? The muffin I'd eaten for breakfast swirled.

My thoughts crept to my sister. She would absolutely sneak into a place if she didn't get the answers she wanted. Once her investigator switch flipped, not much was off limits.

Stop. That didn't mean she was in there. *If you knew anyone . . .* the firefighter had said. *Anyone* could be a janitor or another employee I hadn't met.

"Sure thing." Waiting until he'd gone back across the street, I started toward my car feeling like a metal band had been strapped around my chest.

Bystanders had gathered on the main thoroughfare, their eyes glued on the fire trucks. I recognized a few faces from my initial visit—they'd come from the NA meeting. Then I spotted Rhonda with her black hair pulled back.

My instincts said to get the hell out of there before those detectives showed. The other part said Rhonda might have more information and we should chat again.

Before I decided which voice to listen to, she saw me and started walking away at a fast pace.

Her actions clinched my choice. "Hey," I said, catching up with her before the end of the block. Her stride increased. "Remember me from the other day?"

"Yeah, Fancy Pants, I remember."

Unsure of how to respond to that, I just nodded. "Did you see what happened at the adoption agency?"

Hands tucked into her front pockets, her head remained down, eyes locked onto the street. "Yup. Probably no meeting today, and I have places to be."

"The fire didn't reach your part of the building though."

She shrugged.

Her excuse would have been more convincing had she not taken off the moment our eyes met. "Rhonda." Winded, I reached for her arm. "Please stop." Sitting at a desk all day played hell with my stamina. "Let me buy you breakfast."

It might have been presumptuous to think she hadn't eaten, but her ratty dress and thin body suggested food might not always be a given. She stopped after a couple more steps and stared at my hand. "What do you want from me?"

"Information. That's all. I'm looking for my sister."

"You think I can help you with that? Why? Is she homeless? On the streets? It's not like we all know each other."

Everything I said seemed to offend this girl. "No, neither. Her name's Lindsay and she's a reporter. I believe she was at the agency asking questions before I was."

"And?"

"And when you said they didn't like questions there, I wondered if you knew more about that or if you'd seen her."

"I've had friends deal with them. That's how I know." She folded her arms over her chest. "What's your sister look like?"

"Red hair, and . . ." I reached into my purse for my cell and pulled up a picture taken last Easter.

Rhonda glanced at my sister's smiling face. "Maybe."

Maybe was enough because something else had caught my attention—the fact she'd had friends go into the agency. "Then let me buy you breakfast. Something weird is happening there. I just can't put my finger on what."

"Well, don't buy the sweet act from that front desk chick. She's all about sucking you in. Once she finds out more about you, she reports back to that old hag on whether you're acceptable."

"You mean Bailey?"

"You've met her? Yeah, she's a piece of work."

Rhonda might have had a different interaction than me. Bailey had brought the midwife's name on a piece of paper . . . Unless it wasn't real information? What did *acceptable* mean? "I've met her, and almost watched her die when a car tried to take her out yesterday."

The color drained from Rhonda's face.

With a response like that, she had to know something. "Please, I just want to find my sister." My voice cracked, and I held my breath waiting for her answer.

CHAPTER 17

After a few seconds of speculating which way Rhonda would go, she finally said, "I like pancakes."

We were close to a small retro diner—retro in the sense the dingy black and white Formica tiles reflected decades of customers across them. I waited until we'd ordered a short stack, two eggs over easy, a side of bacon and sausage for Rhonda. I opted for a bagel and lox with cream cheese and a fruit bowl.

Rhonda shook her head. "Fancy Pants," she muttered before leaning back in the booth. "So, that red hair chick, that's your sister?"

"Yes."

"Anyone ever mention you two don't look alike?"

"I've been told." Although not as often as in the last few days. Or perhaps it stuck out more. "Anyway, I believe she was at the agency asking questions. The problem is, I don't have absolute proof she was there."

"Yeah, you do."

I straightened. "You talked to her?"

She nodded. "She caught me coming out of a meeting like you did. She didn't offer to buy me breakfast though." She took a sip of OJ.

"When was that?"

"Few weeks ago. Probably."

"Did she say why she went there?"

"Doing a story on adoption agencies. Except that Bailey chick must not have been there that day because she'd run into that old woman, who shut her down."

Odd that Lindsay hadn't laid out that she was looking for her birth parents from the start. "You don't think much of Bailey?"

"Her job's to butter you up for info. See what you make, if you're drug addicted, where your family's at, what your resources are." She frowned. "Nosy."

"Was she doing that for people looking to adopt?"

"No, pregos."

"Pregnant women?"

She smirked. "Uh, yeah."

I ignored the snark. "If you're there asking about adoption, that seems like relevant information."

She chugged the juice. "Fancy, people don't go there for that. They look for you."

"What do you mean 'they look for you'?"

"They want women who have nowhere else to turn."

I tried to wrap my brain around whether that was good or bad. Rhonda's time on the street could have distorted her perception, making her jaded. Offers of help could be seen as threatening her way of life.

Bailey had been so excited at the resources that Ms. Ottoman provided expectant mothers—healthcare and the midwife to save them money. That didn't sound bad, especially for someone with limited resources. If I could find Bailey, I could ask her, but with the fire and no last name, that seemed impossible. Then I thought of a body potentially inside the building and her near miss yesterday. I cringed at the thought it could be her in there. Either way, it might be best if I didn't involve her anymore.

"Did your friend have that experience with the agency?" I asked.

"They tried. But she had someone to talk to. Me. And I told her to run like hell. Anyone wants to help you like that, there's a string attached. Or a chain."

The pancakes arrived and Rhonda dug in without another word for several minutes. I nibbled on my bagel. She rolled her eyes, and I took a couple of voracious bites to avoid further judgment.

"Did you tell my sister all of this?" I said when I'd finished chewing.

Rhonda chomped on another piece of bacon. "Yeah. She seemed interested in that last part."

I bet she did. If Lindsay believed her birth mother had gone there, she'd want to know more about what led her to that agency in the first place. She'd also want to find her. If her mother had been homeless, that could be difficult. Where did one even start?

And none of that explained the tragedy at Alliance this morning. It could be as simple as an electrical fire, I supposed. But the timing . . .

We chatted until Rhonda finished her last bite, but she'd shut down and offered nothing else. At the register, she eyed the bowl of takeaways next to it. I grabbed three apple strudels and a blueberry muffin from a wicker basket, along with an orange, and handed them to Rhonda, who shoved them in her backpack.

"We'll take those," I said to the cashier.

Outside, I retrieved one of my cards for the firm from my purse and jotted my cell number on the back. "If you hear anything more about the agency . . . or just want to talk . . ."

"Don't wait up. But thanks for the chow and snacks, Fancy," she said, slinging her backpack over her shoulder. She trotted to the crosswalk and waited for the light. I scanned the area for a black sedan and then kept my eyes on her until she'd made it across.

I appreciated Rhonda trusting me enough to share what she knew. Now I hoped it hadn't put her in danger.

Rhonda's safety and our conversation were on my mind when I rounded the corner back on the street with the fire trucks. Those thoughts were interrupted when I spotted Detective Matson peering into the driver's side of my car. Right before he saw me.

With nowhere to run, I straightened. "Detective."

"Let's talk, shall we." It wasn't a request. He strode to his department-assigned tan Chrysler and motioned me in.

My throat tightened. I circled the car and slid into the passenger seat, reminding myself we were both on the same side of the law, even if the detective and my father might not see it that way.

"First time, I understand. Mr. Bartell was murdered at work during an office party," he said. "Even buy the second time with Ms. Perez." He must have come by Alliance yesterday if he knew Bailey's last name. "Now you're at the scene of the fire of the same adoption agency you mentioned."

When he put it that way, it didn't sound great.

"Either you're horrific luck to those around you, or you're the direct cause. Regardless, I suggest you tell me what's going on before I arrest you until I figure it out on my own. Not even your daddy will be able to help you out of that one."

The muscles across my back spasmed. I could call my dad and lawyer up. But it might only make things worse. "Who's dead inside that building?"

He leaned his head back on the headrest. Frustrated? When his jaw twitched, it left no doubt. "How do you know someone is?" He massaged the space between his eyes. If I weren't the focus of his annoyance, I'd almost find that trait attractive. "Start talking, Ms. Ralston, and don't stop until I tell you."

Except I was the focus, and his tone reflected the seriousness of the situation.

"I didn't know about the body," I said. "One of the firefighters told me to stay put if 'I knew someone who'd worked there.' I put two and two together. Who is it? I'm not talking until I know it's not Lindsay."

He drew in a breath. "We don't have a positive ID. Why would you think it'd be your sister?"

Not having a positive ID didn't mean anything. Still, I had to believe it wasn't Lindsay . . . if for no other reason than to keep going. "Because, like I'd mentioned, I think she was working on a story," I said.

"What kind of story?"

The DNA test would put unnecessary focus on my family, but I had to give him something. I wanted to. This burden had grown heavier by the minute. And a part of me liked the detective and his tenacity, despite Dad's warnings. "From what I've gathered, adoption agencies. I don't know if in general, or this one in particular because they serve a low-income popula-tion. As for where Lindsay was in her investigation, or what it centered around, I have no idea. That's why I've been trying to retrace her steps."

"That's led you to believe she could be in that building?"

"She can be dogged when she wants information. I'm not saying it's her. I'm making sure it's not."

He seemed to think about that. "Was she at the law firm that night to see Mr. Bartell specifically then? Were they working on an investigation together?"

"No idea. I'd invited her to the party. Until you told me about the cameras, I thought she'd ghosted me. Which she's done before when working a story." A fine line of truth, but chasing her meant nothing—I hadn't caught her. And he'd likely decided that already based on the video. "Anyway, this agency was the last lead I had on her. That's why I came here."

He tapped the steering wheel. "Your sister . . . Let's say she didn't talk with Mr. Bartell. Is there anyone else at the firm she might have seen?"

Not my father . . . so he'd claimed. "Beats me." The truth, but I didn't correct him. She had come for Craig, likely for help in finding her birth parents. Telling him led to the DNA questions though. I'd come as clean as I could for now. "You said you saw her leaving," I said. "That means you saw everyone coming and going from the firm that night. You must have other suspects?"

He shot me a sideways glance. "Should I?"

"I've been thinking of that car that nearly hit Bailey and the black sedan down in the parking structure the night Craig died. The guy had dark hair, dark eyes. Creepy. In replaying the past few days, it's possible they're one and the same. That's all." I mentioned being followed this time too. When put together, it had to be related.

He shifted. "Unfortunately, there are countless black sedans in this city. As far as guests, it's a slow process. We're going through the camera feed and confirming identifications. We will find Mr. Bartell's killer."

I wished that would be soon and not include Lindsay in any way. "Did the license plates pan out?"

"Stolen."

Not surprising. Anyone so bold as to attempt a hit-and-run, not to mention murder, had certainly thought of the street cameras. The skin on my arms tingled. "I have to tell you, these last two days have me concerned for Lindsay. Whether she gets consumed with her investigations or not, I'd have expected her to reach out by now. I think she's in trouble."

"She's definitely someone we intend to talk to."

I shook my head. "I mean in danger. If she was investigating Alliance, and someone did try to hurt Bailey and now burn the place down . . . and the body . . ."

"It could be a homeless person in that building. The nighttime temps have been dipping and they're known for starting fires to keep warm. Until the body's transported and a post is done, we don't know what happened here."

His words didn't ring true for a homicide detective. "If the medical examiner believed that, you wouldn't have been called."

He didn't answer; I didn't expect he would.

"Am I free to go?" I said.

"You tell me. Anything else you'd like to share? Because interfering with homicide investigations will land you in jail. Your time at a law firm must have taught you that."

"There's nothing else."

He waved his hand, shooing me from the car. "Until we meet again," he said. "I have a feeling we will."

I stepped out of his car, shivering from the burst of cool wind.

Lindsay might not be in that building, but I didn't buy his homeless theory either. Not with a fire and a body on the heels of an attempted hit-and-run. Had my questions scared someone? Although I'd barely even started asking them. Maybe the detective's visit yesterday . . .

Or was someone concerned with whatever Lindsay had uncovered?

All this time I'd worked under the assumption that Lindsay was too consumed with her investigation to reach out.

What if she couldn't? What if she'd concerned someone enough that they were covering their tracks? Acid formed at the back of my throat that they might have started by removing her first.

CHAPTER 18

The frightening prospect of Lindsay not being alive had me driving faster than the posted speed limit to the law firm.

The man in the black car had been downstairs during the party. My sister had not gone down into that parking lot; she'd gone to see Kai at the bar at closing—a fact he failed to mention. It might be nothing. Or it could be everything. I'd circle back to him one way or another and find out.

My father's lies had to be dealt with first. I'd put it off for as long as I could. He'd seen Lindsay the morning of the party. They'd argued. She must have confronted him about what she'd learned. It couldn't be a coincidence that after their argument Craig was murdered, Lindsay went missing, and the agency Lindsay might have been adopted through had been burned.

There were connections. While I hadn't put them all together yet, I felt certain my father could. I tried not to think about what that would mean since finding Lindsay was all that mattered.

I parked in my usual space and rode the elevator to the penthouse on the thirty-ninth floor. A new face who hadn't been brought up to speed about my relationship with The Big Cheese sat at the receptionist desk. With no time for niceties, I waved to her on my way by before she could ask who I was there to see.

The administrative offices consumed the west wing, and offices for the named partners, including my semi-retired father, took up a portion of the east. I strode into my dad's corner suite expecting to see him on the phone, his feet on the desk. Instead, it was empty.

Damn it. Determined to get answers, I didn't think to call first. He could be gone for the day or in a board meeting . . .

Crossing to his desk, I intended to check his calendar to find out, but was drawn to the window and the view of Mt. Hood that graced the skyline. The Willamette River sat below with numerous bridges that connected the east and west parts of the city. I pressed my forehead against the glass, watching the dots of people below moving like ants, thinking about the Alliance Agency and my parents.

My conversation with Rhonda and what I'd learned about the agency didn't mesh with a man who could afford a multimillion-dollar view. If Lindsay's mother had come from an agency of low income or destitute women, how had my parents even known about them?

My parents weren't as well off thirty-plus years ago, but he'd still been the head of his law firm.

"Excuse me," came a voice from behind.

I whipped around. "Ms. Pierson," I said to my dad's assistant. "I was looking for my father."

"He's not here." She strode in and went to his desk, pushing the chair under and straightening the blotter. "HR said you were out for the week?"

"I am. I need a break."

She checked his file drawers. Locked. "Understandable. After Craig . . . But like I said, your father's out."

"You happen to know his schedule?" I spotted the day-planner on his desk.

"The Rotary Club invited him to speak. He might come back after."

Always campaigning. "Do you know where that's taking place?"

"Well . . ." She hesitated. She was my father's gatekeeper. Every business had one, I supposed . . . But I was his daughter.

I smiled in case I'd come on too strong. "I'd love to hear him talk about plans for the city. And he'd get a kick out of seeing me in the audience."

Her shoulders lowered. "I bet he would. It's at the Hilton. You should hurry though. It starts in less than an hour."

"Thank you." I headed to the door, then turned back. "Ms. Pierson, you've worked with my dad for years."

Her eyes narrowed. "I have."

"And you know my mother."

That got a smile. "Shelby, yes. Lovely woman."

Except when she was shutting me down. I nodded. "When she was pregnant with Lindsay, did you see her much?"

The smile froze on her face. "Once, I believe."

"Did the firm throw a shower for her?"

Ms. Pierson gazed out the window. "Oh, yes. Any chance to take a few minutes and celebrate such an occasion is welcome around here."

I laughed. "Any reason to have cake."

"Absolutely."

"I bet she was really showing then too."

Her face scrunched. "I'm sure she would've been. I don't recall."

That didn't tell me much—but expecting someone to remember something that happened thirty-three years ago was a big ask.

I hurried out of my dad's office, determined not to miss him. On the way down, the elevator stopped on the thirty-sixth floor and Mandy stepped in, her eyes glued to a file.

"Hey," I said.

Her gaze shot up and she stiffened. *Busted.* I expected a quick apology for her no-show. Instead she said, "Hey, yourself. What the heck? I thought you were out sick?"

"Just needing time off."

She punched the button for thirty-four. "That doesn't sound like you, but we all need that, right?"

It didn't. She didn't sound like herself either. "We do. What happened yesterday, by the way?"

Her brow wrinkled.

"Coffee? Five thirty?" *She wanted to be there for me. Right.*

"Oh my God." She enunciated each word. "I totally forgot. I'm so sorry."

Mandy wouldn't forget. Was she lying? "Did a big project get dumped on you?"

"No. Yeah. Craig's work went to my boss, and since you weren't here . . ." She let out a weary sigh. "My workload has doubled."

I grimaced, having made assumptions. The work didn't disappear because Craig died and I was on a fool's errand, as Nova would say. At least it felt like I was covering the same ground and getting almost nowhere.

"Now I'm sorry," I said.

"Don't be. Take care of yourself. Keep in touch, okay?" The elevator arrived on her floor. She stepped out and disappeared before I could even say "sure."

On my quest to find Lindsay, I'd become a person I barely recognized—someone who let people down. Until my sister was safe, though, it might remain that way, which meant my father and I needed that chat.

At the Hilton, the valet parked my car, and I hustled to the upstairs conference rooms. The largest of the spaces had been transformed for the luncheon with large round tables and white linen tablecloths. Waitstaff hurried about, setting silver and filling crystal water glasses.

A mixture of men and women, all dressed in business suits and bathed in strong colognes, gathered in small circles outside the room immersed in deep conversations. I searched the lobby for my father and spotted him at the far end in one of those deep conversations with Judge Elizabeth Johnson, who I recognized from the party. Their heads were together, and their shoulders touched. Unlike that night, they weren't laughing, but seemed quite close. Had my parents not had a tiff at brunch, I would have thought nothing of his proximity to an attractive woman. Now I wasn't sure what to make of it.

The look on my face as I marched in his direction must have read *serious business* because he excused himself from the judge, who integrated into another small group a good distance away.

Not at all suspicious.

My father flashed a sincere smile as I approached, happy to see me. "Beth, what a pleasant surprise."

That was about to change. "We need to talk."

He frowned. "Now is not the place."

"It's now, Dad."

He drew in a breath and guided me farther away from the crowd into a corner. "What is so important that it can't wait?"

"How about we start with why you didn't mention speaking with Lindsay the morning of the party."

He blanched before composing himself. "You've spoken with Lindsay?"

"No. But you have."

"Where'd you get that idea? And why aren't you working, sweetheart? Keeping busy . . ."

My shoulders inched up. "Quit stonewalling me. Why'd you lie?" I wanted to ask what had prompted his comment that Nova overheard—*Lindsay, what have you done?*—but it would be bad enough if he figured out Nova had told me about seeing Lindsay in the first place, let alone that she'd been eavesdropping.

"I didn't. It slipped my mind." His focus drifted to the crowd. He flashed another smile to someone behind me. He had that politician thing down pat. "It was about a donation she wanted for one of her causes."

"Bullshit."

He waved at someone else, then stepped me even farther away from his constituents. "Don't talk to me like that."

This wasn't the best place, but I couldn't wait for the right moment. "I know Lindsay is adopted. She went to a place called Alliance Agency to find her birth parents, and shady stuff is happening there because someone coming to meet me nearly died and the place was set on fire. I'd like you to at least come clean about something here."

He straightened. "You don't know what you're talking about. I'd advise you to stay the hell away from it."

His tone took me aback. "Lindsay's my sister. Your daughter. Until she's home, I won't. I can't." I couldn't keep the desperation about how much I wanted her home out of my voice. We were sisters, despite our differences. There was no me without her. "And Detective Matson—"

Dad's eyes widened; his voice tight. "You haven't been talking with him about any of this, I hope?"

He needed to get over it. "Some. He came to see me. He doesn't know about Lindsay being adopted, but he does know about the agency and my theory that Lindsay was investigating something there."

"I told you—"

"Dad, I'm not a suspect. I don't need your protection."

The blood drained from his face. "I'm ordering you to stop. No more talking to the detective. I've got everything handled." His teeth clenched now. His chin quivered. It would have been imperceptible to most, but I'd seen it once before. "Get back to the law firm and put in your hours. You are not the reporter."

His words cut deep, making my heart pound. That's right—I wasn't my sister. And I'd never be as good as her. But I'd damn well try. That was more than he could say.

Before I verbalized that, a hand gripped my shoulder and his henchwoman, Ericka, was at my side. She flashed a fake smile and then focused on my father. "It's time, Frederick. Your public awaits."

"I must go," he said. He hesitated and sighed, bending to kiss my cheek. "I love you, Beth. But I mean it. Stop."

"Dad."

He put his finger up and Ericka ushered him a few strides down the hallway. One of his constituents nabbed him and started talking.

Ericka strode back to me. "You should go. You're a distraction at these events."

Her tone was no better than my father's and it sent my blood pumping into overdrive. "Well, by all means, pencil me in on his calendar then." He had gatekeepers all over the place.

She leaned in. "Your father's going to be the next mayor of this town. If you want to help with that, great. If not, stay away from him until after the election."

She walked away, heels clicking, and grabbed my father by the arm, leading him into the banquet room.

Dumbstruck, I didn't move. Who did that woman think she was?

A few minutes later a glass clinked, and Ericka introduced the fantastic *Frederick Ralston the Third*. When he started talking, he sounded confident. In charge.

Yet, I knew better. While my father felt like a different creature to me, I recognized one thing in his voice when he told me to go away: fear. His chin had betrayed him.

When Lindsay was nine and I was six, Lindsay dove into the pool on a frosty spring morning. Not nearly as daring, I'd held at the edge, refusing to join her.

The icy cold had hit Lindsay, robbing her ability to move the moment she'd entered. She went under. I screamed and my father came running and pulled her out. He'd begun CPR as her lips turned blue and her skin translucent.

For a moment, he thought he'd lost her, and his chin quivered as dread covered his face. It was then I vowed to keep Lindsay safe because she was almost reckless in the risks she took, and the decisions she made, and I . . . well, I wasn't.

I'd never seen that quiver again on my father—until now. He was scared. I had every belief he knew where Lindsay had gone. Perhaps he feared what she was digging up—or that he couldn't save her this time.

I was terrified of the same things.

CHAPTER 19

There'd been such a deluge of information rushing toward me, I needed time to sit and unpack it. I had some certainty in what I'd uncovered—my sister was adopted, and there had to be a link to Alliance as the adoption agency—but little else. And Alliance had been torched, but I only had assumptions as to why. What had Lindsay uncovered there that would scare someone into that kind of extreme action?

My brain shot to human trafficking. While Lindsay's passion was the climate, she'd never turn away from a story like that—especially if children were being sold into sexual slavery or an exploitation ring. Rhonda's words still echoed in my head—*they look for you.*

But how was my father linked to that agency? The sole connection had to be that my parents went through the agency to adopt Lindsay. As a respected lawyer, and someone I loved, I couldn't envision him being associated with anything illegal. Although it wouldn't matter whether he was aware of the agency's dark side or not. The media would eat him alive for the simple association. Scandal equaled lost votes. My father hated to lose. That could be the basis of his frazzled demeanor, and the concerns of his bull-dog campaign manager.

As to why Lindsay went to Craig—maybe he'd offered to help her decipher what she'd found. That part remained unknown. But according to the Meta's other bartender, Lindsay had gone to see Kai near closing the night Craig was murdered. Kai might not have mentioned it before because the interaction was insignificant and not worth remembering. With any luck, she'd dropped a hint that he didn't think relevant at the time.

I'd take anything at this point. Which meant even though he'd creeped me out by hanging around my car, I had to see him.

Taking the chance that a bartender would be home in the middle of the day, I pulled into Lindsay's parking spot.

A cherry red motorcycle was parked in 405's stall. A good sign.

On the fourth floor, I knocked on Kai's door. A woman from down the hallway peeked her head out and then disappeared before I could ask if she'd seen Kai around. I rang the doorbell this time and pressed my ear against the wood. There were no footfalls or indications from the other side that he was home.

Shoot. A note to call me would have to suffice. I'd started digging through my purse to find a pen and paper when Kai strode down the hall, dripping in sweat. His T-shirt was slung over his bare shoulder where the python tattoo hung out, and he wore gray shorts and running shoes.

"Whatcha doing?" he said.

"Hey." I shoved the items back in my purse. "Got time for a chat?"

He smiled and pumped his eyebrows when he caught me glancing at his abs.

Nothing like being obvious, Beth.

"Sure."

I'd made plenty of room for him, but he brushed my shoulder as he stepped between me and his door. He smelled of musk and perspiration—not an unpleasant scent—but his T-shirt slipped, and the tongue of the snake met me at eye level. I stepped back and he winked, entering his apartment without a key.

Good thing I hadn't checked the handle. Knowing my luck, I would've had half my body in looking around at the precise moment he came home.

I hesitated at the doorway. So much had happened since finding Craig, the image of him churning acid in my gut every time. Who to trust wasn't as clear cut anymore.

"You coming in?" Kai headed straight to the kitchen.

Answers wouldn't be forthcoming from the hallway though.

He withdrew a jug of milk from the fridge and held it up to me as I shut the door. "Want some?"

"No thanks."

He took a long drink and used his shirt to wipe his mouth. I could see my sister liking this guy, despite his caveman ways. He had a wildness to him that she'd find attractive. It would make Dad crazy. And Mom . . . I almost smiled at how that introduction dinner might go. Lindsay loved the bad boys. Although, he'd said they weren't an item . . .

"You hear anything from Lindsay?" he asked, bringing my attention back.

"No. Hoping you had."

He frowned. "Not a word." He pulled a toaster out from a cubby. "Want a slice?"

"No thanks." I climbed onto one of the two stools at the eating bar between the dining area and the kitchen. "But she did come see you last Friday around close, correct?"

He popped two slices of bread into the slots. "You been by the bar?"

"Yeah. It's near my apartment."

"Hmmm," he said.

"The other bartender there said he'd recognized Lindsay when she came to see you that night."

"Okay."

"Okay? You didn't mention that before."

"You sure?"

Answering questions with questions meant he was hiding something. "Positive. In fact, what you said is you'd seen her running out Friday morning. You even threw in that she disappeared sometimes for days. You said nothing about seeing her at two o'clock Saturday morning."

"Huh." He leaned against his stove, the smell of toasting bread filling the space between us.

"So?" I said.

"Sure you don't want some milk?"

Now he was stalling. "Kai, cut the crap. I don't have time for this. You know my sister well enough to have a key to her place and use her shower. Why are you lying about having seen her that night? Please tell me what she said. Better yet, where is she?"

"That I don't know," he said.

"Then think. She's been MIA for several days, and you appear to be the last person who saw her."

In reply, he flicked the release button and two lightly toasted pieces of bread popped up. He took one and buttered it.

Blood rushed into my face. Did no one else care about bringing Lindsay home? "Kai, this is serious. Whatever Lindsay was doing has caused some problems. My boss is dead, for one. A woman who was to meet me from an adoption agency was nearly run down. That agency burned up with a body inside. It could be Lindsay's as far as I know." Or Bailey's. Neither would be something I could live with. The weight of fear and potential loss crushed my chest as the words came out in a torrent. "I'm sure I'm not doing myself any favors by trying to find my sister." Or even telling Kai all this. Although Lindsay thought enough of him to visit him at two in the morning. "But I have to. I need to." My voice cracked for the second time today.

Kai's face creased. He blew out a long breath and shook his head. He strode out of the kitchen and disappeared into his bedroom. If he came back with a joint and told me to chill, hand to God, I'd slap him.

Instead, he returned with a key that he set on the counter before sliding onto the barstool next to me. He'd slipped his shirt back on and added a sweatshirt.

"What's this?" I said.

"You wanted to know why Lindsay came to see me at the bar. This is it."

It didn't have the wide gaps a safety deposit box might require, or the head of a house key. "What's it belong to?"

"No clue." He rested his elbows on the counter.

I swiveled in his direction, gripping the bronze key. It was round, slightly smaller perhaps than the average key. "Postal?"

He shrugged. "Your guess is as good as mine."

"Why are you only bringing this to me now?"

"She told me not to tell anyone—for a while. But after what you've just said . . . if it helps you figure out where she's at sooner, you know . . ."

While frustrated that he'd delayed showing me this, I understood. Lindsay could be convincing when she wanted something done. "Start from the minute she walked into the bar. How did she seem?"

"In a hurry. A little stressed. Not much different than normal."

I would have expected her to be freaking out after she'd seen Craig. Although she'd had a few hours to process it . . . "Okay, continue."

"That's about it. When she came in, I was restocking and, except for Mike, the bar had emptied out."

"Then what? What did you mean 'for a while' you weren't supposed to say anything?"

He sighed. "She shoves this key into my hand and says if she's not back in a week I was to retrieve it and get it to her editor at the paper. Then right before she walked out, she said to give it to you instead. Which I'm doing, ahead of schedule."

If Lindsay had suggested her editor first, it could be for a PO box that the editor could access. Its contents could relate to whatever she'd been investigating. But why give it to me if that were the case? Had she not really meant her *don't ask, follow, or tell* directive literally? "You didn't think to question her about *why* she'd ask such a thing?" A week was a long time—and the term *if I'm not back* should have been a red flag.

"Like I said, it's not unlike her to disappear for a few days at a time when she's on a story."

I had to give him that. "Did she give you any indicators about what she was investigating? If not that night, at any time before?"

"Nope. I asked if it was a big deal though since there was so much secrecy. All she said was she was onto something that she never expected, and the story needed to be told no matter what."

Did *no matter what* mean at the risk of her own safety? She'd applied for a gun permit. She'd stolen my stash and left me her phone, making her untraceable. She'd also had a contingency if she didn't make it back . . . It had been less than a week since she disappeared, but I couldn't wait to find out if she showed or not.

I slid off the stool and grabbed that pen and paper from my purse. I set it on Kai's dining table and jotted down my number. "If you hear from her again, call me."

"Okay," he said.

It was then I noticed a dark rain jacket hanging over the chair. It was boxy . . . and familiar. My throat muscles tightened; my eyes locked onto it. I swayed. It was Oregon though. It rained here. A lot.

When I glanced up, Kai had come out of the kitchen, taking long strides toward me.

I stepped away from the table creating space between us, my heartbeat ticking up.

He froze. "Are you okay? You look like you saw a ghost."

"I'm good." The uptick turned into pounding.

He eased the coat off the chair. "Just coming to put this away. I'll be in touch if I hear from your sister. I promise."

Lindsay being MIA was taking its toll on me. I nodded, but my arms shook as I headed to the door. That's when I spotted the coat tree next to it, a pair of rain slicker pants dangling from a hook. They matched the coat.

I flung open the door and ran to my car, not once looking back.

CHAPTER 20

Had Kai been the man who'd watched me from the park? I gripped the steering wheel to stop from trembling as I left the apartment complex. He'd been to the bar an hour before I'd gotten there the other night.

Why would he though? Had Lindsay asked him to keep an eye out for me? If she was frightened enough for her own life, she could be afraid I'd ignore her *don't ask, don't follow* directive. Although she'd directed him to give me the key at the one-week point, and that alone would have ensured that I'd do just that.

On the flip side, Kai could be involved. Except turning over the key my sister gave him made no sense unless his sudden desire to help was intended to get me off track. Finding out what the key belonged to could resolve that uncertainty.

I found the nearest grocery store, parking in a middle slot surrounded by other cars facing the entry, and called Steve at the paper. Voicemail. I left a message for a callback.

Whatever the answer, I'd been too lax in my movements, not absorbing the seriousness of being followed. *Maybe you're the target.* Detective Matson had raised that question, and I'd disregarded it because I'd only begun to inquire. Either that alone was enough, or they truly thought I could lead them to Lindsay as I'd first thought.

Whatever the case, I had to be more careful. And the sooner I found Lindsay, the sooner this nightmare would go away.

From my phone I launched Google, deciding not to wait for Steve. He could be busy or out all day. The key had an alphanumeric serial number on it. A locksmith would be the fastest way to narrow my search.

The closest was two miles away. My GPS led me to the closet-sized shop located next to a pot dispensary and a resale store that focused on hippie clothes. The smell of patchouli about knocked me on my ass when I got out. Even inside the locksmith, the scent wafted in.

Thankfully, my stay was brief, and my belief confirmed. The key belonged to a postal box. That only put me halfway there. Because every post office had its own serial numbers, I'd have to check with each to find out where it fit.

My first three calls sent me navigating through phone trees and on hold for what felt like an hour, only to be told that the serial number didn't match their keys. My fourth call was a success, and I backtracked it to the postal building about three miles from Lindsay's apartment complex in the opposite direction.

I fell in behind a long line of patrons carrying small packages to large envelopes and those needing to buy a stamp. All the while willing them to move faster. More so after the two clerks became one at break time.

When I got to the front counter, I set the key down. "I think this is one of yours."

The older woman slipped on the rhinestone-tipped glasses that hung on a beaded cord around her neck. She flipped it over and her manicured nails clicked on the keyboard. "Sure is."

"Can you tell me which box it opens?"

"Can't do that."

I'd expected that, although I was fairly certain all that clicking on the keyboard had pulled up the information on her screen. "The owner's my sister. We have the same last name. I can show you my ID."

"Won't help unless your name's on the box, hon. Happy to take the key and get it to the rightful owner. Best I can do." She wrapped her hand around the key, her eyes flicking to the next person in line, dismissing me.

That, I hadn't expected. "That's okay." I whipped out my hand, palm up.

She hesitated.

"Dorothy?" Another clerk called the woman who was holding my key hostage. "Did you want me to grab you a coffee while I'm out?"

Dorothy turned long enough to acknowledge her coworker and place her order, and I leaned on the counter, catching a glimpse of the screen.

When she turned back, I smiled. "To be honest, I'm not certain this belongs to my sister. If it does, she wouldn't appreciate me losing it. I'll go home tonight and ask her first."

She seemed satisfied with that and dropped the key into my waiting hand. "Next," she yelled.

I rushed out of the service area and into the lobby. When I'd first come in, I hadn't noticed where the mailboxes were situated.

Now I went down the short hall. The mail room was on the right and filled with wall-to-wall and floor-to-about-six-feet-high rows of silver boxes.

It would take a month to go through them, but I'd seen enough of the box number on the computer screen to narrow my search. The 1900 series included about fifty manila envelope–sized boxes on the right near the bottom and that's where I'd start.

If Lindsay had a PO box at all, it was to keep it separate from her home life, and that suggested it would be work-related. A four-by-four box would be too small if she was receiving files or research items. Not that those bigger items couldn't be held by the clerk, but having to retrieve them during limited post office hours didn't seem Lindsay-like.

Relying on there being no law against trying PO boxes with someone else's key, I got to work. A few times I stopped when someone entered the room. I smiled and they gestured a hello, went straight to their mailbox, and disappeared with their mail. I half expected them to report a woman loitering, but no one came to check on me.

By the time I'd tried my fifteenth box, however, I began to think this was impossible. Then I realized the pattern of numbers—1950 to 2000. If Lindsay could pick one, there'd be one choice.

Her birth year. A long shot, maybe, but it beat opening twenty more boxes only to discover I was right. I found the box near the end of the row and inserted the key. It turned.

Yes. I'd been thinking I didn't know my sister anymore. While true in many ways, I did at least know some of her quirks.

What I didn't understand at first glance was what I pulled from the box—an envelope from Lindsay's return address at the newspaper to Lindsay's PO Box here. Then I realized what she'd done—she'd mailed the items to herself.

Giddy with success, and anxious about what was inside the envelope, I clutched it to my chest and secured the box. Next stop: somewhere safe to look at the contents. My office at the firm had once been that place. Craig's murder had destroyed that.

I ended up at the Lewis & Clark Law School, nestled into the forest on Terwilliger Boulevard. The law library was open to the public, and I'd come here a few times for Craig to research some old case law, to hang out with my dad while he worked, and even to put in some of my own billable hours in the peace and quiet. If I did go to law school, this would be my first choice—the Pacific Northwest vibe was everywhere, and I fit in here. But until I found Lindsay, that future felt like a lifetime away.

The heady smell of the hundreds of thousands of books that lined the shelves hit my nose the moment I entered. My muscles unraveled at the sight of the wall of windows that looked out onto a deck and then beyond that a slew of towering fir trees.

It was late afternoon, and a few students were making use of the quiet. I grazed my fingers across the spines of the environmental law section for Lindsay on my way to a remote corner table and comfy chair I'd melted into a few times to read.

My whole world had been surrounded by justice and books and law. Because of my father, sure, but I'd become enamored by it early on. A desire to have things orderly and in place—for things to make sense and have a reason for being—had long been inside me.

Lindsay's world had never been that. She thrived on chaos. Conflict. Wanting to right the world by forcing it into change.

There were times she challenged me and thought I judged her for that trait. She had it wrong. I wanted to be her. To have her courage. My heart squeezed. I'd tell her that now if she were here. But I'd often wondered how two people raised by the same parents could be so different. Maybe having different DNAs contributed, but I'd known other siblings that were nothing alike too.

One thing we absolutely shared was our persistence. Despite my father's wishes that I return to work and leave finding Lindsay alone, I'd keep pushing until I succeeded. He had called me his *stubborn girl* after all.

No one else had claimed the back corner chair and I plopped into it, letting the serenity of the place prepare me for what I might find. With the envelope on my lap, I pulled out the contents—a bright green folder.

Inside was layer upon layer of newspaper clippings that centered around missing children, their ages ranging between three and eight. Some had disappeared from parks and shopping malls. Some from their own front yards.

Heartbreaking—both for the reasons of their disappearances and the sheer number. As I dug into the stack, the articles turned from older children to infants. An entire piece had profiled two babies taken from a hospital nursery. The stories below that moved away from missing under suspicious circumstances to obvious claims of abduction.

I settled deeper into the chair, deciphering why Lindsay would have this, why she'd wanted me to have the key, and how it tied to what I thought I knew so far. Did she think the agency was involved in adopting out missing and abducted children? I checked the date. The hospital incident had occurred twenty years ago.

Perhaps after learning that Alliance had been involved in her adoption, Lindsay had dug deeper into the agency. They didn't like her questions, and on her way out, she'd spoken to Rhonda.

Did that conversation take her to this place we were at right now? Which was where? Craig dying? Her on the run? My father worried? At first, I thought his fear stemmed from being connected to a questionable agency . . . but another troubling thought emerged. What if Lindsay herself had been abducted and that's what my father feared would be uncovered? No. I had no proof of that. And recent interactions with my parents said the truth wouldn't come from either of them.

I kept lifting the articles one by one, trying to figure out why she would have wanted me to ultimately find this. Until something caught my attention.

A note in Lindsay's handwriting. A couple of years ago, a woman had come through St. Luke's Legal Clinic claiming she'd been told her child had died during childbirth. Certain that was a lie, she'd sought their help. The word "Alliance" was jotted next to it. But St. Luke's was what made me pause.

There'd been a file labeled that in Craig's desk drawer, which I'd dismissed as his medical file since it hung next to his taxes and bills folders.

I had to get back to Craig's place—I just had to maneuver around one obstacle first.

CHAPTER 21

I called Detective Matson from the law library's deck. Craig's house could have been deemed a crime scene by now and that would make it off limits. Crossing the detective on that aspect might land me in jail, making it impossible to search for Lindsay.

A light mist floated in the air, cooling my warmed face. Typical Portland weather—and not enough to send me running for cover or to deter a group of women entering the trailhead that led through Tryon Creek. The law school preached balance and wellness, encouraging students to make time for self-care. Someday I'd heed that kind of advice and take advantage of the lush forestland and greenery of this area. Until then, I enjoyed it from a distance, with a laptop, while being productive.

I'd never questioned my choices. Now, on the verge of my entire world coming undone, my sister in hiding, my parents less than forthcoming, I wondered what the hell I'd been trying to prove by making no life for myself outside of work.

Detective Matson answered before I could ponder that more. "Ms. Ralston, I hope you have not stumbled upon any more potential crime scenes?"

"No, sir. Avoiding those."

"Good to hear." His tone lifted.

I smiled at that. Briefly. "Have you identified the body at the adoption agency?"

"I can't discuss an active investigation, Ms. Ralston." His tone was back to the one I'd come to expect. "Am I to take it you still haven't heard from your sister?"

"That's correct." Lindsay wasn't in that building or he wouldn't have asked. A small win. Now to hope it wasn't Bailey.

"So why are you calling?" he said.

"I'd like to get into Craig's place and wanted the okay."

"Why would you need to do that?"

"Murphy." Any other reason would have raised suspicion. "That night I took him, I grabbed the basics. I'd like to get the rest."

"Pet stores are all over this city. Even I have a cat, Ms. Ralston. I'm sure you can find what you need in one of them."

I cleared my throat, imagining a cat might be the lone thing capable of loving Detective Matson. He didn't wear a ring. "True, but they don't have his medication . . ." If he asked me the name of it, I'd be screwed.

The women hikers came back from the woods, moving at a fast clip. Mountain lions had been seen on the trail in the past. Their faces were pinched. Serious.

He let me wait it out before he said, "Fine."

"Appreciate it. I won't—"

He clicked off.

The day was getting late. I'd better go if I intended to be at Craig's before dark. I hustled through the library and held the glass door open for the women hikers as they approached. "Everything okay?"

"Some creep's right off the trail with binoculars and watching the library."

I gripped the door tighter. It could be anyone, even a bird-watcher. You didn't have to be a student to hike the trail. Campus security had chased off a few pervs hanging out over the years. "What did he look like?"

"Hard telling. He had some dark rain slicker thing on."

Kai? My shoulders bunched. "Did you say anything to him?"

"Yeah. We told him we were calling security and he took off running into the trail."

Why would Kai follow me here? That didn't make sense . . . unless it wasn't him. Not waiting around to find out, I sprinted to the parking lot, anxiety stealing my breath with every step. How did he or anyone even know where I'd be? I'd glanced in my rear-view every minute while driving. When I'd parked, the lot was empty of black sedans. The long trek to the library had been quiet. No one stood out as not belonging on campus.

A heart attack at worst, or a panic attack at least, was guaranteed at this rate. Because more frightening was the thought that it might not be Kai at all. Someone had known where Bailey was headed to meet me. They'd known when I was home and staked out the park. How?! No one could watch a person's every move, could they?

By the time I neared my Honda, panic had my breaths coming in gasps. It was like they could read my thoughts. My cell. If they put on a tracker, would they need access to it? It had never left my sight. That might not mean anything.

I approached my car from the other side and froze. A sickening wave rippled through me.

I bent to inspect the undercarriage but couldn't get a good visual without getting on my hands and knees. In the rain, I wasn't quite ready to do that.

Instead, I rounded to the front and ran my hand underneath the front bumper. Clear. At the back end I crouched and slid my palm under, stopping against cold metal.

What the hell? I pushed against it. It moved—barely. Magnetic. I grasped it and yanked out a black box. Goose bumps covered my skin. A GPS tracker had been placed on my car. My throat tightened.

I had to get out of this parking lot. I tossed the tracker onto the passenger seat like it was on fire, got in, and drove off campus with one clear goal.

The minute I hit the bridge, I rolled down the window. With a primal scream that would have woken the dead, I sent the box sailing into the Willamette River.

*   *   *

The sun had set, and mist hung around Craig's house by the time I arrived. I blasted the car vents' warm air onto my face trying to stop the adrenaline-induced shaking that had continued since finding the GPS unit. I'd make this fast—get what I came for and go home to Murphy. There I could close the shade and at least feel a little safer.

Entering through the front, I shuddered at the eeriness of the cold and quiet space.

At some point, someone in Craig's family would clear out the house and put it up for sale. I'd heard nothing about a funeral yet, or whether Craig's body had been released.

The paralegal part of me wanted details. The woman who'd worked with the man for five years, and thought we were friends, did not. That could also be the sister who felt betrayed by both him and Lindsay for never mentioning their working relationship. There'd been little time to admit that or even give it much thought.

Why hadn't they trusted me? It had done nothing but leave me exposed as I searched for answers. Searched for Lindsay.

She had to have known her stupid directive wouldn't detour me. Like the night when we were kids and she'd jumped out of the window to meet her friends at the train trestle.

Despite being afraid that my father would come in and find us gone, I'd followed. I couldn't believe she'd taken that trail down to our private place. That she'd lied by omission. A part of me wanted to confront her. Wanted her to get caught.

When I got to our special place, she and her friends were out in the middle of the trestle with their flashlights nestled in the rock between the wood tracks and pointed skyward. Someone's iPod squeaked out some song by New Kids on the Block. Lindsay was tossing her hair about. Her girlfriends giggled, their feet dangling toward the water, and passed around that flask I'd seen in my sister's purse. A flask filled with whiskey she'd stolen from Dad's liquor cabinet.

She'd hopped up on the edge of the narrow steel rail, swaying and teetering, with clearly too much of that whiskey in her. She balanced on one foot, and then the other, throwing her head back, all near the edge. Too close to the water. Being too cocky for her friends.

She hadn't seen me watching, but I saw when her foot turned. Her friends continued to laugh, unaware, as she slipped and slid over the trestle's edge, hanging by her fingertips. Her shoe dropping into the freezing water.

I'd come running, screaming for them to help her as I clawed for her wrists. Something to get hold of. I held her firm as they finally realized the danger.

Once back on the tracks, I got a *thanks, but I have it, now go home.* Which I did. Alone. But the next night, she'd crawled in next to me and set her head on my shoulder.

Thank you, she'd whispered in my ear before falling asleep, our hands clasped. I'd been right to ignore her directive and she'd been thankful. I tried never to think about what would have happened to Lindsay if I'd stayed beneath the covers that night. Dad never found out; we never spoke of it again.

Realization settled into me. She *did* know I'd follow by leaving me that message on her phone. That's why she'd dropped it in my purse. Not only for that message, but to see the connection between her and Craig. Maybe like the key she'd given to Kai, and the envelope she'd mailed to herself, I was her fail-safe—like I had been that night.

She could be afraid, even with her confidence, that she didn't have it all figured out this time, and that's what scared me the most. The fact my strong, fearless sister might be scared.

I shook my head, releasing any annoyance over being iced out. My sister needed me. I had no idea what had happened. She could be out there praying I was on my way.

That thought alone would propel me through my fear.

I locked the door behind me to avoid any neighborly drop-ins and went straight to Craig's desk. The blotter had been turned to its side, and the drawer opened a crack. The police had been here.

Whoever the office had assigned to secure client-privileged documents would have been sent here too.

Shoot. If St. Luke's was a legal file, it might have already been pulled to be returned. Going to the legal clinic would do no good if that were the case. Attorney/client privilege held strong, even at a free clinic. Hopefully, the special master had overlooked it like I had the first time.

I opened the drawer that held Craig's tax filings and tingled with relief when I found the clinic file still hanging next to those returns. Anxious to see what it held, I set the file on the desk and skimmed the contents. The handwritten notes of case law to review were a clear indication that the file related to legal work.

The file also contained handwritten notes from a conversation Craig had had with an Ellen Sullivan. She claimed she'd given birth to a girl over thirty years ago—a child that had died during the birth process. Or so she'd been told by the midwife. She'd never believed it.

The hairs on my arms pricked up. Alliance Adoption used a midwife. Sherry Smith. I searched for the midwife's name and found a reference to a Jodi, no Sherry. But this was thirty years ago—it wouldn't likely be the same person.

Had Lindsay suspected she was that child? I scanned the paperwork. The birth year didn't match Lindsay's.

On the next page, another woman had come to the legal clinic claiming the same thing had happened to her twenty years ago. And another woman five years ago. A definite pattern, but none of them indicated the agency they'd worked with. It could be Alliance, given Lindsay's notes in her file. What I could confirm was that the stories were similar—all children lost at birth. All three dealing with a midwife, although the other two didn't list a name.

I couldn't discount that the midwife or -wives might have worked with the adoption agency too, but separately. Freelance maybe? But how did the women and the midwife get connected in the first place?

Sherry Smith could answer that question if I could find her, but I'd already gone down that road to a dead end.

Lindsay might have had better luck. More likely, she'd started with the women on the list, which she must know about if she and Craig were working together and based on what I'd found in her postal box. If finding these women would lead me to Lindsay, it was worth a shot for me to try as well.

In the kitchen, I grabbed the rest of Murphy's food, and his dish from the cupboard. He had a couple of catnip toys in a drawer, which I dropped into my purse next to the St. Luke's file.

I flicked off the lights and secured Craig's house, not expecting to return here. I rested my palm against the door, sorry that whatever Lindsay and Craig were involved in might have resulted in his murder. Of course, Craig and Lindsay made decisions for themselves. But finding out that Craig had been involved in helping others through the clinic made me feel the loss of him even more.

Across the street, a white and tan corgi ran the fence line. A porch light illuminated the walk. What was that neighbor's name? Harold? No, Henry. He'd kept an eye on Craig's house and was quite observant that first night I came through. It could be worth checking whether Lindsay had come back. Or anyone else besides the police. With Lindsay's articles on abduction cases, and Craig's on women who'd come to the legal clinic, I had an uneasy feeling that others might want the information too.

I ignored the yipping and rang the doorbell. A few minutes later, a slightly hunched gray-haired woman answered. "Sorry to bother you," I said.

"No bother. Just watching a game show. What can I do for you?"

"Is Henry available?"

"Who?"

Had I misheard him? "Henry. I thought that's what he told me his name was. He's a little shorter than me. Brown hair. Brown eyes."

She shook her head. "No one lives here but me."

"Grandson?" I asked.

"Lives back east."

My tongue suddenly felt thick. "You're sure there's no Henry?"

She smiled. "I've lived in this neighborhood for years. Mr. Stalling lives next door with his wife. They have no children though, so it wouldn't have been anyone from his house. Barbara lives next to them. Her kids have been in Hawaii for the past couple of weeks. Mr. Bartell lives . . . lived across the way." She closed her eyes and crossed herself. "God rest his soul."

I nodded. "That's where I just came from. I was Craig's paralegal."

Her eyes softened. "Oh dear, I'm sorry for your loss. So sad. I wish I could help you find this Henry you speak of, but he doesn't sound like he's from the neighborhood."

I thanked her for her time, and then hurried to my car.

If not a neighbor, who had been in Craig's house with me that night? He'd asked about the redhead who'd come by earlier. He'd thought I was her when he came over. He wasn't there to see me . . . he was there for Lindsay.

My face broke out in perspiration.

Had I been in the house with Craig's killer?

CHAPTER 22

Aching pain radiated through my body from the stress of the last couple of hours—from the last several days—as I left Craig's house.

It was possible I'd been followed from the first night I'd come here. Henry could have put the GPS unit on my car after he'd tested my knowledge of the redhead who'd come by. He might have known who I was even then.

Although if he recognized me in the parking garage when I'd gone to find Lindsay, he could have gotten to my car at the firm.

Or when I was at Lindsay's place. Henry could also have gotten to my car at my apartment, where there was no secured parking. It would take but a second to attach a magnet under my bumper.

However the GPS tracker got there, it explained his appearance at the coffee shop. Whether Bailey was targeted, or to serve as a warning, one thing was clear: searching for Lindsay had put a target on my back, and anyone I spoke to in my search for Lindsay was at risk. And attaching another tracker could happen again too easily.

It killed me to admit it, but my pride and joy had become a liability.

Whoever was after Lindsay knew what I drove and what I looked like. While I had an inkling of what Lindsay's investigation had focused on, I didn't know who would be after her. Henry, obviously—he'd been in far too many places now to think otherwise—but that didn't tell me his true identity or how he fit. And he might not be acting alone.

Opting for the backroads of Marine Drive, I headed to the Portland airport. A calm settled over me as a plan formed to keep myself, and ultimately Lindsay, safe. I secured my vehicle in the long-term lot and hitched a ride with a car rental shuttle.

A half hour later, I left in a small black SUV feeling more in control than I had in days, although aware only part of the issue had been fixed. If my apartment was being watched, it wouldn't take long to figure out I'd changed vehicles. Someone could be there now since I'd taken away their ability to track me. They could also be wandering the bridge thinking I'd crashed into the Willamette River. A smile crept onto my face despite the seriousness of this situation.

Ideal or not, though, I had to go home. Murphy had to eat. If he yowled for dinner and my landlord heard, there'd be no place for us to live when this was over.

On my way, I spotted the University of Oregon Duck Store on Couch and pulled in front. After purchasing a green and yellow *Go Ducks* sweatshirt, stocking cap, and scarf, I slipped the items on before arriving in my neighborhood. I barely recognized myself in the mirror.

I ditched the SUV a couple of blocks away. With my hair tucked under the knit cap, scarf up to my nose, and head down, I hustled through the courtyard at the back of my apartment building. I'd entered the first two numbers of the five-digit code on the digital pad when I heard shuffling. My fingers stumbled. I restarted. Another shuffle. Hit the wrong key. One more time.

"Excuse me," a male voice said from behind.

My hand froze, along with the rest of me. "Yes?"

"You having a problem, miss?"

"No, sir. Going to see my uncle."

"Turn around," he said. "Slowly."

It had to be security who came through once a night. I did as directed. "I have the code, sir."

"Why aren't you using the front like most guests then?"

A security logo was blazoned across his gray jacket. I breathed again, but I wasn't in the clear yet. "This is closer to get to his apartment." And mine.

"Who's your uncle?"

"Harold Logan."

The guard winced. Guess Mr. Logan had a way of charming everyone he met.

"I'm already late for dinner. Way late. He's going to kill me."

"Go." He waved me on. "Next time use the front door."

"Yes, sir."

I scurried up the back stairs and secured myself in my apartment before anyone else stopped me. But I hadn't been as sly as I thought. For the short term, I might not be able to come back here.

Murphy purred by his dish in the kitchen. Keeping the lights off, I filled his bowl with pâté. While he ate, I grabbed a duffel bag from my bedroom closet, completing the college student look.

I stuffed some clean underclothing, pj's, a pair of jeans, and a sweatshirt inside. I folded in a pair of dress pants and blouse to be safe and slid my laptop into the side pocket.

With that done, my focus rested on Murphy, who'd finished his dinner and taken to licking his paws without a care in the world. Lucky him.

"I'd better apologize now," I said. "You're not going to like this idea one bit, buddy."

* * *

Murphy waited until I made it down the stairs and out of the building before letting out his first protest. I'd tucked him and some of his necessities into the duffel on top of everything else. If Henry was in the vicinity, he'd have recognized the crate and me right away.

Clutching the bag to my side, I speed-walked to the SUV and swiped my hand under the bumper for any trackers before I got in. All clear. I set the bag in the passenger seat and unzipped it enough for Murphy's head to pop out. In the dark, I inspected the passing cars, the drivers, and the people on the sidewalk. I scanned the park. No lurkers or indications that anyone had been waiting for me outside.

Now I had to figure out where to go next. I couldn't stay at Lindsay's place. Kai was out—I hadn't decided whether I could trust him yet. Same with Mandy, given her flakiness. Sleeping at the law firm wasn't an option.

After my unsettling interaction with my father, I couldn't stay with my parents either. At least directly. That left one place to get some sleep tonight—if she didn't mind.

Nova lived in a room above the detached garage on my parents' property. I'd long suspected that at some point she'd leave to create a family and life of her own. She never had.

When I was a kid and wanted to get away—usually because Lindsay was spending the night elsewhere—I snuck out to Nova's room. It had been years since I'd done that, but I hoped she wouldn't mind the intrusion, or Murphy. She'd had a cat of her own a few years ago. At least she didn't have an aversion to them, like old man Logan.

Murphy and I knocked on her door around ten o'clock after leaving the SUV behind the garage and out of sight. My parents' darkened house indicated they were out anyway. They were prone to late nights, ten o'clock far too early for them to be in bed.

Nova answered in her robe with a wide-eyed look of surprise on her face.

"It's me, Nova." I yanked the hat off my head and unwrapped the scarf from around my neck.

Her surprise turned to a worried frown. "What's wrong?"

"Everything." Unexpected tears stung my eyes. "Can I stay here tonight?"

Her gaze flicked toward my parents' place. Fear? Concern?

On cue, Murphy meowed.

She blew out a breath. "Come in." She bolted the door behind me and slid a chain across for good measure.

I relaxed immediately. Nova had always made me feel safe.

"Tea?" she said.

"I'd love some. Let me get it."

"Nonsense." She waved me off. "Settle in. You know where your bedding is. There's a box in the utility closet for your friend."

Thankfully, she hadn't thrown everything away, and I'd brought Murphy's litter.

Her apartment was a thirty-by-thirty, but she made good use of the space. An aisle kitchen ran along the back. A small bedroom and bath were off the main living area. It almost mirrored my apartment. No doubt that's why I'd been attracted to my place the first day I walked in.

Her blinds were drawn, and I turned off a couple of lights that cast shadows so that no one from a distance could make out two people moving about.

Murphy found Nova more interesting and had sauntered into the kitchen while I grabbed a sheet and blanket from the closet and tucked them into the sofa.

"I know when you're anxious," Nova said as she placed a teapot on the burner. "And you are my unflappable one." She came out into the dinette area, where she took a seat. "Come. Sit. Talk to me."

She knew me better than I wanted to admit. I was brave and driven and had my father's stoic traits. I'd convinced the world, and often myself, that I was strong and capable. Tonight, I felt anything but. A tear rolled down my cheek. I couldn't even find my sister. My parents were keeping secrets. And Craig . . .

I wiped my eyes and slid into a chair next to her. I hesitated as I thought of Bailey and the body in Alliance's building. If anything happened to Nova . . . But I hadn't been followed here and I had nowhere else to turn.

I started from the beginning, when Lindsay had run from the office and down the elevator, to reliving the moment I'd walked in to find Craig dead. She knew I'd found him, but not the details. Nobody did. I finished with Lindsay putting her phone in my purse with the don't ask, don't follow directive, and how I'd not told a soul until this moment.

More than once I swallowed down the acid climbing in my throat as Nova paled at my recounting of events. I didn't add that the man following me could be a killer. No sense having Nova terrified for my well-being on top of everything.

She listened, her hands clasped near her chest, nodding and frowning.

"All I want is my sister," I said. "But she's not even my birth sister."

Nova leaned back. "You'd asked about adoption before. What makes you say that now?"

"DNA tests. I saw them with my own eyes in her personal email. She's a different nationality. You know my parents are so proud of their full Scandinavian heritage, and Lindsay is part Spanish. My parents adopted her, even if they refuse to come clean about that. And the agency that she likely came from seems shady. The place had a fire, and someone was dead inside." It didn't matter who. It was tragic, nonetheless. "At first, I thought, who would do that? Who'd ever give up their children to a shady adoption agency?"

"Ah," she said raising her finger. "Don't judge. I had a sister once who was pregnant." She averted her eyes.

My face flushed in embarrassment. "I'm sorry. I wasn't . . . I didn't know."

"It's no matter now. It's been so long, and it was after she'd come to this country illegally—before I could find her. People give up the things they love for many reasons. For my sister, she'd spent years in addiction and was fearful of being deported. She trusted the wrong people." Tears filled Nova's eyes. She cleared her throat.

Of course, it still mattered. Did one ever get over losing a sister? My chest tightened. I wouldn't. I held her hand. "Well, that's where I was going . . . the wrong people. I soon realized that Lindsay thought something bad was happening to these women and their babies."

I laid out my theory that Lindsay must have started investigating her own adoption, and it turned into finding that children associated with the agency—or really the midwives—had been abducted. But there had to be connections to an official agency that I hadn't found yet.

"She might even believe *she* was abducted," I said. Or all those things could be true. "Whatever she's uncovered has her in danger, though, and I can't keep her safe while she's out there." I pushed away the fear of it already being too late.

"You've always tried to take good care of her." She gripped my hand firmer. "But if you are being followed, you don't want to end up like the agency. Or Mr. Bartell." She cringed. My description had shaken her more than I'd thought it would.

"No. But if they wanted me dead, they could've done that by now. I've been careless. Too confident. I can't be certain, but I've felt for a while that they believe I'll lead them to Lindsay." Tears brimmed again. We both knew that I'd find that far worse than anything happening to me. "That's why I came here."

The teapot hissed on its way to a whistle. I motioned for Nova to stay, but she stood with a look that said *don't argue*. She pulled two mugs from the kitchen cupboard. Her shoulders slumped and her hand shook as she poured the water over the teabags. I shouldn't have dumped all of this on her.

She returned with the tea.

"I'm sorry, Nova. I didn't mean to upset you."

"You didn't. But Lindsay could be wrong about herself. I don't believe she was adopted."

"How can you be sure? You didn't work for my parents then."

"Yes. But Lindsay is very much like your father in personality and mannerisms."

"Don't tell her that." I chuckled, trying for a moment of levity as I wiped my eyes. Nova smiled. Although she was right. "I have to tell you though, my father has me so annoyed at the moment. This campaign for Mayor has him thinking like a politician, not a parent. He ordered me to stay out of it and stay in my lane because I wasn't the reporter in the family. His campaign manager is also a real piece of work. She called me a distraction to his campaign."

Nova's face hardened.

"What'd I say?" I asked.

"She is something else." She slurped her tea. "I wasn't supposed to overhear their conversation, but when they saw I had, they were not happy and told me to be silent."

"What did you overhear?"

She inhaled. "Mr. Bartell's funeral's tomorrow."

Seriously? "Why wouldn't they tell me?"

She shook her head. "I'd like to think it's because they realize how traumatizing his death was for you."

"It was. And not finding Lindsay yet is equally so." Along with the countless things that had happened since. "But I'm not a child." I bristled. "Was that Ericka's idea or my parents'?"

"Both, I believe."

My father might have agreed, but Ericka had probably suggested it. "Regardless, I'm going. He was my boss, and more importantly, my friend." And if there was even the slightest chance that Lindsay would show . . .

When I looked up, Nova's face was creased with worry. "I won't tell them you told me," I said. "Promise."

She drew in a shaky breath and nodded. "Please don't. I can't be sent back."

My arms dropped to my sides. "Sent back?"

She rose and retrieved the teapot from the kitchen, topping both of our cups.

I wasn't sure I could take any more bombshells. But this was Nova. "Please, Nova, what do you mean?"

"I'm not a U.S. citizen, Beth. I'm no longer legally in this country." She said it all in one rushed breath.

Stunned, I searched her face. What did she mean, *no longer*? "How's that possible?"

"The opportunity got away from us, from me, I guess. Your father was to take care of it when my visa was set to expire. But he got involved in a trial"—she looked away—"and forgot. After months went by, I was afraid they'd send me back if I came forward."

I sat straight, angry that this had happened to her. "I will help you, Nova. I'll find someone to guide us through the process, or help you directly if I can't."

She clutched my hand and met my eye. "Now is not the time."

Heat crept into my face that my parents, my father, would do this to her. But as much as I wanted to help her, I agreed. If it came out during the campaign, everything would fall apart. Not an unwelcome thought for people who had essentially enslaved Nova to work for them. It answered so many questions on why she'd never gone anywhere else. Hurt for her and rage at them raced through me.

To bring that down now though, with Lindsay missing, could ensure her deportation.

Not a risk I'd take.

"Fine, but when this is over . . ."

She patted my hand. "Yes, when this is over."

She got up, kissing me on the cheek, and dumped out her tea. "Let's talk in the morning."

I nodded and she disappeared into her room. My chest tightened again as I dropped onto the couch, exhausted.

When this was over . . .

Did I believe there would be an over? Because I had no idea where any of us would be at the end. Two people I loved without measure were suffering, and I wasn't sure I could save either one of them.

CHAPTER 23

Moss dripped from the limbs of the towering knotty oaks and horned owls screeched. A pea soup–thick fog rose from a lake in the distance. Lindsay stood tall at its edge before diving into the water. The impending doom of the cold and the realization that the shock would kill her gripped me. I ran with everything I had, the distance between us growing with each step. Out of breath and face wet with tears, I reached the water only to find Lindsay floating face down near the middle. Too far out to reach. Panicked, I waded in and trudged the distance, the blood cementing in my legs.

When I reached Lindsay, I screamed her name and flipped her body over.

Her eyes shot open. Empty—then accusing.

"It's all your fault."

I flew backwards, waking from the nightmare when my body smacked the floor. Tangled in sheets and drenched in sweat, my eyes locked onto the ceiling. *Nova's apartment—I'm okay.* But I was far from okay. Lindsay's words of blame settled over me like a weighted blanket. I'd convinced myself yesterday that Lindsay wanted me to find her. What if my not heeding her directive to stay away had brought something far worse upon her?

Murphy perched on the top sofa cushion and stared at me. He had no answer to that either.

"Nova?" I wiggled off the floor and settled onto the couch.

Sunlight peeked through the blinds, lightening the space. Nova's bedroom door was open. My cell phone read nine o'clock.

She'd be in the main house by now. My parents would have expected breakfast at eight sharp, and she'd have started her chores. Without meaning to, I'd triggered painful memories of her past and hoped to make things right this morning.

My apology would have to wait. Nova had left a note, anchored by an apple, on the dinette table.

Funeral, 11am, Church of God. Leave Murphy with me.

Church of God had been the family church for as long as I could remember. Lindsay had gone a few times—I'd gone less. A child running through the pews would have been a distraction to my parents, I assumed. They never said.

Because of that, my relationship with God was tenuous, at best. So even now, if God could help, what could I say? Talking to Him only when I wanted something didn't feel right.

Still shaking off the remnants of my nightmare, I peeked out the front window. *My fault*, Lindsay had said. If based on not finding her yet, that's because she'd left me little to go on. But I'd keep pushing; I wouldn't fail her.

Landscapers buzzed about doing winter pruning and running twinkling lights around trees. I stayed hidden in Nova's apartment, took a shower, and got ready.

With time to spare, I retrieved the St. Luke's file from my duffel. I'd planned to dig into it last night, except I'd passed out the minute my butt hit the sofa.

Now, in the quiet of Nova's space, I curled on the couch and flipped through the pages—my focus being on Ellen Sullivan, the woman who'd claimed her child had been taken from her thirty years ago. The other cases would have proven that the practice still occurred, but I sensed Lindsay would be homing in on the time frame around her own adoption.

Craig had left several notes on each of the cases, along with some contact information. Ellen Sullivan lived on North Chautauqua off Columbia Boulevard. It had been years since I'd been down that way, but even then it had a substantial transient community.

I punched in Ellen's number; it went to voicemail. A woman's voice, though no identifiers. I took a chance.

"Ms. Sullivan, my name's Beth Ralston. I have a file that suggests you were working with a Mr. Bartell from the St. Luke's Legal Clinic." I wavered. "You might have spoken with Lindsay Ralston as well. I'd like a moment of your time. It's important." I left my number.

Since the call pertained to her child and the reason for her visit to St. Luke's in the first place, she should call back.

My parents finally departed around ten thirty, with my father driving. They were running behind. With no time to say goodbye to Nova, I scribbled out a note: *Thanks for keeping Murphy. Be in touch soon.* Since Nova had hung onto her previous cat's supplies, she might welcome Murphy's company long-term. It would solve my landlord's *no cats allowed* policy, and Murphy needed somewhere safe and stable, even if it would be weird without him.

Twenty-five minutes later, I arrived at the church. My parents had parked in a nearby lot and gone in by the time I'd arrived. My "shadow" might expect me to be here, so I parked farther away and blended in with a group walking in the same direction.

A black sedan was parked at the curb. My step faltered. I couldn't see the face underneath the chauffeur's hat as the driver had it buried in a novel. Until the man glanced up and turned the page. Gray hair and a mottled hand.

I hurried up the stairs and into the church, taking a breath when the towering door closed behind me. Funeral programs had been splayed on the outer table. Craig's mussed brown hair and kind smile pierced me. The photo had likely been taken after one of his long runs. He looked happy, relaxed—confident. I'd miss that. The easiness about him. I'd also miss how I'd always felt his equal. He didn't often pull rank, except for that night at the party.

In retrospect, he acted so out of character that I should've recognized something was wrong. Had I talked with him, instead of heeding my father's beck and call, Craig might be alive. At the least, he might have told me what had him so concerned. Or how Lindsay was involved.

I tucked a program into my purse and stole into the sanctuary where I slid into a pew at the back. That bench, and the two ahead and across the aisle, were all that remained empty. The rest were filled with many faces I didn't recognize.

Mandy sat near the middle, along with several staff from the firm. They were focused on the closed flower-draped casket. I scanned the front pews for Craig's family.

Judge Johnson, dressed in black and wearing a fifties-style box hat with netting across her face, sat closest to the casket. Odd that she'd be in the family section. Perhaps she'd been the judge Craig had clerked for when he attended law school. That didn't explain why she'd be in front.

My parents were in the pew behind the judge, my father's hand resting on her shoulder. I stiffened at the sight. My mother conversed with the woman to her right, indifferent. The firm's administrator, Phil Garrett, sat at one end, along with other men in black suits; one of them being another attorney from the firm. They had the official look of pallbearers.

The minister, complete with a white priest's collar, shuffled to the pulpit and began to talk. A hush overtook the crowd. I listened to the man's words that were supposed to comfort and felt irritation instead. At my parents for lying to me. At the situation with Nova. That someone had murdered Craig. That Lindsay had put herself in danger. That I hadn't found her.

My thoughts were interrupted when Judge Johnson stood. She approached the oak pulpit, the minister offering his hand to her.

With tear-filled eyes, she began. "My son was a good boy."

Son? I heard little else as the shock of her words tumbled in my head. Craig's mother was Judge Johnson? Was that why he'd never spoken about his parents?

In some ways, I understood his secrecy. Being a judge's son could garner him special treatment. With Craig's work ethic and desire to be recognized on his own merits, he'd have cringed at the thought. He and I were alike in that.

Still, I was surprised it had never come up when I visited my parents. Did my father not know . . . ?

Once she'd finished, a few lawyers from the firm spoke, evoking tears mixed with laughter throughout the crowd. But the revelation had me in such a daze that when Mandy broke my thoughts by sliding next to me, I jumped.

"Sorry. What're you doing here?" she whispered as the rows of people emptied and moved toward the front to give their condolences to Judge Johnson standing at the casket.

"Why wouldn't I be here?" Did I appear that fragile? My father had made it to the front of the line and was hugging the judge, my mother's hand on his back. The last couple of interactions I'd mistook as Dad and Judge Johnson being too close. Now I realized, at least at the Rotary meeting, he'd been comforting her.

"That came out wrong," she said, her hand on my shoulder. "I meant, how are you doing? With all the trauma around seeing Craig . . . you know . . . dead, we thought you'd want to stay away. I mean, you haven't come back to work."

"He was my friend." I softened—their confusion making sense. I'd always been predictable in my drive to work and suddenly I'd gone MIA with my energies directed elsewhere.

"Of course he was." She shifted. "What have you been up to?"

I wanted to tell her, but after her no-show for coffee and our weird exchange in the elevator, I didn't know who to confide in. That person had always been Lindsay. Despite our differences. And I needed her home—now.

"Look, I have to go."

She frowned as I stood and scooted past her, joining the line to the judge. My parents were walking back when they spotted me and motioned me over.

As much as I didn't want to lose my place, I had to know why they'd kept Craig's funeral time from me. "Hey," I said, approaching. "Good thing they announce funerals in the paper, or I'd have missed this."

My father flushed, and my mother gave me a brisk hug. "Ericka thought it might be best . . ."

"Right, Ericka. Does that woman ever think of anything but your campaign?"

My father squared his shoulders. I'm sure he didn't like this new me that questioned him. And Ericka was nowhere close to shield him from me this time.

My mother rubbed my forearm. "Darling, let's not make a scene. For Craig's sake. His mother is a mess."

"Yes, about that," I said to my father, "did you know Craig was her son when you hired him?"

"Yes, dear," he said. "I know most things that happen in the firm."

"Then you do know what Craig and Lindsay were working on and where Lindsay has gone?"

His eye twitched. My mother's eyes filled with sadness at the mention of Lindsay's name. Another couple drew near, and my parents shifted their attention to them and took a step away from me.

Wow. Guess we were done talking. Did they not care that their daughter was missing? I studied my parents' faces for signs they were as freaked out as I was. But other than the flash of emotion my mother had shown, her stare was cold, and my father's lips were tight.

Appearances might mean everything to my parents, but their lack of concern for Lindsay left me wanting answers even more.

The line to the judge had shortened. Despite everyone being "surprised" I'd shown, I had worked next to her son and intended to give her my condolences. Perhaps that would mean something to her.

When my turn came, I reached out my hand. "I'm so sorry for your loss."

"Thank you," she said, her grip cool and shaky.

"I was your son's paralegal."

"Thank you for coming." She looked past me, her eyes flitting back and forth. Searching? The couple that had been in line behind me got sidetracked by another couple and had stepped out, leaving just the two of us.

"Craig never mentioned that he was your son," I said, taking advantage of the extra time. There was no resemblance either. Judge Johnson had sharp features. Craig's were softer. His hair wavier. Since I hated being compared to Lindsay in that way, I kept that to myself. "You must've been proud."

"Very." She cleared her throat.

"He was easy to work with and I truly enjoyed our time."

She nodded. "I appreciate your sharing."

I didn't move on. Conflicted. Timing couldn't be worse, but there might not be another opportunity. My intention wasn't to overwhelm her with the adoption agency stuff or women losing their babies, but if I got the ball rolling, she might have information to share with me. "I'm curious, did Craig talk to you about any recent cases he was working on?"

Her eyes flicked to the side this time. "Client confidentiality would have barred that, even if I am a judge."

Uncertain that what he and Lindsay were doing qualified for that, I leaned in, keeping my voice low. "I'm sorry, but the reason I ask is he and my sister were investigating something on the side. I'm fairly sure it had to do with an adoption agency. With your background, and access to information, I'm hoping he mentioned what exactly that investigation was about."

Her eyes flashed this time before she blanched and stumbled back. The minister had been nearby, watching. He marched to her aid, steadying her, and shot a scowl at me as he hustled her away.

CHAPTER 24

The judge's reaction left me dumbfounded. Okay—the timing of the question was inappropriate—but her son had been murdered. She should want answers as to why. But I had no time to think on that more as the church had nearly emptied. Leaving with a crowd would make me less noticeable if anyone was watching.

Before I'd made it halfway down the aisle, the minister appeared at my side. "Ms. Ralston," he said. "You're welcome here any time. Your parents are fine people and in good standing here." Translation: they give lots of money to the church. "That welcome will not extend to you if your intent is to harass other members."

"I wasn't harassing—"

His hand shot up. "Evelyn is grieving. She's a good woman. She's a pillar to this church and the community it advocates for."

"I'd only asked if her son had worked with someone I know." My voice chilled a few degrees. His defense had me on the offense.

"Now is not the time or the place for questions of any kind."

Maybe, but he couldn't take issue with this one. "What kind of advocating does Judge Johnson do?"

As I'd hoped, his tone lightened. "Women's causes, addiction programs, children's resources. She's been an absolute angel to them and to us. I won't allow anyone to treat her like she's anything otherwise."

"I didn't mean to upset her," I said, absorbing what he'd said. It came as no surprise that Craig came from a philanthropic family with his own volunteering at St. Luke's Legal Clinic. But women's and children's services? That struck me as too great a coincidence.

His message delivered and received, the priest nodded and veered off.

I hurried out of the church, my focus on the sidewalk void of people, and lamented that I'd let the priest slow me down.

"Surprised to still see you here," Detective Matson said from the base of the stairs, startling me.

"Hey," I said, relieved it was him. "That seems to have been the general opinion as to my attendance. I didn't expect to see you at all." Although I had to admit, I was glad he was here. And not only because I didn't want to run out on the street by myself.

"Homicide detecting 101. Attend the funeral. Never know who might attend." He smiled. A bit unnerving. Had something changed?

"Ah," I said, realizing he thought the murderer would show. "You still think Lindsay's involved."

He shrugged. *Right, looking at all angles.* "Where you headed?" he said.

Good question. Until Ellen Sullivan called, I had no Plan B. Although I did have her address. Standing out here, however, wasn't the best idea. "You have a minute to chat?" I said.

"Sure." He joined me at the top of the stairs and we went inside the church, grabbing a pew at the back.

A cleaning woman—I assumed, based on her blue apron and hair up under a bandana—shifted the plants to one side of the casket up front. She pressed her hands on the mahogany box, her face drawn, tired . . . sad. How many funerals had she cleaned up after?

Two men I recognized from the service joined her. They gathered the flowers off the casket and secured it.

"Have you decided if there's a connection between Craig's murder and what happened at the adoption agency?" I said, averting my eyes from the scene.

He arched an eyebrow.

"Right." No sharing during an active investigation. The hardwood dug into my shoulders. "Can you at least say if anything has surprised you?"

"After twenty years in this job, not much does anymore. The question is what have you found out, Ms. Ralston?"

Too much. "For starters, that Craig's mother was Judge Evelyn Johnson. Guess I should have known something was up when he'd recused himself from files assigned to her, but I had no idea. There's not even a slight resemblance between the two."

"He never spoke to you about his family history?"

"Not at all. I . . ." The way he said that sounded odd and my skin pricked. It would make perfect sense. "Was he adopted?"

He didn't answer, but his eyes had shifted.

"I'm right, aren't I?" Lindsay and Craig both being adopted had to be why they were working together.

He shrugged. "It could be a line of inquiry."

Wow, I would've thought Craig would've mentioned that . . . but why would he? He hadn't told me anything else. Unless . . . "Was he aware?"

"We've found evidence to the contrary, although we believe Mr. Bartell suspected."

I read that to mean the judge had been no more forthcoming with Craig than my parents were with Lindsay. That had to be relevant and could explain her reaction to my questions. I shifted to face the detective. "What kind of evidence?"

He shook his head.

I sighed. He'd said what he had to gauge my knowledge. "Can you at least tell me what his mother said about it?"

He pressed his lips together.

"Please. It could be important to something I found."

He cleared his throat. "Okay. I'll bite. She was quite surprised we were questioning her and whipped out his birth certificate to prove it."

That seemed a bit theatrical. "But you're not convinced?"

"Politicians always spin things in a way that shows them in the best light. It's not shocking she'd want to control the narrative. Let's say we're looking into a few things around it, and they're not panning out in her favor."

I'd ask him for details but doubted he'd embellish. "That's good you're looking," I said, more to myself.

"Your turn," he said. "Why is it important?"

I shifted. "Will you throw me in jail for withholding information?"

"You mean for obstruction?"

I didn't respond, or flinch.

He settled into the bench. "Have you done anything overtly illegal?"

Had I? "Not that I know of."

"I suspect you'd know, Ms. Ralston." I didn't blame him for being sarcastic, but he finally let out a long breath. "You're safe, for the moment."

I'd find out soon enough if he was true to his word. "Lindsay was there that night at the law firm, like the tape showed."

"Tell me something I haven't figured out already."

"Fine, but I don't know why she was there. She'd run from Craig's office and out the back before I could ask."

"Have you spoken to her since?"

"No. But she has to be on an investigation, and . . ." I closed my eyes. Time to jump, even if my father would be furious. He didn't have anything handled from what I could tell. "Lindsay was also adopted. The agency Lindsay was looking into was Alliance, and while I don't have absolute proof, it feels like it's at the center of everything."

"I'd buy that."

I straightened. "You would?"

"Not about Lindsay and Craig being connected to the agency. We didn't have the information to get that far." His stare was hard and lasted far too long. The wood pew became unbearable. "But there's something going on at the agency that's a few degrees shy of proper."

"You've identified the body, haven't you?"

"It was announced this morning on the news. The victim was Sherry Smith—at least that had been her most recent name. She was purportedly a midwife."

My shoulders inched up. Bailey had been bringing me her name and now Sherry was dead. She must have known something . . . "What do you mean *recent name*?"

"She's had a few aliases over the years."

I thought back to the reference of a Jodi in one of the files. "Like?"

"Can't say." He might not, but it explained Sherry not showing up in any databases. She might not even be licensed since he'd said *purportedly*.

Fine. "The important thing is it lends credibility to my theory that the agency is involved in something weird with Lindsay and Craig."

"Not necessarily. Someone could have been upset about a botched adoption and decided to retaliate."

I hadn't thought of that. "Is that what Ms. Ottoman thinks?"

"She believes it's a possibility. The agency has had vandalism issues in the past."

"Is she concerned for her safety?"

"Yes, and she's staying with family."

Still . . . "You have to admit, even if they had issues in the past, how likely is it that my sister is investigating them at the same time as one of their employees almost gets hit by a car right before their building is burned down with a midwife inside, who has a 'few' aliases?" I air quoted the word *few*. "Not to mention Craig's murder, and that might have been because he was getting too close to something they didn't want found out."

The detective's face remained impassive.

Either he wasn't convinced, or he had no intention of letting me in on his investigation. Neither of us were good at sharing. "Anyway—I'm just saying it's odd because all of that transpired right after my sister learned that she's adopted and started poking around," I added.

"Her adoption wasn't common knowledge?"

"Not by her or me. My parents are holding to their story that she isn't—like the judge with Craig."

"How'd she find out?"

"I, well . . ." I shifted to get comfortable, not sure what more to tell him. Knowing Lindsay wouldn't want me to . . . But she'd also left me the key, which led to the file and back to Craig's house. If I was her fail-safe, she'd have to trust me. It was on me to make these decisions now.

"Ms. Ralston, it could be important. How?"

He was right, it could be important. "A DNA test. I found a copy of the report in Lindsay's email."

He folded his arms over his chest. "Interesting."

"What is?"

He ignored my question. "I want a copy of that report. What's the name of the lab?"

Finally, some leverage. "Tell me what's interesting first."

"There's no *first*, Ms. Ralston," he said. "Do you get that? I can subpoena records. I can throw you in jail. The reason I haven't done so, yet, is because I think you're trying to find your sister and the truth. But my patience is thinning."

I lifted my chin, defiant. "That's all true. Except your subpoena could take weeks, and I have what you want now. Working together could benefit us both." Wasn't I a walking contradiction? He knew it too. "Look, all I'm asking is why you find it so interesting."

Our eyes met in a contest that I'd lose, but I refused to give an inch. Every part of me thought I knew the answer and wanted confirmation.

"We found a DNA report in Mr. Bartell's possessions," he said.

I pressed the heel of my hands onto my eyes, thinking. When Lindsay went to Craig for advice, that could have prompted him to get one of his own tests—for curiosity reasons if nothing else. If they compared and recognized the similarities . . . and him at the clinic . . . I didn't know the steps after that, but there'd been a few to get here.

"When can I expect that report, Ms. Ralston?" he said.

"This afternoon. I do have one ask about the adoption stuff, and that is that it remains confidential. My father's campaigning." Why I cared about protecting him eluded me. Perhaps blood ties ran deep, and I wasn't prepared to destroy my entire world in one stroke.

"I don't see the need for that to come out at this point," he said.

"Thank you." He didn't have to accommodate that request. "I'll find a Wi-Fi connection and send it." I could go back to my apartment and send from there, but I hadn't intended to return yet. What was my plan anyway? Stay at Nova's place indefinitely or find someplace else?

"Why the frown?" he said.

"When I went to Craig's yesterday, I realized the man that had probably been down in the parking garage—and tried to run down Bailey—had been at Craig's house right after his murder that night."

"What makes you say that?"

"Because I'd run into the guy."

He shook his head, annoyed. "Why didn't you say something when you came to the precinct or when we spoke outside the agency after the fire?"

"He told me he was a neighbor, and I didn't connect him then. Now I'm convinced he put a tracker on my car in hopes I'd lead him to Lindsay." The reality sent an ache through my already tensed shoulders.

"Give me the tracker. We can trace it back to who purchased it."

I winced, wishing I'd thought of that. "It's at the bottom of the Willamette."

He sighed.

"At the time, I just wanted it far away from me." I didn't regret my decision. Every second I had it, I could be tracked and taking it to the police then meant answering questions I wasn't ready to answer. I was scared—a feeling I didn't admit to easily and had a hard time with now. "Anyway, I feel no closer to finding Lindsay than I did that first night. Maybe she's not even in town. She stole money from my apartment the night of Craig's murder, which means she could be holding up and not want to use her own credit cards." I swallowed. "Or she can't."

"We haven't found any evidence that she's dead."

"How about that she's alive?"

He shook his head.

A tremor ran through me. I'd seen no evidence of that either. The key given to me by Kai was a *just in case* measure. Nothing had pointed me in her direction in real time.

"Look, I'll have an officer make your building part of his rounds. That's the best I can do."

I nodded, grateful for that much.

His phone rang. He glanced at the screen and got up to answer, walking away. When he returned, his face had hardened. "I need to go, and you've done enough. Go home." I only nodded. He must have sensed my reluctance because he added, "At least keep me in the loop."

That I could do. He walked me out before running to his car. I hadn't mentioned Ellen Sullivan, who hadn't called back. There was no reason to loop him in on that until I heard what she had to say. Not knowing her relationship with the police, I didn't want to scare her off. As for the St. Luke's file, it was a work product of the clinic, and privileged.

I'd report back after seeing Ellen. Asking the detective for forgiveness might become our thing.

As I was about to run across the street at the corner, a woman's raised voice caught my attention. I whipped my head around. Judge Johnson was in a heated conversation with the driver of a black sedan parked at the curb. My insides jellied and I stepped back out of their sight.

Judge Johnson's voice raised again as she waved her hands with emphasis, her face tight with stress. I was too far away to hear their words. She slapped her hand on the driver's closing window, and the car sped off.

Unsure of her connection to the person looking for Lindsay, I remained hidden as the judge ran across the street to a limo similar to the one I'd seen in front of the church earlier. She was shaking and crying. The chauffeur got out. Devon. The driver who'd taken my mother and me to the MAC.

My parents and the judge were closer than I'd ever known. Enough that they shared the same car service. Maybe that was common, but the fact that both Craig and Lindsay were adopted, that there was so much secrecy around it, and the closeness of our parents, suggested our worlds were intertwined in a way I'd never been privy to.

That was about to change.

CHAPTER 25

After leaving Detective Matson, I ran by a Starbucks and borrowed their Wi-Fi long enough to shoot the DNA report to him and dig through the file for Ellen Sullivan's home address.

The two-story shack had a plastic tarp draped over one part of the moss-covered roof and anchored by bricks. The semi-enclosed porch drooped on one side, a rusted-out washing machine and piles upon piles of plastic bags overflowing with pop cans underneath that. Despite the house's dilapidated appearance, it was in better shape than most of its neighbors.

The white metal Christmas tree illuminated in the front window almost gave it a homey feel, suggesting someone cared—and might be home.

I hoped that "someone" was Ellen Sullivan.

Making sure that no black sedans had followed me, I knocked. The door opened a crack, large enough for a woman's face to poke out and for me to see she was dressed in an oversized plain sweatshirt and jeans that hung from her small frame. From the light lines on her face, I'd put her at mid-forties. When I'd read it had been thirty years since Ellen lost her child, I assumed she'd be much older.

"Yes," she said. She chewed the side of her thumb, with the other arm wrapped around her middle and supporting her elbow.

"Ellen Sullivan?" Her gaze stretched beyond me, scanning the street, nervous. "I left you a message earlier," I said. "I'm Beth Ralston. I work for Craig Bartell."

She scoffed. "Another representative who makes house calls?"

"No," I said, not sure what she meant. "When's the last time you went to the clinic to see him?" His notes hadn't specified.

"Saturday, but he wasn't there." Her jaw tightened. "He promised to help me figure out what happened to my baby and then stood me up."

If only that were the case. "Does the name Lindsay Ralston mean anything to you?"

"Yeah, the lawyer wanted me to meet her. I spoke to her on the phone briefly and told her some stuff." Lindsay *had* started here. "She's another flake," Ellen continued. "We were to meet here Monday, but she's like all the rest who make promises they don't keep."

"It's not like that. I think something's happened to her." The words rushed out. I'd felt that way for a while now—hadn't wanted to believe it even though I'd said similar words to the detective. But hearing Lindsay had been on a story and hadn't followed through made the words real. "I'm her sister. Would you be willing to talk to me instead?"

Ellen must have heard the strain in my voice because she softened. "I don't know if it'll do any good, but whatever. You probably won't show next time either."

Too many had let her down; I didn't intend to be one of them. Lindsay wouldn't have if she could help it, which had my stomach in knots. "You have my word that won't happen."

Her living room was set up like a studio. Her bed shoved in the corner had boxes set on it and her sofa next to that. At least the sofa was clear. A thirteen-inch TV teetered on a rickety table. Plastic bags inside bags littered the floor. Beyond that, the stairs were blocked with books and more boxes.

"You can sit anywhere." She dropped onto the couch and resumed chewing her thumb.

I perched on the edge of the sofa. "You said Mr. Bartell wanted you to meet Lindsay?"

She nodded.

"Why?"

"He said he'd heard from a few women like me who'd claimed their babies had been stolen and Lindsay was a reporter. She'd be very interested in hearing more about that." Her arm once again strapped around her middle, she nodded—and rocked.

I wondered if Ellen had an addiction issue, or a mental one. "How long ago was it that you lost your baby?" I asked.

"Thirty-two years, four months, six days, and . . ." She glanced at a clock. "Three hours."

My heart squeezed at how much Ellen had suffered since that moment. "You must have been so young."

Her eyes rimmed with tears. "An uncle decided to have 'fun' with me one night at my parents' New Year's kegger and I got pregnant." Her face paled. "Then I got the boot for upsetting the family. I'm the bad guy and out on the street with few options."

"I'm sorry."

She shrugged but her rocking increased. "You find ways to survive. I found a place in Portland to hang out."

"Where was that?"

"A shelter on Burnside. That's where some guy approached me at the chow line and told me he had someone who could help me."

"Help you with housing?"

"No. Having the baby." She chewed her thumb too hard and winced. "There was some lady they worked with that would give me free vitamins."

"A midwife?" Had I found the connection that easily?

"No. She didn't deliver my baby. She set me up with who did."

"Sherry Smith?"

"No, Wanda something."

"The woman or the midwife?"

"Yeah."

Neither name matched anything I'd seen, but it could be one of Sherry's aliases. Would have been nice had the detective shared information. "What can you tell me about the lady who arranged that? Was she with an agency?"

"She was a bitch—I can tell you that much. She kept telling me to give up my baby, but I said no way. I could do better than my parents. Sure as hell couldn't do worse."

I pushed myself even further to the edge of the couch. "Ellen, it's important. Did she belong to an adoption agency? Maybe Alliance?"

She shook her head. "Doesn't sound right." She massaged the chewed thumb into her other palm. "All I remember is having my baby in some old building and the pain split me in two. Like, it was bad. Wanda gave me something for it, and then . . ." She started rocking again.

I set my hand on Ellen's knee.

She drew in a shaky breath. "Then my baby was gone." Her voice had gotten small and quiet. "Wanda said my little girl died."

Her face crumpled. "I don't remember having her, but I could tell I did." She rested her hand on her abdomen. "When I asked to hold her, Wanda said it had been a terrible delivery and it would be too traumatic . . . I tried to tell people. No one listened. Until Mr. Bartell. He listened because other women had said the same thing."

I wanted to believe her story. I *did* believe her. "Why do you think the baby hadn't died?"

"Because they wouldn't let me see her." She straightened. "I watch TV. I've seen movies. You always get to hold the baby even if they're dead. Like for closure." She looked away, struggling to control her breaths. "It was a year later when I heard rumors that the same thing happened to another woman. But she woke during the delivery for a second and swears she remembers seeing someone coming to take her babies."

"But they told her they died?"

"Yeah, and they wouldn't let her see them."

The idea of that sent a wave of indignation through me. How could anyone be so cruel to another human being? "Did she go to the police?"

Her lip curled. "Police don't listen to people like us. She was into drugs and slept her highs off behind dumpsters. No one believed her when she did talk about it, even when she came to the shelter." She looked down. "People just said she'd been hallucinating."

In the way she spoke those last words, I wondered if they'd thought that of her as well. "Did she go to the same shelter on Burnside as you then?"

"No. I met her at the food place."

"They're not the same?" I had no idea how the system worked.

"It's up the road. A church ran it back then, so anyone could go. Sometimes meals aren't guaranteed on the street. If there's an opportunity to hit a couple of lines, you do."

I'd do the same thing. "You think they're still there?" It had been thirty years, but the houseless issue had only grown since then.

"No idea. I go to the food bank for supplies now."

I nodded. "I know it's a long shot, but do you remember the guy's name that you'd met at the time? Maybe your friend encountered the same person."

"I don't. I'm sorry."

"No worries." It probably didn't matter. Churches rotated in and out helping the homeless all over the area. There must be many, along with countless volunteers. "Are you still in contact with that woman who believed her babies had been stolen?"

She shook her head. "One day she disappeared. The heroin might have got her. It does that, you know."

I didn't know. I lived in an insulated world that didn't expose me to drugs or poverty and was fine with that. Not Lindsay though. She'd spent her adult life digging deeper, trying to make a difference with everything she touched. While I was content to tread at the surface of life, more involved in my own goals, too busy to connect, she sought out a way to shine a light, hoping to make a difference.

Ellen Sullivan's story crushed me, as much as the realization I had to do better.

But after a few more questions, I didn't get any further. The pieces and players were muddled and not connecting. There could be a church, an agency, and another midwife completely unrelated to Alliance.

"And you told Craig all of this and he still wanted you to meet Lindsay?"

"Yeah, he said something about patterns."

There could be. They just might not lead to whoever I thought. I stood. "Thank you for sharing your story, Ellen." I dug into my purse, coming up with my card. Crossing out the law firm number, I wrote my cell on the back. "If you think of anything else, please call."

She scanned it. "Paralegal, huh?"

"Yeah."

"Fancy." I'd heard that a few times now. She walked me to the door.

"One thing . . ." I said, stepping out. "You mentioned delivering your baby at an old building . . . do you remember where that was located?"

"I don't. Only that it was somewhere around warehouses. Stupid me didn't pay attention."

My heart ached that she'd see herself that way. She'd been a victim. Traumatized. I squeezed her arm gently. "You're anything but stupid, Ellen." And while it offered no real proof, Alliance Adoption Agency was in the warehouse district. Ellen's event might have happened thirty years ago, but it didn't feel like a coincidence. Before leaving, I wanted to reassure her. "I will be back to help you, I promise. Until then, please don't talk to anyone else about this."

"Well, yeah, unless they send another representative for Mr. Bartell."

She'd alluded to another visitor when I first arrived. "Did someone else come talk with you?"

She nodded. "Some guy in a suit. Made me feel awkward, but he insisted he was from the legal clinic, so I let him in."

I lifted my hand so as not to scare her by pressing too hard. "What did he look like?"

"Weird hair. I mean, weird. Reminded me of that tan color that . . ."

My heart thumped. "Like a Shetland pony?"

She lit up. "That's it. And dark eyes that seemed empty. Creeped me out. It's like he saw me but didn't see me. You know what I mean?"

My mouth went dry as I nodded. "What did you tell him?"

"That his boss was sending a reporter to take my story." Her eyes narrowed. "At the time, I thought it was strange he'd come for information the day before my meeting with Mr. Bartell. But he said it was part of their process since the lawyers at the clinic had full-time jobs."

"That was last Friday morning?"

"Yeah."

My heart was pounding as I left her with another promise, and her assurance that she'd keep her door locked and not talk to anyone until I was back in touch.

CHAPTER 26

hit the I-84 and sped fast and far out of the city. My thoughts blurred as I weaved in and out of afternoon traffic with no clear direction. At some point, a horn blasted behind me, snapping me out of my fog and putting my already stressed heart rate into over-drive. I'd cut a semi off and the woman behind the wheel flipped me off, rightly so.

But Henry, the man who'd been at every turn in the past few days, had come to see Ellen on the same day Craig was murdered. The day my world turned upside down. He'd gotten her story and must not have liked that Craig and Lindsay planned to help her. And she said there'd been other women, which Lindsay's folder confirmed.

Had he decided to kill Craig at that point? Had he been look-ing for Lindsay to do the same to her?

I stayed in the right lane as the semi steamed past me. I needed to collect myself before I caused an accident.

The Multnomah Falls parking lot came into view, my thoughts flipping to Bailey and the midwife, and thankful Henry hadn't tried to kill Ellen. But he was clearly gathering information and silencing people for someone. Who? Alliance and Margaret

Ottoman? Maybe. But so far, I'd found no direct links. There could be someone else I hadn't discovered yet.

Someone else that Lindsay was running from.

Parked now, I melted into my seat. On the run would be best-case scenario. I'd gone back and forth with worry, but despite what I'd told Ellen, I had to believe Lindsay was alive and would hold onto that for as long as I could. Otherwise, what the hell was I doing? My father was right about one thing—Lindsay was the investigator in the family, not me. I was only a little sister desperate to get her sibling back.

But that counted for something.

Beginning to feel centered again, I scanned the full parking lot. Even in the winter, people came to hike the trails that led to multiple waterfalls. The summer Lindsay got her license, we'd come here every week. A cold, clear pool sat at the end of one of the trails near the top. Most tourists never went that far—not many locals either. We'd claimed it and immersed ourselves for hours on end.

We would do that again. I'd find Lindsay and we'd come back next year, together, when the leaves were green, and the sun burned our skin. We'd reconnect, talk, promise to never let time and work separate us. I'd even attend a march, or two or three, or whatever of her choosing, just to see her smile.

I rested my eyes, hearing Lindsay's laughter, feeling the splash of water, remembering the joy, taking in the reprieve. When I reopened them, I pulled the St. Luke's file onto my lap. Lindsay had to be investigating the women with stories like Ellen's. Finding those women might help me locate Lindsay—even though I had no idea how far she'd gotten on the list. Or whether Ellen was her first contact—or the last.

What I had was their numbers, and if not their numbers, their last known addresses. I'd start with those that listed cell contact information first.

The first number I chose had a note that the woman claimed she'd had a child five years ago. I immediately got a *number disconnected* message. The second number rang and rang, with no voicemail. That woman reported to have had a child over seven years ago.

The third woman I dialed answered. My heart jumped with anticipation until she followed her hello with, "This is Cheryl."

The paperwork reflected a different name. "Is Berniece available?"

"Wrong number."

"I—"

Click.

Not to be deterred, I dialed another contact. No answer again. The phone numbers turned out to be a bust, but there was still the last-known addresses to try.

I headed back into Portland with a clear goal, changing lanes several times, and taking a couple of random exits before dropping back onto the highway. I never stopped checking my rearview. No one followed that I could tell—or else they were damn good at it.

A few miles later, I took the Sandy Boulevard exit for real this time. The first address listed was off 33rd. The neighborhood was a mixture of new construction and homes built in the '30s or '40s. I pulled up to a well-cared-for ranch house and double-checked the file. According to the notes, Camille Jackson should live here.

I approached the front door but hadn't knocked before a woman about my age burst outside, her eyes wide and her face contorted. "What do you want?"

I stepped back to create distance. "I'm looking for Camille Jackson?"

"Why do you want her?"

"I'm . . ." How did I phrase this to a woman who was already on the defense? "I'm here on behalf of St. Luke's Legal Clinic."

"Don't trust lawyers."

"I'm not a lawyer. I'm an assistant. Camille's name showed up in a file regarding a claim that her child had been taken from her."

"She's not here."

"Camille, get in the house." A man appeared behind the woman. Tall, older, her father perhaps. "And you . . ." He pointed at me. ". . . leave before I call the police."

"I'm sorry. I'm here on behalf of—

"I heard you. Same with the other guy."

My stomach clenched. "The other guy?"

"Yeah, whatever he said to my daughter put her in a tailspin. We'd just gotten her meds taken care of, now look at her." He grimaced. "Camille, hon, go."

Her eyes flicked in my direction before she ran inside. He started to close the door.

"I just have a few questions," I said. "Please."

He stepped out onto the stoop and closed the door behind him. "She's not well."

"I understand, but she's claimed her child was taken from her."

"She's claimed aliens abducted her while she lived on the street too, and then ran tests on her before bringing her back to earth."

This lead did not sound promising. "Was she ever pregnant?"

He closed his eyes. "I'm serious about having you removed."

I stood my ground. "I'm trying to help. There are others like Camille, and I believe my sister, Lindsay, wanted to help them. Now she's missing."

He let out a breath, and when his eyes opened, they were red. "I'm sorry to hear that, but I have my own sorrows. I've tried to be a good father, but I lost track of my girl for a year when she disappeared onto the Portland streets. I searched. God, I searched. She's been ill since childhood. We institutionalized her for a while until funding stopped for some of the state hospitals. I couldn't afford it after and, well, her mother died. Her dying wish was I'd take care of Camille. So that's what I'm doing." His jaw twitched. "You coming around has no doubt put her into another breakdown that I'll have to deal with." His face turned red to match his eyes.

"It's just my sister . . . I'd hoped she might have been here before me." I wanted that to be true; to confirm I was on the right track.

"No one's come around but that man last week. And I made a foolish mistake by letting him talk with her." He went back into the house.

"I'm sorry," I said, as the door slammed.

Even if Lindsay had come here, she likely wouldn't have gotten any further. The alien abduction was an interesting twist, though. Camille could be trying to reconcile what happened to her, because her name wouldn't be in Lindsay's file or Craig's list if she hadn't had a child—or they at least believed that to be true.

The next address proved no better—the house was boarded up tight and had been for some time. The address after that didn't appear to exist—my GPS ran me around in circles until I came upon an empty lot.

Another two hours of searching left me hungry and exhausted. I pulled into a Burgerville drive-thru and ordered a chicken sandwich, then drove to the last address.

The neighborhood had tall and solid oak trees that would create a beautiful canopy come spring. Now their gnarly branches reached for the sky. Pines and firs intermingled. The homes had been established for at least a couple of decades, and the area had *tight-knit community* written all over it. I half expected Neighborhood Watch signs to be posted.

Toward the far end of the street, the homes were older, except for a two-story office-like building nestled between a couple of ranch-style homes. That building matched the address in the file for a Toni Thompson who claimed her baby girl had been stolen six months ago while being drugged during childbirth.

Despicable. Lindsay was probably here, investigating ongoing patterns.

I approached the glass door and rang the bell.

A woman in her fifties answered with a warm smile. "Can I help you?"

"I hope so." I introduced myself and asked for Toni.

"May I ask what for?"

"Her name's in a file I'm working on from St. Luke's Legal Clinic."

Her face lightened. "Do come in." She opened the door wider. "My name's Angela, by the way."

Angela's welcoming demeanor was a relief after the experience at Camille's house. "Thank you."

A kitchen off to the right had a long communal-type dining table. The main area was covered with warm maple flooring and boasted soft pillowy couches with chenille throws. It all added to the happy and airy feeling of the space. Although not quite home-like.

"Coffee?" she asked.

"Please." I set my purse on the dining table. "What is this place?"

"We're a sober living facility. Take a seat."

I pulled out one of the dining room chairs. "Has Toni been here long?"

"About four months now and doing incredibly well."

"That's great."

She returned with two ceramic mugs and set one in front of me while taking the seat across the table. "Tell me a little bit more about your file? You mentioned St. Luke's Legal Clinic?"

"Yes, they work with clients on a sliding scale based on income," I said. "Quite often they do pro bono work. My boss—" I stopped and almost corrected, then decided not to. "My boss, Craig Bartell, volunteered at the Clinic."

"His name sounds familiar," she said, then frowned. "He was on the news."

I nodded and gave her the rundown of his murder and what I'd found about women claiming their children were taken from them. "And my sister was helping him, or at least that's what I believe."

"You don't know?"

"I haven't been able to find her."

Angela placed her hand on my forearm. "I hope she's okay."

Her kindness lodged a rock in my throat. I cleared it. "Do you know if she came here to talk with Toni?"

"What does she look like?"

I showed her the same Easter picture I'd shown Rhonda.

She leaned in. "She certainly did. And Toni felt hopeful after speaking with her. In fact, I'd eavesdropped a bit as they were concluding their conversation. I was under the impression they might meet again."

I smiled, glad I hadn't given up. "Do you know if they did?"

She shook her head, taking a drink of coffee. "I don't. I do know Toni seemed quite upset a few nights back but refused to talk about it. Of course, it could have been work-related, I suppose. Though she generally talks about those topics with ease. It's the personal stuff . . ."

"Did Toni give you any indication of what my sister and she spoke about?"

"No. But my impression was they'd been talking about Toni's time before arriving here at the facility."

"When she was pregnant?"

Angela took a sip. "She's never said she was."

She'd been here four months though—so unless Toni talked about it, Angela might not know. I was anxious to find out more about Toni's conversation with my sister. "Is Toni here now?"

"She's not. Forgive me. I should've said that from the beginning, but I wanted to understand why you were asking for her first. I protect my girls."

That made me feel better for Toni. "I get it."

She nodded. "I do think she'd like to speak with you though. She's working late tonight, but scheduled for housekeeping chores between ten and noon tomorrow. We share the duties . . . it's part of the rehabilitation process. Come back during that time if you want to chat. Otherwise, she'll be leaving after that for some volunteer work."

"Will do. I appreciate your talking with me—and the coffee."
Although I hadn't taken a sip; I felt too amped already.

She smiled. "I'll let her know to expect you."

At the door, I turned with one last question. "Has anyone else
come here saying they're from the clinic?"

"No, ma'am, and I'm the only one that allows people entrance
into the facility."

I'd hoped that was the case when she'd told me she protected
her girls. Henry could show later though. "If anyone does, don't
let them in. They're not who they claim to be."

Her face wrinkled. "Should I be concerned?"

"More like cautious."

"Our doors always remain locked. Toni will be fine."

That Toni seemed to be in good hands gave me a sense of hope
I hadn't felt since the night of Craig's murder. I didn't have
answers yet, but Toni could have important information to share
that might lead me to Lindsay. At least she'd spoken with my sister in person.

I'd just clicked in my seat belt when my phone rang. I didn't
recognize the number—until I did.

"Detective Matson," I said. "Promise I'm being good, and we
should probably talk." Feeling like I was on the right path had me
almost giddy.

The detective cleared his throat. "Ms. Ralston. We found
Lindsay's car."

CHAPTER 27

The phone tumbled from my grasp. My fingers were thick and clumsy as I groped the floorboard and gulped back the sobs. Once I found my cell, I hit SPEAKER long enough to find out where Lindsay's car had been discovered.

U-turning the SUV, the tires squealed on the dry pavement. The news had ripped away my hope, crushing my insides. It took every ounce of inner strength to get back to the other side of town near my parents' house.

Lindsay's car hadn't been found on their property. Far worse— it was at the train trestle. The trestle where we'd gone countless times to talk away our problems. To complain about our parents. To navigate our relationships.

If Lindsay had been there the entire time . . . I punched the window down, sucking in fresh air.

It was almost dusk when I arrived, and a team of official-looking people scoured the area beneath the trestle and on the shoreline. Detective Matson, hands in the pockets of his parka, stood on the tracks, gazing down at the water churning fifteen to twenty feet below. A young couple huddled on the other side, talking with a uniformed officer. I approached the detective, my legs shaking and unsteady.

Catching sight of me, he closed the distance. By the time he reached me, my whole body trembled from the cold and the fear. The bitter wind bit through the cotton fabric of the slacks and blouse I still had on from the funeral.

Detective Matson slid out of his coat and wrapped it around my shoulders. I didn't see my parents anywhere.

"Have you found her?" I braced for the worst.

"Not yet."

I nearly dropped with relief. "How did you find the car?"

"The couple with the officer were kayaking and saw a purse in the brush. They found the wallet was intact and hadn't been out in the elements for long. They could see the car from the water, and that no one was in it."

"A concerned citizen call," I said, matter-of-fact.

"Correct." And like when he'd been notified of my 911 call, he would have been alerted.

My eyes scoured the water and the embankment. "You haven't found any other traces of her though?"

"We're still searching."

So, no. "Any idea what happened here?"

He shook his head. "Your sister's car was unlocked. There's no visual evidence of blood or hair inside or out, which might indicate a fight of some kind."

No blood was good, but it didn't mean much. "Well, something happened."

"Did she ever seem depressed?"

What kind of question was that? "What are you implying?"

He didn't say it. He didn't have to.

"Lindsay didn't jump off the bridge." Despite the cold, my face burned. "She would never do that."

His face softened. "People change. From what I've gathered these past days, Lindsay has to the point even you've been confused."

If this was the demeanor he used when dealing with families of potential suicide victims, he needed to be retrained. "She wouldn't kill herself. What's your other theory?"

"I understand you'd feel that way."

"There's nothing to 'understand.'" I folded my arms over my chest. "What else?"

He drew in a breath with no intention of sharing further theories. "You should go," he said. "There's nothing for you to do here and my focus is to get an answer to that question."

"I can't," I said, lifting my chin. Three men climbed out of a county-issued police van carrying neoprene suits. My legs turned into wet noodles, my defiance faltering.

"It wasn't a suggestion, Ms. Ralston."

I fought to keep the rising panic from taking hold and gripped the detective's forearm to steady myself. "Have you contacted my parents?"

"I called your father's phone. Ericka Hough answered and said he was unavailable."

"Oh really." Campaigning. Again. I couldn't keep the sarcasm out of my voice.

"History?"

"Hmmm. Did she say when she'd give my father the message?" My irritation at Ericka gave me a shot of strength. Along with frustration at my dad who should have insisted any call from the detective be put through. I let go of the detective's arm.

"She didn't. But she promised to relay it at her earliest opportunity."

Right. I stood firm as the men with the wet suits began pulling on their gloves and retrieving their diving gear. "What are they doing?" I said, although I knew.

"Go, Ms. Ralston."

"I . . ."

"Beth." He removed his jacket from around my shoulders and slid his arms back through the sleeves. "This search could take anywhere from an hour to a week or more. The water through here is fast and deep this time of year. I'll let you know the moment I have something definitive."

My feet were entrenched. How could I leave my sister if she was nearby? I closed my eyes to feel her. *Where are you, Lindsay?* A shiver rattled through me. The money. "Did you search her car for everything?"

"We did."

"Did you find any large amounts of cash in her purse?"

He shook his head. "Just credit cards and small bills."

"Then where's the money she took from me?"

"It might be on her."

I scoffed. "She wouldn't kill herself with a few thousand dollars stuffed in her pockets. That makes no sense, does it?"

"I'll be playing the part of detective this evening, Ms. Ralston." His lips pressed into a hard line. "Go. I'll be in touch."

He left me and approached the divers. The young couple that had found the purse were removing their kayaks from the river. An officer appeared to be assisting them, likely on getting them back to their vehicle.

I trudged to my SUV and staggered in. My hands gripped the steering wheel, holding on for dear life. The detective was wrong.

Lindsay wouldn't kill herself. And his suggestion that she had the money on her was ludicrous. But where would it be?

And why come here at all? *Did you come to meet someone, Lindsay?*

It would make sense if she wanted a quiet area where she'd feel safe. She could also have come here to think, and then been attacked. Or this whole thing could be a ploy to have people think she'd died. Had she left her car and taken off to continue investigating in the shadows?

Whatever the answers, I'd search until I had them. Because no way she was in that water.

That meant continuing to follow what I thought were her steps over the last week and looking further into the adoption agency. They were at the center of this. I had to find the connection. At some point, I'd know with certainty what Lindsay had found—and that would provide her whereabouts. In my core, I believed Lindsay was counting on me for that.

I drove, numb, to my parents' house, hoping they'd come home by now. I didn't trust Ericka to tell my father anything that would interrupt or distract from his campaigning. If Detective Matson hadn't told her specifically why he'd called, she might not think it was important enough to repeat it to my dad. But they needed to know that Lindsay . . .

My throat tightened. She wasn't dead—I wouldn't accept that.

When I arrived at the main house, the windows were dark. Fighting disappointment, I continued along the drive, pulling behind Nova's apartment. I ran up the stairs.

Nova answered in a fluffy pink robe. Since this was the regular dinner hour, my parents must not be expected back until late.

"Beth." She sounded surprised. "Are you here for the night?"

"No. Do you know where my parents are?"

Her hands shook before she buried them into her robe's pockets. "A fundraiser, but they left a couple of hours ago. How was the funeral?"

"It was . . ." What was it? "Illuminating."

"I'm sorry," she said as an afterthought. "Come in. It's just been hectic at the house with the holiday preparations. Have you had dinner?" The smell of chicken wafted through her tiny house.

I still had half a sandwich in my car, and the idea of eating anything made my stomach turn. Besides, Nova was visibly tired and had no idea they'd found Lindsay's car. After our last conversation that had left her shaken, I couldn't tell her. I'd save Nova from the grief and terror of it until we knew more.

Also true was that getting into it right now might stop me cold. Falling apart was a luxury I couldn't afford, even if every cell wanted to curl in a ball and do just that.

"Thank you, but I'm good. And I need to get to the office for work."

Her shoulders eased down. "Good. You need to get back—what do they say?—in the saddle?" A crash came from her kitchen. She glanced behind her.

"Murphy?" I said.

She nodded. "He's a bit of a rascal."

"I'm sorry. It won't be long, and I'll take him off your hands."

Her brow creased. "No hurry. I rather enjoy his company."

I leaned in and gave her a long hug.

When I stepped back, her face was ashen. "What was that for?"

"I don't tell you enough how much you mean to me, Nova. You mean the world, and I was serious when I said we'll get your citizenship figured out."

She cleared her throat. "I know you will. All of this with Lindsay and the campaign . . . it's been hard on everyone."

"Except on my parents as it pertains to my sister." At least that's how it had felt from the beginning.

"They're focused."

They were something, all right. "Did they happen to say when they'd be home?" I asked.

"They didn't, but no doubt another late night."

I glanced back at the unlit house, an idea forming. Murphy appeared at Nova's feet and rubbed innocently against her shin.

She scooped him up and nuzzled his neck. "My little troublemaker. So sweet. See? We're getting along just fine, aren't we, Murphy?"

His purr vibrated the fur on his chest. I'd made at least one good decision by leaving him here. I kissed Nova on the cheek. "I'll see you soon then." Very soon if the detective found Lindsay.

I crushed the thought and trotted down the stairs, scanning the quiet grounds. My parents would be gone for at least a few hours. What had first been disappointing might be an opportunity.

Based on my father's sketchy behavior, he knew more than he'd been telling about Lindsay. He'd been concerned enough to warn me away and to avoid my questions. He'd even insisted that I not speak with the detective because *he had it handled.* What did that mean?

More troubling, he and my mother wouldn't admit that Lindsay had been adopted. The reasons for that had my stomach in a twist. If I could find out why they wanted to hide that, or even what my father and Lindsay had been arguing about, I'd feel less in the dark.

His office might hold those answers.

Along with bringing home legal files, he'd long kept the family's personal records, birth certificates, and passports in there. It was worth checking because, given his previous responses, he wouldn't be volunteering information.

Leaving my SUV behind the garage, I ran across the grounds to the back of the house and let myself in through the employee entrance using Nova's code.

The entrance led through the kitchen pantry and into the chef's kitchen. As kids, Lindsay and I would sit on the counter waiting for Nova to make us grilled cheese sandwiches and tomato soup. Or at night, saltine crackers and cocoa. The thought of not having Lindsay to share those memories with constricted my lungs, making it hard to breathe.

But I couldn't go there. I didn't care what the detective said. He wouldn't find her in that river.

Refocused on the dark room, I was surprised the green clock light on the microwave was off. Under-cabinet lights usually lit the kitchen. Nova must have shut them down for the night. Or a fuse blew. I opted not to flick on the lights to check so as not to concern Nova.

I felt my way along the counter and entered the hallway on my way to the foyer where a sliver of moonlight shone through the window above the entry. My dad's office door was closed, and, a tap of the handle confirmed, locked. Of course it would be. Why had I thought it would be different with the staff gone for the night?

Think. No one carried their keys all the time. There had to be a spare nearby. I ran my fingers over the doorframe. Clear. I searched the foyer. A tall palm sat in the corner. I checked there. Only moss and dirt.

Where would you put it? Nowhere as obvious as the two places I'd checked, but I would have a backup for sure. Maybe above a door that the key wouldn't open?

Rising on my toes, I ran my hand along the frame at the entry and touched against metal. The key. My heart pounded at the discovery. Now what? It was one thing to contemplate invading Dad's sanctuary and going through his files. It was another to do it.

But there'd been too many secrets . . . and Lindsay. The key was in the lock in seconds. Once inside, I secured the door behind me and took a breath. The windows here didn't face Nova's apartment, but I thought better of announcing my presence. I clicked the flashlight app on my cell instead.

My father's private space hadn't changed since I was a child. A large mahogany desk anchored the room with a matching credenza running parallel to it. Family photos, awards, plaques of recognition covered that long strip of wood and plastered the walls.

Happy family, or so it would appear when you first walked in. That couldn't be said anymore. Had it ever been true?

At my dad's desk, I tried the drawers. Also locked. I swiveled the chair and pulled the credenza drawers. One slid out. The mechanism was ticked up . . . like it hadn't shut all the way and latched. My father must have been in a hurry and didn't notice. Whatever the reason, I'd take it. I set my phone on the credenza so that the light aimed toward the drawer filled with hanging files.

I immediately grabbed one labeled PLACEMENT POTEN-TIAL. Not very legal-sounding. The word *placement* had my face tingling. I opened the file and flipped through the pages, all filled with last names—none familiar. Nothing indicated who

they were, where they lived, or why he would have a list of surnames at all.

I slipped the file back into place and pulled out another labeled
HAVEN ADOPTION. Half-expecting "Haven" to be someone's last
name, I found instead it was an adoption agency in northeast
Portland. I took a picture of the address with my phone. The second page listed surnames again. No first. No addresses. Nothing
indicating who they were or how to contact them.

Frustrated, I shoved the file back in and fingered through the
other files, about to pull one more out. HEAVENLY ADOPTIONS.
Another agency, perhaps.

As I lifted it from the drawer, a sound came from the entry. A
click. My throat tightened. The front door had opened.

CHAPTER 28

My insides melted as I eased the drawer back into the cabinet, leaving the file behind. I had no idea who'd come into the house, but Nova would have used the back entrance.

If it were my parents, Mom would be feigning exhaustion and the need to get right to bed, and Dad would be complaining about the lack of lights as he dropped his keys into the pottery bowl on the entry table. I'd heard none of that, and it was far too early for them to be home from a campaigning event.

Dad could have forgotten something though and sent Ericka back. If that were the case, explaining how I got into my dad's locked office could be awkward at best. I ducked under the desk, silenced my phone, and made myself small, pulling the chair close to conceal me. Until the person left, I was trapped.

The handle on my dad's door shifted, followed by scratching noises. Metal on metal. A key. It must be Ericka. I curled, shrinking smaller. The scratching continued, taking too long. Someone was picking the lock?

Not good. I had two options: confront whoever was on the other side or stay hidden. If found, I'd have a harder time defending myself from the cubby. Could I do any better in the small office space? The door creaked open, making the decision for me.

I held my breath as a flashlight beam darted against the walls. Not Ericka or anyone who should be here. Whoever had entered hadn't even tried to turn on the overhead lights.

The urge to run skittered through me again, but I forced myself to remain still and dropped into information gathering mode—a skill I used as a paralegal. I could do that.

Who was here and why? The response to one of those questions came in the form of glass shattering. One of the framed photos had been smashed against the credenza. A gloved hand snatched another picture, followed by a muffled thunk as it hit the floor.

I pulled my knees into my chest, hoping they had no intention of going through my father's desk.

A hissing sound came next. Long. Short. Long.

The pungent and toxic smell of paint wafted into the room.

My heart crashed and my ears felt stuffed with cotton, making the sounds in the office far away like I was in a tunnel. My head throbbed from the fumes. I needed to get out of there. Before I could move, the vandal walked out of the room and closed the door. Footsteps followed. A squeak on the tile. Tennis shoes?

My jaw locked as my brain registered having heard that sound before. The front door shut.

I scrambled out from under the desk, smacking my head on the drawer, and flicked the light switch. Nothing happened. The power had been out—or it had been taken out.

Opening the office door allowed enough moonlight from the foyer to reveal the damage. CHOOSE WISELY had been painted on my dad's office wall where his Lawyer of the Year plaque lay in pieces on the floor below it.

Determined to confirm the ID of who'd done this, I raced into the entry. Through the side-panels, the sole streetlamp allowed me to catch a glimpse of a man sprinting to the edge of the property. The vandal had parked on the road.

I could do nothing about the office. When Dad reported it, I'd learn more. But if I could catch up with who'd caused it, I could turn the tables and follow him for a change. I went out the back and sprinted to the SUV. As far as I knew, no one had caught on to my new ride, so I had that going for me.

I cleared my parents' long drive ducked low in the seat and hit my high beams so there'd be little chance of anyone on the receiving end seeing who was behind the wheel.

The all-too-familiar car turned left at the far end of the road, the streetlamp confirming it was indeed a four-door dark sedan. I punched the accelerator, but at the end of the road, I had to wait for a VW Bug to pass. As soon as it did, I hit the gas again and swerved around it, waving a "sorry" at my erratic behavior. By then, the road ahead was empty.

I kept driving, searching the side streets. Nothing. I slammed the heel of my hand onto the wheel.

But whether I caught up with him or not, the silhouette of the vehicle and the squeak of those shoes left me no doubt. Henry had sent my father a message.

The question was: what choice did my father have to make *wisely*?

*   *   *

It was after eight when I pulled under the law firm's building and parked in my assigned spot near the security booth. The message on the wall had unsettled me and rolled in my mind like rocks in a tumbler. Deciding not to call the detective, I'd driven to Portland instead.

I'd planned to come here to do research on Alliance and whether there'd been any cases filed against them for shady adoptions. Ellen Sullivan, whose story of her lost child thirty years ago had not let go of my heart, had said she hadn't dealt with Alliance, but now I had the name of two other agencies. It could be there was a network of them that worked together. Whatever the case, my father kept the files in a drawer in his office separate from his legal files, leading me to believe this wasn't firm related.

The adrenaline in my body, while dissipating some, remained in the background. It had no chance of disappearing with the detective still searching for Lindsay. Shaky, and desperate to keep my mind busy, I had to keep pushing for my own answers.

I rode the elevator to the main floor, withdrew my pass card from my purse, and approached the elevators to the suites. After hours, the card was required to gain access to any of the firm's floors and storage facilities.

Inside the next elevator, I swiped my card across the red beam of light. At the same time, I pushed the button for the thirty-fifth floor, anxious to get to the research library. The elevator didn't move. I repeated the motion again, like I'd done every day for years when I worked late.

The security guard shadowed the opening. Charlie's barrel chest and muscular arms left no doubt he could bench-press me, or just about anyone, with one arm. But he'd never been anything but pleasant to me.

"Evening, Ms. Ralston," he said. "Got problems with the card?"

"It appears so," I said with another swiping motion across the red light. Once, twice, three times. *Come on.*

He held out his hand. "Let me try."

He took the card and tried it with no luck, then handed it back. He reached for his own pass card before his hand stopped and fell to his side.

"Let's go check yours at the front. Could have been demagnetized."

"Could have been." While some could deactivate if close to a cell phone, mine had never had that problem in the past.

I started to follow him to the security desk, thinking about that message on my dad's wall: *Choose Wisely.* That phrase kept niggling in all the wrong ways. It implied my dad could be involved in something that he shouldn't be.

From the very beginning, he'd told me to stop trying to find Lindsay. Lindsay, whose car had been found—the river being searched. Bile clawed into my throat along with the rising anxiety.

Both of my parents were lying to me. They didn't tell me about Craig's funeral and weren't happy when I showed. A funeral where I'd learned Judge Johnson was Craig's mom. Now there were files regarding adoption agencies in Dad's home office.

My card had always worked here. Always. Would my father be concerned that I'd come here to do more digging and try to stop me? Shutting me out of the firm would be one sure way to restrict my options.

Charlie might be pleasant, but he took his job seriously. My throat constricted. I couldn't let him check that pass card.

At that moment, Gladys, who I'd known for years, was rolling her janitorial cart stocked with cleaning supplies in our direction.

"Gladys," I said, my voice lilting up. "How are you?" Charlie stopped and nodded a greeting to the sixty-something crew lead.

"Ms. Ralston." She smiled. "Good to see you. Are you back working late again? Sure sorry to hear about Mr. Bartell."

"I am." I turned to Charlie. "I'll just be a minute."

He nodded and returned to his desk.

I waited until he'd rounded the corner. "You wouldn't happen to be heading to the firm, would you?" I'd lowered my voice.

She chuckled. "You know I always start at the top and work down. Helps me keep track of the crew."

"I do remember you telling me that." It wasn't protocol, but I banked on the fact that she knew me well. "Mind if I catch a ride with you to thirty-five? My card's being weird, and I have a pile of work to get started on."

"Honey, you work too much."

"I wouldn't normally ask, but because I've been gone . . . I'm feeling pressured."

Her eyes darted toward the security desk. "Guess that would be fine, Ms. Ralston. It's not like your father doesn't own the place."

"Thank you," I said. "Be right back." I jogged to the security desk as she rolled her cart into the elevator and held it. I didn't want to put Charlie in an awkward position, or to inspire him to check my credentials by disappearing.

"Hey, Charlie, my card worked. Must've been a computer glitch."

An alarm beeped on one of the screens that monitored the front entrance. "Computers," he said, preoccupied with punching a few buttons.

"You know it." I took advantage of his distraction and hurried back to Gladys.

We talked all the way up about the weather and that she'd be heading home to Idaho for the holidays with hopes for a white Christmas.

When I stepped out onto the thirty-fifth floor, I gave her a quick wave. I almost let out an audible sigh, until I heard footsteps.

The firm's administrator, Phil Garrett, was coming down the hall.

CHAPTER 29

The question of whether I'd been officially taken off the access list could be readily answered by Mr. Garrett. Depending on the answer, it also could get me escorted out of the building.

The split second between stepping off the elevator and realizing the big boss had his eyes glued to his phone required a decision. I escaped into the women's bathroom near the elevator bay—and hid. That seemed to be happening too often in the last few hours.

A moment later, the elevator chimed. A cell rang—Mr. Garrett's, I assumed, as the sound muffled when the elevator doors closed on it and him.

Heart pounding in my ears, I eased open the restroom door and strained to listen for anyone else coming down the hall. Confident I was alone, I beelined it to the research library where I settled in at a corner desk.

Now to see if my login credentials still worked. I typed in my name and password . . . and stopped. The minute I began searching, I'd leave a digital footprint of what I'd been looking for. Did it matter at this point? Screw it. I hit ENTER.

The icon swirled, giving me hope, then returned to the user and password page. I worked my fingers and retyped in the information.

Same result.

I'd been locked out of the computers too. *Un-effing-believable.* The pass card was no fluke. *Thanks, Dad. Or was that Ericka's idea as well?*

Fine. I had another option—Craig's password. I keyed in his username and Murphy123. He'd thought I'd get a kick out of him naming it after his furball and he'd shared it with me. The information stuck.

I was in. Apparently only the living needed to be iced out of the database.

My first search on the State of Oregon corporation website was directed at Alliance. I typed in the name and waited. And waited. Nothing came up. It could be a *doing business as* listing, but I would have thought the parent corporation would show. Unless it hadn't been registered through Oregon? I tried Washington and California. Even Delaware, a popular place to incorporate businesses for legal reasons. Same result.

Okay, just because I didn't find them registered, that didn't mean a legal action hadn't been started against them.

I switched over to West Law and searched for any cases pertaining to Alliance. Again nothing. And then OJIN, the website that listed state court filings.

That icon swirled for a full minute. Optimistic, I leaned back in the chair, expecting I'd hit on something.

A minute later it cleared and came back as *No Results Found.*

The WHOIS database was up next to find out who owned the Alliance Adoption Agency website.

The website came back as available to purchase.

So, the agency existed in physical form, but nowhere else? There had to be something—or did there? If the agency was up to no good, conducting themselves as a credible business would be the least of their concerns. The women they dealt with were homeless, addicted, and who knew what else? And if Alliance was involved in any way with stealing babies, they'd be operating under the radar—and desperate to keep that quiet.

But again—where was the link? Registered or not, no one had ever reported a problem. No one had sued them. There'd been no external investigations I could find.

Maybe I needed a different approach. Bailey had said Ms. Ottoman started the agency, but she didn't know how long ago. She also hadn't said the agency itself. Had there been others?

I pulled up the photo of the file I'd taken in my dad's office. HAVEN ADOPTION. I punched that into the corporate website. Nothing came up. *Think* . . .

The file I'd put back. What had it said? Not Haven. Heaven. Heavenly. I typed that into the corporate offices. The screen populated. *Finally.* It had been in business several years. It was a PO box, but interestingly the registered agent was itself. But there'd been no complaints.

I flipped back to West Law to confirm and found no case law referencing them.

Feeling like a Ping-Pong ball, I returned to the Oregon State courts site and entered the agency name. Success. A complaint had been filed against Heavenly. I searched for the plaintiff. Rebecca Sheer. I recognized her name—she'd been on Craig's list of women who'd said their child had been taken. But that didn't do much good. Her phone had been disconnected, and she'd been listed as an occupant of one of the boarded-up houses I'd gone past earlier.

The complaint essentially reflected the notes—she believed there'd been wrongdoing. She'd filed on her own behalf using a form complaint she'd probably bought online.

I cleared that document and found the next one filed in the case.

A Motion to Dismiss, followed by an Order of Dismissal.

I opened the motion first to identify Heavenly Adoption Agency's attorney of record. It was per se by the principal member of the agency—Heavenly had represented itself in the form of Margaret Ottoman, Alliance's owner.

If she owned both Heavenly and Alliance, she might have owned Haven too.

Businesses didn't generally represent themselves, but it made sense if the company was doing illegal activities. It also didn't surprise me that the business name kept changing. That could be to stay ahead of complaints and charges of misconduct. Complaints from people like Ellen Sullivan. Change the name, and someone who didn't understand the system might give up. According to Detective Matson, the midwife had different aliases, so why not the agency? With all this maneuvering in the shadows, fraud could be added to anything else these people were doing.

I pulled up the last document in the case, the Order of Dismissal. The judge had wasted no time on ruling on the motion. There'd been no hearing, or rebuttal. It took all of one day for the judge to decide in favor of Heavenly. That judge was Evelyn Johnson.

I stretched my arms overhead to loosen the tension about to bust my shoulder blades. The judge who had an adopted son—a murdered adopted son—had been involved in the one case against Ms. Ottoman and her now defunct agency. While I had no proof that Craig and Lindsay had been adopted through Alliance, or whatever it called itself back then, the strings attached to it couldn't be ignored.

I printed out the Order. While I waited for it to spool, I entered Margaret Ottoman's name in a people finder. I put her on my list of people to see, although Detective Matson had said she'd gone to stay with family. He hadn't been specific.

But the search produced nothing local. There were Margaret Ottomans in Louisiana, New York, and Colorado. Nothing in Oregon. My jaw tensed. Her name could also be an alias. I didn't know how to find her. And did I want to?

She'd been closed off and rather hostile during our first inter-action. She'd already shut Lindsay down, and given the activity surrounding her and her illegally operating agencies, she had to be involved. The fact Lindsay had even gone there in the first place might have started the dominoes falling.

But that was a guess because I still didn't have a direct con-nection. Until I did, no one would believe me any more than they'd believed the women who'd tried to accuse them in the past.

I also had no idea where Lindsay could be based on any of this. As far as computer searching, I'd gone as far as I could.

The printer stopped and I retrieved the paperwork before log-ging out of the systems. I'd just gathered my purse when the library door swung open.

"Ms. Ralston," Phil Garrett said from the doorway. He'd exchanged his business suit for gray sweatpants and a plain black sweatshirt. "What brings you here at such a late hour?"

The computer clock read midnight. I'd fallen down the rabbit hole of research and time had slipped by. The question was, what had brought *him* in at such a late hour? When I logged in as Craig, an alert could have been sent out. Or it could have been my failed attempts as myself. It was also possible Charlie had double-checked my pass card.

Playing dumb might be my only way out. "Just getting some billables in. Before Craig died, he'd asked that I do some research on a matter. I know I've been assigned to a senior partner . . ."

"That's not the case any longer, Ms. Ralston. You've been put on a temporary leave of absence."

"By?"

"It was decided by the senior partner."

My father. "But the lawyer I'm going to work for . . ."

"Ms. Perkins has been assigned instead."

"Mandy?" *Wow.* "When did that happen?"

"Monday. HR was supposed to inform you."

"They haven't," I said, curtly. That explained Mandy's weirdness when she saw me in the elevator—and why she hadn't bothered to show for our coffee. "I appreciate the concern, but I don't want a leave of absence, Mr. Garrett."

"Your father has said you need time off, and what he says goes. Please get your things together."

"I'd like to go to my office first." This whole situation didn't set right. It didn't even seem legal.

"Your items have been boxed for you."

"*Boxed* hardly sounds like a leave of absence." My father had fired me? It was one thing to slow me down, but to terminate my position was low, even for him.

"I'm sorry, Ms. Ralston. You must leave."

Arguing would only get Charlie up here. I had what I needed anyway. "Fine."

My phone rang. *Speak of the devil.* "Hey, Dad," I said, following Mr. Garrett out of the library. The back of his sweatshirt read *God's Got Your Back.* Wish someone had mine. "What's this about me being fired?"

Silence hung between us.

"Dad, I think I deserve an answer."

"Come home, Beth." His voice strained. "Lindsay's dead."

CHAPTER 30

My father was in the kitchen, hunched over the dinette, nursing tea. Nova, still in her fluffy pink robe, tended a teapot on the stove. How I got from the firm to my parents' house was a blur. One minute Mr. Garrett stood next to me on the ride down the elevator, and the next I was stumbling through the mahogany front door. I only remember believing it had to be a mistake.

I wasn't adept at dealing with death in my family—our parents had always protected us from the tragedies. Grandparents on both sides had died before I came along, but there were family friends, and those instances were met with "that's terrible" or "God had a different plan." I couldn't imagine what plan God could possibly have when it deprived the living of a loved one.

I'd rationalized, theorized, and shoved aside every emotion to get here. Now the sight of my father and Nova hollowed me.

My father rose from the chair—his body stiff, his chin tilted upward—and wrapped me into a hug. He kissed the top of my head. "Oh, Beth."

"Where's Mom?" I held him tight.

"Migraine. The medicine knocked her out."

I could only nod.

I'd never thought much about our lives and our family being so sheltered until we were the only ones gathered in the wake of Lindsay's death. Mine had consciously been made small and consisted of my parents, Lindsay, and Nova.

And now Lindsay . . . A ball of emotion stuck in my throat.

Nova had yet to acknowledge me. Her drawn face and red-rimmed eyes had my own tears pushing to spill out. I gave her a hug. The wedge of grief and loss now threatened to cut off my air, but I couldn't let myself break without understanding what happened.

I turned to my dad. "Where's Detective Matson?"

"He'll be back. He wanted us together when he disclosed the details."

While I'd expected a call directly, I understood why he'd tell my parents first. "They found her at the river?"

He shook his head.

I straightened. "Someplace else?"

"No."

What? "Then why did you tell me she was dead?"

"Beth, he'll explain."

Explain what? He'd either found her or he hadn't. I wrapped my arms around my middle to steady myself. I had no idea what Detective Matson would be detailing, but anything short of a body . . .

A knock sounded on the front door. Nova moved to answer it.

"I've got it," I said.

My father raked his hand through his thinning hair. I'd never seen him look so old and tired. I passed his closed office and answered the door.

"What are you doing here?" I said, unable to dredge up an ounce of politeness.

Ericka strode past me to the kitchen, and I followed.

"Frederick," she said the moment she saw my father. He didn't rise to greet her. "I'm so sorry." She sat in my mother's chair and reached her hand out in front of her, resting it on the table.

He almost bristled. "You didn't need to come."

She'd pulled her dark hair into a neat bun, with tendrils draped down her neck. Her cashmere white sweater and floral scent were too much. Even in the middle of the night, she looked camera ready. I couldn't stand to be around her.

"I'll be upstairs," I said. More than anything, I couldn't watch their interaction or deal with my response to it. I'd hoped to get my father alone to talk about the message on his office wall— about Lindsay. Maybe his gatekeeper wouldn't stay long. "Nova, will you let me know when the detective arrives?"

She nodded and I dragged my body up to Lindsay's room. It had long since been repurposed for guests. We'd each had our own domain, but a storage cubby had separated the two rooms. A door on each side gave us access, and we'd had many overnights where we slept in the between space with the doors closed, Lindsay telling ghost stories. I'd spend the rest of the night staring at the ceiling, waiting for hands to yank me into some black abyss while she drifted off to sleep without a care in the world.

It's where she'd hidden that boy she'd snuck in that night and asked me to cover for her. The irritation of that gone without a trace. I'd replay that moment and take the heat a million times if it would bring her back. The tug in my sinuses had returned, this time followed by tears.

I dropped into the overstuffed corner chair, grabbing one of Lindsay's old teddy bears that hadn't found its way to a donation pile, and held it against my chest. Having to exist without my sister had never entered my mind. Someday we'd both be married, and live close. Perhaps when I had children, after law school and my career had started, they'd visit Aunty Lindsay for cookies. Hear stories of how boring I'd been as a kid.

I'd attend her award ceremonies as she collected accolades for shining a light on corrupt corporations determined to decimate our world.

I'd drive her to her doctor appointments when she got old and decrepit and we'd laugh about how our parts sagged and what a pain our parents had been, but how we missed them and loved them anyway.

Fresh tears flowed. We were supposed to grow old together. Who would grow old with me now?

No one else "got me" on the level she did. Our shared childhood. Our shared experiences. Were they really gone?

A soft tap came at the door as I buried my head in the soft fabric of the bear, wiping my tears. Nova. "Detective Matson is here."

I hopped out of the chair and dropped the bear in the corner. Before heading down, I opened my parents' bedroom door and peeked in. My mother stirred.

"Detective Matson's here," I said, willing a response.

Soft snores came back to me instead.

Many times, I'd envied my mother's ability to escape through sleep. Now the idea of it tightened the muscles in my jaw. I eased the door closed and reemerged in the kitchen, ready to hear what the police knew about Lindsay.

"Ms. Ralston," Detective Matson said as I leaned against the counter. Only my father and Ericka were present—Nova had gone back to her apartment.

"So, where'd you find her? Or have you? I'm confused," I said, steeling myself for what came next.

"We haven't. But we believe it's a matter of time and wanted to let you know what we did find."

I shook my head. "You told me you'd come by when you had something definitive. What's convinced you she's . . ." I couldn't say it.

"A bright blue tennis shoe was found downstream."

There must be a million of those in the world, still, my stomach tightened. "How do you know it's Lindsay's?"

"It matches those worn by the woman in the elevator. The one you've confirmed was your sister."

My mind raced. They were slip-ons. The shoe could easily have come off. "Is that all you've got? Really?"

"Beth," my father said, his face pale. "Please."

"The man's only doing his job," Ericka said.

"No, he's not. He's here instead of trying to find Lindsay. Why are you here?" I demanded, ignoring every bit of etiquette I'd ever been taught.

For once, Ericka had nothing to say in response.

"That's all we know for now," the detective said. "But I felt it was enough reason to update you. I'll keep you apprised as things progress."

He turned to leave. I followed, wanting to drill him. Find out more. Tell him to keep looking—to stop looking. He wouldn't find her in that water, and he should be doing something else. Anything else.

"Beth," my father called after me. "Please..."

I met his eye on my way out and shook my head. No more secrets. Because of my unspoken agreement with Lindsay and trying to please my father, I'd done as asked. Don't tell. I feared now for too long. If my decision to do that ended with Lindsay gone forever...

No. That time was over.

He couldn't stop me from talking to Detective Matson anymore. He must have sensed it because he looked away.

The detective and I descended the stairs toward his car in silence.

My thin jacket did nothing against the cold, but I pulled it tighter around me to quell a tremor. "I need you to do better, Detective," I said. "A found shoe won't stop me from continuing my search for her."

"I suspect that's true. It won't stop me either."

I believed that we did have that in common, but his admission stunned me.

"Thank you for sending the DNA report," he said.

"Was it anything like what you'd found in Craig's belongings?"

His lips pressed together. "It was more than that."

"How so?"

"Mr. Bartell and your sister were closely related."

I stepped back. "Closely related? Like siblings?"

"Potentially."

How? "But Lindsay is three years older than Craig."

He shrugged. "I can only tell you what the DNA report showed. Perhaps their mother wasn't in a position either time in her life to raise a child."

The wind whooshed out of me. Once Lindsay and Craig had their tests, they would have known of their connection. They might have even gotten one of those notices that said *you have a DNA match*.

Lindsay finding her own brother dead that night in his office, having just learned of their connection, must have devastated her. I might have run too—and never looked back.

"I guess that could be true," I finally said. "Judge Johnson can't deny the fact that Craig was adopted now. And Alliance, or some version of them, could certainly be implicated."

"Given some other evidence we've found, I'd agree with that," he said. "What do you mean 'some version'?'"

"I did some research at the firm and Ms. Ottoman has done business under other agency names. In fact, I didn't find Alliance at all, but the judge's signature was on dismissal papers of a complaint for wrongdoing brought against one of those defunct agencies. The judge and Ms. Ottoman must be involved together . . ." I was rambling. "What did the judge say when you confronted her?"

"I haven't yet." He scanned my face. "And you won't either."

"What?"

"I can tell by the concentration lines between your eyes that you're thinking about what to do next. Despite what I said earlier, I'm telling you—you're to do nothing. We are pursuing all leads. Now let me do my job."

"Yes, but—"

"There's no *but*, Ms. Ralston."

Except there was. "There are too many angles here, Detective. Bailey's near miss. Craig's murder. The midwife, dead. Have you circled back to Ms. Ottoman? She's been at the head of these fraudulent agencies . . ." At least two confirmed. "When are you planning to confront my father about his role now that you know that Lindsay was adopted? If you can believe it, he actually shut me out of the firm tonight."

"Stop. There's nothing to confront. Not telling your children they're adopted isn't a crime."

"It's wrong." And stealing them was a crime—which I didn't have proof of. Yet. Only notes in a file. Theories. Ellen Sullivan, who might or might not be reliable, but who lived a shell of a life. Camille Jackson, whose thoughts of alien abduction also left her unreliable. But there were others to check. They couldn't all be wrong. Lindsay believed them. That was enough for me.

"I'm not the morality police," he said.

"Well, someone broke into his office here tonight. The man I told you had followed me—he was here and spray-painted a message on my dad's office wall. Did my dad tell you about that yet?"

"No, but are you sure it was the same man? You saw him?"

I shifted feet. "Not up close, but I heard him. I was pretty sure . . ."

He put his hand up to silence me. "Your father clearly isn't concerned enough to report it. And without that . . ."

"You're going to do nothing?" I snapped.

He frowned. "Don't make me regret having shared information with you." He drew in a breath and softened. "Go take care of your family. They need you. And I need to get back to the scene so I can provide solid answers next time."

"You won't find her, Detective."

His eyes were saddened. "Why do you believe that?"

"There's no blood. I know Lindsay." I thought back to the bouncer she'd beaten all those years ago. "If she was fighting for her life, you'd see signs of that."

"What are you saying? That she was taken?" he said.

"I'd rather believe that than what you're telling me."

He didn't respond, instead dropping into his car without another glance my way. I tracked him to the edge of the property. His taillights dimmed and then disappeared when he turned onto the main road.

The detective's words that I was to do nothing ran through my mind as I stared back at the house. But there was so much more to it at this point, and I sensed the detective had held back on all he suspected. I felt helpless at that moment. And while I didn't believe they'd find Lindsay, where had she gone? Why had she gone to the trestle in the first place? Had Henry taken her? Had someone else? How would I ever find her?

Defeated, I plodded back inside. My father had gone to bed. It was nearly four o'clock in the morning. Ericka hadn't taken the hint to go home—she sat in a chair with her eyes closed. Did campaigns truly dictate this much dedication?

The idea sickened me. A few minutes later, I slipped into Nova's apartment and curled up on the couch, afraid to sleep. But sleep pulled me under, despite my best efforts.

I woke with a jolt, sending Murphy, who'd been stretched across my chest, flying.

My father was outside screaming.

CHAPTER 31

Frederick, you must go. What can I possibly tell them if you don't?" Ericka said. She stood at the base of my parents' stairs, hands planted on her hips. Even at eight o'clock, she was camera-ready and raring to go.

My father, on the other hand, seemed to have aged twenty years since I'd seen him four short hours ago. "You can tell them I don't feel well," he said.

"There will be a thousand-plus voters at this event. If you tell them what's happening in your family, the sympathy factor alone will secure you a spot on that ballot."

He grimaced. "Is that all you think of?"

Go Dad. I'd been eavesdropping from Nova's front door and held back a cheer that at last he'd pushed back on this success-obsessed woman who ran his life. I crept down the steps to get closer.

"It's what you pay me for, Frederick. Optics are everything." She used a voice I'd expect when addressing a small child.

"That might be, but I can't perform. Not today. Maybe not ever."

Her head whipped back like he'd slapped her. "Oh no you don't. You aren't giving up."

"I'm . . ." He sucked in a trembling breath.

She climbed the stairs and placed her hand on his forearm. "Frederick. Everything's been handled. Go get dressed. The distraction will do you good."

"But Shelby . . ."

". . . has already taken medication for her migraine. She was up before you and said she'd be spending the day in bed. You'll do the most good for her and yourself if you keep moving. Someone must stay strong. That someone is you."

My eyes rolled back, and my heart sank as she followed him into the house. Dad had never run for office. I'd always thought that leading the law firm had been his pinnacle. At some point, that hadn't been enough. I'd been so busy living my own life—college, working overtime—to notice when that happened. Our conversations at holidays and Sunday brunches centered on dull and superficial topics. Another part of my life I didn't dig too deep into. No better than polite strangers in many respects. I wondered now if I'd ever truly known them. Did they feel the same about me?

Inside, my father had already gone upstairs, and I found Nova in the kitchen preparing breakfast. I kissed her cheek.

"Good morning," she said. "How are you?"

Every muscle in my body felt weighted, but my determination to keep moving was strong. "As good as can be expected. No word from the detective?"

She shook her head.

Good. Every minute they didn't find Lindsay confirmed she was somewhere else, alive. In trouble . . . or in hiding? That I couldn't be sure of.

Ericka sipped a cup of coffee at the dining table. I poured myself a cup and sat across from her. "You should go a little easier on him. We're all shaken from last night."

"Exactly why I am pushing him. He wants to be mayor and run this town."

"Opportunistic, don't you think?" I said.

"When moments present themselves, there's no other choice. Your father has a penchant for the community, and opportunities for human connection, of grief, must be taken when they arrive."

She really believed her bullshit. "Except a shoe isn't a body. I'm sure the police won't want him talking in public on the subject until they have more."

"I'm not asking him to commit to any theories. Just play it up where he can."

"Politicians love that non-committal thing, don't they?" Sarcasm dripped from my voice.

She sniffed and sipped her coffee.

"Don't you have a family to go home to?" I knew little about Ericka except that she was cold and had far too much influence over my father.

"The people I help win elections, and the team I build to make that happen . . . they're my family."

"When they don't need you anymore, what then?"

She took a long drink this time. "There will always be an angle to spin or a situation to make go away." She checked her hair. "I'm serious about you staying away from the campaign."

"I'm sure you are." Her words sounded like a veiled threat. I refused to look away.

But she did. Her phone rang. She disappeared through the back door to answer.

I took the opportunity to find my father and see if I could get a real answer on what he knew about Lindsay. Given the message on his wall, he knew something, and I hoped that included who put it there.

I was halfway up the stairs when my father appeared at the top of them, frowning and texting. "You okay?" I asked.

He looked up from the screen and quickly tucked his phone away. "The show must go on." The words didn't match his anguished tone.

Is that what they said when one's missing daughter's car and shoe were found by the police? "You don't have to do what she tells you."

With a weak smile, he took a step down.

"Dad, what are you involved in that you have to *choose*? What does that mean? Is it about Lindsay? The adoption agency? What are you into, Dad?"

His eyes narrowed as he took another step. "Whatever are you talking about?"

"I was here."

"Where?"

"In the house. Last night."

He stepped past me like I was a ghost before he turned. "I have no idea what you think you know. I've said that before, but it's true. I'm fine. You're fine. Lindsay . . ." The muscles in his throat and jaw tightened.

"Dad, both Lindsay and Craig were adopted," I whispered. "*That's* what I know. Please trust me that whatever is happening, I can help."

He swayed and the blood drained from his face. He clutched my arm. "Beth, stop. Please stop. I can't protect you if you continue with this . . . this insanity. It will get you nowhere. Do you understand?"

His fear penetrated my skin; my heart pounded. "Protect me from what, Dad? Is that why you fired me?"

"What?"

"My pass card. Telling me to leave the office . . ."

"I don't understand."

Did he ever tell the truth? "Don't shut me out. Let me help. Tell me what the message means. Who's the guy that did it? Who's he work for? Could he have taken Lindsay? He was down in the parking garage the night Craig was murdered."

His grip tightened.

"If something's going on with the firm, or that Alliance agency, you have to at least tell the detective so he can—"

He lifted his hand off me like I'd burned him. "My God, is that why you followed him last night? Don't tell me you've told him any of this? I begged you . . ."

I crumpled at his tone. At what his denials meant.

"Everything okay?" Ericka said from the bottom of the stairs.

"Fine," he snapped.

"Chop-chop then. We must go." She glanced at her wrist for effect. "Like ten minutes ago."

He sucked in a breath and cupped my stunned face. "Please, go home. We'll talk later." He trotted to the bottom.

I held back tears. "Will we, Dad?"

He acted like he hadn't heard a word. Ericka had his overcoat waiting and they walked out together. I followed and peered through the side windows. Devon waited at the limo with the door ready.

Nova appeared behind me with a wrapped breakfast sandwich. "You need to eat, get some fresh clothes, and rest. If the detective comes by, I'll call you right away."

I nodded. The detective also had my number. I took the sandwich, although I had no appetite. And rest? Impossible. I could no more do that than I could wait idly for answers or his call, despite Detective Matson's directive to stay away from the case.

I'd been swept aside by my father and his little yapper dog Ericka since the beginning. There wouldn't be any talk later, no matter what he said. He was scared, and I had my theories as to why.

Too much about our lives had been a lie. The lie was collapsing and out of his control. He was happy to let the Erickas of the world dictate his moves.

When had it become this way? Had it always been, and I didn't see it?

It didn't matter. Only finding Lindsay did. If my father didn't want to talk about the whole adoption business, maybe Judge Johnson would.

CHAPTER 32

Taking Nova's advice, I ran home to change clothes. Entry into the courthouse would be easy enough even with the heightened security around it these days. Entry into the judge's chambers, however, would be difficult if I didn't look the part.

There'd been no marked or unmarked police cars patrolling near the building when I sprinted through the front door of my apartment building. Not that I expected any. Resources were low in Portland as it was. Detective Matson had only said he'd do his best to have a patrol, which could be hit or miss.

I remained on guard until I was on my floor. While unsure of what had happened to Lindsay at the trestle, it hadn't been good. She could be in hiding—but I didn't truly believe that anymore. She would have found a way to communicate by now, and there'd been nothing. I had to assume she'd been taken. And after the last few days, I believed that "Henry" could be involved.

If he had her, I might be off his radar. But I also couldn't be complacent. People who kidnapped and murdered, and tried to take out receptionists on street corners, would think nothing of ending me if they thought I was a threat. Until Henry was in a jail cell, I couldn't feel safe.

I stepped out of the elevator and only made it halfway to my door before my landlord hobbled into the hallway, his cane thumping the floor with each step. "My allergies seem to have disappeared as of two nights ago."

"Wonderful," I said, reaching inside my purse for the key.

"Funny thing, it was the same night I saw you running off in a college sweatshirt and a duffel bag."

"Weird." I dug to the bottom of my bag, coming up short. I wouldn't make the mistake of not having them out again. "What a coincidence."

"Hmmm."

"Everything been good here?" *Where're my damn keys?*

"Good enough," he said. "Seems I've inherited myself a niece, however."

Damn. The security guard. "Had no idea you had one?"

"Don't." His eyes narrowed. "Don't want one either."

I forced a smile. "Yes, relatives that pop up out of nowhere can be troublesome."

"Hmmm. We're a quiet building, Ms. Ralston. We let you in because you come from a good family, and you work at a reputable law firm. We're far too old for shenanigans. Am I making myself clear?"

I didn't correct him on my employment status, and any other time, I would've just taken his crankiness. But with Lindsay missing, my tolerance was nil. "Crystal clear. And believe me, I'm too old for that too," I said, my voice taut.

He stepped back. "Everything okay, Ms. Ralston?"

"I don't know yet." My voice faltered unexpectedly. If I didn't find Lindsay safe, they might never be okay. My hand patted the bottom of the bag now, desperate to get out of that hallway.

His face softened. "Well, I hope you figure it out soon. Until then, do we have an understanding that things will go back to normal?"

I almost laughed at the lunacy of the question. There'd been too many lies to believe that was attainable. "Yes, sir." My fingertips found the key ring. I yanked it out like I'd found a winning lottery ticket and shoved the key into the lock. Before he could say more, I stepped inside and shut the door behind me, resting my back against the hard wood.

How did I intend to function when I could barely get through an interaction with Mr. Logan?

Eyes closed, I sucked in a shaky breath. I had no choice. I had—

"Don't be alarmed."

My eyes flew open searching for where the familiar voice came from and landed on Kai perched on my couch. "What are you doing here?" I reached around to the knob—ready to bolt.

"We need to talk," he said, his lean face drawn. "You've got a problem."

I followed his gaze to the shelves in my dining area where books were tossed on the floor, and cupboards and drawers lay open. At my desk, paperwork had been strewn about, some on the floor.

My heartbeat inched skyward as I reached for the doorknob.

"I didn't do this," he said. "I swear."

I didn't remove my hand. "Who did, then?"

"No clue. But they came through your fire escape, the same way I did."

I'd locked that window after the park-bench stalker. Clearly, feeling safe in my apartment had been an illusion.

"Why are you here?" I said.

"Because I believe Lindsay's dead."

The pounding in my chest turned into a tight pull of dread. My sister's shoe being found hadn't made any news. I turned the knob.

He stood. "Please. It's not what you think."

"What do I think, Kai? Because I'm trying to figure out why you'd say Lindsay's dead, and how you knew where I lived in the first place." The rain gear. My stomach tightened. "It *was* you at the park, and the law school."

He winced. "Yes." I arched my brow. "Only because Lindsay asked me to."

"Why would she do that?"

He dropped back onto the couch and ran his hand through his hair.

"She thought you'd be in danger if you ignored her message." He hesitated. "That's not actually true. She *knew* you would, and she wanted me to watch out for you."

That did sound like Lindsay, and I'd already concluded that the message on her phone had been intended for me to follow. That didn't explain everything.

"I found a tracker on my car . . ." My voice teetered.

His face reddened. "That was Lindsay too. I swear. Since I work, she thought it would make it easier. She made me promise not to lose you. She said it could be life or death."

It had been for Craig. The midwife. And Lindsay . . . ? My grip remained tight on the handle. "You haven't said why you believe she's dead."

He hung his head. "The money."

"What money?" I played dumb.

"She brought a wad of cash at the same time she brought that key to me and asked that I put the money in a locker at the Union Station. Which I did."

"What was the money for?"

"She planned to meet someone at a bridge close to your parents' place. She didn't say who or even when, but she wanted the money at the station so she could put them on the train out of town."

She'd only do that if she thought they'd be in danger. "Did they meet?"

He shook his head. "No idea. But like with the key, she said if I hadn't heard from her in a week, I should check the locker. If the money was there, something had gone wrong and that's when I should give you the key. I didn't go at first, but when you sounded so upset and I gave you the key sooner, I thought you'd find her anyway. Then you disappeared off the grid, and I worried something happened to you. I panicked and checked."

"It was there?"

"Every penny."

My inkling that she'd been planning to meet someone at the bridge was right, but that didn't tell me much else. "Where's the money now?"

He retrieved the envelope from his jacket and set it next to him. "Since it belonged to Lindsay, you should have it."

I nodded, but his concern seemed premature since he didn't have details on when the meeting would take place. "You believe she's dead because of this?"

He blew out a stream of air. "That, and I went by that bridge. She'd talked about it a few times. Said she'd always felt safe there." Tears stung my eyes. "Her car was near the tracks."

The image of her empty car had rattled me too. "It was, but they've only found her shoe, nothing else."

The shoe seemed to be enough for him as he buried his head in his hands, defeated.

I swiped my eyes, refusing to give up. "What else do you know, Kai? For someone who denied knowing anything, this is twice now. You seem to dole out information at your convenience."

"That's it. I wish I knew more, but . . . she loved you, Beth, and whatever she was into scared her—enough to create these safeguards. I couldn't tell you—I expected her to come back and she'd be furious at me if I did. And Lindsay furious . . ."

I chuckled, even with nothing to laugh about. He laughed too, and his eyes filled with more tears.

"You love her, don't you?" I said.

He nodded. "But she didn't feel the same about me."

"I wouldn't be so sure. She trusts you. That speaks volumes about what she feels. And please quit talking about her in the past tense. She's not gone, Kai."

His chin trembled. "The shoe?"

"Proves nothing." He gave me a pitiful look. My skin crawled. "Don't look at me like that."

"Denial's not healthy."

I stood taller. "Look, I can't be propping you up and keeping myself grounded at the same time."

He seemed to think about that. "Fine. What do we do now?"

Good question. My hand slipped off the knob. I went into the kitchen and pulled out a container of orange juice, lifting the jar to him. He nodded.

Joining Kai in the living room with two glasses, I handed him one and took the chair where Detective Matson had sat a few short days ago. How everything had changed in my life since that moment.

"I need to figure out who she planned to meet at the trestle," I said. "Lindsay obviously believed the information was important.

And if she was willing to pay their way out of town, she must have thought it would put the person at risk." My heart sank. If she'd already gotten that information, Henry might have it now and then what? I scanned my room. It felt like he'd been the one here—but what was he looking for?

"How're you planning to do that?" he said, breaking my thoughts.

I took a long drink of the juice; I rubbed my eyes. Would going to the judge at this point get me answers or more denials? It was after ten. She'd be at work . . .

Toni Thompson.

God, I'd almost forgotten that she'd be at the sober living house until noon—two hours from now. She'd met with Lindsay, and Angela thought they'd planned to meet again. If that meeting took place, she might know what happened to my sister.

I'd circle back to the judge later at her home.

"I have a meeting to get to. But a guy who calls himself Henry, drives a black sedan, has been popping up during my search for Lindsay. This was likely his handiwork." I nodded to the mess. "I also think he murdered my boss, Craig." I hesitated. I had no idea who to trust anymore, but Kai, while misguided, had at least been trying to do right by Lindsay. If nothing else, we had that in common. "You still want to keep that promise to Lindsay?"

His eyes widened. "You trust me?"

"If Lindsay does, then I do. Just be careful. Obviously, Lindsay is onto something that people will kill to keep quiet."

He glanced at the fallen books. "Let's roll."

CHAPTER 33

Kai followed me to the other side of town and to the sober living house. He continued past me, circling his index finger in the air to indicate he'd be driving around.

Someone watching out for me, in a good way, left me with an odd sensation. Truthfully, he'd been watching off and on from the beginning. He would've saved me a lot of stress had he come clean from the start. Now his presence, even in the vicinity, boosted my confidence.

Though it might be short-lived. He'd only be able to watch my back for a few hours. It was Thursday and only one of us was unemployed—a fact that still rankled me, along with Dad acting so damn innocent about it.

At the glass door of the facility, I rang the bell and waited for the woman on the other side vacuuming to acknowledge me. I waved, getting her attention, and she lifted her chin. She pulled off her rubber gloves and opened the door ajar. "Yes?"

Angela had said she personally manned the door. She must be busy. "I'm Beth Ralston. Toni Thompson's expecting me." Perhaps two people were assigned housekeeping duties and Toni was upstairs.

She frowned, her mouth trembling. "Hold on."

The door shut without an invitation to come inside. I shifted feet. Waiting again. An uneasy feeling crept up my spine, which slowed when I saw Angela through the glass on the phone. She flashed me the peace sign. Two minutes.

Okay. Things were okay. So much hadn't been, I'd lost my ability to discern with any certainty.

Another couple of minutes passed after the original two before she came out, her complexion ashen. "Toni's not here. She . . ." She drew in a breath.

Shoot. She didn't want to talk to me after all.

Angela put her hand on my arm.

My stomach dropped. It was more than that. "Is she all right?"

"She's alive, but . . ." she said. "I'm sorry. It's just been a shocking twelve hours."

For us both. "Please start over. What's happened?"

"Toni was mugged on her way home last night."

Mugged? "Did they get the guy?"

She shook her head. "Witnesses saw her get off the bus, but no one heard her screams until the attacker was long gone."

"Was she able to give a description?" It could be random. No one had followed me here. I'd made sure of that. Unless Angela had been talking about my visit, Henry couldn't know about it. But I also didn't believe in coincidences.

"Not yet. She's been in and out of consciousness since the attack," she said. "I'm sorry."

I nodded, numb with shock and unsure what to say. "Where is she being treated?" I finally managed.

"Legacy Emanuel. They have a wonderful trauma center."

There was no better place to be. "Will they call you if she improves?"

"I'm not sure. She has a next of kin back east, but they're not close. I want to see her. Give her a friendly face and assure her that she'll be okay, but I can't leave right now."

"I'll go, if you'd like," I said. "I can at least report back to you." And hope Toni would be awake enough to talk.

Angela's shoulders drooped almost with relief. "I'd so appreciate that. She's in 504 on the fifth floor."

"I'll be in touch." I started to walk away.

"Wait," Angela called after me with a bag in her hand. "Would you mind taking this to her? Her clothes have blood on them and . . ."

"Of course," I said, flinching. No one should have to put on the same clothes they'd been assaulted in.

"If they give you any problems about seeing her, tell them I sent you with them."

"I promise, if possible, they'll be hand-delivered."

"Thank you," she said. "Any word on your sister?"

Her thoughtful question had my emotions and resolve teetering. But I wouldn't scare her with details. "We don't know anything for sure yet."

"I hope soon."

She and I both.

I hurried to my rental, but lost track of Kai on the twenty-minute drive to Emanuel. My brain wrestled with the unsettling thought that my visit had caused Toni's mugging. If so, was Ellen Sullivan okay? Or Camille Jackson? Had I brought danger on them by trying to find my sister?

I shook my head to clear those thoughts. I had no idea who'd hurt Toni, and I couldn't get lost in guilt. Henry had visited both Ellen and Camille's homes long before I showed up asking questions. If he perceived them as a threat, he would have done something to them already. I had to believe both women were okay.

Kai rejoined me at some point because he passed by as I pulled into the parking garage. He was better at this following gig than I realized.

At the fifth-floor nurse's station, I approached the forty-something nurse, dressed in a frog-covered smock. "I'm here to see Toni Thompson."

"You family?"

I lifted the bag of clothes. "Friend."

She smiled. "Good. She's going to need all she can get. Don't be alarmed when you see her. Despite appearances, she's improving."

The blinds had been shifted enough that light filtered in, warming Toni's stark white room. A single carnation in a vase had been placed on the table.

A steady beep from the machine above Toni's head reported her pulse was steady and her oxygen levels good, but she was not awake. The bandage across her skull and the black under both eyes indicated a brutal attack. My jaw tensed with anger for her.

I placed the duffel on the guest chair, hesitating to get closer. She'd never met me, and I didn't resemble my sister. I searched her face for signs she might wake soon. Nothing indicated that.

A nurse walked in with a stethoscope hung around her neck. "How's my patient today?" She went straight to Toni who didn't respond. "You her sister?" she said to me as she checked Toni's vitals.

"Just a concerned friend."

She smiled. "You and the other girl that just left. That's nice."

The other nurse hadn't mentioned another visitor. "What other girl?"

"I didn't catch her name. Pretty black hair. She'd stepped out of the restroom as I walked in here."

Curious, I glanced from the door toward the restrooms. A woman waited nearby at the elevator. Her jet-black hair poked out from under a stocking cap, and a familiar backpack hung from her shoulder.

"Rhonda?" I hollered, jogging in her direction. The nurse who'd greeted me scowled. "Sorry," I said.

Rhonda didn't turn. Instead, she took a sharp left and punched the door to the stairs.

She'd already cleared the first floor by the time my feet were on the top tread. "Rhonda, wait."

She didn't answer.

"Why are you always running away? This is ridiculous."

She stopped on the next landing and whipped around to face me. "What are you doing here?"

"The same thing you're doing, apparently. Checking on Toni."

"Not the same. Toni's my friend. How do you know her?"

"I don't. But my sister does."

She smirked. "Ah yeah. The sister who's on a big story."

"Exactly. And she'd spoken with Toni."

"So, this is her fault." I didn't blame Rhonda for being angry. I shared it. "You and your sister need to stay far away from my friends. You're nothing but trouble."

It must seem that way. "I can't. Lindsay's in danger." The words rushed out. "Toni and I were supposed to talk today."

"And now she's lying in a hospital bed."

I nodded. "It can't be a coincidence."

Rhonda's face slacked. Her backpack slid off her shoulder and smacked the floor.

"Please, Rhonda. Is Toni the friend you'd spoken about? The one you got away from the agency?"

Her eyes narrowed in distrust.

"Look. I know she had a child six months ago. She must have gone to the law clinic for help from my boss because her name was in his file."

"She's not the friend that had a kid. I saved that one. I couldn't save Toni in time. I met her after and introduced her to Angela where she got sober."

"Helping people we care about is something we have in common then. I hear your frustration in being too late for Toni, but I think she planned to meet up with my sister again. Do you know if they did or why they'd have arranged to meet a second time?"

She sighed. "She'd mentioned the plan to meet someone . . . she didn't say who or when. But something upset her about it."

"What?"

She shrugged. "She only said it didn't pan out. After that, she shut down."

So close. I needed Toni to wake up.

Rhonda swooped her backpack from the floor and repositioned it on her shoulder. "Wish I had more for you, but I don't."

"I think you do though," I said, desperate for more information. "You've known people who went to that agency, which has to be at the center of what's been going down. You've worked to get your friends away from them. Which means you must know how they're getting sucked into the agency in the first place. And their babies. Why are they being taken away? Is it against their will? Are they being abducted?"

She shook her head. "I have no plans to end up like Toni, thanks."

"Please, Rhonda. There's a thread. Help me find it. You said the agency . . . you said they look for you. Where are these women? Where do they look?"

Her leg bounced. "If I tell you, will you promise to just leave me alone?"

"Yes." I'd try anyway.

She huffed. "There's a soup kitchen on Burnside. That's where I met Toni. It's where my friend had gone."

Ellen Sullivan had said something about a soup kitchen, but I'd failed to ask more particulars. Blood rushed into my face. "Does a church run it?"

She nodded.

"Where on Burnside?"

"22nd." She checked her phone. "They open in a couple of hours, but the line starts as soon as someone arrives to start cooking."

"You still go there?"

"Nah. I stay at a shelter across town. They feed us on the regular." She sighed. "Can I go smoke now? I want to get back to Toni."

"Of course." I retrieved a twenty from my purse and held it out to her. "For your dinner."

She scoffed. "I don't take handouts, Fancy."

"It's not. You've given me valuable information. It's worth something."

She shrugged. "At least you're not acting like you want to save the day. I'm over do-gooders."

I pressed the twenty into her hand and fought the urge to pull her in for a hug. Her tough façade reminded me of Lindsay.

Before I could say another word, Rhonda leapt down the stairs and disappeared through the door leading to the next floor. I proceeded to the bottom and entered the lobby while texting Kai.

Heading to 22nd and Burnside.

Behind you, he replied.

CHAPTER 34

A tall man dressed in a dingy winter coat and jeans that pooled at his feet was already in the soup line when I arrived. His hat, something more akin to what you'd see in the Australian outback, sat snug on his gray covered head. Pleasant conversation had me learning that Faith-Centered Ministries ran the service.

"When do they open?" I asked.

"In thirty." He tapped his watch and leaned into me. "Sometimes they let us in early."

I ignored the days-old grime and sweat that filled my nose. "Any idea where to go if I'm not here for a meal?"

He gave me the once-over, then pointed to the back of the building. "Staff come and go from there. Don't forget old man Farley here's waiting when you bust on in." He winked. "Maybe you can squeeze me in ahead of the crowd."

"Sure will if I can," I said and thanked him for the help.

Before I'd made it around to the back, Kai whizzed by on his motorcycle. Seconds later, he texted that he had to peel out for work. He'd be at my service later.

I hated to see him go. But being at a church-funded food line felt safe enough, and there'd been no signs of a suspicious black sedan since leaving my apartment. Or since leaving my parents' the night of someone scrawling that message on Dad's office wall, for that matter. The fact someone had been in my apartment, however, hadn't left my mind. Henry, likely, although I still couldn't imagine what he thought he'd find.

To my surprise, the back door into the kitchen was unlocked. A snowy-haired woman wearing a chef coat hanging to mid-thigh tended three large stock pots on the stove. The smell of stew, meaty and satisfying, drifted through the space. My stomach growled. Nova's sandwich was somewhere in my purse and squished by now, and except for orange juice, I'd eaten nothing since last night.

"Can I help you?" The voice came from the side.

I turned to find a young woman holding a large tray filled with rolls. Her name tag read BREE and was pinned to her black T-shirt.

"Yeah, I . . ." I'd run headfirst into this so fast I hadn't developed a strategy to get information. Identifying myself as the sister of a reporter might shut the conversation down. So could saying I was investigating, especially if there was a connection to Alliance. "I was thinking of volunteering," I said. "I saw the line and—"

She set the tray on the chunky wood prep table between us. "Geez, that's awesome of you," Bree said. "We're actually all set for help."

What charity didn't welcome more feet on the floor or at least the cleaning crew? "I'm happy to do whatever's needed." Willingness to integrate into the ranks could be the best way to learn more.

"Yeah, our leader's pretty particular about who he lets help out."

A little controlling—or like a group that wanted to keep what they did to a few. If they were targeting young pregnant women, that made sense. "I just want to get involved."

She flashed a sweet smile. "If you're serious about helping, you'd have to join the church, take some classes, get approved. It's a long process."

Approved? It couldn't take much knowledge to hand someone a roll or fill their soup bowl. Or scrub a toilet, for that matter. "Awesome," I said, mirroring her earlier enthusiasm. "Where's that?"

"Church of God on Lombard. Are you familiar?"

The hairs on my neck rose. The church was where Craig's funeral had been held. Where the minister had touted Judge Johnson's work with homeless women and children. Where my parents had attended Sunday services for years. "Vaguely." I struggled to process the information. "So, this is part of the Church?"

"Faith-Centered is an outreach." She looked past me to the wall above. "Time for me to get back at it. Lots of hungry souls to feed. And to save."

An obvious cue she intended to wrap up our conversation. "I appreciate the info because it sounds like an incredible organization."

"We have a great reputation."

A timer chimed behind her. She grabbed a set of oven mitts off the counter and withdrew a tray of perfectly browned and fluffy rolls.

The back of her T-shirt read: *God's Got Your Back.*

The tingles on my neck started again. "Love your shirt," I said, racking my memory of where I'd seen one like it before. "Where can I get one?"

"They're for the volunteers so the homeless know we're part of the same team."

"Only volunteers?"

"Yeah. Boss man's strict on that too." She slid the next tray into the waiting oven. "I'm sorry. I really need to get busy. Thank you for stopping by. Get to the church if you're serious."

Damn it. The connection was right here, just out of reach. I couldn't leave until I had it. "Your reputation . . . I've heard it's especially good among pregnant homeless women. Is that true? What do you offer them that's so great?" I searched her face as I said the words.

The smiled remained frozen on her lips, but the warmth had drained from her eyes. "What did you say your name was?"

"I didn't."

She hesitated. Perhaps she'd been warned about answering questions that delved into the population they served. But the way her face pinched . . .

"Has someone been here before me asking the same questions?" I asked.

Her shoulders dropped. "Yes, and I'll tell you the same thing I told her. Brother Phillip runs our outreach and he's here on weekends. If you want to know more, come back and speak with him."

The memory clicked in. That night in the law library. "Brother Phillip runs this?"

"Yes." She let out a sigh that held far too much reverence for a mortal. "He's wonderful."

I had to confirm, even though I knew. Just like I knew the other inquirer had been Lindsay. "Does he have a last name?"

"Garrett."

*　*　*

My legs could barely move fast enough to get me out of there. Phil Garrett, the firm's administrator, was a link. But to what? He served the homeless that came through the line and picked out the isolated pregnant women. Rhonda had said just that—they targeted the women who didn't have anyone on their side. Alone, they could be taken advantage of. Taken advantage meant linking them with the midwife.

Lindsay had been here. Her similar questions meant she'd learned that much, and she would have connected the midwife too. After speaking with the women, the child stealing would be the next connection.

Had Lindsay gone to Phil Garrett to push for answers at that point? Was she looking to bring the agency down, or to find her mother—Craig's mother—their mother? I still hadn't truly absorbed the idea that they could be siblings.

If Lindsay went to the firm to confront Phil, she must have believed that she and Craig were among the abducted, as I'd thought earlier. I didn't want to think that my father also knew that part. The buzz in my head turned into a full-blown headache. He had to have known. He'd hired Phil and worked with him all those years. They were members of the same church.

I didn't have all the links though—like how Phil knew Margaret Ottoman or why he'd send women to the midwife. And did that midwife connect to an agency? Other than Sherry's body being in the building, her name wasn't in any file—and had not come up otherwise. And whoever Phil referred the women to, did he know that an adoption agency became involved after that? *Don't be naïve.* He knew. This could very well be a whole ring of people doing bad things. Which means he could know where Lindsay was right now.

Another unsettling thought erupted. Had Phil Garrett been a part of Craig's murder? He'd been the first one in Craig's office after I screamed that night. He'd taken control with his calm and authoritative demeanor. If he had anything to do with Craig, he could be involved in everything else that had happened since.

My father firing me might not have to do with my investigation. He could be protecting me from Phil Garrett.

The OJ in my stomach burned into my throat as I debated what to do with the new information. I could go to Judge Johnson and see if I could push her to talk, or go to the law firm and confront Phil Garrett. Both could potentially have information about Lindsay.

It was midafternoon—the judge wouldn't be out of the courthouse yet. If she was part of the corruption, she could claim I was harassing her like she had at the funeral. That would get me arrested pronto—a risk I couldn't take.

The firm, however, was within regular operating hours, and I couldn't envision Phil having me arrested, fired or not, at my own father's practice.

I turned the SUV in the direction of downtown, pondering a third choice—call Detective Matson. While he'd said to stay away from the judge, he'd said nothing about the law firm or Phil Garrett. Because he didn't know.

But calling him would only get me shut down because there was no irrefutable proof yet. No connection. That said, I wasn't stupid. I'd put my fact finder skills to use, learn what I could, then hand it all over to the detective.

I opted to park in a different spot in the parking garage this time. I might have made a mistake before if Henry had been watching, and I couldn't afford any more of those. I rode the elevator to the main lobby. With pass cards only necessary after hours, and Phil unaware of what I'd just learned, getting into the firm should be no problem.

Still, when I saw Charlie working the security desk, I hung back in the parking garage lift. It might be smarter to go back down a floor where the archive files were kept and see if I could access the stairway there. A long climb that my lungs would take issue with.

Before I could decide, Charlie turned his attention to an elderly gentleman asking directions to an investment firm located down the street. I strode across the hall and stepped into the main building's elevator, barely breathing until I reached the penthouse.

Now to get past the office gatekeeper.

A receptionist who'd been with the firm for a couple of years sat behind the desk, a crease forming between her eyes. Oh yeah, she knew my employment status.

"Hey, Lacey," I said.

"Beth." She shuffled a stack of billing statements to one side. "I've been asked to inform you that your final check was sent by mail."

I tapped my hands on the counter. I bet she had. Checking in first and not sprinting down the hall to Mr. Garrett's office had been a good decision. "Appreciate that. Is Mr. Garrett available?"

She grabbed that stack of paperwork she'd pushed away. "He's not here. I'll tell him you stopped by."

That was unexpected. "Is he coming back?"

Her eyes never once glanced at her computer, where his schedule would be on the master calendar. "No."

I didn't believe her. Phil Garrett lived at this office, except for on weekends apparently, when he was targeting young women. "Okay. How about my dad?"

She shook her head.

That I *did* expect. His office was at the opposite end of Mr. Garrett's, but I had no intention of leaving the building without answers. "Shoot. He asked me to pick up his dry cleaning. I'll be right back."

"Well—"

Pretending I didn't hear her, I kept walking and disappeared into my dad's corner office. My heartbeat in my throat, I only let out my breath once I'd closed the door.

"You okay?"

I startled. "Mandy?"

"Hey, what's up?" she said while reshelving some law books on his shelf.

"I was about to ask you the same thing."

"Just returning some borrowed items . . ." She nodded to the revised statutes she'd shelved and the two in her hand. "You?"

"Grabbing my dad's dry cleaning." I made a show of searching for it—only his overcoat hung from the coatrack in the corner.

"Cool. I heard you're not coming back to us, that you found something better. I'm bummed you never mentioned it."

Was that the story going around? "Actually, I was fired."

"By your dad?"

Maybe. "Yup. All the better for you though, right?"

"Excuse me?" Her face crinkled.

"The senior partner you now work for. I'd heard you got the job." The one I supposedly had, but there was no sense in alienating her.

Her neck turned bright red. "I planned to . . ."

"Tell me?"

She looked away. We both knew she'd had a few opportunities.

"No worries. You had places to go in this firm and you clearly thought my relationship with *upper management* would help you get there." Okay, maybe I was fine with alienating her a tiny bit.

She pushed a book into my dad's shelf with emphasis. "It wasn't like that."

"You mean at first?"

"I didn't think I'd ever have a chance to be considered. You're the golden child, and I couldn't compete with the hours you put in."

"Until I didn't put them in."

She nodded, barely.

I'd be embarrassed too if I took advantage of a friend's situation like that. Although I understood her drive to get ahead. Maybe I was being too hard on her. After all, she'd done me a favor. "Don't sweat it. We're all good."

"Really?" Her eyes narrowed.

"Don't look so serious. Really. Coming back here after what happened to Craig would be too hard anyway. You made it easier."

She nodded, fully this time.

"But I need your help. I'd like to get to the other end of the hall, but Lacey . . ."

She chuckled. "A bit of a bulldog, isn't she?"

That was putting it mildly. "And you know, firm protocol, yadda yadda. But if you could get her away from her desk for five minutes..."

She smiled. "I can do that. Suggestion though. Most people think you quit, so be prepared if they ask where you're working now. I'd also make it quick on whatever you're wanting on that end too. Mr. Garrett has issues if we loiter."

I had no intention of dallying, but appreciated the heads-up. "Thanks. I will."

She crossed to the door. "Give me ten seconds. She can't resist croissants, and they're in the lunchroom today." Mandy winked and disappeared down the hall. "Lacey," I heard her say. "Follow me. You won't want to miss this."

Their voices faded as the glass doors to the elevator lobby closed. I waited a few seconds and then sped to the other end of the hall, pretending to look at my phone until I reached Phil's office.

Certain Lacey had lied, I expected him to be sitting smug behind his desk, working away in his cocoon of a world.

His office was empty.

I went in anyway and closed the door. In my years here, I'd never stepped foot in Mr. Garrett's private domain. My daily life of piling up hours and conducting research gave me no reason to interact with him. Another department handled HR.

At half the size of the senior partners', Phil's office had a view of the Portland hills instead of the beautiful water views the attorneys enjoyed. My eyes moved from the windows to the framed photos lining the cabinet behind the administrator's oversized desk.

I hadn't realized Mr. Garrett—Phil—was a family man. The pictures reflected a happy one at that, with his wife and three grown children, and a couple of grandchildren. Other pictures showed him at Communion where he stood with the minister who'd accosted me about talking with the judge. Another, of Mr. Garrett sporting that same black sweatshirt I'd seen him in that night—*God's Got Your Back.*

Next to that, a picture of a much younger Phil and a young woman. The photo's gold antique frame reminded me of those around my parents' house containing images from their youth. The woman looked familiar, though I couldn't place her.

Heavy footsteps sounded from the hall and grew louder. *Shoot.* More than a couple of people were headed my way.

Mr. Garrett was back, or Lacey had returned too soon. Trusting Mandy might have been the wrong move.

Either way—my time was up. I snapped a couple of pictures of the credenza with my phone. Getting back here again would be a no-go.

The door swung open with some force and Lacey shadowed the doorway, hands on her hips, with Charlie and another security guard I didn't recognize at her back.

I smiled with all the innocence of a kid caught with chocolate stains on her face. "Hey, Lace, thought I saw Mr. Garrett returning to his office. You'd left, or I would've asked you to ring ahead."

Lacey didn't answer, her jaw set at being duped.

"Sorry, Ms. Ralston," Charlie said. "You're no longer welcome here."

I met his eye, and his cohort's whose hand rested on his belt like there should be a gun there. Good thing there wasn't, given the dark look he gave me.

"That's okay," I said. "The feeling's mutual."

They escorted me down the hall. Mandy had conveniently disappeared, and Lacey shook her head as my personal security detail rode with me down the elevator and to the parking garage.

"Goodbye, Ms. Ralston. It's been a pleasure to have known you."

I waved goodbye to Charlie and gave him a sad smile, my bravado tumbling away as the elevator doors closed. At one time, I'd enjoyed working here. I'd liked Craig, and the sense of accomplishment of working the cases. Of being part of something bigger.

Everything I thought I knew had changed. Including the people who'd once felt like my family and friends.

Dejected, I slipped back into my vehicle, unsure of how to find Lindsay or get the answers I was desperate for, when my phone dinged with a text.

Angela from the sober living home.

Toni's awake!

CHAPTER 35

Toni's bed had been raised enough that she saw me enter her hospital room.

"You Beth?" she said in a small voice before I'd introduced myself.

"Yes. Angela told you about me?"

She nodded, then winced. "She said you had some questions." Her face collapsed in pain as she pushed herself up further in the bed. "Thanks for bringing my stuff."

"Absolutely. You okay to talk, though?" Color had returned to her face, but she looked like she needed a week of sleep.

"I'll be okay."

I hadn't realized until she said it just how worried I'd been. Grateful, I approached. "Mind if I sit, then?"

"Nah."

I pulled the lone chair from the corner and drew it close to the bed. "I was so sorry to hear you'd been attacked last night."

"You and me both." She looked past me, her eyes on the closed blinds. "I kept feeling like I was being followed. Never saw anyone though. Figured I was being silly, you know?"

"I do."

"Should've been watching the alleys instead of behind me. I got yanked so fast off the sidewalk." Her eyes moistened.

"It could happen to anyone." Her face crumpled. It was probably best to get off that topic. "I'm Lindsay's sister."

She sniffed. "Yeah, Angela mentioned that too. Sounds like you thought I was supposed to meet her?"

"Yes." *Sounds like?* "You weren't?"

"Not me. My friend."

Rhonda had gotten that wrong. "Okay." How did that make sense though? Toni had been on the list. "Did you have a baby six months ago?"

"Yeah. I put him up for adoption."

As in voluntary? I hesitated. "You weren't told your child died?"

Her chin trembled. "God, no. I mean, that didn't happen to me. My baby was alive and well."

Had I misunderstood Lindsay's notes? "How did Lindsay or Mr. Bartell at the legal clinic get your name, then?"

"A girl I knew, Rebecca, mentioned me to Mr. Bartell. He was looking for other women who'd had similar stories."

Rebecca Scheer maybe? She was the one who'd filed the complaint that had been dismissed by Judge Johnson. The woman whose number had been disconnected. "You said *knew*?"

"She OD'd a while back."

I nodded, my heart hurting for her. "I'm sorry."

"Me too."

"So did you visit the soup kitchen on Burnside that Faith-Centered Ministries runs?" Or was Rhonda wrong about that part as well?

"Yeah. That's why Rebecca gave my name in the first place and it's where I met Brother PG." She tried to smile, then cringed. "He's a good guy."

PG. "Phil Garrett?"

She shrugged. "I just call him PG. His first name's Phil though."

"What did he do for you?"

"He runs the ministry and serves food—that's how we got talking in the first place. He saw I was pregnant and felt concerned. That was over a year ago now, I guess. He asked me if I was set up okay for after the birth. And before."

"Were you?"

She frowned. "Hell no. I was a mess. I mean, I'm in a sober house. That should tell you something."

"But you're good now?"

"Yeah. And I managed to stop when I found out I was pregnant. I even thought for sure I'd keep my baby. Like I'd be stronger if I had someone helpless relying on me. But at the time, I had no stable place to live. PG kept telling me I had a better chance of success if I placed the baby for adoption."

Even when he appeared to be doing the right thing, he wasn't. "And you did?"

Her gaze fell to her lap. "At first, I said no. Then he introduced me to Sherry, who took care of me. Once she gave me the lowdown, you know . . ." She turned her head now.

"The lowdown?"

"That I owed it to my baby to give him the best chance, given my track record . . ."

"Sherry's a midwife?" I leaned in.

"Yeah."

"Nothing ever seemed off to you about the way either Phil or she pushed for you to go the adoption route?" It would set all kinds of red flags waving for me. The biggest one being that reputable agencies didn't go around approaching women to place their children, and certainly didn't try to convince them when they were told no, regardless of the woman's track record. There had to be laws against that, especially when targeting already vulnerable women.

"No. She was great to me. I never had to go through all the hoops of figuring out appointments, insurance stuff, hospital check-ins. Like, do you know how crazy that system is for those of us with nothing? Anyway, I was okay with it, knowing my baby was with another family and they'd take good care of him. Give him opportunities I could only dream about. Truth is, right after the baby was born, I started drinking again. PG had been right about me. Then." She ground her teeth and flinched.

"You said you *were* okay with it. Not now?"

"Well, I'm better, you know. I'm sober. Working." She sniffed. "I've been trying to get hold of Sherry the last couple of days to tell her that I'm better and I've changed my mind, but she hasn't answered."

Not wanting to scare her, I didn't tell her she wouldn't. "What do you mean you've changed your mind?" I said, afraid the answer explained her attack last night.

"I want my baby back. Or at least to be able to visit. You know, open adoption if nothing else."

That wouldn't have gone over well. "Did you leave Sherry a message?"

"A couple. Then, after work last night, I went up to find PG. That's where I was coming from when I got jumped. I hoped he'd help me since he told me about her in the first place."

My stomach tightened. "Did you talk with him?"

"Nah, he wasn't there."

She stared at her bandaged hand. "Anyway, I don't mean to be ungrateful to them."

"Sure." My mind reeled. "I have a question about the process, though. Did you have any paperwork to sign releasing your rights?" Something official could be an irrefutable link to hand over to the detective.

She shook her head. "Nothing like that. Sherry said it was better that way because they could just do their own paperwork without involving me."

"So, you verbally agreed?"

"Yeah, otherwise, I might have to go to court and sign stuff. That's why I thought maybe they'd let me see the baby. Since, you know, I could say I didn't mean it."

My shoulders inched up. "Did you tell Sherry any of that on the message?"

"Sort of."

I drew in a breath, not wanting to scare her. These people did nothing but take advantage of these young women. Of their addictions. Of their naiveté of the system. Of course Alliance, who wasn't even a legit corporation, wouldn't want the birth mother's name involved anywhere in writing. Then they could go about creating a false record of birth and anything else they needed.

I didn't know how it worked, but there was an entire Vital Records division in the state that housed such documents, and there must be a few rules about who could file and when. But as to the actual birth, it didn't even sound like some of these women knew an agency existed behind the midwife. That kept the agency safe to barter or sell or whatever they did to these children under the radar.

Until someone like Toni tried to create a problem.

My teeth were grinding now, for all these women had endured and that I still had no tie from Phil to the adoption agency. I'd already suspected he knew the midwife—who was now dead. That midwife had to have worked for Alliance—why else would she have been in their building. Detective Matson must know more on that. Also clear, Phil and Sherry had an agenda when they approached and handled these women. But Toni was the first person who'd admitted to dealing with either of them, and she offered no solid connection to Alliance. Toni hadn't seen her attacker, so no connection to Henry. She hadn't met my sister a second time, so no idea where Lindsay would be or where she'd gone.

My search for Lindsay felt futile, but I started the conversation back from the beginning in my head. Toni's change of heart was recent. I realized I'd missed something.

"You'd said that it wasn't you. That your friend was to meet my sister. Did I hear that right?"

"She's kind of my friend, yeah. We met at the soup kitchen."

"Did you refer her to Lindsay?"

"Yeah. Lindsay asked me about my situation. When I told her, she gave me that same look you've been using. Expecting something dark and tragic, I guess. Anyway, this other girl, she had a totally different experience with Sherry. She claimed Sherry had lied to her about her baby being dead and that she'd stolen him from her. I figured your sister would want to talk with her about it."

She didn't sound convinced. "You don't believe your friend?"

"It's just not what happened to me, and Camille can be a little different."

My breath caught. "Camille?"

"Yeah. Jackson."

The one whose father ordered me off her property yesterday. She'd gone to see my sister? What did *different* mean? "When did Camille see Lindsay?"

"Sunday night—well, Monday morning. Your sister wanted to meet at some train track outside of town, and I went with her."

I sat straighter. She hadn't mentioned that part. The lump grew in my throat. "Did you walk with Camille out to the trestle?"

"I waited in the car." She let out an exhausted sigh. "Please don't tell Angela. Sneaking out is against the rules and I've felt guilty ever since, especially when she kept asking me if I was okay."

That explained why Angela had thought Toni was upset. "Did Camille talk to my sister?" She hadn't appeared capable of carrying on any conversation when I'd seen her.

"I assume so, but not for long. She was only gone about ten minutes before she came running back."

"How did she seem afterward?"

Her face grew serious. "Upset, I guess, now that I think about it."

I worked my bottom lip with my teeth. Upset didn't sound good. "She say anything more?"

Toni's eyelids sagged, our conversation taking a toll. "No. In fact, for being a chatty person, she was quiet the whole way back. I thought reliving *her drama*, as she's referred to it, had been too much for her."

I feared it was more than that. "Have you seen her since?"

"Uh-uh." Her eyes closed.

I leaned forward, knowing Toni needed to rest. "This is going to sound weird, but does your friend have any mental issues?"

She grimaced. "Told you, she's a little off."

Off could mean so many things. I stood. "Thank you, Toni."

"Uh-huh." She yawned, wincing. Her head drifted to the side, and I crept out of the room. Had Camille been lying, or did she have a psychiatric disorder?

If so—could she have hurt Lindsay? Anxiety inched across my skin. Had she pushed Lindsay off the bridge?

I didn't want to believe Camille would lash out at someone who could help her, but I couldn't make assumptions any longer.

An hour later, my stomach in knots, I found myself at Camille Jackson's door. Her dad answered with a deep frown, his T-shirt stained with coffee, and a cigarette dangling from his other hand. "You again?"

"I have to speak with Camille."

"She's too fragile. I won't let you put her into another state, which lasted hours last time you dropped by."

Determined that he not shut the door on me, I said, "I know she went to see my sister." That might not do much good. "Tell her Toni thinks we need to talk."

His eyes narrowed. A small hand touched his shoulder from behind. He startled. "Go inside, Camille. I've got this."

"It's okay, Dad." She blew out a shaky breath. "Maybe she can help."

He folded his arms over his broad chest, not convinced. "I won't let you stand out here in the cold and talk."

"I'd like to speak with her privately," Camille said. His lips pressed together. "Please?" Gone was the wild-eyed woman I'd witnessed before. Were her medications balanced now, or had it been an act?

"Fine. Wood bin needs filling anyway," her father said.

"Thanks, Daddy."

He disappeared into the house and reappeared within seconds wearing a wool coat, hat, and a pair of work gloves.

Once her father had cleared the corner and moved out of earshot, she stared at me. "Well, you want to know, so are you in or out?"

CHAPTER 36

As much as I wanted to hear Camille's story, and why she seemed quite sane standing in front of me, I didn't move. She might have been the last person to see Lindsay. My body was leaden with fear—afraid of what she would tell me. Terrified she'd confirm Detective Matson's theory that Lindsay was dead.

But Lindsay had gone to meet Camille for a reason. No other option existed but to play this out to the end.

Inside, the home was simply decorated, and clean, except around a leather recliner facing the TV. Sports magazines surrounded the chair, and an ashtray in need of emptying teetered on the armrest. Mr. Jackson had his own man cave smack in the living room.

"Sit," Camille said, heading for the sofa where she hopped onto the brown cushions and sat with her legs crisscrossed in front of her. *Crisscross applesauce.* Lindsay's voice was in my head before I realized it. Such an innocent movement had a lump filling my throat once again. I'd been pushing and running from the potential pain of Lindsay being gone, but it was right there, ready and all too willing to bury me.

"If you don't sit, I'm not talking. You make me nervous."

I plopped down on the edge of the love seat across from her. "So, I'm confused."

She picked at the skin around her nails. "I'm not crazy, if that's what you thought. I'm bipolar. There's a difference."

Of course, but . . . "Your dad . . ."

"We didn't know who you were."

"I'd told you, I'm Lindsay's sister."

Her demeanor shifted at Lindsay's name. Her chin trembled. "Yeah?"

Her tremble clutched my heart. *You have to know, Beth.* "You were supposed to meet her."

She focused on her hangnail.

"Did you?" My chest tightened. While sitting across from her now I didn't sense she'd hurt my sister, she could hold the answers of who had. She could also hold the answers I'd been searching for since Lindsay ran out of the office that night—wherever they might lead. She could know Lindsay's location at this very moment.

Instead, she shook her head.

Frustrated tears pushed into my eyes. Another dead end? I wouldn't believe that. I almost jumped off the love seat. *Sit.* "Was she not there when you arrived at the train tracks?"

She swallowed, hard, her throat muscles rippling.

My shoulders bunched. "You saw her there, though, didn't you?"

She nodded.

"Was she alone?"

Her face reddened in response, amping up my already skyrocketing blood pressure.

"Look, you invited me in. Toni says you believe someone stole your baby, and I believe you're telling the truth. But if you don't tell me what you know . . ."

Anger flashed across her face. "Yeah, that hasn't worked out so well for other people, has it?" She met my gaze.

"No, it hasn't." I wouldn't lie to her. "It's time it didn't work out for the right people. The people who took advantage of your trust." The anguish of wanting to know what happened to my sister on that bridge and where she'd gone swelled like a wave, threatening to drag me to the murky bottom. I straightened. "Please. What did you see?"

"Why would you believe anything I'd say anyway? Toni doesn't, not really."

"Because my sister did . . . does. And that's because she was one of those abducted children." At least that's what everything so far had suggested.

Camille wilted into the sofa.

I clamped my hands together. "Anything you'd be willing to share, I'll take. Because right now, I'm lost."

Her shoulders slumped, perhaps with the weight of what she knew. But just as quickly, her jaw set with what seemed like a determination to get rid of it. She started from the beginning.

I'd already learned part of her story from Toni and had learned more from visiting Faith-Centered Ministries. She'd been alone, no friends, and the tall man who often served the soup had approached her. His kindness lowered her walls, and he'd offered her assistance. Except, unlike Toni, she could not be convinced to give up her child.

"You took his recommendation for the midwife anyway?"

She looked down, embarrassed. "It was free, and they have this birthing suite that's comfortable. They take good care of you all the way through. Or that's the bait, right? Because they're only manipulating you the entire time."

"Where's that suite located?"

"Back of some warehouse. Outside doesn't do it justice though. I mean, it's nice and big."

It could be the same place Ellen spoke of. "Who is *they*?"

She frowned. "Sherry. She's the only one who took care of me."

These people were smart. Making sure the victims only interacted with a few. But Sherry didn't act alone, or she wouldn't be dead. She must have done something that made people concerned she would talk—that would follow the pattern.

Someone had to be in charge. Margaret Ottoman? With Sherry's body in her building, who else would it be? If I was right about Sherry potentially talking, they'd kill her so she couldn't be leveraged against the agency. Toni was beaten because she came back asking for her baby. These people didn't like anyone making waves. Craig and my sister were looking to generate a tsunami.

"What did Sherry say happened during the birth?" I asked.

Her chin trembled again, and this time tears followed. "That my baby died."

After several minutes of pulling herself together, I learned it was essentially what Ellen Sullivan had described—they wouldn't let Camille see the baby after.

It was all I could do not to cry with her. So much loss. A mother who'd lost her child—it clearly had crushed her. And I thought of Lindsay, a child who'd begun with the innocent wish of finding her own mother. The quest to uncover the corruption had ended up taking her newfound brother's life and sending her on the run. Nausea swept through me.

"As soon as I could after the delivery, I went back to the damn kitchen and found that guy and raised hell," Camille said, snapping me out of my grief. "And that same night, on my way home, some black freaking car nearly ran me over."

My jaw twitched. "Black sedan?"

"Yeah. If I hadn't dove into a ditch . . . And don't look at me like I'm being dramatic. He was gunning for me."

"I believe you. One hundred percent. What did you do?"

"Well, after he reversed, fast, it didn't sit right," she said, like she hadn't heard me. "Most people would get out of their car, panicked, to see if I was okay. This guy was far too collected. He got out, all right, cocky, strutting his way over. Expecting to find me dead, no doubt. Or to finish me off. I hid, not planning to find out. But I had a feeling it was all connected to my baby, so I stayed out of sight for a while. Stayed away from my dad, and never went back to that soup kitchen."

That move had probably saved her life. "Did you get a look at him, the guy in the car?"

"You bet I laid eyes on that creepy, brown-haired asshole."

Along with the black sedan, it had to be Henry. *Unbelievable.* Even before Lindsay had picked up on the investigation, he'd been at every turn, wreaking havoc. "And my sister found you through Toni?"

She nodded. "When I was raising hell at the soup line, Toni'd talked me down and we became friends. Anyway, when your sister went to talk to her, Toni knew I'd had a different version of events and she gave her my number." That was what Toni had said, but with so many stories not lining up, I had to make sure. "We chatted then, and she insisted we meet. I told her it had to be somewhere safe. That she had to pay my way out of the city once I gave her what she wanted, because it was absolute proof that those jerks were involved in something dark and shitty. But I had to watch out for myself and my dad, even if I wanted to bring them down. That's why she suggested the tracks."

My stomach churned, feeling on the verge of the truth. "What happened out there?"

Her eyes clouded. "I heard a commotion as I got closer. A white car was parked, and two people were standing on the other side. At first, I couldn't make out who they were, but one had long red hair. I figured that was Lindsay." She swallowed again. "But the person behind her had his arms wrapped around her neck. She struggled at first and then she went limp." She looked away. "I froze, and then . . ." Her breath shook.

Every muscle in my body clenched, constricting my chest, my lungs. Surrounded by oxygen and I was suffocating. "Did he throw her in the river?" I asked.

"I assume he did."

What? "You assume?"

Her eyes glistened now. "I ran."

"You ran?" My voice cracked.

"I'm sorry. I shouldn't have. But I was in shock. And . . ."

I tried to keep the judgment out of my tone. Camille must have been terrified. "And what, Camille?"

"I recognized him. It was the same man that had tried to run me down. The same man that came last week asking questions. That's when I got the idea to act crazy. I told my dad to go with it, and as you saw, he sold it better than me." She picked at her hangnail again. "Anyway, I couldn't let him think I remembered him. When I saw him with your sister, I knew he'd come after me. I couldn't risk that. He knows where I live, you know? I'm really sorry."

"I don't blame you, Camille." I didn't, but the truth was, she didn't know if Lindsay had been killed or not. The way she described the attack sounded like he'd put a sleeper hold on my sister. Camille hadn't seen her go over the bridge. The only sign of Lindsay was her purse and one shoe. Those items could easily be lost during a struggle.

Lindsay could still be alive.

CHOOSE WISELY on my father's wall. Did he know where Lindsay was? What were his choices?

Only he could answer that, but as for Camille . . .

"There's one thing I don't get. You haven't told me anything different than I've heard from others. What do you have that my sister would pay your way out of town for?"

She tapped in a few numbers on her phone, bringing it to life. She scrolled through photos, picked a video, and handed the phone to me.

The image of Judge Elizabeth Johnson and Margaret Ottoman arguing played across the screen. A moment later, they disappeared from view and the image became a solid white door, the voices quieter in the background. While muffled, it was clear that Margaret was telling the judge to back off and shut up.

"Is she out?" Margaret's voice rose. She had to be talking to someone else in the room.

"Like a light," a woman said. It had to be the midwife. Sherry?

"Well, then hurry it up," Margaret said.

"Like you can hurry childbirth. You're an insensitive bitch." Elizabeth's voice rose. "And I won't let you do this to the girls. It's insanity."

"I'll ruin you first," Margaret said.

A long silence and then Elizabeth's voice grew cold. "Don't threaten me. Or I will end it my way."

The midwife was talking smoothly to Camille. "Don't you worry about them. They argue all the time. But no one ever gets out of this," she said. "We just need to get that baby out of you safe and sound so it can find its way to a better life."

Her words sent a chill through me. "When was this taken?"

"Last year."

I straightened. "You witnessed this interaction?"

Camille shook her head. "I threw my phone on top of my purse next to me. I didn't realize it had recorded anything until later. They'd given me something to relax because the pain was so bad. I was out the minute they put whatever that was into my IV. Next thing I know, I'm awake, sore, and Sherry had this devastated look on her face." Her jaw clenched.

"Telling you the baby had died?"

She nodded. "But I'd felt my baby kick right up until that IV. Sherry lied. My baby was alive."

"And the police wouldn't listen?"

"I didn't try." She hung her head. "I have a record. Fraud. Theft. A few stays in a psych ward." She sighed. "I didn't think anyone would believe me. As for the video, no one knows it exists— except Lindsay. But whoever that old woman was kept saying 'judge.' Don't know about you, but my experience with the law has never worked out."

I decided not to tell her what I did—or had done—for a living. I no longer saw billable hours in my future anyway. What I felt certain of was that Margaret Ottoman was absolutely involved— and Judge Johnson was in deep with her.

"I need this video," I said.

"It won't go by text. The file's too big. Lindsay wanted me to upload it to some website I'd never heard of, so I wasn't about to do that. I'd only been able to send your sister a still photo."

I'd scanned Lindsay's texts and seen nothing like that on her phone. "Where did you send the picture?"

She pulled up her log and showed me. I didn't recognize the number. Lindsay had another phone?

I yanked my cell out of my purse and pushed in the numbers, pressing SEND and holding my breath. One ring later, a message came on that the voicemail had not been set up. It was off or the battery had died. Either way, useless to me at the moment. I refocused on Camille. "A photo won't be good enough anyway. I need the video."

She shook her head. "I'll tell you what I told her. The best I'd do was let her watch it and we'd figure out what to do after that. That didn't happen—and I told you I don't want that guy back here."

I moved from the love seat to sit next to her. "You don't know me, I get that. But this is proof that these people are into some terrible stuff." It also provided proof of who some of the players were.

Whether the women signed anything or not, acquiring a new life into a home would require legal documents to be filed and the judge's signature would make them official. The agency wouldn't be able to make things look legitimate for new parents without them. It would also require a certificate of birth—I didn't think an unlicensed midwife, or an unlicensed agency, could file something like that. While not sure of exactly how it worked, it must have many working parts.

Parts that the judge didn't want to be involved with anymore. She'd argued with someone who might have been Henry in that black sedan at Craig's funeral. Craig's murder could have been a message suggesting what the video had—there was no getting out.

And my sister had been investigating all of this with Craig, putting her into grave danger. Detective Matson might finally be compelled to stop looking at the river and help me find my sister based on this.

"Could I borrow your phone for a couple of days? I'll get it back to you after I show the video to the right people. I'll protect your identity. I promise."

"I—"

"Camille. It's important. For Lindsay."

She hesitated for a long minute and then slumped into the cushions. "It's not like I have anyone to call anyhow."

Her father offered a wan wave as I pulled away. I did the same but held back from rolling down my window to tell him it would be okay. I didn't know if it would be. If I could get Elizabeth Johnson on my side, there might be a chance. They'd killed her son—I wanted to believe she'd talk to me if I got her alone. With her involvement, perhaps she'd know where Lindsay was.

Detective Matson needed to see this video.

Maybe together we could get some answers.

CHAPTER 37

After four rings, Detective Matson's phone went to voicemail. The time to record a message would only last so long, and without context . . . I'd have to hit the high points. At least this way it would give him time to digest the information before he called.

"I'm heading to Elizabeth Johnson's house. I have a video and proof that she's involved with Alliance and Margaret Ottoman. They're doing illegal activities concerning women and their babies, Detective, and it has to be connected to Craig's and the midwife's murders—and Lindsay's disappearance." I didn't care if he thought I hadn't faced reality with that last part. Nothing would stand in my way of finding her. I was Lindsay's fail-safe, and that meant no giving up. "Call me."

I'd never broken so many speed laws in my life, but my foot never let off the gas until I was in the Laurelhurst neighborhood and a block away from Judge Johnson's home. When Detective Matson called to say he was on his way, I'd be nearby.

The street lamps illuminated the quiet, long-established neighborhood. In the spring, maple trees provided quite an entrance into the area. The judge's long, rambling driveway was ahead on the right. Rock pillars framed the entry, along with a tree of life design centered in the middle of a sturdy wrought iron gate. Towering evergreens often found in Tuscany paintings lined her driveway and obscured any visibility of her house from the main road.

Parking at the curb, I killed my lights and drummed my hands on the steering wheel. It was after six. I'd expected Detective Matson to call by now. Though, unlike me, he might have a personal life. He had a cat—perhaps he had a wife and kids as well. Or a bowling league. I stared at my phone. *Call, damn it.*

Stuck, I pulled out Camille's phone and punched in her code to get to the video and replayed it once. Then again. I'd gleaned no more information by the third run-through, except that whatever was happening in this abduction ring, there were several people involved. The midwife, obviously. Margaret. Phil, at least as far as suggesting the women contact the midwife. The judge.

My mother? Her entire life had centered around committees and social status. I didn't see how she'd be involved—even though she couldn't be oblivious to certain truths.

But my father?

Someone had to file the legal documents for the judge to sign, and Phil Garrett wasn't a lawyer. Was I kidding myself to think my father was innocent? My head hurt thinking about it, trying to understand why he'd go along with anything so evil.

Headlight beams coming down the judge's driveway grabbed my focus. I sank low and to the side in my seat, keeping my eyes on the approaching car. The judge might be heading to a meeting, or a late dinner. Or to work out. I knew as much about her life as I did the detective's.

I'd been told not to interfere—and I'd already pushed the boundaries enough in this case. However, if the judge and I happened to travel in the same direction and our paths crossed when she got out of the car . . . Random things like that occurred. Detective Matson would be glad I had more proof for him in the end.

But that line of thought was for nothing when the car came into full view and idled on the other side of the opening gate. My heart jolted at the sight of the black sedan and the driver wearing a ski mask. It might be cold out, but it wasn't that cold.

The driver didn't seem to notice me as he accelerated the moment the gate cleared and hit the main drag while ripping the mask off his head.

Henry. I gripped the steering wheel, debating whether to follow—but the ski mask had me concerned. Why was he wearing one?

People only hid themselves when . . .

My heart raced. What had he done to Judge Johnson?

No time to rationalize whether I should wait for Detective Matson. The gate would only remain open for another few seconds.

The SUV's engine cranked to life, and I swerved into the driveway. The tires squealed as I cleared the gate just as it began to close. Judge Johnson's two-story plantation house came into view. I parked, hurried up the steps, and rang the bell.

A gong chimed. No footfalls came from the other side.

I reached for the doorknob but hesitated, not wanting to get ahead of myself. Henry could have come here to spray-paint a warning on the judge's wall. It might be better to go back out to the street and wait for the detective.

But if it was far worse than spray paint, and I learned later that the judge had been harmed, and I could have helped . . .

I knocked lightly at first, then pounded with my fist. "Judge Johnson? Are you here?" I yelled. "It's Beth Ralston. Frederick and Shelby's daughter."

Pressing my ear to the door, I willed a response.

Nothing. I tried again. "Are you okay?" If she was monitoring a security camera, she could be afraid to answer. I straightened and went back to knocking lightly. "Judge, I'm here to help. I saw that car leaving, and he's been to my dad's place recently, and mine too."

Still no footsteps. This time, I tried the door. Unlocked. I stuck my head in, anxiety prickling my scalp. "Judge Johnson? Are you here?"

"Help." A small voice; high pitched.

Upstairs? I could have imagined it. I listened closer.

Something crashed to the floor. Not my imagination.

I rushed into the white marbled foyer and took the stairs two at a time. "Judge? Where are you?"

From the top, a moan came, louder this time.

A hall of doors mocked me. Where to start?

"Help." The plea came again. The room at the end.

Elizabeth was on the floor, her back propped against the bed, her breath coming in short shallow surges. Her hand was pressed against the side of her stomach where a bloodstain had spread on her white shirt.

The image of Craig's death crashed back. Dizzy, my hands shaking, I found my phone and had my finger on the numbers.

"Stop," she said.

"But . . ."

She shook her head. "It's too late."

I wouldn't admit that. Maybe because she'd lost her son, she'd lost her will. But I wasn't about to let Craig's mother die no matter what she'd done. I dialed 911 and ran to her bathroom, grabbed a towel, and dropped to the floor next to her, covering what appeared to be a bullet wound to her side.

The operator came on. "What's your emergency?"

"A woman's been shot at—" My eyes darted around the room to find an address. I should have used the landline. "Judge, what's your address?"

She didn't answer.

Panic pushed me. "I'm at Judge Elizabeth Johnson's home off Royal. Send an ambulance." I disconnected and pressed on the wound.

She reached out a bloodied hand to my face, dropping it short. "I'm sorry," she said. "We were trying to do the right thing."

A lump lodged in my throat. "Who's *we*?"

"You don't know?" Her face creased in pain. "I thought that's why you'd come." She took a deep breath, wincing. "Thought you'd seen the baby pictures. That you'd figured it out. Like Lindsay." Her breaths were back to short gasps. "It's always been a matter of time. I told them."

"Baby pictures?" The photo albums in my parents' living room held a few of our childhood photos. Lindsay had gone through them? I closed my eyes. "Who's *we*?" I said, desperate for confirmation. "Phil Garrett? My father? Margaret Ottoman? Please, Judge, tell me what you know." The blood seeped through the towel. I pushed harder to stop the flow. "Is Lindsay still alive?"

"I'm sorry," she whispered.

I nearly crumpled. Was she sorry because Lindsay was dead? *You don't know that.* "I saw the video of you and Margaret at the birth of one of the girls," I said. "You wanted out of lying and stealing from these mothers, didn't you? That's what was happening, right? Who else is involved?"

Her eyes filled with tears. "I thought that losing my career would be the worst of it, but my boy . . ."

My panic swelled higher. I needed answers. I changed direction, looking for confirmation. "Was Craig abducted too? I know he and Lindsay were siblings, so it makes sense, right?"

She gazed at me, her eyes narrowed—confusion?—then her eyes closed. She wasn't dead. I'd seen dead. But the loss of blood was weakening her.

I pulled her away from the bed and laid her flat. "Judge?" My voice squeaked. "Stay awake. Help is coming." Her eyes opened again, and she placed her hand over mine, pressing into the wound.

"Tell your father," she said.

"Tell him what?"

She looked away, but her eyes remained open. Her grip firm on the towel against her stomach. "Go. Danger."

Danger? Was Henry cleaning up the mess—systematically eliminating anyone who could incriminate—who? Him? Margaret? Phil?

CHOOSE WISELY. A warning to my father. Had he chosen, and Elizabeth being shot was the result? Was my father next on the list of people to silence?

That had to be what Elizabeth was trying to tell me. I pulled the phone close to the judge and put a fresh towel on her wound. "They're almost here. Can you hold on?"

She nodded and I stood, backing out of the room into the hallway. I punched my dad's number in my cell and paced the corridor waiting for the call to connect, my own stomach tight with dread, my hands covered in blood. The coppery smell made my insides roil. The phone rang and rang. He didn't answer.

Home. He must be there.

Nova picked up right away.

"Where's Dad? I need to speak with him," I said, squashing the tremble in my voice so as not to scare her.

"He's upstairs and running late. The tux just arrived for his event this evening."

An event? "Put him on the phone, please. It's important."

"Mr. Ralston," she hollered with her hand over the receiver, I assumed, since I could hear voices in the background, but not what they said.

When she came back on, she cleared her throat. "Your father says whatever it is, it'll have to wait."

Damn him. I looked in on Elizabeth. Her eyes were open. A good sign.

I wanted to warn him—but I needed him on the phone to do that. "Please tell him he doesn't have it handled. That someone's been hurt. Tell him I need to talk with him. Now."

"Oh dear. Are you okay? What's happened?"

Exasperated, I squeezed the phone tighter. "Not me. I'm fine. Please tell him."

More muffled voices and then she came back on the line whispering, "He's asking for my help, Beth. I need to go."

What? No. "Did you tell him?"

"I did."

My father was hollering. "Nova where's my . . ."

"I have to go."

I crushed the END button and almost threw my cell down the hall. Henry could be coming for him next, and he wasn't listening.

Back in the bedroom, I returned to Elizabeth's side. Her grasp was firm on the towel she held against her wound, the color coming back into her face at the blood loss slowing.

I wanted to stay until help arrived, but my father might not have time. "I have to go."

"I know," she whispered and gave me a sad smile.

Still, I hesitated to leave. "Help is on its way."

Her eyes still open, she nodded. "Please go. Tell him."

Forcing myself out of the room, I sprinted down the stairs. Once outside, I sucked in the cold night air—clearing my head—and raced to the SUV. The squeal of sirens in the distance cut through the quiet. If I stayed until they arrived, I could tell the officers that my father was in danger. They might send help with me. But if Detective Matson was among the responders, he'd force me to sit it out. Worse, he might arrest me to ensure that.

That can't happen. I had to get to my dad to make him understand that he could be next. And then I'd press him until he spilled the truth. All of it.

I was a mile from my parents' when my phone rang. Detective Matson.

"What the hell happened here?" he barked into the phone. "Where are you?"

"You're at the judge's house?"

"Yes. And I want you back here."

"I can't. Will she be okay?"

"She's conscious and they've stopped the bleeding." Relief flooded through me. "But I want to know every goddamn thing you know at this point."

"The man who shot Elizabeth is the same one who tried to run down Bailey. Probably who killed the midwife. Who murdered Craig." My voice caught. "He attacked Lindsay a few nights ago too, Detective. I have a witness . . . I don't believe Lindsay's dead."

There was a heavy silence. "You might be right. We've only found the other shoe."

Finally. "Then you understand."

"I do, Beth," he said. "So, get back here and let's find her and the man who did this. Together."

I wanted to believe that he wouldn't try to lock me down, but I couldn't bank on him being true to his word with Lindsay out there and my father at risk.

"I'm afraid my father could be next."

"Beth . . ."

I disconnected and silenced the ringer, my parents' driveway coming into view.

CHAPTER 38

'd used the Ducks sweatshirt to clean up the blood before running into the house. It might make an impact on my father, but it might also give Nova a heart attack. Hopefully, when I told Dad that Elizabeth had been shot, that would be enough to get his attention and to get him talking.

But when I rushed inside, the foyer was dark, and a small table lamp in the adjoining living room cast an amber hue. A wall clock ticked out of sync with my pounding heart. A chill crept over me that Henry had already been here.

A rock formed in my throat. I checked Dad's office, only to find it locked. I hurried to the kitchen. Unlike last time I'd been here at night, the under-cabinet lights were on, but dinner had been cleaned up. Not even a dish in the sink. Nova had finished her nightly chores and left.

I returned to the foyer and listened for any sounds as I raced up the stairs. When I reached the top, I hollered. "Dad, are you here?" Nothing. "Mom?"

The rooms were empty, and my parents' bedroom door closed. I pressed my ear to the door, not hearing anything. I eased it open to find my mother snoring on her side of the bed. The lump in my throat eased just a bit. She was likely three migraine pills in and sound asleep.

Tonight, I'd take that.

Heading back down the stairs, I noticed the empty coat tree. My father's overcoat often hung there when he was home.

I closed my eyes. I'd missed him, but if Henry had intended to hurt my dad before he left, it meant Henry had missed him too. At least Dad was with Ericka. Despite my thoughts about her, she'd keep him on task and her eyes on him. He'd also be harder to get to at a political event with hordes of people around. Henry seemed to attack when people were isolated.

Which meant I had some time to wait. I stood at the edge of the living room and eyed the photo albums that might contain the photo Elizabeth had been talking about. Lindsay had found it and the judge thought I had as well. In thinking back, I couldn't remember any photos that had triggered suspicion at the time. Although I wouldn't have been looking for anything either, and it had been years since I'd looked through any of these books.

I sat on the floor and grabbed a few, thumbing through them for something that would have grabbed Lindsay's attention.

The first album contained pictures of my sister's school years, all the way through college graduation. I traced the photo of a beaming Lindsay in her cap and gown with my finger, her entire life ahead. *I will find you, Sis.*

I flipped the pages further, scanning photo after photo for what the judge meant, but only found random pictures of scenic locations and events at the law firm I hadn't attended. Several had Judge Johnson in them, but none with children.

The next album centered around my mother's college years. Her beauty had never faded. She'd been the president of her sorority and her debate team, and a princess at homecoming. I'd seen snippets of that woman in the way she led her garden groups and planned galas, but that woman hadn't shown up much in our home. When had it become easier for her to escape than to deal with reality?

I shifted the third and last album onto my lap. This time, I started from the back. It took only minutes to find the photo that the judge must have been talking about.

My youthful mother held a newborn while sitting in a dining chair in their current house. Next to her, Elizabeth Johnson cuddled another newborn in her arms. Loving smiles lit their faces.

Newborns. Not one. *Two.* I pulled the album closer, scanning the entire photo and the images of the babies reflected back. In the limited light, I'd made out a woman standing to the left with a toddler, but not who the woman was. Another woman standing nearest the judge sent tingles up my arms.

Pulling up the photos on my phone that I'd taken of Phil Garrett's credenza, I zoomed in on the picture in the antique frame of a young Phil sitting next to a woman. In comparing that picture to the one in the photo album, it was obvious they were the same person. I focused on the bright red lipstick she wore in the baby photo, and the reason for the familiarity I'd felt earlier became clear.

The woman was a young Margaret Ottoman.

Phil and Margaret were related? I'd seen the pictures of Phil's family—she wasn't his wife. But Phil and Margaret were close in age and shared similar facial features. The same shaped nose. The same smile. Phil must be her brother. He had to be.

There was no denying the connection between Judge Johnson's family and ours, and that Margaret was part of it. Now I understood why Phil would send women to the midwife linked to the agency. He was sending them so that Margaret, his own sister, could orchestrate placing or selling the stolen children elsewhere. When Lindsay began to dig, she must have seen this photo. Elizabeth had said as much. Lindsay putting it together might have begun right then.

Once she'd gone to the soup line, as the young woman Bree there had suggested, then Lindsay would have learned that Phil Garrett was in charge. That might not have made a lot of sense unless she went to Phil and confronted him . . . I could see that. And if she'd seen the same picture of Margaret in his office, and if Camille had sent her the still shots from the video too, along with everything Craig had learned from the women at the clinic, the connections would have come together in no time.

While I didn't know how far she'd gotten or how much she'd uncovered, it was enough that these people had been compelled to murder. Henry appeared to be the trigger guy, but I wasn't sure how else he fit. Was he part of executing the abductions, or did he take orders from someone like Margaret or Phil . . . or both?

What I didn't understand is why they hadn't come for me yet. Or maybe they had . . . someone had been in my apartment looking for something. Was it the video?

Did they think Lindsay had already gotten it? Did they think I had?

Wait—they didn't know about the video if Camille had only told Lindsay.

The skin on my arms prickled. There was only one way they'd know about it. They *had* Lindsay. And if I knew my sister—she wouldn't go quietly. She would have told them she had proof to take them down—she might have told them at least some of what was on the video. It could explain why Sherry and Elizabeth had been targeted. If they didn't have the video, was it better to kill those in it?

Except the video was still out there and Lindsay hadn't told them who had taken it—or Camille would be dead.

Of course, I didn't know if any of that was true. When my father came home, I'd be asking him those hard questions because, while he could be next on the hit list, he could also be dirty like the rest of them.

CHOOSE WISELY. Were they blackmailing him? Or leveraging him? Lindsay could still be alive, but for how long?

"Beth? Is that you?"

A small voice floated in from the foyer, where my mother was inching down the stairs with a bottle of wine in one hand and a half-filled glass in the other.

"Mom." My mouth felt dry with anxiety.

"Thought I heard someone down here. I hoped that was you and not some burglar," she said with a small laugh as she passed by me, her eyes glazed, on her way to the sofa.

She curled at the end, and topped off her glass, nearly emptying the bottle that she now placed on the coffee table. Her usual perfected hair hung across her forehead and her flawless makeup was smudged.

My chest gripped at her pain and brokenness. She'd given up on Lindsay the night the detective found her shoe.

Despite my resolve, I hesitated to move. Had my parents been up front with Lindsay from the beginning, this situation might have been avoided. Their need to hide everything, to be involved in whatever this was—those were the sources of my mother's distress. I wouldn't be stopped by it.

The photo album tucked under my arm, I settled onto the sofa next to her. She laid her head on my shoulder, the smell of too much wine and grief drifting off her.

"We need to talk."

She lifted her head and straightened. "What about, dear?"

Her protective walls were on the rise. Balancing the photo album on my lap, I flipped to the page with the picture.

"I know almost everything, Mom. I want—no, I need to hear it from you."

She flattened her palm against her chest. "What do you think you know?"

My face grew hot with frustration. "That Alliance Agency is involved in abducting children from their mothers who are either homeless, alone, or addicted." I didn't have the exact profile. "Or at least Margaret Ottoman is, since she seems to have changed her business name a couple of times to avoid detection."

"I—"

"That Phil, Dad's right-hand at the firm and Margaret's brother, sends these women into that den, acting like he's helping them. But coercion is illegal. And Lindsay knew about it, or at least enough that it concerned everyone enough to murder Craig. To harm Lindsay." I did believe that much. "And they attacked Elizabeth—Judge Johnson—tonight."

My mother sucked down a long drink of wine. The blood drained from her face. "Is she okay?"

"She's alive, but she was shot."

My mother swallowed hard.

"Mom, why'd you do this? Why would you be involved in targeting these already vulnerable women, lying to them, stealing their babies?" She started to cry, and angry tears stung my eyes. "And why didn't you tell Lindsay who she was from the beginning?"

Her chin trembled.

"Tell me, Mom. Is any of this getting through? If they're willing to kill Elizabeth, Dad could be in danger."

Her face grew impassive. She glanced at the photo—lifted her chin. "It's not Lindsay."

"Of course it's Lindsay."

She shook her head.

A weight pressed against my chest. "What do you mean?"

She peeled back the plastic that held the baby photo in place and set it onto the surface, pointing to the baby in her arms. The baby that had the same brown curly hair as the baby in Elizabeth's arms. "That's not Lindsay."

"Then who is it?"

She looked at me, her eyes widened, silently answering.

The pressure mounted, sinking me back into the sofa with the realization of what my mother was saying. What I'd sensed the moment I'd seen the photo of two newborns but refused to believe, afraid to destroy the last remaining shreds of a life I thought I knew.

"I'm the one who was taken?" I said the words but couldn't isolate my emotion. Numb. Shock. Realization. My whole life had been a lie?

In the better light, the woman on the left side of the photo became visible. Nova? My jaw clenched. Had the woman whom I'd associated my warm childhood memories with known all along? The betrayal of that sent nausea ripping through me.

"My God, why do you keep saying *taken* or *stolen*?" my mother snapped, bringing me back. "We're not monsters, Beth."

I shook my head. "Then what are you?"

My mother yanked the wine bottle off the coffee table and poured the small amount remaining into her glass. She swallowed it in one gulp and cringed. "We're saviors. And we saved you, for goodness' sake."

"Saved?"

"Yes. Your mother, she was an addicted mess. All of the babies come from broken women who have no business having children. They couldn't care for a baby if they tried. So yes, we saved you. But try telling that to your determined sister."

"How did she even—?" My brain spun so fast I couldn't get the questions out.

"She wanted to surprise you for Christmas; that's how it started." She laughed bitterly. "Getting DNA tests is all the rage, apparently, and she asked what I thought of the idea. I told her, 'Get one on yourself. It will bore you. You're Scandinavian.' But no. She wanted to have yours done so you could have it to share with your children someday."

How was that possible? "The test. I found had her name on it."

"Because you can't run a DNA test on whomever you want. And she wanted it to be a surprise."

"Then . . ."

"She got your hair from a brush and turned it into some lab under her name."

"Like Ancestry?" I asked, numb.

"Oh, she wanted better than that. More foolproof. Honestly, when she hadn't said anything more, I thought she'd forgotten about it. But I made the mistake of reiterating that it was a bad idea. I'm sure it was then that she wondered if something was amiss."

Lindsay's investigative tendencies didn't just extend to strangers. Had my mother left it alone, Lindsay might have dismissed it. When she didn't, she would've taken it to mean Mom was hiding something. So, she found out that I had a different DNA . . . "How did she know about Craig?"

"That's on your father. Lindsay told him what she'd found. He made some mention that people were adopted all the time and it was our choice not to tell you. That in fact your own boss didn't know he was adopted." She waved her hand. "I'm sure he was trying to say it was normal and to throw her away from where she inevitably went, but it backfired."

"And it led to Craig."

"Who did a test on himself, and they soon figured out you two were related. That's when she remembered seeing this silly picture from years ago, confirming you and Craig were"—she looked at her hands—"twins. I should have burned that photo long ago. I'd meant to, but forgot about it, honestly, and then . . ."

I bent over, putting my head down between my legs, feeling dizzy, angry, confused, and so sad my heart ached. I'd been taken or stolen. Or "saved" as my mother kept saying. Was that true? Or had the woman who birthed me been made to feel inadequate like Toni? Or worse, had she been told Craig and I died?

My head pounded. Regardless of how I came to be in the family, my mother was more concerned about her failure to burn the proof. And Craig? All these years I'd been working with my brother. My twin. No wonder we'd connected so easily—that I'd felt sisterly toward him. My heart squeezed. I'd lost him without ever knowing.

I rubbed my eyes. "None of that explains how you got me."

"I told you. The woman who birthed you was new to the country and a complete mess. You'd be dead if we hadn't stepped in."

"But why you?"

She stared ahead with empty eyes. Shame? "I was content with Lindsay, with no desire for more children. I never had a good relationship with my mother or sister, and I didn't want the same for Lindsay." Her chin trembled. "Not that I didn't grow to love you. I did. I do. But your father envisioned more children. When the opportunity arose . . ." She cleared her throat. "Well, he stayed up half the night thinking how horrible your life would be if we didn't intercept. Thankfully, he only wanted one more."

Yes, thank God, Mother. "And Elizabeth?"

"She'd wanted children for so long but couldn't conceive. She'd lost a marriage over it actually, and there were two of you that needed a home. But had I known . . ."

Every fiber in my body bristled. "What? You'd have insisted I be taken to some other family? Is that how it worked?" I knew them not wanting me to attend the funeral felt off. They didn't think I was fragile. They'd been afraid I'd put it together.

"That's not what I meant, Beth. But clearly, it's all come at a great cost."

The cost was my brother, and now, quite possibly, my sister. If they were cleaning up the mess, they wouldn't let Lindsay live much longer—if they hadn't already killed her.

In one moment, the image of my entire family had been shattered. The way Mom talked about *the cost*, I couldn't be sure if she counted losing me among any of it. More likely she was concerned that she'd lose the way of life she'd grown to love. Her committees. Her board appointments. Her Garden Society.

I wanted to scream. "Even if what you say is true, I've met the devastated women that were told their children died and know that was a complete lie. You act like you're helping these women, but you're playing God when you deem them unworthy to be mothers and set out to do something about it."

"It's not—"

"It's exactly what you did." When Lindsay's investigation led her to that same conclusion, and I believed she had gotten to it, there'd have been no stopping her. "What exactly happens to those babies that are taken? Where do they go?"

"I'm not certain what happens to them all. But adoption can take years for some couples, if they even qualify. It's not fair. If they're good churchgoing couples with money to spend, why should they wait?"

Money. Privilege. Greed. I gritted my teeth so hard I thought I might break a tooth.

"But those others are beside the point," my mother continued. "Your mother couldn't raise you and we were there." She lifted her chin. "You'll see that everything your father did was for the right reasons, for the children. Including you, my darling. You'd have had no life otherwise."

"So, Dad was part of it all?"

She looked away. Sadness nearly caved my chest. I'd known on some level all along, but her non-response confirmed it.

I pulled away from her. I'd always believed my parents loved me the best they could. A part of me still wanted to believe that. But this was too much to unpack.

I couldn't sit here another second or wait until my father returned to drill him. "When will Dad be home?"

"Late, I assume. The car came for him before you got here. Off with Ericka to some event, as usual." She looked past me, her eyes glassy, sad. "I think they're having an affair, you know. Like Lindsay, he'll eventually leave me too." She fell back into the couch rubbing her temples. "I need my migraine medicine."

She wanted sympathy; I had none to give. It had been her escape for far too long.

The doorbell rang. Detective Matson had no doubt come to find me. I'd apologize for hanging up on him. Show him the video. Get my mother to confess again. Stop this hell that these people had been putting helpless women through all these years. And pray he meant it when he said he'd help me find Lindsay.

I answered the door.

Devon?

"Can I help you?" I said.

"I'm here to retrieve Mr. Ralston for the campaign drive this evening."

My mother appeared at the edge of the living room.

I turned to her, shaking. "You said Dad had already been picked up."

"Yes. A car came for him like it always does." She seemed to just notice Devon. "Did someone take your place tonight?"

"No, ma'am. Ericka asked me to come for him."

"Was it a black car?" I asked my mother.

"Well, yes."

My stomach tightened. "Did you see the driver?" My voice inched up.

"I was busy at the time and just glanced out the window."

"Dad seem okay then?"

"He . . . No, I guess not. He looked back at the house. We'd had words. I figured that's why his face was red, and . . ." She wrapped her arms around herself. "Do you think something has happened to your father?"

"I don't know." But Henry had come for him after he'd shot Elizabeth. I hadn't missed Henry at all. He'd beat me here, and the image of the judge's wounds had me gripping the door. I could only imagine what Henry would do to my father. While I didn't have time to process my parents' betrayals, they were all I knew. All I'd ever known. I wouldn't let my father die if I had the ability to save him. But even more reason to find him—he could know where they had Lindsay.

I ran past Devon on the way to my car, unsure where Henry would take him. I punched in my father's number. *Answer.* It went straight to voicemail. So did my next call to Detective Matson.

I was on my own. *Think.* Detective Matson had said Margaret was staying with family. That could mean her brother, who I believed was Phil. But they wouldn't go there. Phil had a family, at least according to the photos in his office.

The agency had been set on fire—but they might take him there. It was in the warehouse district and businesses would be closed at this time of night. Or would they go to the birthing center that Ellen Sullivan and Toni had spoken about? Maybe, but they'd only known it was in the warehouse district. Nothing more specific.

In truth, they could have taken my father to any remote location if they planned to kill him.

My phone lit up as I started the car. Kai's name scrolled across the screen.

"Where are you?" he said out of breath when I answered.

"Leaving my parents' place. Where are you?"

"Sitting outside some warehouse in northeast Portland. I got off early and tried to call. When you didn't pick up, I drove around your usual haunts to see if I could find you."

"Sorry. I'd silenced my phone," I said.

"Way to give a guy a heart attack. Anyway, I was approaching your parents' house when a black sedan raced out of their driveway. You'd mentioned a black car had been following you and it felt suspicious the way he flew onto the street. So, I followed."

"God bless you, Kai. You said warehouse . . . Are you on Russell Street where Alliance is located?"

"No. Loring Street." He gave me the exact address.

My throat tightened. Loring Street ran perpendicular to Russell. That could be where the birthing center was located. It would make sense to have it close to the adoption agency, and that was literally the back side of the Alliance building.

"And, Beth," he said. "The driver just took some old guy into the building. He didn't look happy."

A shudder ran through me. "Stay there. I'm on my way."

CHAPTER 39

The block where the building was located was dark and desolate. I approached on Russell, the street running parallel to Loring, where the adoption agency had once done business. The door where I'd first seen Rhonda emerge from the NA meeting was shut. I cruised by the burned-out agency's storefront. Plywood sheets now covered the windows.

Rain began spitting on my windshield. Not even the homeless milled about tonight. I checked my phone. There'd been no sign of Kai and he hadn't texted since we spoke. Detective Matson also hadn't returned my call. I'd tried twice more on my way here and it went straight to voicemail again. This time I'd left two urgent messages.

Where the hell is everybody?

I passed the lamppost with the missing children's posters that had sparked sadness in me days ago. Anger now replaced it knowing that Alliance could have been at the root of some of them. And while I couldn't be sure my mother's version was accurate, or if my birth mother had been told Craig and I had died at birth, I sensed everything Lindsay had done was to find my truth. Not hers.

This entire time, I'd acted in a way to protect her from the trouble she'd stirred up for herself. But she'd been trying to protect me—to find out who I was. If she'd only told me what she'd found, or what she'd planned to do, I would've told her to leave it alone. Nothing was worth risking her life over.

The thought clutched my throat. I'd hoped she was leveraging information—but now I couldn't imagine a scenario where they would let her live . . . not after Elizabeth. Not now that they'd come for our father. The tenuous rope I'd dangled from until this moment had frayed to a snapping point.

The reality was they'd see her as a threat. Once she realized my parents' deception, nothing could have stopped her from confronting our father. As my mother had reported, that led her to Craig, his test, and his work at the free clinic, then to meeting women who claimed their children had been abducted. And ultimately the Alliance Agency. By that point, she would have been a freight train with no brakes.

It would have ceased being about me at all—her focus turning to find and bring down every perpetrator.

A fact they'd know about her.

That thought fueled my determination to finish what she'd started. I had to know why. Saving my father could be the way to those answers.

Once on Loring, I spotted the familiar black sedan parked on the opposite side, facing my direction. No one was inside.

I still hadn't seen Kai's motorcycle though as I cruised past the door that likely led into the birth center, given it was almost in line with the adoption agency on the other side. They could be connected in some way. Although the entire building hadn't been shut down or condemned after the agency's fire. Firewalls might safeguard the other businesses.

At the end of the block, I turned the corner and parked out of sight. I texted Kai.

I'm here.

While I waited for his response, I texted Detective Matson the address of the warehouse. Hopefully he'd get this message.

Please come and send reinforcements. They've taken my father. The wedge in my throat was suffocating. *I'm going in.*

The idea of that started my heart slapping against my chest so hard I thought it might burst. I wasn't made for this. I was the thinker in the family, not the fighter. That was Lindsay's role. If she hadn't survived, what chance did I have?

It might already be too late.

I messaged Kai again.

Where are you?

As my phone sat silent, fear crept over me that maybe Kai *couldn't* respond. With or without him, I had to move.

My breath hung in the air as I scanned the street. Drips from the building broke the eerie silence, along with the crackle of a sole overhead streetlight. I forced myself forward, searching for Kai on my way back toward the sedan and finding no sign of him or his motorcycle. If he was circling, he might not hear his phone.

I wanted to believe that, until halfway down the block I spotted a narrow opening in the building. An alley of sorts, although it didn't go all the way through. A half-moon security light gave an amber hue at the farthest point where a dumpster butted against a brick wall.

If I were on a motorbike, it's where I would have parked.

I flicked on my phone's flashlight and swung the beam back and forth. A rounded form slouched against the wall. Garbage? A homeless man sleeping off his liquor? Unsure, I walked toward the image, slowly at first, and then recognized the leather jacket. Racing to Kai, I dropped next to him.

"Are you okay?" I said close to his ear. No blood seeped through his clothes. No obvious gunshot or stab wounds. I shook his shoulder. "Wake up."

He toppled to the side revealing a deep gash on the back of his head and swelling around his left eye.

Panicked, I pressed my palm on his cool face. Not cold though. I leaned in and felt his warm shallow breath on my cheek. A small relief because he was still hurt and needed help. Help was on its way, I hoped, but I couldn't wait any longer.

I backed out of the alley and approached the birth center, before deciding that entering the same way as my father might not be the best approach.

My hunch could be right and there was another way in.

I sprinted to the other side of the building.

CHAPTER 40

I f the detective had gotten my numerous messages, he, along with police backup, should be charging in my direction any time. I prayed they were while I pried loose a piece of plywood from the agency's window and shifted it enough to squeeze myself into the space.

My pant leg caught, and a nail dug into the side of my thigh. I squelched a yelp, rolling backward and forward before falling through the opening, landing on my side. Pain ricocheted through my leg.

Afraid my grand entrance had alerted someone, I didn't move. Margaret had gone to the back of this office the first day and left through a door. At the time, I'd thought it might lead outside. Logistically, that would only have been about half the length of the building. While I believed the birth center was on the other side, I didn't know if or how it connected.

A minute passed with no approaching footsteps. Thigh stinging, I stood and rubbed my leg, feeling dampness, warm and sticky, on my palm. My eyes adjusted to the dark. The blood trickling down the outside of my leg had seeped through. I might never look the same in a bathing suit, but I'd survive.

To avoid getting hung up on another nail or worse, I clicked on my cell light and swept the beam over the room. Soot covered the counter and desks; smoky black streaks snaked the walls. I made my way around the desks on the way to the back, passing the front left office. The amount of ax marks and skeletal frames suggested the fire had been set in there.

The idea of the midwife's body having been inside sent a violent tremor rippling through me.

Careful where I stepped, I maneuvered around downed insulation and wiring.

The hall ended at a metal door. I pressed my ear against it. Sharp sounds followed low ones, all indistinguishable as to whether they were voices or normal building noises. Whatever the source, they were muffled and likely not coming right from the other side.

Easing open the door, a strip of yellow caution tape strung across the opening stopped me. Once removed, I stepped into a concrete hallway. A small green light on my right identified the two restrooms located several yards in that direction and illuminated an electrical box anchored to the wall. A couple of uncharred desks and office chairs had been brought out into the hallway. A closed door across and down from where I stood could be the janitor's closet. Or the birth center?

Keeping the agency door ajar with the wadded caution tape, I crept in that direction. The muffled sounds became clearer voices. Louder now. And angrier.

"Don't be ridiculous. I'm not Elizabeth. But we should've stopped this long ago. I've made no attempts to hide that fact, Margaret."

My father.

"Don't take the high road with me, Frederick. You got a daughter who's just like you out of the deal." A woman's voice. Older. Margaret's. It had to be.

"Regardless. I'd only ever agreed to help with the paperwork of women who willingly placed their children. Even then, we were breaking the law with falsifying birth records so you could stay disconnected from the transactions. But you decided to change everything, and I would've never agreed to get involved had I known that was the plan."

"There is a need for babies, Frederick," Margaret said. "Supply and demand. You're a businessman. You should understand that."

He snorted in what might be disbelief. "Yes, and resorting to stealing them and lining your pockets was the answer to that? Christ, Margaret. Telling mothers their babies were dead is immoral. You've taken what started with good intentions and made it an abomination."

"That's not true," Margaret said. "These women had no business having babies. And while I won't deny that desperate couples pay handsomely to avoid the years of delays and red tape of traditional adoption, the children are the true beneficiaries, which was always our mission."

"Except the money was to go back into creating resources to help these women who had no one."

"Some money did. Right, Phil?"

Phil Garrett.

"That's right," Phil said. "How else do you think the vitamins and other medical items given to the pregnant women were paid for?"

My father snickered. "Right. Feed the money back enough to keep the cycle going." His voice was tight. "But you screwed up when you took Lindsay."

His words horrified me with the confirmation that he'd known. All along. And that she was what—dead? *No, Dad.*

"Lindsay will destroy everything, but we have her stored away for now. What happens next to her is up to you."

That's what the message had meant on my father's wall. Lindsay was alive. I clasped my hand over my mouth, afraid I might scream.

"You need to let her go," my father said.

"Once she tells you who took that video, then we'll consider it. Until that loose end is snipped, none of us are safe."

Camille's video. I'd been right. Lindsay might have used the threat of it being released if anything happened to her to keep herself alive. That's why they'd come to my apartment. They thought I had it.

As to my father getting Lindsay to cooperate—he and I both knew he had no control over her. My chest burned with just how dire this situation had become.

My father cleared his throat. "I understand, and I believe she'll talk to me," he said. "But she'll be much more likely to cooperate if you let her go."

"We can't do that," Margaret said.

He scoffed. "I won't help unless you do."

Phil tsked and drew in a breath, exhaling loudly enough to leave no doubt he was annoyed. "We don't want to hurt you, my old friend," he said. "We've come so far in this. We can keep going, together, but that choice is yours."

"Then why is he here?" My father's tone was incredulous.

"We thought you might need encouragement to do the right thing," Margaret said.

Henry. If he was in that room, so was a gun. If I ran in now, I'd get Dad and me both killed. My heartbeat swooshed in my ears.

My father laughed, but it held fear. Despite his misdeeds, I was afraid for him. He was closest to me, to the door, but I didn't know how to help him.

"Right," he said. "And if I refuse, you'll kill me, like you did the others? Then what? You need me. So let Lindsay go, let me talk with her, and let's work this out."

"My nephew had no choice but to kill Sherry," Phil said. The connection. Henry was Margaret's son. "When Lindsay came sniffing around, Sherry decided she could leverage that. She knew where the bodies were buried, as they say, and when she'd heard about people questioning the agency, she wanted a bigger cut to keep her mouth shut."

She hadn't taken her own words to heart: there was no getting out, and it had cost her.

"And Craig?" My father's voice shook.

"Well, you know that one, don't you? Unlike Sherry who simply wanted more money, Elizabeth had decided she was through with us, and with Craig helping Lindsay . . . We had to silence him—make him an example of what happens to those who don't listen. Now Elizabeth is silenced as well. Are you listening, Frederick?"

"You've killed Elizabeth?" My father's voice had grown small.

"An unfortunate turn, but that doesn't have to be your fate. You've always understood our mission. And you won't hurt or destroy us. You'll talk to Lindsay. Find out who took that video, and then she'll go home."

Panic welled again. They would never let her go.

"Why would it matter? You can't truly expect to continue this charade after the one person whose signature was needed to finalize the paperwork is dead."

Phil laughed. "We have and always have had another judge in our pocket. And I'll level with you, old friend. We have several other attorneys willing to help as well."

My father scoffed. "So, you've lured them into thinking they'll be doing some goddamn good deed and you'll blackmail them, too."

"They see the good we do. That these children need saving and we're giving them a better chance at life. No blackmail necessary."

"For now, perhaps. They'll see you're only about the money and what you're willing to do to get it soon enough."

A long silence followed as I strained to listen. A standoff?

"I'm sorry you feel that way," Phil said. "We'll get Lindsay to talk one way or another. Rest assured, with or without you, things will remain the way they've always been."

Phil's tone had turned as cold as the dread rising in me.

My father was out of time and Lindsay would be next. I had to do something now.

The lights. *Henry can't shoot what he can't see.* I started in that direction.

"What the hell is going on here?" A woman's screeching voice pierced the air, stopping me in mid-step.

Ericka? My God, was she involved?

"Ericka, get out of here," my father yelled.

I recovered and raced to the electrical box. Flipping it open, searching for the switch that would do the trick. Aiming for the largest lever, I yanked it down in one motion.

The building went black.

Clambering and swearing came from the room as I sprinted back to the birthing center. A gunshot blasted. I swung open the door and recognized my father's form, still standing, near enough to grab him by the arm.

"What the—?"

"Come with me," I said.

"But Ericka—"

Perhaps killing the lights had bought her an opportunity to get out, but I couldn't save us all. My father didn't argue as he slammed the door shut behind him.

"Let's go." I kept my cell light focused on the ground.

"I'm so sorry, Beth."

"Later."

I hurried him across to the agency while keying in 911 and hitting SEND.

"What the hell's going on?" Margaret snapped. "Get the damn lights."

I almost had the agency door closed when Henry was on the other side, his foot square against it. He punched it, and the force sent me reeling to the floor.

My father had made it to the boarded window and had popped one plank off, letting in light from the street. He stopped when I went down and rushed back, ducking behind a desk. Before Henry got inside, I managed to get to my feet and scramble toward my father. Finding cover under a desk across from him, I searched, frantic, for something to use as a weapon.

"Hiding won't save you with that nice trail of blood to follow," Henry said, his footsteps heavy and advancing.

I had a narrowed view of him through a hole used for computer wires in the desk. He was almost on top of us. A box of office supplies sat nearby. I clutched a stapler and hurled it over the desktop at him. He stepped back.

"The next time she fires something at you, it will be a bullet," my father said. "She has a gun, and she's well trained to use it."

My father nodded at me like the confidence in his words would help.

Henry paused.

"It's over, Henry," I said. "The police are on their way." Detective Matson should have gotten the text. I glanced at my phone. My 911 call had failed. The flashlight had drained my already low battery. Had my earlier text failed too? "It's just a matter of time before they get here. You should get out now if you want to save yourself."

"Unlike you, I protect my family. I don't destroy it."

I scoffed. "You have destroyed it. The police know everything that Lindsay was investigating. They know what I've found. You can kill us, but it won't change anything. Your mother and uncle will go to prison." My jaw tensed. "And you'll fry for all the crimes you've committed."

He laughed, deep and wicked. "And your sister will die too because only I know where she is."

My jaw trembled, afraid for Lindsay. For us. At the hatred I felt for Henry. I looked across at my father, who had paled. Scared.

Frail. But for Lindsay's sake, we couldn't die here in this room. I had to buy time and pray that by some miracle the police were coming.

"How did you stomach all of this? What kind of person would kill to protect a woman that ripped children away from their own mothers?"

Henry sneered. "Are you kidding me? I was one of those children and my mother was an addicted whore. A nothing with no future. Whether the women had to be persuaded, or the decision made for them, Margaret gave me, gave all of us, a chance at a better life. You and Craig clearly did okay for yourselves. Why would you be anything but grateful?"

His words of loathing for the woman who'd birthed him made my skin crawl, as did his admission that everything they'd done was to manipulate the vulnerable women they came into contact with. "If Margaret is so altruistic, then she can't possibly approve of all the crimes you've committed in protecting her secret. Or did you do that on your own?"

He smiled. "Me, Mother, my uncle, we do God's work. Your father was doing God's work too, and the judge—until they lost their way."

He didn't answer the question. "The midwife—did she lose her way? And Craig? You killed him like it was nothing."

He shrugged. "We do whatever's necessary. Just like now. Eliminating you and your father will ensure that what we created continues."

Delusional. "God's will, too, or is it about the money?" My father had implied that.

"The American away, right? But still, we are givers and it's unfortunate that the women don't see the gift we gave them by making sure they are healthy through the birth. It is on them that their choices make them unworthy to keep their children."

These people were crazy. Their twisted view of the world. Of their place in it. Pure insanity.

"Come out here with that gun," Henry said. "Or I'll take my chances."

My father's weary eyes had filled with tears. He wasn't a bad man, just misguided—and he'd cost us our family. He'd cost himself everything.

"Done waiting," Henry said.

The time my father had bought us was up.

I grasped the box of supplies in one hand, a three-hole punch in the other, and bolted up from my hiding spot. I hurled the punch at Henry and followed it with the heavy box. It hit his arm. He faltered. With an advantage, I charged headfirst and rammed my shoulder into his stomach. He flew onto his back, hitting the floor and shooting off a round into the ceiling.

Sirens squealed in the distance. My relief was short-lived. Henry, wild-eyed with rage, leveled his gun at me.

My father moved in front of me as the blast hit my ears. He shoved me out of the way as a bullet exploded into his back, his eyes wide and hollow.

I reached out to him and screamed.

He crumpled like a deflated balloon. The rage at everything Henry had done burned through me. Henry must have sensed it because he rushed to get to his feet. I came at him, pushing him forward. The gun flew from his hand.

I scratched and crawled over him, lunging for the weapon. He had me by the ankle and yanked me back. My fingertips brushed the gun enough to scoot it in my direction. I clutched it like a lifeline.

He flipped me and came face-to-face with the metal barrel. My extended arms trembled. "Get off me."

He lifted his hands in surrender and backed away as I got upright. He stepped over my father on his way to the window.

"Stop," I said.

"You don't have it in you to kill. You don't have the fight—any more than Lindsay." He laughed.

My finger pressured the trigger one notch. My brain had shut down. The safety was off. "Where is she?"

Henry smirked.

"Where the fuck is she?" I screamed.

"That's enough, Ms. Ralston," Detective Matson ordered from behind me. "We'll take it from here."

I didn't move, the gun lasered in on Henry. "He's got Lindsay, Detective. He killed Craig, my brother. My dad." My voice broke.

"We heard everything." Detective Matson was beside me, his hand on top of the gun, lowering the muzzle toward the floor. I nearly dropped it with relief into his waiting hand.

Two uniformed officers made quick work of taking Henry into custody; he didn't put up a fight.

My eyes went to my father, lying on the floor, bleeding. I knelt at his side, put my head on his shoulder, and cried.

CHAPTER 41

I sat inside an ambulance parked outside the birthing center, my feet hanging out, pressing a gauze bandage against one leg while bouncing the other. Lindsay was alive. Even though Henry had smiled at me in a way that still had my insides squirming, Phil had told my father they hadn't killed her. With all of them now in custody, I believed she was at least safe from *them*.

That didn't mean she was "safe." I didn't know if they'd given her food or water. Or if she'd been hurt. If nothing else, she had to be terrified.

Sitting here tending to a stupid cut felt wrong, but I had no idea where to begin looking for her now. Detective Matson, busy pressing for answers, hadn't made it back to me yet with an update.

The uniformed officers, medical personnel, and even firemen running around the scene, looked like an ant colony, working together to bring order to the chaos.

Kai had been whisked away in another ambulance, but he was conscious. Our eyes had met for a moment.

"Thank you," I'd mouthed. It was hardly enough for what he'd done—what he'd risked. When this was over, Lindsay and I would make it up to him. I believed that would happen. We would find her.

Ericka barked orders at the ambulance attendants to hurry with my father, who hadn't died from the gunshot. Dodging bullets hadn't blemished her camera-ready look. She wore a short black dress and high heels, her hair smooth as silk and not a strand out of place.

"This is the future mayor of this town," she'd told them more than once. "You make sure he survives. Do you hear me?"

Unbelievable. At least she'd made it out without a scratch. And her interruption had bought me the seconds I'd needed to reach the lights.

"She'll be changing that tune as soon as I put the cuffs on him," Detective Matson said, coming toward me.

I blinked, his image coming into focus. "She has no idea?"

"Not yet. I'll update her when I take her statement. She's the one who brought the cavalry in since I hadn't seen your messages right away. Apparently, she tracks your father's every move using a phone finder app. When Devon called to report that he'd left with someone else, she blew up 911 to get a response out to this location."

Her being annoyingly clingy to my dad had paid off. I thought about what my mother had said—that they were having an affair. I'd never gotten that vibe before, or now. She managed Dad and made him feel special. After our conversation about her dedication to her candidates, I believe she did that for every campaign she oversaw.

My father would miss that when she disappeared from his life. He'd miss myriads of things sitting in a jail cell—if he survived.

"She won't stick around long once she realizes the Ralston boat has sunk."

He nodded. "I haven't known many political types who would."

Margaret and Phil were handcuffed and marched to separate cruisers. "They're not talking yet, are they?" I said.

He frowned, folding his arms over his chest. "No. But we're just getting started. So far Margaret has stone cold down pat, and Phil's already trying to structure a deal saying he had no idea what they were doing. He simply 'encouraged' the women from the shelter to contact the midwife and she did the rest. Also, no surprise, he insists Henry acted on his own."

"That's not true. Henry said they acted together, and Phil had to have let Henry into the law firm that night to kill Craig. He would've known my security code. He was right there when I screamed."

"Don't worry," Detective Matson said. "I have no doubts he was involved. We'll have a warrant for his personal files and computers soon."

They'd kept so many secrets over the years, it didn't surprise me they were holding out. "Phil also said they had Lindsay, and Henry specifically said he knew where she was. Anything on that?"

He drew in a breath. "Henry's clamming up too. He's quite loyal to his mother. But we'll work on him." He looked straight at me. "If Lindsay is out there, we'll find her."

I hoped so and thought of the phone number Camille had used to send my sister the photo. I pulled it up on my screen, telling him how I'd come by it. "I don't know if this will help, but maybe you can ping it for her last location."

"It's worth a shot," he said jotting it down.

"Isn't family grand?" I said, with a weariness that settled into every fiber. I longed for this to be over. To hug Lindsay again. To sleep for the next week.

"Want to talk about it?"

"I wouldn't know where to start. All this time I thought Lindsay was the child that had been taken from her mother at birth. Turns out, it was me. And Craig." My head pounded, still in disbelief that he was my brother.

"I know."

"When?" My voice lilted with surprise.

"The subpoena for the lab records came through earlier. Your sister used her name to run the test, but she had a friend in the lab who knew the truth and pushed it through. I intended to share that information, but someone apparently beat me to it."

"Yeah, my mom, when forced into a corner. I'm not sure she ever would have, and I haven't decided what to do with that yet." Except Sunday brunches were off the calendar for a while.

"Sorry it came to this." His tone turned serious. "All that aside, if you ever disregard my directives in the future . . ."

"You're right," I said. "I should've shared more sooner." Between my promise to Lindsay to *not tell* and my father's objections to my trusting the detective, I'd felt torn. I prayed now the price wasn't Lindsay. "I apologize."

He nodded, and I sensed some amusement in his eyes. Maybe because I'd yet to agree with him about anything. "I will admit, you helped put us on the trail. We were close to bringing in the players based on what we were finding, including someone in Vital Records that seems to have an awfully big bank account. Appears some payouts were happening to push documents through."

"My dad had mentioned falsifying birth certificates."

"Yup," he said. "Again, however, not a free pass on your part."

"Noted."

He softened. "But we're not there yet."

"No, we're not. Not without Lindsay."

He pushed himself off the ambulance, clutching the paper. "I'll check this number. In the interim, time to get them down to the station and turn up the heat. I'll let you know what we find." He rested his hand on my knee, warmth permeating my jeans. "Don't give up."

"I haven't since the moment Lindsay ran out that door."

EMTs approached the ambulance next to me with my father strapped on a gurney. His eyes were open, and Ericka had gone to badger an officer.

"Can I speak to my dad before they take him to the hospital?" I said to the detective.

"Keep it brief. Paramedics said it's amazing the bullet didn't hit any major organs or arteries, but he's lost blood."

I limped my way over. My father's face was pale; perspiration beaded his forehead.

"Thank you," I said. Even though he'd done so much wrong, in the end he'd saved me from Henry's bullet.

"I'm sorry. I've only ever done what I thought was best. And I didn't know the scope." His eyes fluttered. "Until Lindsay . . ."

I wanted to hear more, to understand why he'd become involved, but not now. "That's not what I came to talk about, Dad. Where are they keeping her?"

Tears filled his eyes. "I wish I knew."

My heart sank. "You must have some clue? You know these people. Where could they have taken her?"

He shook his head.

"Did you know when they took her?"

He sighed. "Not until tonight. I knew they were upset with her and Craig, of course—as Lindsay was out asking questions and digging up the women Alliance had helped. But I didn't know what Lindsay had found until that Friday morning."

"Elizabeth knew something was way off because I've seen the video they're talking about."

"She did, but she never shared what she believed with me. Only that she wanted out. But when Lindsay came, I understood why Elizabeth needed it to end. And so did I. I tried to get a handle on the situation at that point, but Craig was murdered that night, and then Lindsay's car was found." Emotion clutched his throat. "I thought she was dead." He winced.

"And it all started because of my DNA test?"

"Yes. She was so indignant that we wouldn't tell you about the adoption. We were afraid it would beg more questions, so we couldn't, you understand . . . But there was no convincing her, and she refused to let it go." A tear trickled onto his cheek. "I hope you believe me that I didn't know the rest of their crimes. I told them I would no longer be part of it, but clearly too late."

I could see his pain. Feel it. But I had no energy to comfort him. Unaware or not, he'd helped to create this mess.

"Was Lindsay taken from her mother by force too?" I didn't know what was real.

"No. She is our blood through and through." He cleared his throat. "And you weren't . . . or Craig. We'd done good once. Yes, your birth certificates were doctored, and your paperwork shoved through the system, but your birth mother had made the decision on her own. Our actions had been well-intentioned, but it took seeing through Lindsay's eyes to understand that we were wrong in how we did it." He looked away. "Then the situation became something else. On some level, I always knew what Phil and Margaret were capable of, and I didn't want them to turn on me and lose the life I worked so hard to create for you, Lindsay, Shelby. But once Lindsay got involved . . ." His voice caught. "Ultimately, it has been destroyed. It didn't start the way it ended."

"What really happened to my birth mother?" A cold chill skittered across me. I wrapped my arms around myself.

Detective Matson approached, his cuffs out. He reached for my father's wrist and secured him to the gurney.

"What's this?" Ericka's shrill voice pierced from behind.

The detective turned his attention to Ericka and hustled her away before she reached us.

"Please, Dad? For once. The truth."

He closed his eyes. "Talk to Nova."

Nova? Flush crept up my neck. I'd hoped she was not involved, but I couldn't unsee that picture.

Another tear slid down his cheek. "I'm sorry."

A tall, uniformed ambulance attendant approached. "We need to transport him, ma'am." He and his partner folded the legs of the gurney under as they lifted my dad into the back of the ambulance.

"Dad?"

The doors slammed as my father's fear-filled eyes darted my way and then closed again.

As the ambulance drove out, a hollow pit of betrayal grew in my stomach.

"You okay?" Detective Matson had returned to my side. Ericka was running to her car to follow the ambulance.

"I'm fine. Do you need me here anymore?"

He put his hand on my arm. "No. I'll be in touch as soon as we have a lead."

Back in my car, I meandered down the streets of Portland lost in thought, my body a ball of turmoil. My dad had said to speak with Nova, but how could I speak to someone who'd kept secrets from me? A larger part of me was terrified to hear what she knew. The thought of another person I loved lying to me all these years would be more than I could take with Lindsay's safety still in the balance.

But despite my anger, I loved Nova. If she'd held back, I wanted to believe she'd done so out of fear of the deportation my parents held over her head. How could I truly blame her when she was a victim herself?

As I drove, another idea took hold. Why had she come to work for my parents in the first place? If Dad had been telling the truth—that he'd intended to help the women whose children they'd taken—was Nova one of those women?

Sometime after eleven, I turned into my parents' driveway. Their house was dark. Ericka had no doubt sent Devon to retrieve my mom to go to the hospital.

I climbed the stairs to Nova's apartment, my heart pounding with each step. A small light warmed the windows and I stared at it for a long time, debating, before knocking. Nova answered the door with her robe wrapped around her, Murphy rubbing against her leg and then mine.

"Beth?" Her voice strained. Did she know what had happened tonight—why I was here? "Come in out of the rain."

I hadn't noticed the rain had started. I searched her face for signs I'd missed. Had they been there all along? Our eyes. The shapes were similar. Craig had her eyes too. How had I not seen our similarities?

Everything about my life had changed in this day, but Nova had been a constant. She'd been there in that photo with me and Craig. And she'd told the story of her addicted sister who'd come to the country illegally. A story similar to the one I'd heard just a few hours ago about the circumstances around my birth mother.

Had the story been about Nova?

"Oh no—" She leaned against the doorframe, deflated. "Did they find Lindsay?"

I shook my head. "Are you my mother?"

Her face creased and my muscles grew taut waiting for her answer. "No, Beth," she finally said. "Please, come in."

Rain droplets streamed down my cheeks. "Do you know who is?"

She hesitated, folding her arms tight around herself.

"My father said to come here, Nova, and there's no reason to be afraid of him anymore. He's going to jail. I'll help you get citizenship. He can't control any part of your life. No one can. Please, no more secrets."

She dropped her hand to her side. Her chin lifted in defiance before she nodded. "It is past time that I tell you everything."

Inside, she grabbed a towel from her bathroom so I could dry my hair and face and put on a teapot to boil. We sat on her couch, Murphy weaving between us before settling on her lap.

"As I'd shared, my sister, Tiana, came to this country before I did. What I told you was true—she had terrible addictions and was here illegally. By the time I found her, she'd just given birth to twins and agreed to let you go to another home. What your mother told you about that is true. But I'm not sure my sister was ever given an opportunity or the information to make any other choice."

I didn't know either, but if Margaret had been involved, I had to think not. I also didn't believe my parents had been part of that process. "So, Tiana was my birth mother, then?"

Nova nodded. "And she was in a terrible way, her addictions turning her into nothing more than a ghost. My focus became finding out what happened to you children. Talk had been that rich people had taken you in, and I scoured the help wanted ads, hopeful, but found nothing there. Then a woman I'd met from the job source said she'd been hired to work for a judge. And that the woman said her lawyer friend who'd also just adopted was looking for live-in help. I quickly applied, and the moment I laid eyes on you, there was no doubt you were my family. Soon after, your mother invited that other woman, the judge, with her new baby." Nova rested her hand over her heart.

"But my father knew that you would have answers for me. How did he know who you were?"

"One night Tiana came to me on drugs. You were two years old at the time, but your father took one look at her and knew. I thought he'd fire me, or worse. I begged to stay, but . . ."

"But instead, he never got your visa, trapping you. Blackmailing your silence." I hurt for her. For Tiana.

She nodded. "I never saw my sister again."

"She's dead?" The reality of that numbed me. I hadn't known her to miss her. Still, the idea of never having the opportunity pressed hard against my chest.

Nova stared at her hands. "I believe she has to be."

I recognized her guilt for not having been able to save her—I could feel my own for not finding Lindsay yet. I hugged her tight. "I'm so sorry, Nova." After a minute, I pulled away. It might be painful to ask, but I had to know. "Do you have a picture of your sister?"

Nova's face lifted. "I do. She was stunning once. And . . . you look like her."

She rose from the sofa, Murphy hopping to the floor, and she disappeared into her room. She returned carrying a shoebox. "I brought these with me." Inside the box, she shuffled through a stack of pictures before handing me a couple from her and Tiana's childhood.

Tiana had to be around eight or ten, and we did look similar. Same curls and a gap between our teeth, though mine had been fixed with braces. I outlined the photo with my fingertip.

Our differences were more obvious as she aged. The lines around her mouth more distinct, but somehow familiar. I saw Craig in her smile.

I thought of all the times I'd been aware of how different I looked from Lindsay . . . and my parents. It was an odd sensation to see where I came from but feel no real connection to that life. My life had been as a Ralston. As Lindsay's little sister—a fact I didn't regret for a second.

I spent the rest of the night with the photo on my chest, racking my brain. As bone tired as I felt, I wouldn't sleep until Lindsay was home.

Shadows played on the ceiling, and I found images in the light and dark. Lindsay and I used to do that as children. We'd laugh too loud at the silly images we came up with. Then we'd get scolded. "Store that laughter for another day, girls," Nova had said more than once.

Those words had meant nothing, until that moment. Store it for those times when the laughter and joy weren't as easy to find. Store it away until you need it.

I needed that memory now; I hoped memories weren't all I had left of Lindsay in the end.

When the sun peeked through at seven thirty, I rolled off Nova's couch, stiff and sore. A text from the detective had come through during the night to say the phone number I'd given them hadn't yielded anything and they were still working through it. I made a half-dozen calls to Detective Matson after with no answer, but left messages each time. Then I changed my leg bandage, although the gouge hadn't seeped much through the night. A half hour later, unable to sit any longer, I left Nova a note that I'd gone to check on a friend at the hospital.

Kai was propped up in bed when I arrived, a nasty stitched cut on his head, and a couple of black eyes.

"You've looked better," I said, lifting the extra coffee I'd brought with me.

"Morning to you too, and thank God, yes. This place serves swill."

"We can't have the hero of the hour drinking swill, that's for sure."

He rolled his eyes. "Yeah, some hero. Right after we hung up, I managed to get jumped and beaten, sending you into a bad situation by yourself."

I pressed the palm of my hand on his forearm. "You did more than most people ever would. If you hadn't let me know where to find my dad, he'd be dead, and so would Lindsay."

Kai tried to sit up, then winced. "She's alive?"

"I think so. I haven't been updated by the detective yet, but I expect he's working on those jerks for information on where they've got her."

"God, she better be okay."

I squeezed his arm, not wanting to think of any other possibility. "You going to make a full recovery?"

"Yeah. But I'll have to put my Harley away for a couple of months until my head injury heals."

I chuckled. "I know how you love that bike."

"I do. Good thing I'll be able to store it in the apartment basement. Hate the thought of it just sitting out . . ."

A tingle started at the base of my neck. "What did you just say?"

"My bike, how much I love it."

That wasn't it. "No, the other part."

"Storing. I was saying our apartment has a basement to keep my bike until I can ride again."

The word yanked me back to last night. *Stored.* Phil had said that word when he spoke about Lindsay.

She was *stored* away.

He'd also turned off my pass card, removing my access to everywhere in the firm.

My heart rate ticked up. My God, had she been there the whole time? While I was upstairs sneaking through the office? That must have been why Phil had come back that night. Why he wanted me out of the firm.

"I've got to go." I kissed his forehead. "Thank you!"

"What did I do?"

"You just might've saved the day again."

I punched in Detective Matson's number on the way to my car. He answered this time. "I might know where Lindsay is. Meet me at the law firm."

I parked on the street in front of the high-rise, replaying the night Phil terminated me. My father acted innocent. At the time, I thought he'd been lying. But he didn't know. It was all Phil. He couldn't risk that I might put it together at some point.

I beat Detective Matson to the lobby of a place I'd known for so long. How had I missed it? Charlie was at the security desk.

"Morning, Ms. Ralston. What brings you here?"

I couldn't wait. "I need access to the firm's archive room."

"Wish I could help, but you're no longer on the firm's authorized list."

Not good enough. "It's an emergency, Charlie."

"I can't—"

Detective Matson approached the desk with an officer and my heart pattered at the sight of him. The image of the white knight on a horse flicked through my mind.

"I hope you have a search warrant," I said.

"I have better." He flashed a plastic card.

"Phil's?"

"Your father's, with permission."

Charlie stepped away from his security desk. "Still going to need to accompany you. I have my orders."

Detective Matson didn't have a problem with that, so neither would I. Charlie led us down to the basement level, the floor right below. The dungeon.

Once on the floor, the detective handed me the pass card and I swiped it across the bright red light of the archive room door. It clicked and we walked inside, cool air wafting out. I shivered. The files were kept at a specific temperature for obvious reasons, but Lindsay must be freezing.

My heart pounded and I wanted to jump out of my skin. I flicked on the light ready to see my sister. Instead, banker boxes cluttered the main part of the storage area, along with paper-filled totes awaiting boxes.

No, no, no. I was so certain she'd be here. Where was she?

Detective Matson shot an odd look at me, and I turned to the fireproof room, another shudder marching through me. The room was eight-by-eight and secured by the same pass card. I was pretty sure. I'd never had reason to go into it.

I swiped the card, every part of me clenched in terror. Afraid of what I'd find—more of what I wouldn't.

When the door swung up, I didn't need a light to see Lindsay, her hands tied, her red hair matted across her face, but her eyes bright and fiery.

"Where the hell have you been, Curls?"

I shook my head and skidded on my knees next to her. "Shut up." And there was no stopping the tears that flowed.

EPILOGUE

Two weeks had passed since I'd watched our father taken away in an ambulance and Lindsay had come home. Two weeks since the police had descended on the law firm, scrutinizing everything related to Frederick Ralston and Phil Garrett, and the duo of destruction that had been hauled away that same night.

Like my father, Judge Johnson had survived the gunshot, and she was cooperating. My guess is they'd both make deals that would limit their jail time. For Elizabeth, having to live without Craig would be far more punishment than anything the justice system could dole out.

Ericka split the moment she'd learned of Dad's fate. And while Mom had been elated that Lindsay was alive, guilt had gotten the best of her. She'd decided to take a "mental health break" and had gone to mend some relationships with family back east.

My guess was she also couldn't stand the spotlight on her in all the wrong ways. She'd been aware of what Margaret and Alliance were about to the same extent as my father, but she hadn't participated and would avoid prosecution. She and I had a long road back to each other. But she was the woman who had raised me—my mother—and I loved her.

Nova and Murphy would live on our parents' property for a while longer. Soon, that too would be sold. While the Ralston nest egg was substantial, legal fees would decimate that in time.

Paperwork had already been filed to get Nova legal status. I'd loved her from the start, and knowing we had a blood connection deepened that bond. I looked forward to hearing more about her life . . . about Tiana's life before they'd come to this country. I was at peace with Tiana's choices, but curious to know more about where I came from.

Now, I sat curled on the couch next to Lindsay in her apartment, so glad I'd ignored her directive to not ask or follow. Lindsay had laid low that Sunday after Craig's murder, rearranging her meeting with Camille. Her hope had been to get the video and take it to the authorities, at the same time releasing an exposé through the newspaper. But Henry had found her at the trestle instead after picking up her trail at some point and following her.

Thank God Camille hadn't arrived yet. I didn't want to think what they would've done to her had they known she had incriminating evidence.

I snuggled closer to Lindsay who'd lost a few pounds during the ordeal. Phil had given her water, but very little to eat. I was having a hard time being away from her—afraid she might go on some new investigation and leave me behind.

"So, what's next?" she asked me, blowing steam off her coffee cup.

"Great question. Not law school," I said, putting my head on her shoulder. "Maybe I'll be your bodyguard."

"Had I only known you had skills." She laughed, flicking her long hair. Aside from a few already healed bumps she'd gotten from her struggle with Henry on that trestle, she'd returned to being flawless.

I soaked in the sound of her laughter, certain there'd never be a sound sweeter. I'd almost lost her, and that adage that you don't know what you have until it's gone had never felt truer.

"But seriously," she said, bumping my shoulder.

"Don't fall over in shock or anything," I said, "but I'm thinking of applying at St. Luke's Legal Clinic as a paralegal."

She faced me, her expression skeptical. "And give up the billable hours and the glory?"

After helping bust open the illegal ring our father had been involved in, I hardly thought of it as giving up anything. "I'm serious. I want to be more like you."

"Girl . . ." She leaned back into the couch.

"Well, maybe without the kidnapping."

She nearly spit out her coffee.

A knock came on her door, and I answered it. Kai.

"Hey, stranger," he said. A slight yellowish bruise remained under one eye but the gash on his head had healed well.

"Hey, yourself. You're looking a lot better than you did in the hospital."

"Feel better too," he said.

"Good to hear." I resisted the urge to pull him in for a hug.

"Lindsay around?"

"Come to use my shower again?" Lindsay hollered from the sofa.

"You planning to be in it?" He sauntered in with a big grin and she laughed. "I mean, it does have better water pressure."

She shook her head, and he plopped down next to her, resting his hand on her leg. Things had progressed in that department, and something told me it might keep progressing. I hoped so. He'd make a decent brother-in-law, python snake tattoo and all.

"Okay, you two, get a room," I said.

"Well . . ." Lindsay shot me a cheesy smile.

"Yeah, yeah." Some things never changed with Lindsay when a cute boy was present. "Luckily, I have places to go anyway. My ride's about to show."

Lindsay looked up, those big eyes peering through all that red hair. That face . . . I took a snapshot in my mind and never intended to let it go. "Thanks, Sis. You know . . ." she said.

"Yeah, I know." I gave her a long hug before heading out.

At the bottom floor, I waited for the unmarked tan sedan that at one point I had tried to avoid. Detective Matson, or Troy as I now called him, pulled up next to me.

"Looking for a ride?"

"Why, yes, sir, I am."

"Then your chariot awaits."

I climbed into the front seat, running my fingers through his dark sideburns.

"You ready?" he said, reaching out his hand.

Interlocking my fingers with his, I nodded.

On the way into northeast Portland, I stared out the window. The fallout from the damage my father and his cohorts had done was far and wide. My mother had said something that had caught my attention during our conversation. She'd said churchgoing people who had money were the recipients of the children. Troy was already neck deep in trying to sort that out and see if those "recipients" came from the Church that Phil, the judge, and my parents attended regularly. He was also helping Camille Jackson and Toni Thompson find their babies. He and Lindsay would be tracking down the others who had similar experiences with Alliance.

I didn't know the odds without Margaret willing to talk—and Bailey Perez was in the wind. I'm sure she wanted to be as far away from Margaret and her group as she could get. Which made me think she knew more than she let on. I wondered if she wanted out too. Otherwise, why bring the midwife's name that day? Or maybe she was naïve. Either way, Troy would do the best he could.

He was a good man. And as we were leaving Toni and the sober living house a week ago, a part of me had cracked open to the possibility of more in my life than work. He'd felt that occur at the same time because, before we'd cleared the stairs, he'd kissed me.

I'd let him.

More than anything, I wanted a fuller life surrounded by people I could trust. And I trusted Troy Matson.

We pulled up in front of Ellen Sullivan's house. The Christmas tree still illuminated the front window. I'd promised her I would bring back someone who would listen, and it was a promise I intended to keep.

When Ellen answered her door, her face was scrunched in confusion.

"Ellen, this is Detective Matson," I said. "He wants to hear your story."

She nearly crumpled in relief. Ellen's children would be adults now with children of their own. But everyone wanted to belong to someone, didn't they? They wanted to belong somewhere. If it was remotely possible, I wanted that for Ellen, too.

I thought of Lindsay and my parents and Nova. DNA binds or not, they were mine, and I was theirs.

ACKNOWLEDGMENTS

Each time I get asked to write acknowledgments, I am reminded of how blessed I am to be living this author life—and of how many people make this life happen.

A heartfelt thank-you to those who buy my books, read and review them, attend my events, engage and encourage, and want to know what's next. You are the reason that I get up each day to create more stories.

Sandy Harding, thank you for being such a wonderfully supportive agent. Your feedback, guidance, and belief in this book has meant the world.

To my team at Oceanview—Bob and Patricia Gussin, Lee, and Faith—thank you for making me feel like a legitimate partner in the process. You are all incredible and I love being part of your Oceanview family.

To my book coach and friend, Dawn Ius. Your belief in me, and this story, has never wavered. You push me to be a better writer, and never let me believe otherwise.

Thank you to my writing friends (too many to name), but each one of you inspires me. A special shout-out to my critique partner Dianne Freeman. Your advice and insight are wonderful, but your friendship over the years has made this journey so much fun.

To Cindy Goyette, Jessica Payne, Jaime Lynn Hendricks, and Heather Chavez, I so appreciate your willingness to read and offer suggestions at a moment's notice—you are my village! To Karenza Corder, Jessica Jett, and Bonnie Matheny, my beta readers, you three are my rock stars.

Thank you to Clark County Sheriff Deputy James Lawrence who helps make the legal aspects of my novels believable. As always, if I got it wrong, it's on me for not asking the right questions!

To my big sister, Marilyn, who's always there to listen to my ups and downs—thank you. I drew from being your little sister to write this story. And if you hadn't shown me the legal world early on, I'm not sure what direction I would have gone in life. But you did, and I embraced it. Now look—I finally used it in a novel!

Lastly, to my husband, Robb. You've championed my writing dream from the moment it was born. When the way was dark, you shined a light. When I was uncertain, or down, you pulled me up, dusted me off, and said try again. More than that, you constantly show me how wonderful life can be. You are my everything. All my love.

Mary Keliikoa
www.marykeliikoa.com

BOOK CLUB DISCUSSION QUESTIONS

1. The book begins with an incident between two adult sisters, where Lindsay, the older sister, leaves her cell phone in Beth's purse with an unsent text that reads, "Don't ask! Don't follow!" The line refers to something Lindsay often told Beth when they were children. Do you think old pacts or promises made between siblings in childhood tend to hold through adulthood? Even in extreme circumstances?

2. There's a point where Beth wonders how far she will go to protect her big sister. Even as it puts her own future in jeopardy. Is there a line when it comes to family?

3. Have you ever felt pressure to cover for a sibling? How did that make you feel? When is it justified to cover for someone—and when is it not?

4. What do you think that Beth's insistence on working as a paralegal, rather than accepting her family's offer to support her in law school, says about her? Do you see this as a strength? Or a weakness?

5. How do you judge Lindsay's choices to not be more forthcoming about what she knew and when? Did you admire her persistence or do you fault her for putting her little sister in danger?

6. What did you think of the decisions made by Beth to investigate on her own? What would you have done differently?

7. How would you characterize Beth's relationship with her mother? Her father? Did it change as the story progressed?

8. What about Lindsay's relationship with her mother? Her father? How did it differ from Beth's? How did that play a role in the story?

9. How did you feel about Kai's decision to listen solely to Lindsay and dole out information in the manner he did? Do you think he should have been more helpful sooner? Do you think he should have followed Beth?

10. Did you feel that Beth should have trusted Detective Matson sooner than she did? Would you trust someone your father/parent/significant other didn't trust?

11. What do you believe Nova's role in the book is?

12. Were you surprised that in the end Beth still felt a connection to her family?

13. Were you happy with how Lindsay and Beth's relationship resolved? What do you see in the future for both of them?

For more information about *DON'T ASK, DON'T FOLLOW* and author Mary Keliikoa visit her website at:

www.marykeliikoa.com